ONE WEEK FRIENDS

MATCHA HAZUKI 2

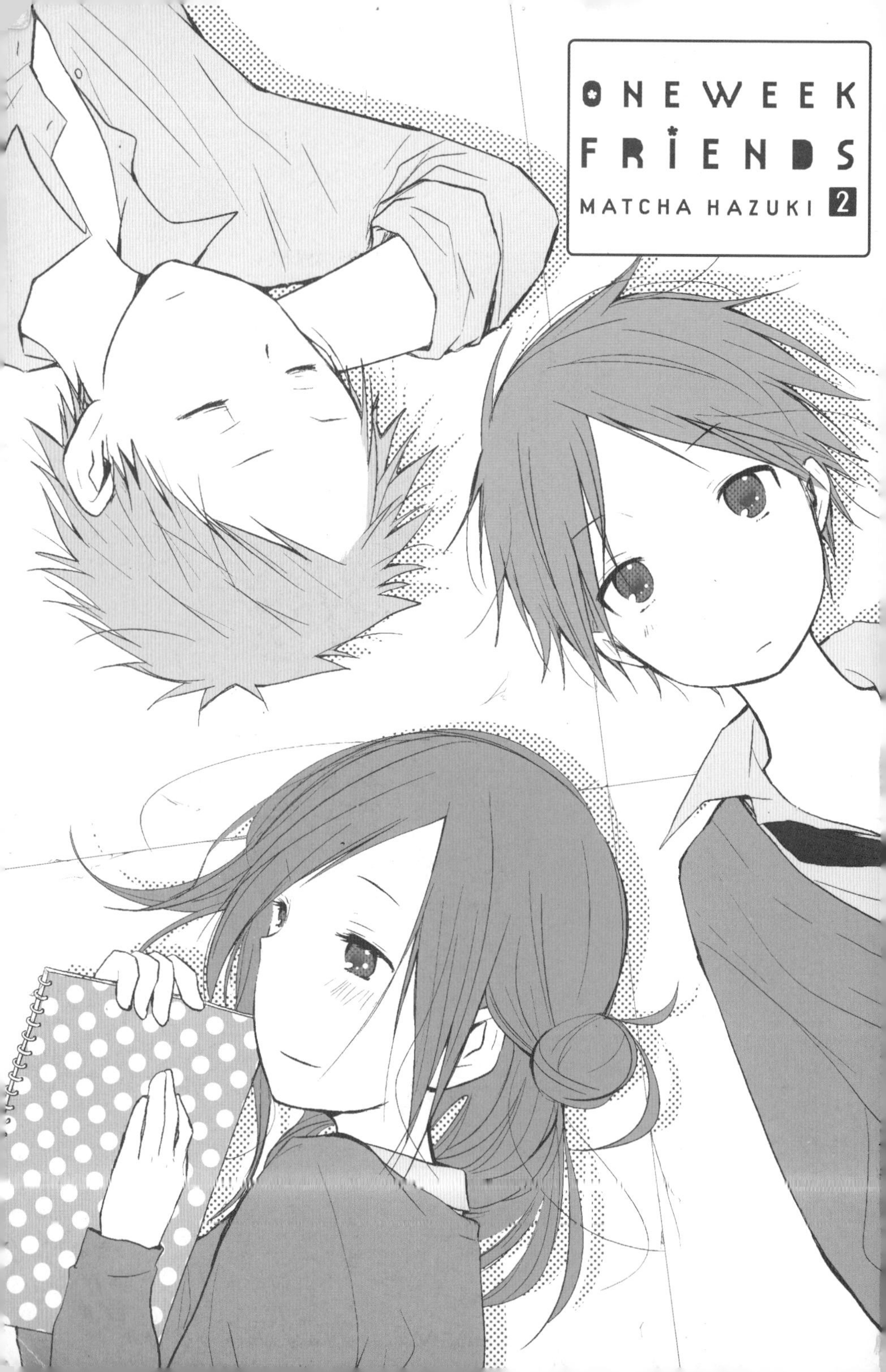

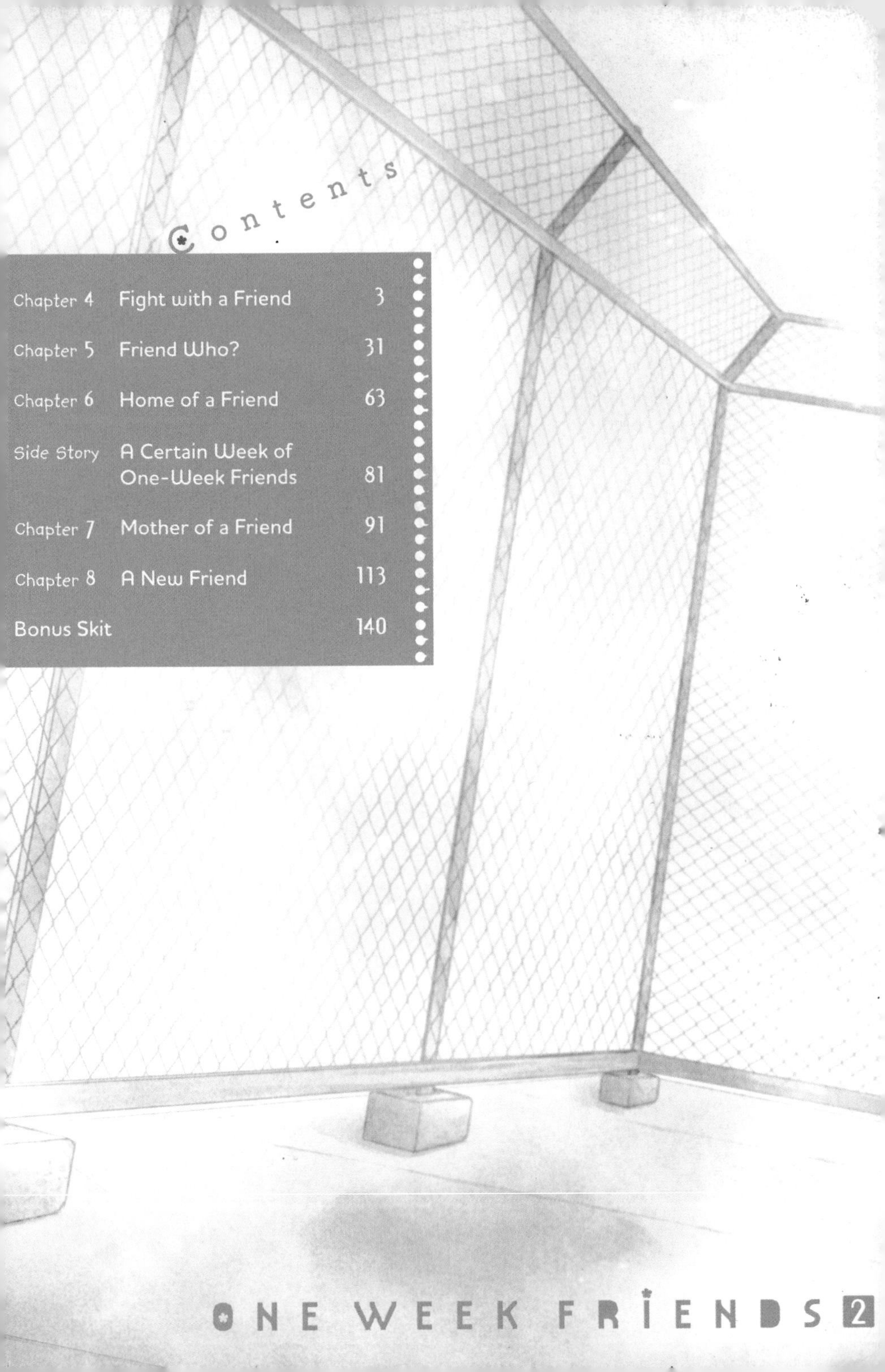

Contents

ONE WEEK FRIENDS 2

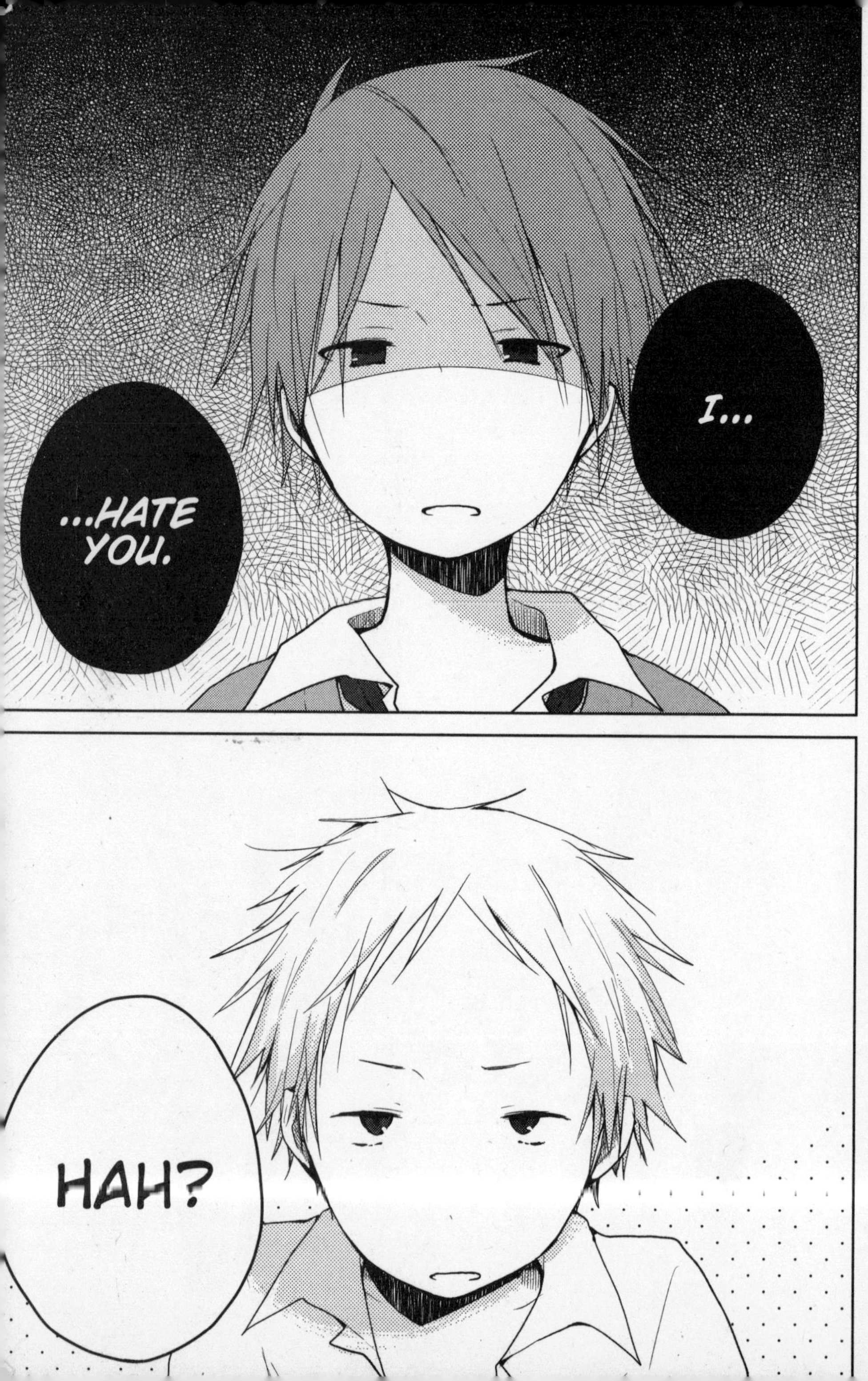
I...
...HATE YOU.
HAH?

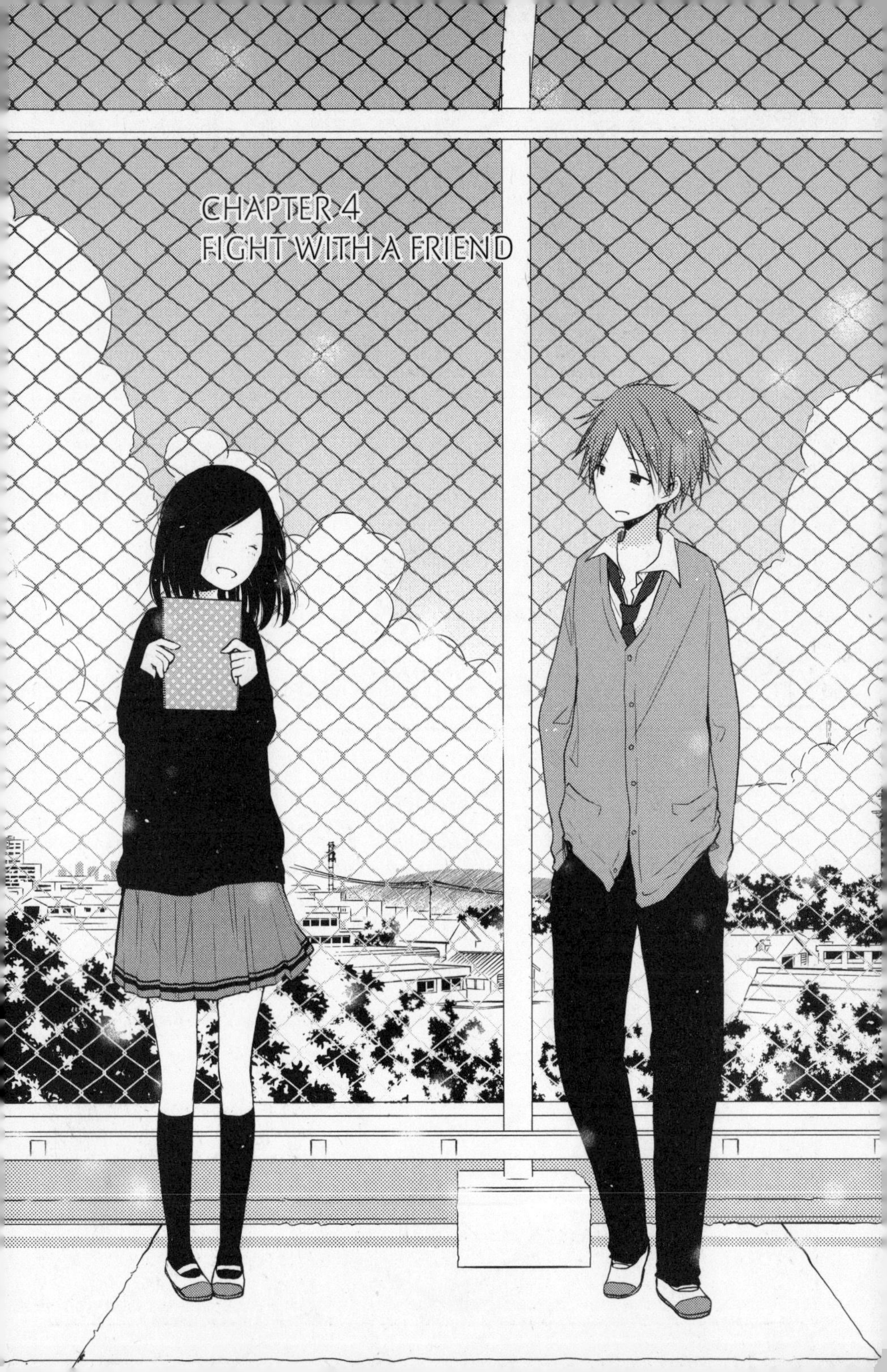
CHAPTER 4
FIGHT WITH A FRIEND

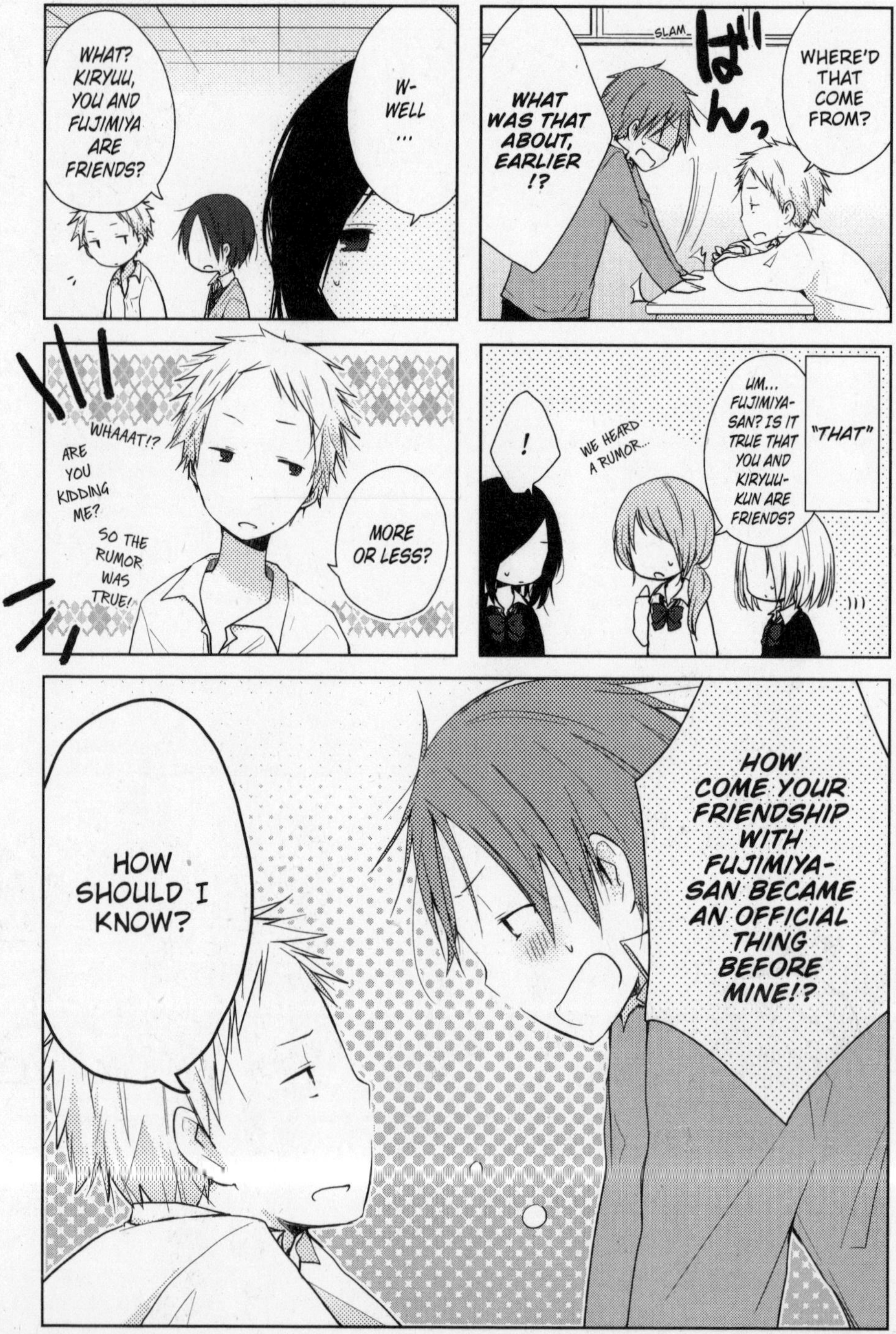
WHERE'D THAT COME FROM?
ばんっ
SLAM
WHAT WAS THAT ABOUT, EARLIER!?
W-WELL...
WHAT? KIRYUU, YOU AND FUJIMIYA ARE FRIENDS?
"THAT"
UM... FUJIMIYA-SAN? IS IT TRUE THAT YOU AND KIRYUU-KUN ARE FRIENDS?
WE HEARD A RUMOR...
!
MORE OR LESS?
WHAAAT!?
ARE YOU KIDDING ME?
SO THE RUMOR WAS TRUE!
HOW COME YOUR FRIENDSHIP WITH FUJIMIYA-SAN BECAME AN OFFICIAL THING BEFORE MINE!?
HOW SHOULD I KNOW?

CAN'T ACCEPT THIS

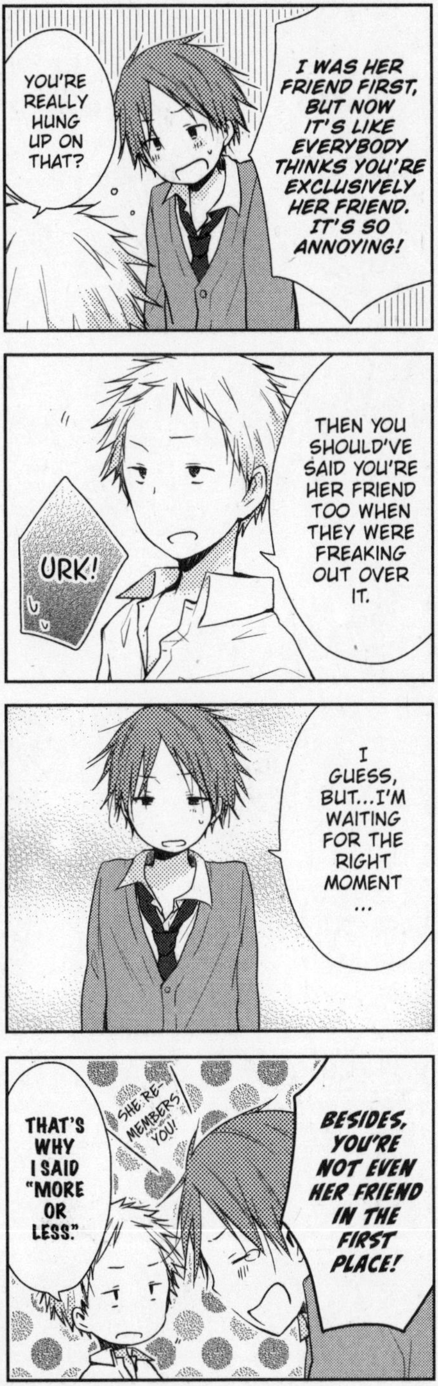
I WAS HER FRIEND FIRST, BUT NOW IT'S LIKE EVERYBODY THINKS YOU'RE EXCLUSIVELY HER FRIEND. IT'S SO ANNOYING!
YOU'RE REALLY HUNG UP ON THAT?
THEN YOU SHOULD'VE SAID YOU'RE HER FRIEND TOO WHEN THEY WERE FREAKING OUT OVER IT.
URK!
I GUESS, BUT...I'M WAITING FOR THE RIGHT MOMENT ...
BESIDES, YOU'RE NOT EVEN HER FRIEND IN THE FIRST PLACE!
SHE RE-MEMBERS YOU!
THAT'S WHY I SAID "MORE OR LESS."

BINGO

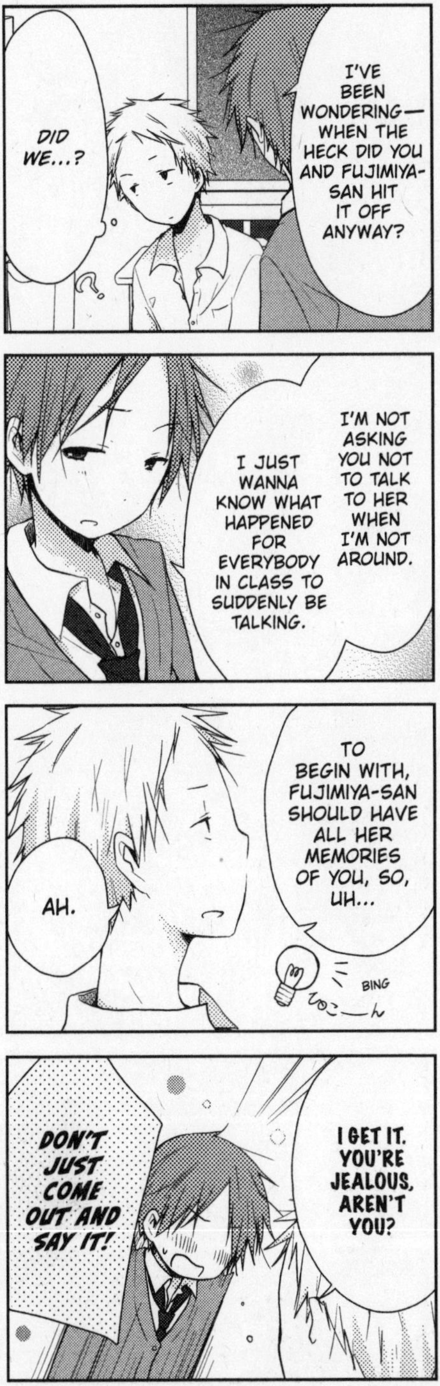
I'VE BEEN WONDERING—WHEN THE HECK DID YOU AND FUJIMIYA-SAN HIT IT OFF ANYWAY?
DID WE...?
I'M NOT ASKING YOU NOT TO TALK TO HER WHEN I'M NOT AROUND.
I JUST WANNA KNOW WHAT HAPPENED FOR EVERYBODY IN CLASS TO SUDDENLY BE TALKING.
TO BEGIN WITH, FUJIMIYA-SAN SHOULD HAVE ALL HER MEMORIES OF YOU, SO, UH...
AH.
BING
I GET IT. YOU'RE JEALOUS, AREN'T YOU?
DON'T JUST COME OUT AND SAY IT!

UNDER THOSE CIRCUMSTANCES

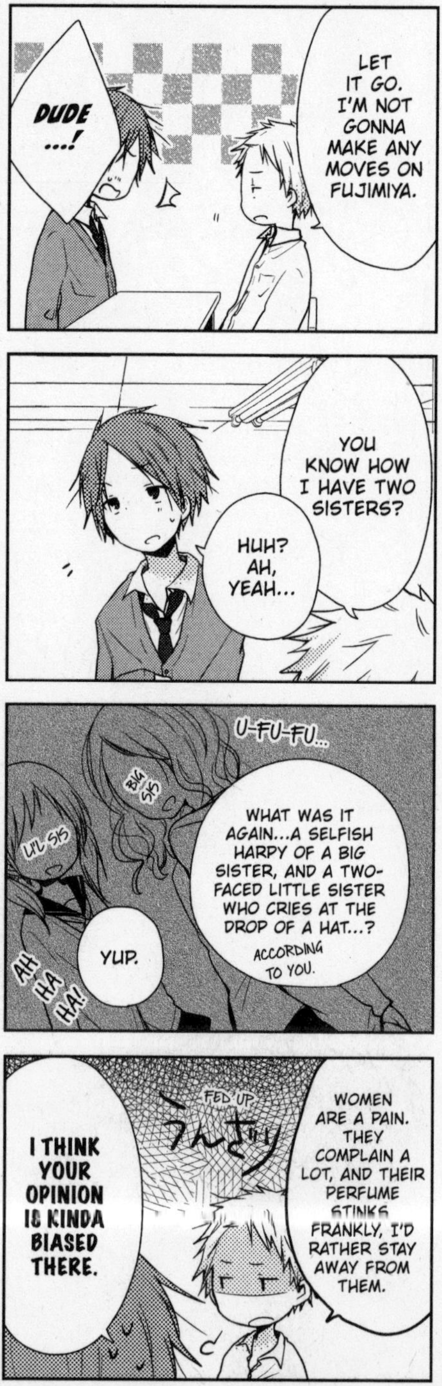
LET IT GO. I'M NOT GONNA MAKE ANY MOVES ON FUJIMIYA.
DUDE...!
YOU KNOW HOW I HAVE TWO SISTERS?
HUH? AH, YEAH...
U-FU-FU...
BIG SIS
WHAT WAS IT AGAIN...A SELFISH HARPY OF A BIG SISTER, AND A TWO-FACED LITTLE SISTER WHO CRIES AT THE DROP OF A HAT...?
ACCORDING TO YOU.
YUP.
LI'L SIS
AH HA HA!
WOMEN ARE A PAIN. THEY COMPLAIN A LOT, AND THEIR PERFUME STINKS. FRANKLY, I'D RATHER STAY AWAY FROM THEM.
FED UP
I THINK YOUR OPINION IS KINDA BIASED THERE.

STAB

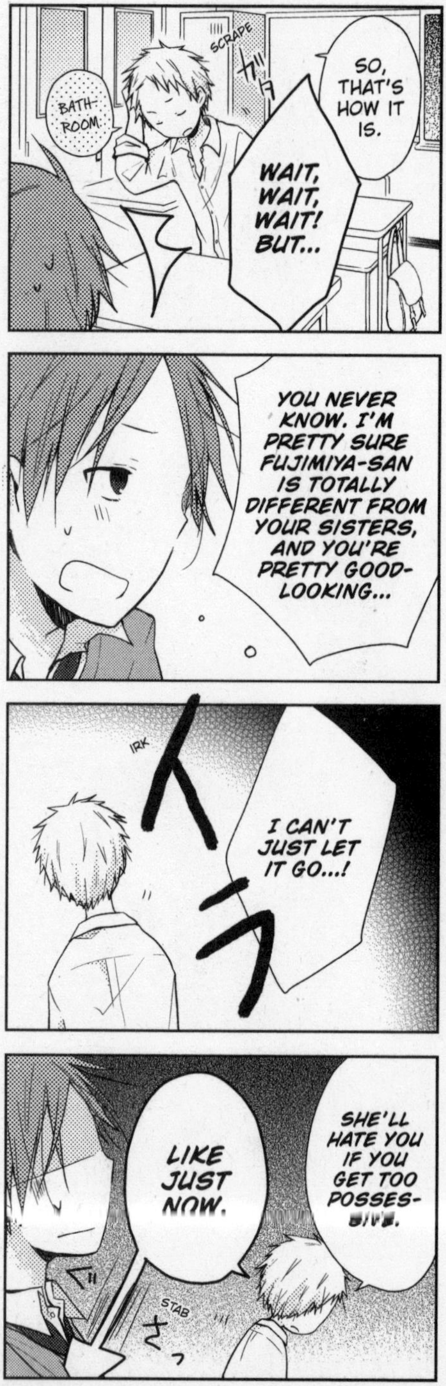
SO, THAT'S HOW IT IS.
SCRAPE
BATHROOM.
WAIT, WAIT, WAIT! BUT...
YOU NEVER KNOW. I'M PRETTY SURE FUJIMIYA-SAN IS TOTALLY DIFFERENT FROM YOUR SISTERS, AND YOU'RE PRETTY GOOD-LOOKING...
I CAN'T JUST LET IT GO...!
IRK
SHE'LL HATE YOU IF YOU GET TOO POSSESSIVE.
LIKE JUST NOW.
STAB

LUNCH BREAK

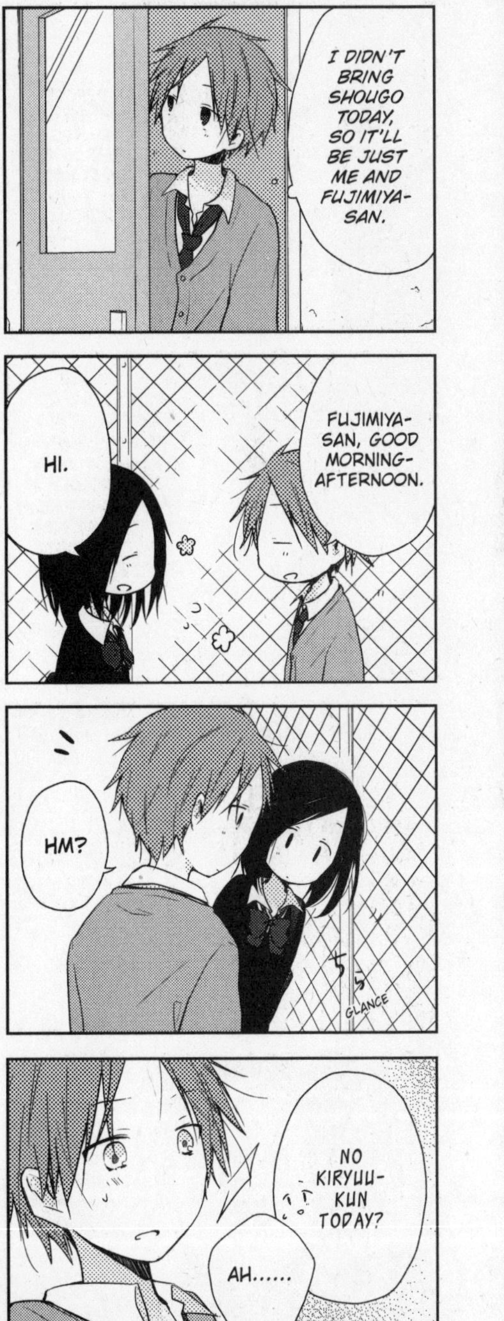
I DIDN'T BRING SHOUGO TODAY, SO IT'LL BE JUST ME AND FUJIMIYA-SAN.
FUJIMIYA-SAN, GOOD MORNING-AFTERNOON.
HI.
HM?
GLANCE
NO KIRYUU-KUN TODAY?
AH......

ON HER MIND

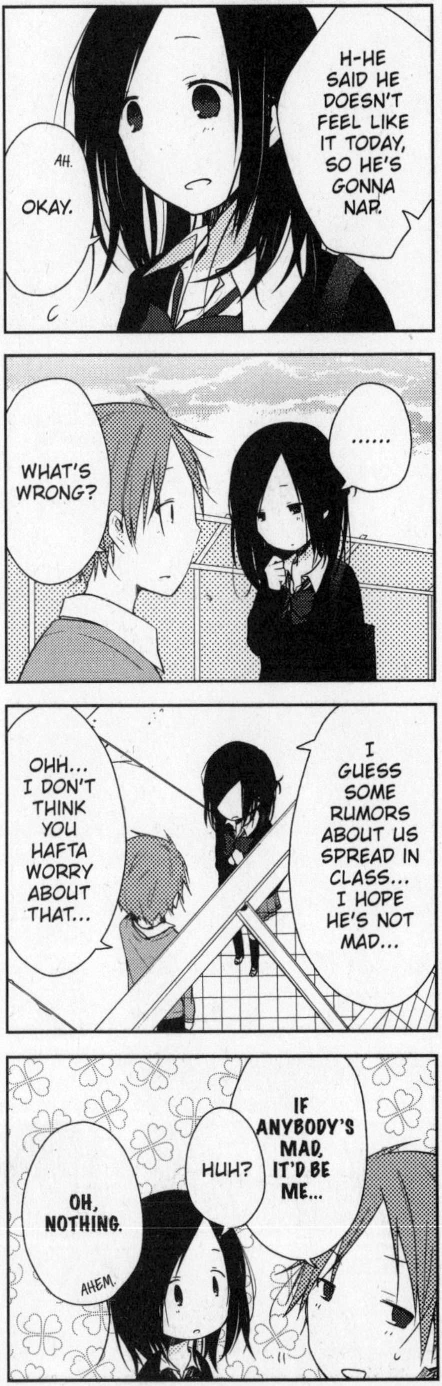
H-HE SAID HE DOESN'T FEEL LIKE IT TODAY, SO HE'S GONNA NAP.
AH.
OKAY.
......
WHAT'S WRONG?
I GUESS SOME RUMORS ABOUT US SPREAD IN CLASS... I HOPE HE'S NOT MAD...
OHH... I DON'T THINK YOU HAFTA WORRY ABOUT THAT...
IF ANYBODY'S MAD, IT'D BE ME...
HUH?
OH, NOTHING.
AHEM.

NATURALLY

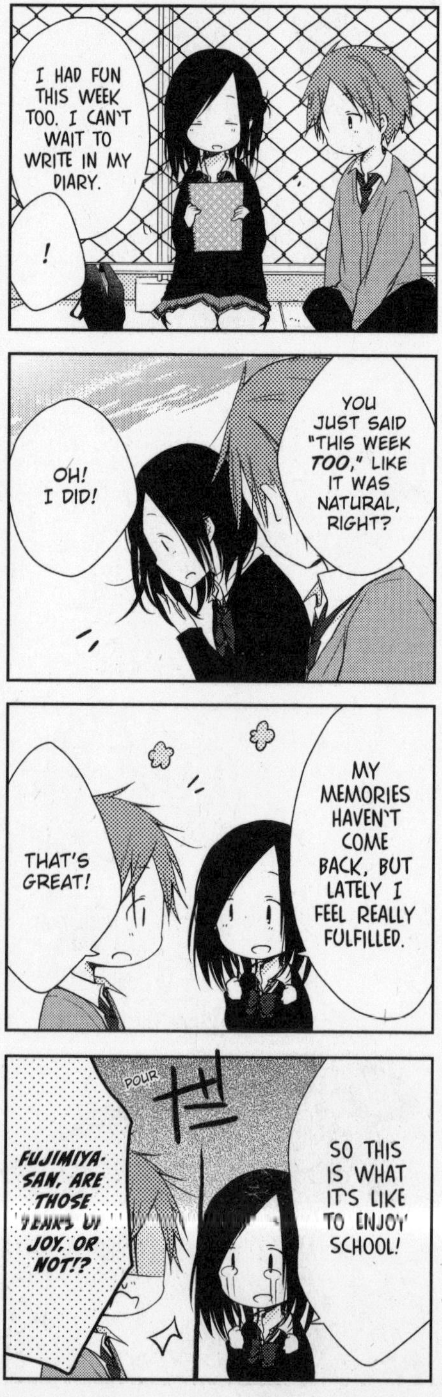
I HAD FUN THIS WEEK TOO. I CAN'T WAIT TO WRITE IN MY DIARY.
!
YOU JUST SAID "THIS WEEK *TOO*," LIKE IT WAS NATURAL, RIGHT?
OH! I DID!
MY MEMORIES HAVEN'T COME BACK, BUT LATELY I FEEL REALLY FULFILLED.
THAT'S GREAT!
SO THIS IS WHAT IT'S LIKE TO ENJOY SCHOOL!
POUR
FUJIMIYA-SAN, ARE THOSE TEARS OF JOY, OR NOT!?

AGAIN

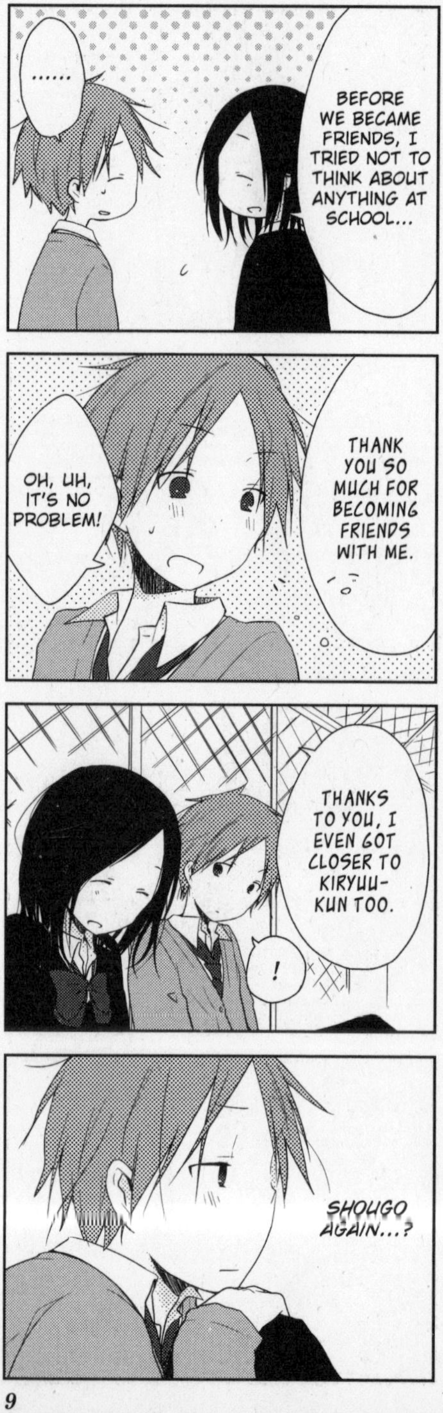
BEFORE WE BECAME FRIENDS, I TRIED NOT TO THINK ABOUT ANYTHING AT SCHOOL...
......
THANK YOU SO MUCH FOR BECOMING FRIENDS WITH ME.
OH, UH, IT'S NO PROBLEM!
THANKS TO YOU, I EVEN GOT CLOSER TO KIRYUU-KUN TOO.
!
SHOUGO AGAIN...?

ABOUT SHOUGO

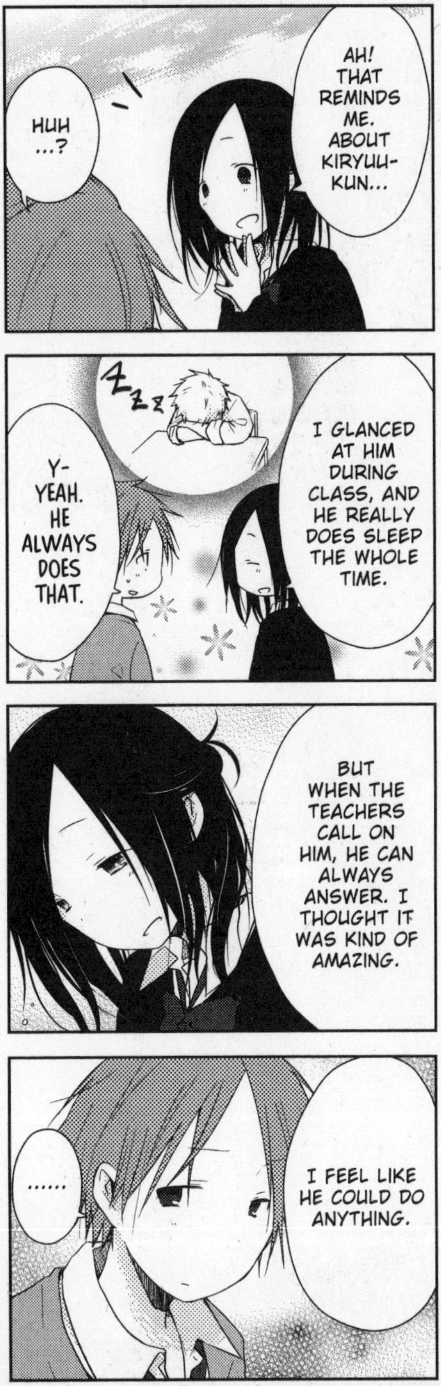
AH! THAT REMINDS ME. ABOUT KIRYUU-KUN...
HUH ...?
I GLANCED AT HIM DURING CLASS, AND HE REALLY DOES SLEEP THE WHOLE TIME.
Z Z Z
Y-YEAH. HE ALWAYS DOES THAT.
BUT WHEN THE TEACHERS CALL ON HIM, HE CAN ALWAYS ANSWER. I THOUGHT IT WAS KIND OF AMAZING.
I FEEL LIKE HE COULD DO ANYTHING.
......

CAN'T HOLD IT IN

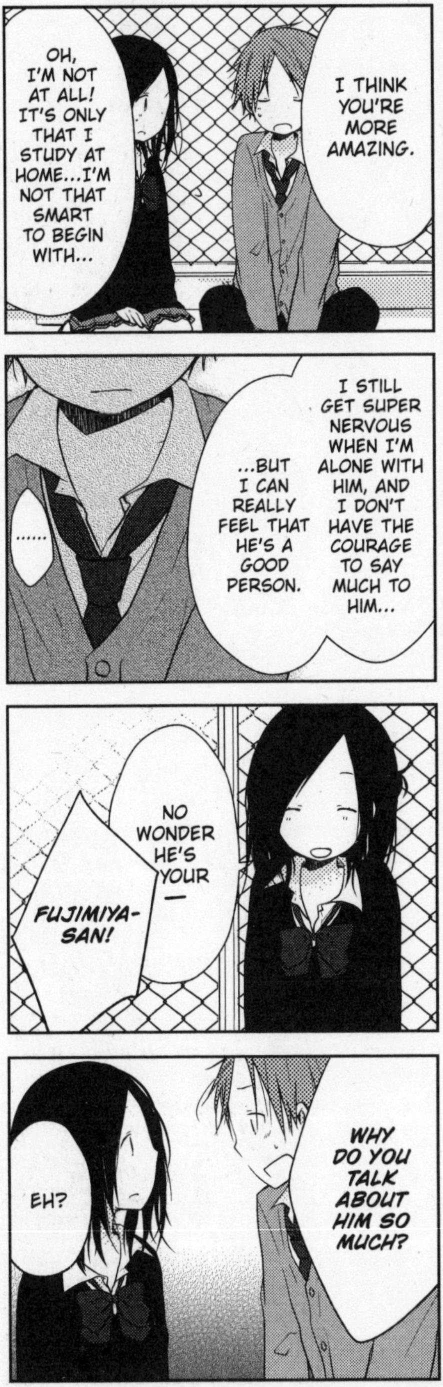
I THINK YOU'RE MORE AMAZING.
OH, I'M NOT AT ALL! IT'S ONLY THAT I STUDY AT HOME...I'M NOT THAT SMART TO BEGIN WITH...
I STILL GET SUPER NERVOUS WHEN I'M ALONE WITH HIM, AND I DON'T HAVE THE COURAGE TO SAY MUCH TO HIM...
...BUT I CAN REALLY FEEL THAT HE'S A GOOD PERSON.
......
NO WONDER HE'S YOUR —
FUJIMIYA-SAN!
WHY DO YOU TALK ABOUT HIM SO MUCH?
EH?

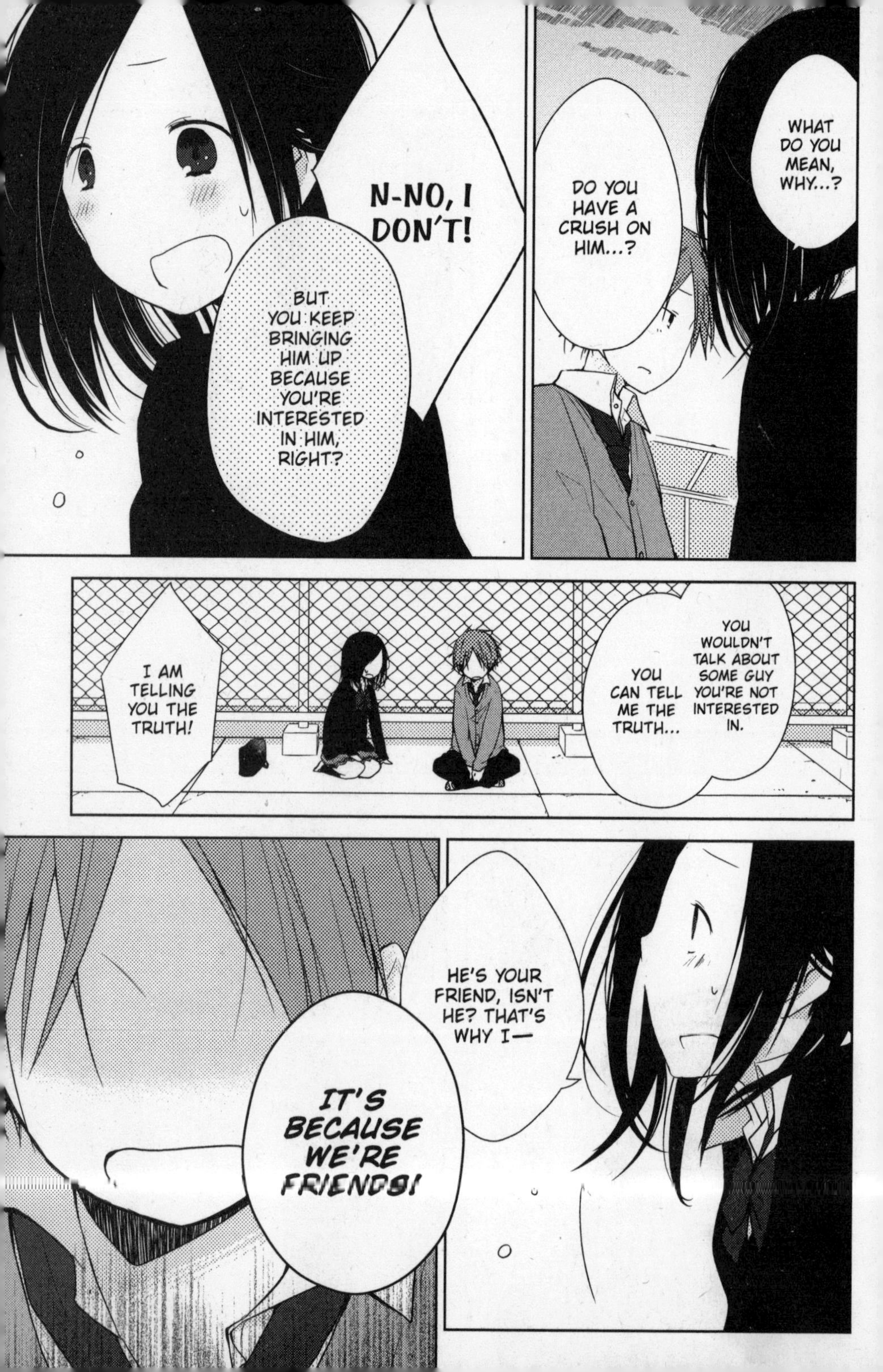
WHAT DO YOU MEAN, WHY...?
DO YOU HAVE A CRUSH ON HIM...?
N-NO, I DON'T!
BUT YOU KEEP BRINGING HIM UP BECAUSE YOU'RE INTERESTED IN HIM, RIGHT?
YOU WOULDN'T TALK ABOUT SOME GUY YOU'RE NOT INTERESTED IN.
YOU CAN TELL ME THE TRUTH...
I AM TELLING YOU THE TRUTH!
HE'S YOUR FRIEND, ISN'T HE? THAT'S WHY I—
IT'S BECAUSE WE'RE FRIENDS!

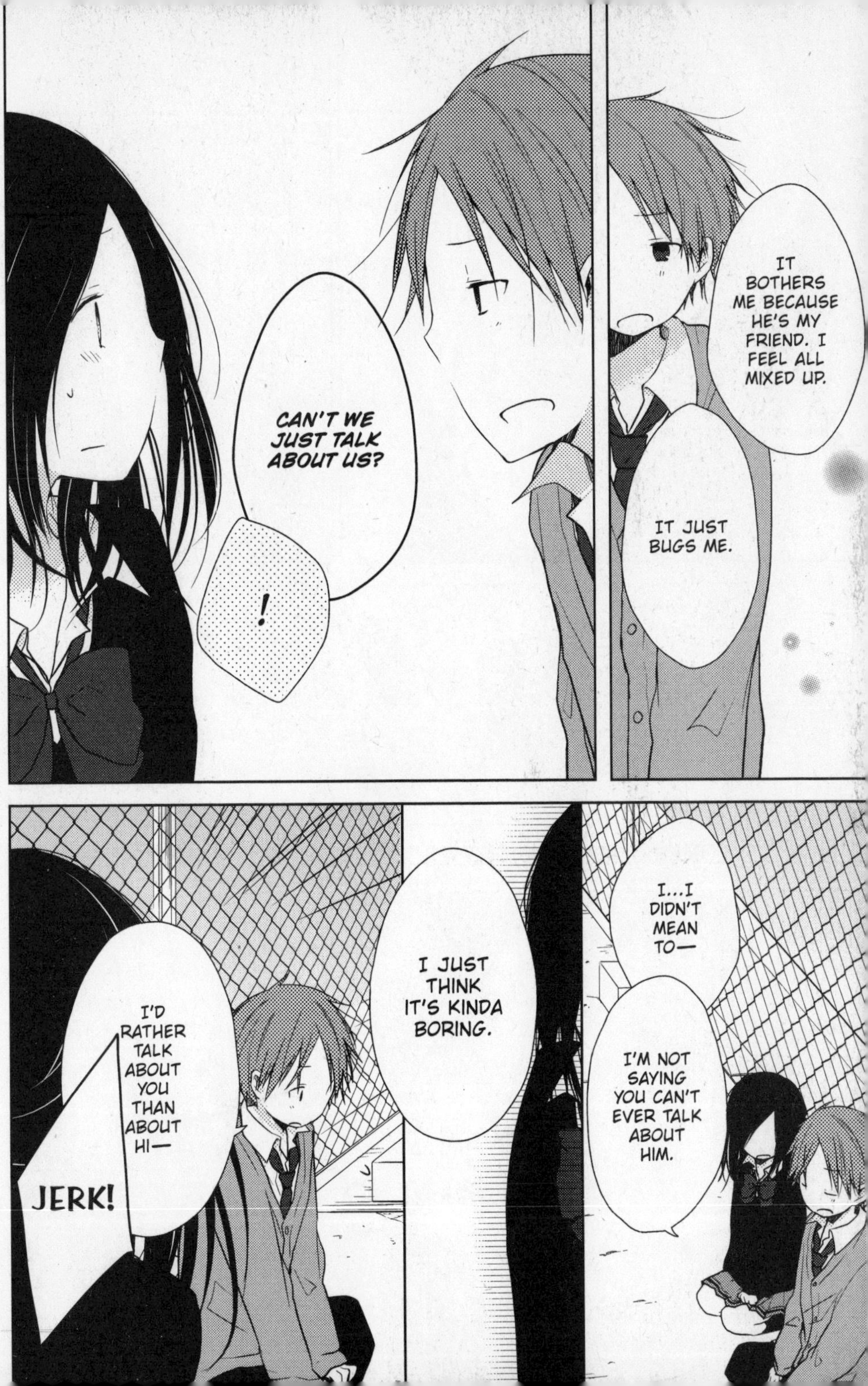
IT BOTHERS ME BECAUSE HE'S MY FRIEND. I FEEL ALL MIXED UP.
IT JUST BUGS ME.
CAN'T WE JUST TALK ABOUT US?
!
I...I DIDN'T MEAN TO—
I'M NOT SAYING YOU CAN'T EVER TALK ABOUT HIM.
I JUST THINK IT'S KINDA BORING.
I'D RATHER TALK ABOUT YOU THAN ABOUT HI—
JERK!

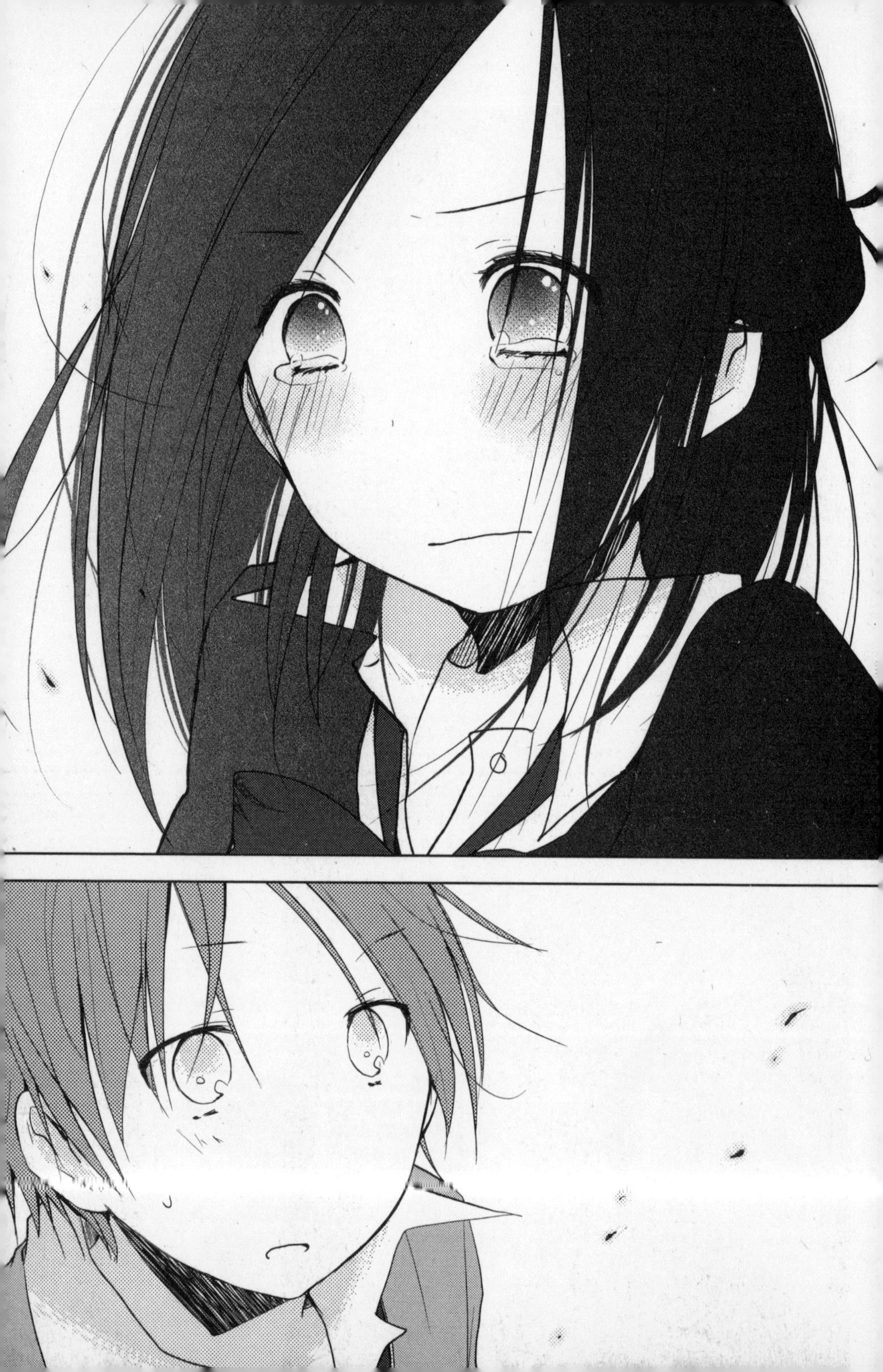

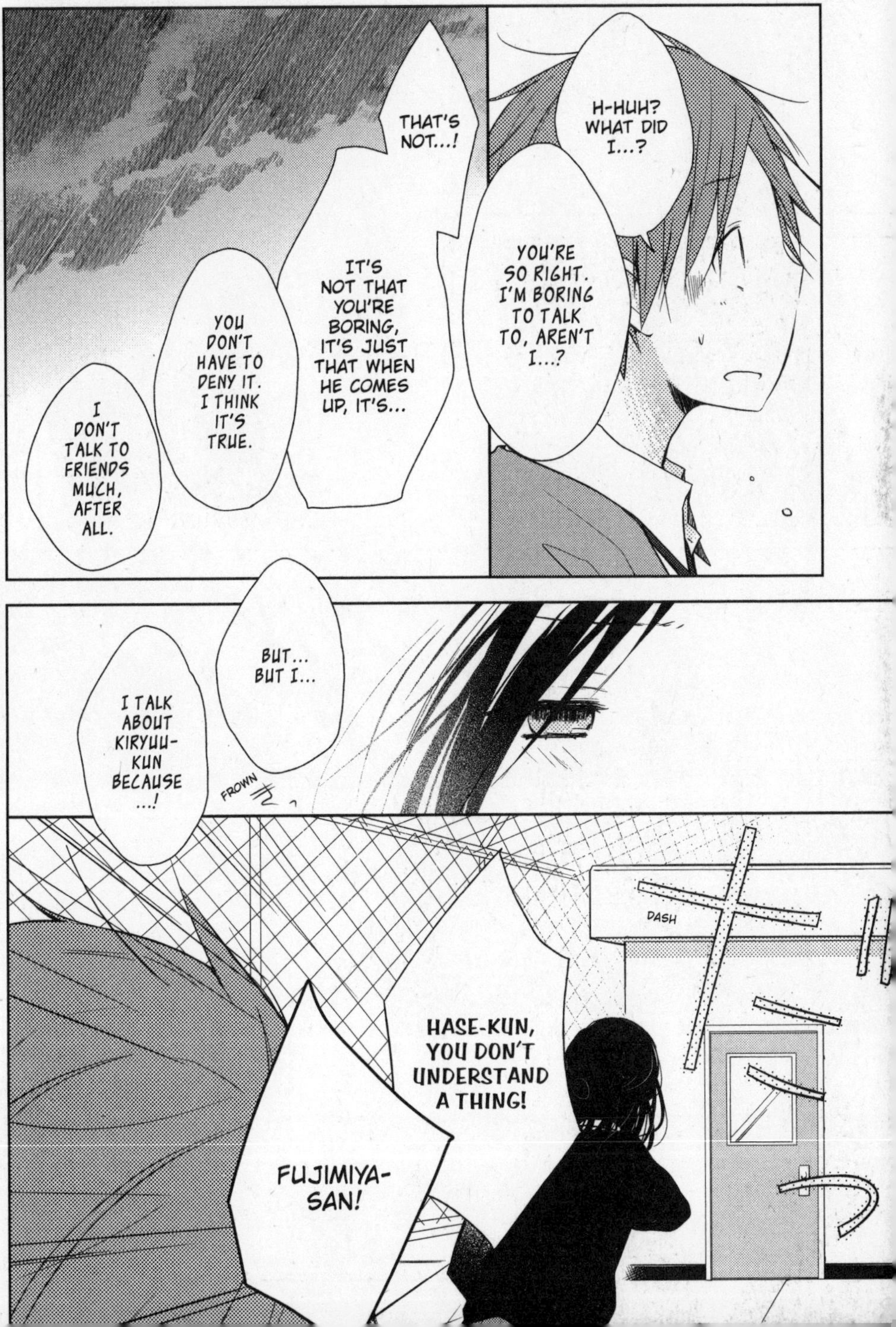
H-HUH? WHAT DID I...?
YOU'RE SO RIGHT. I'M BORING TO TALK TO, AREN'T I...?
THAT'S NOT...!
IT'S NOT THAT YOU'RE BORING, IT'S JUST THAT WHEN HE COMES UP, IT'S...
YOU DON'T HAVE TO DENY IT. I THINK IT'S TRUE.
I DON'T TALK TO FRIENDS MUCH, AFTER ALL.
BUT... BUT I...
FROWN
I TALK ABOUT KIRYUU-KUN BECAUSE ...!
HASE-KUN, YOU DON'T UNDERSTAND A THING!
DASH
FUJIMIYA-SAN!

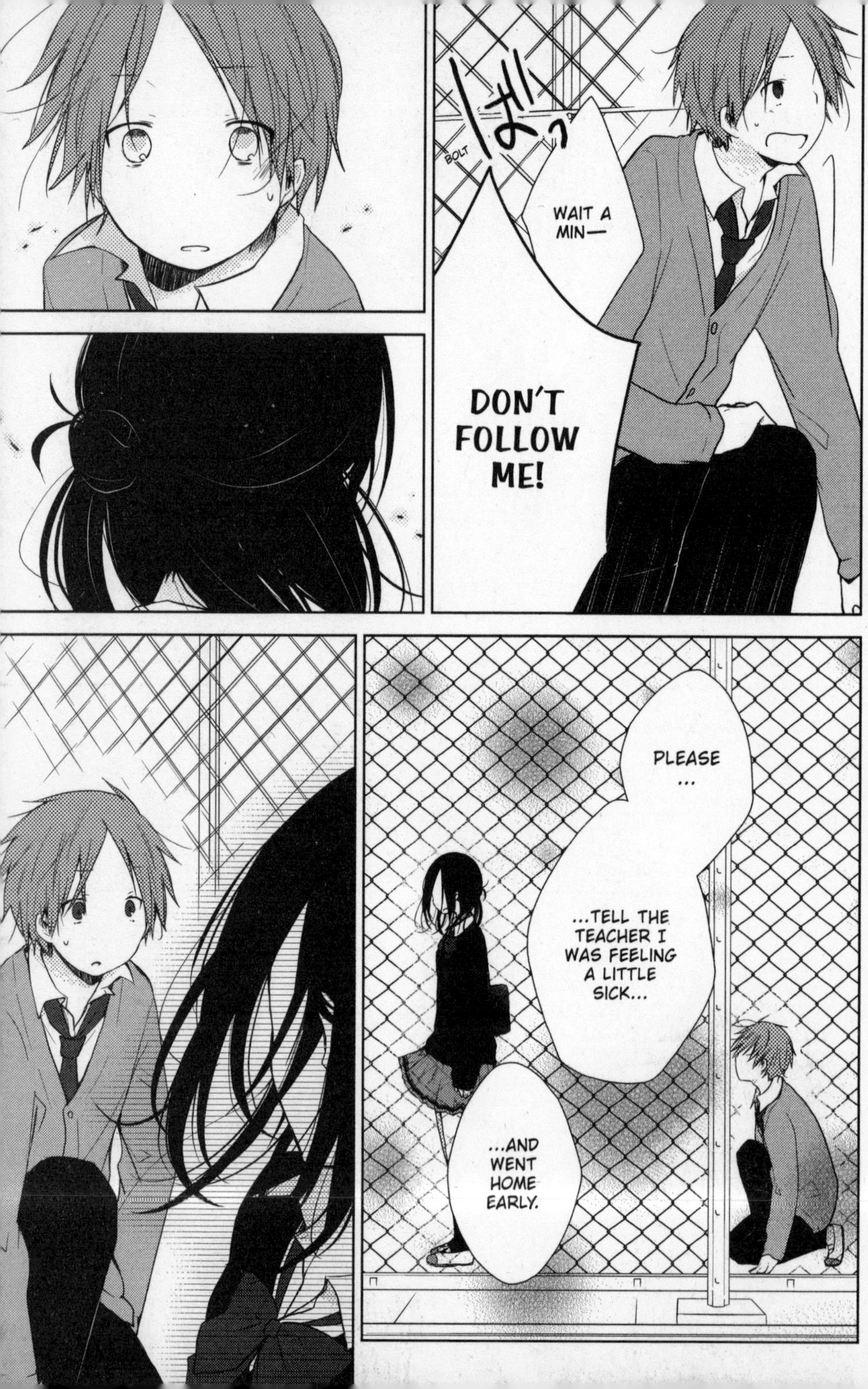
ぱっ
BOLT
WAIT A MIN—
DON'T FOLLOW ME!
PLEASE …
…TELL THE TEACHER I WAS FEELING A LITTLE SICK…
…AND WENT HOME EARLY.

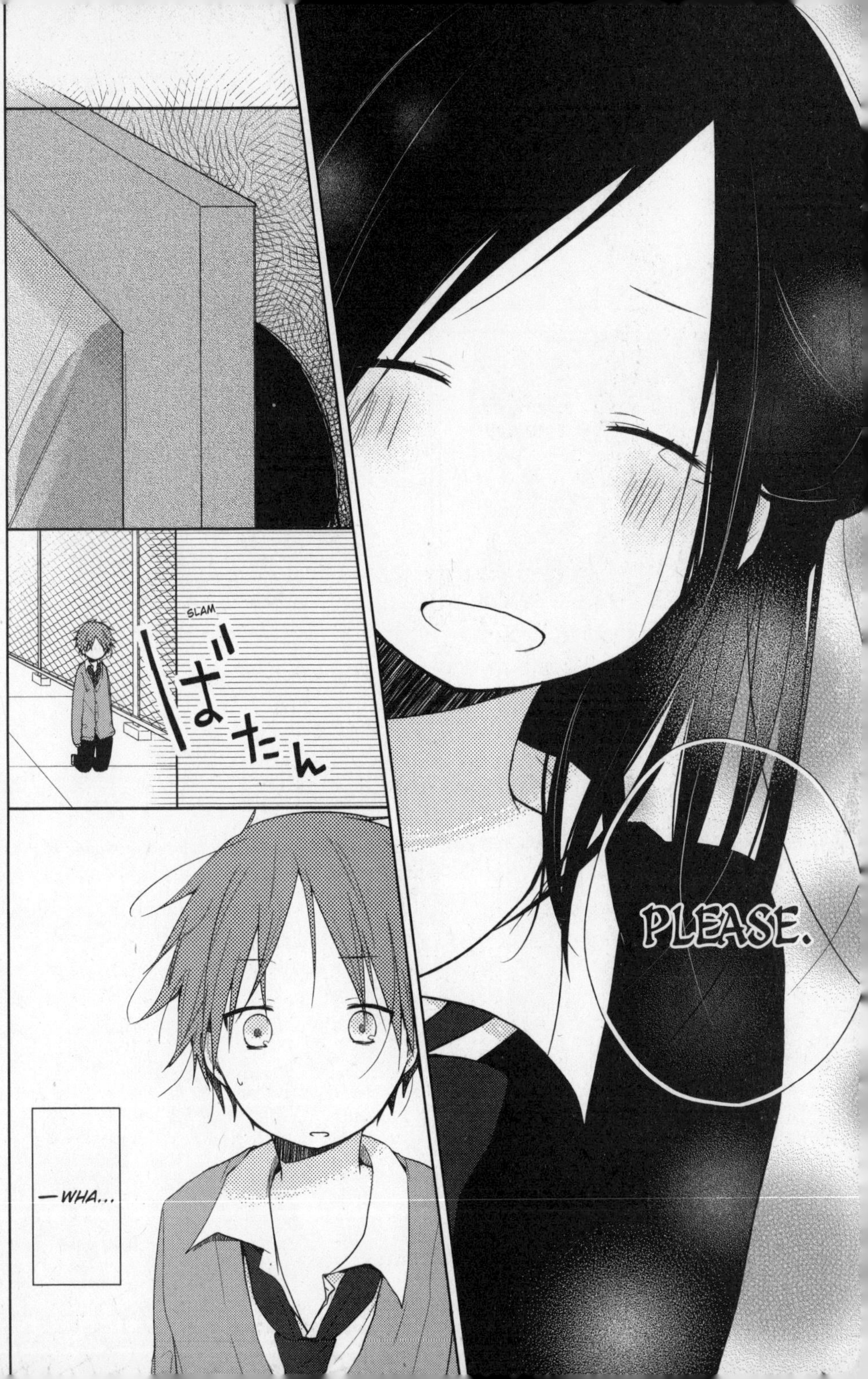
PLEASE.
SLAM
ばたん
—WHA...

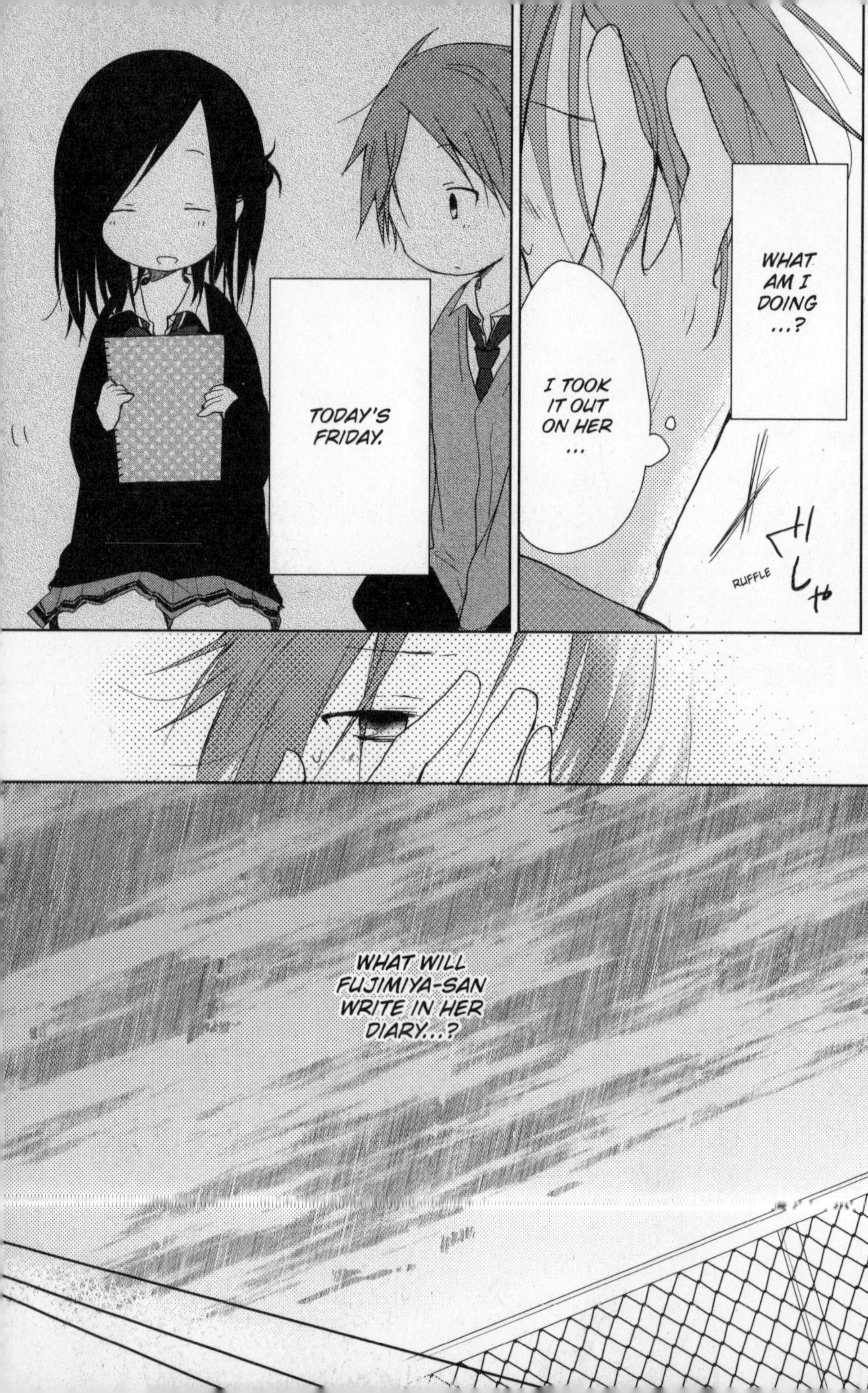
WHAT AM I DOING ...?
I TOOK IT OUT ON HER ...
RUFFLE
TODAY'S FRIDAY.
WHAT WILL FUJIMIYA-SAN WRITE IN HER DIARY...?

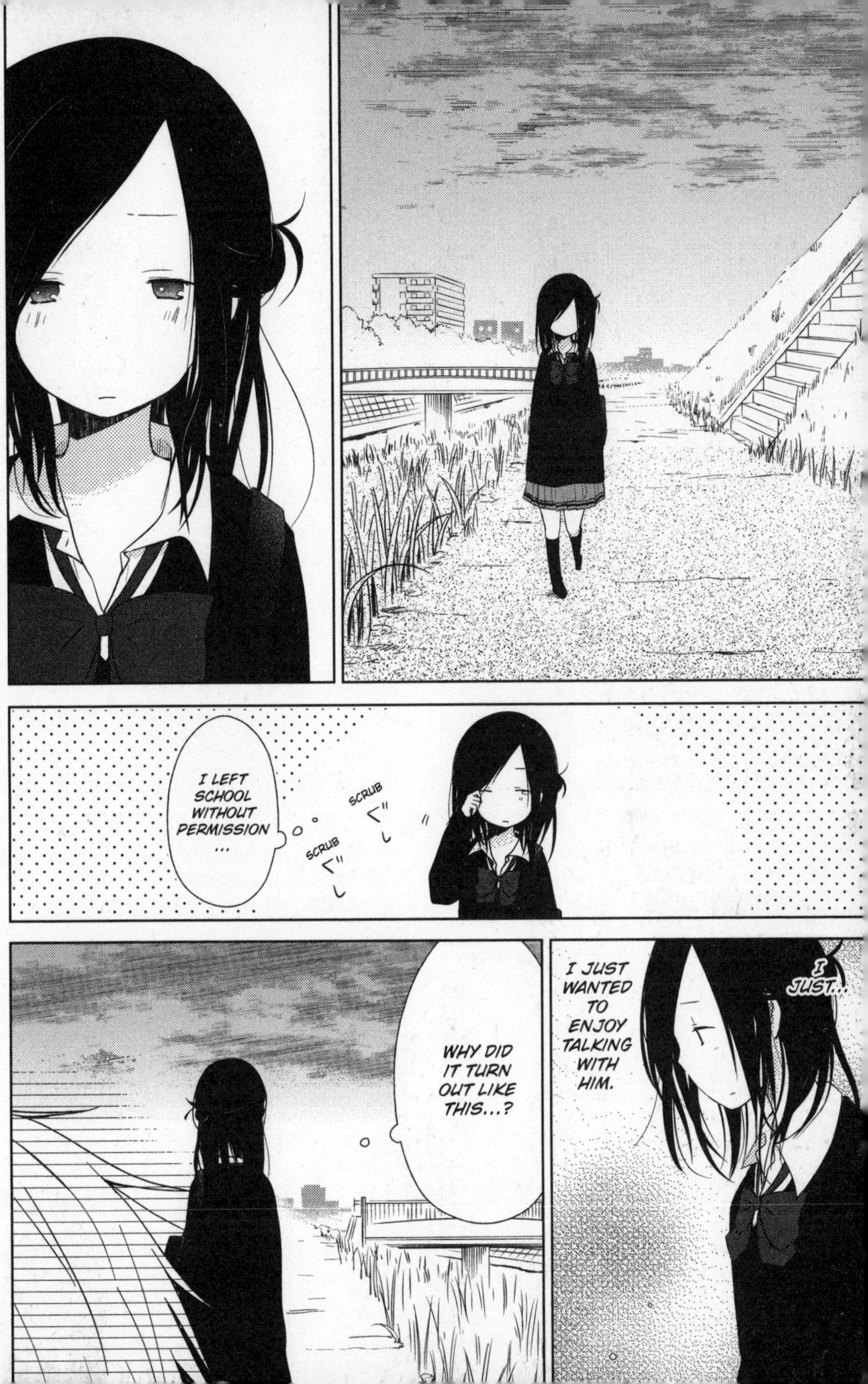
I LEFT SCHOOL WITHOUT PERMISSION...
SCRUB ぐし
SCRUB ぐし
I JUST...
I JUST WANTED TO ENJOY TALKING WITH HIM.
WHY DID IT TURN OUT LIKE THIS...?

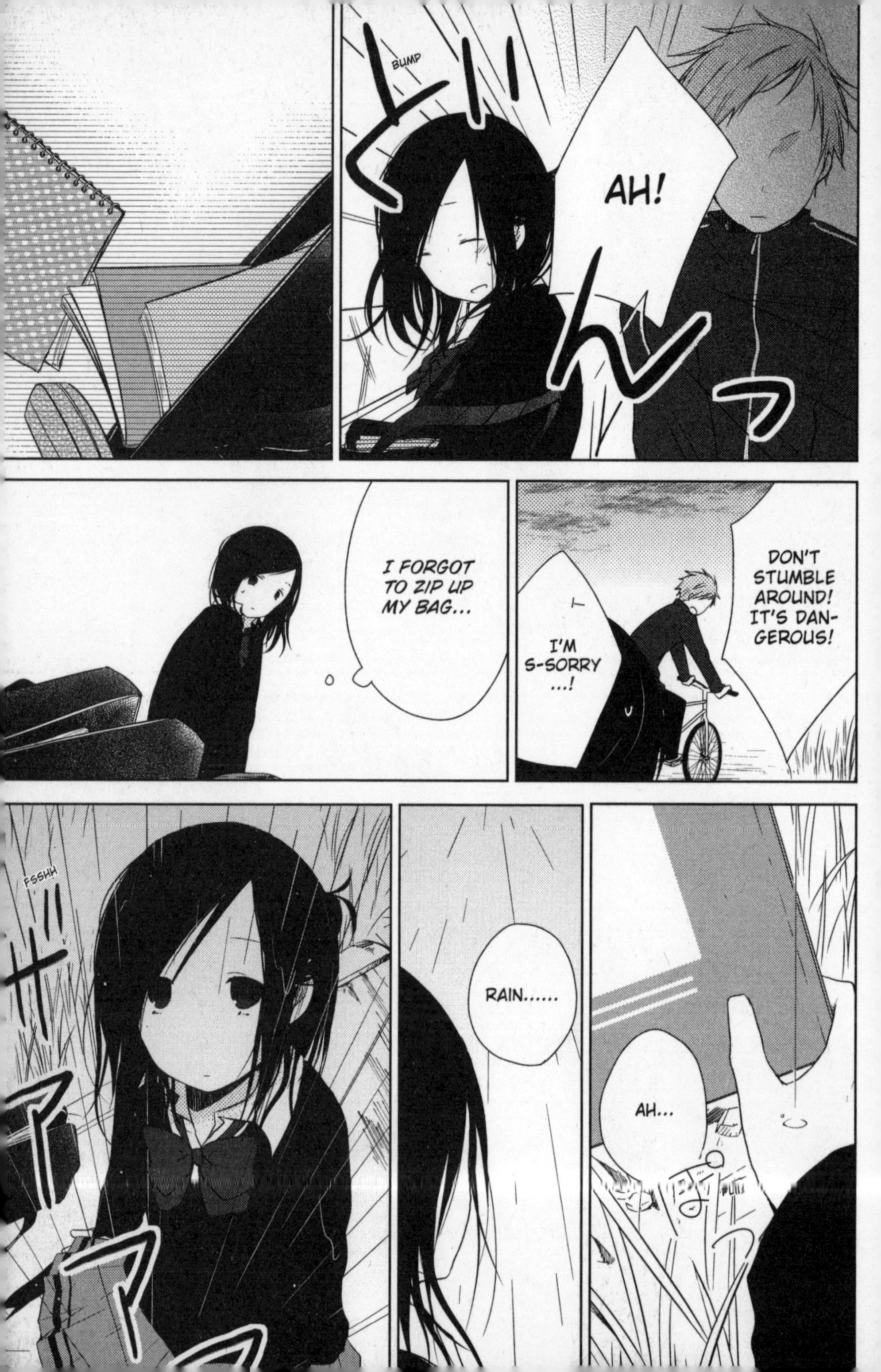
BUMP
AH!
DON'T STUMBLE AROUND! IT'S DAN-GEROUS!
I'M S-SORRY ...!
I FORGOT TO ZIP UP MY BAG...
AH...
RAIN......
FSSHH

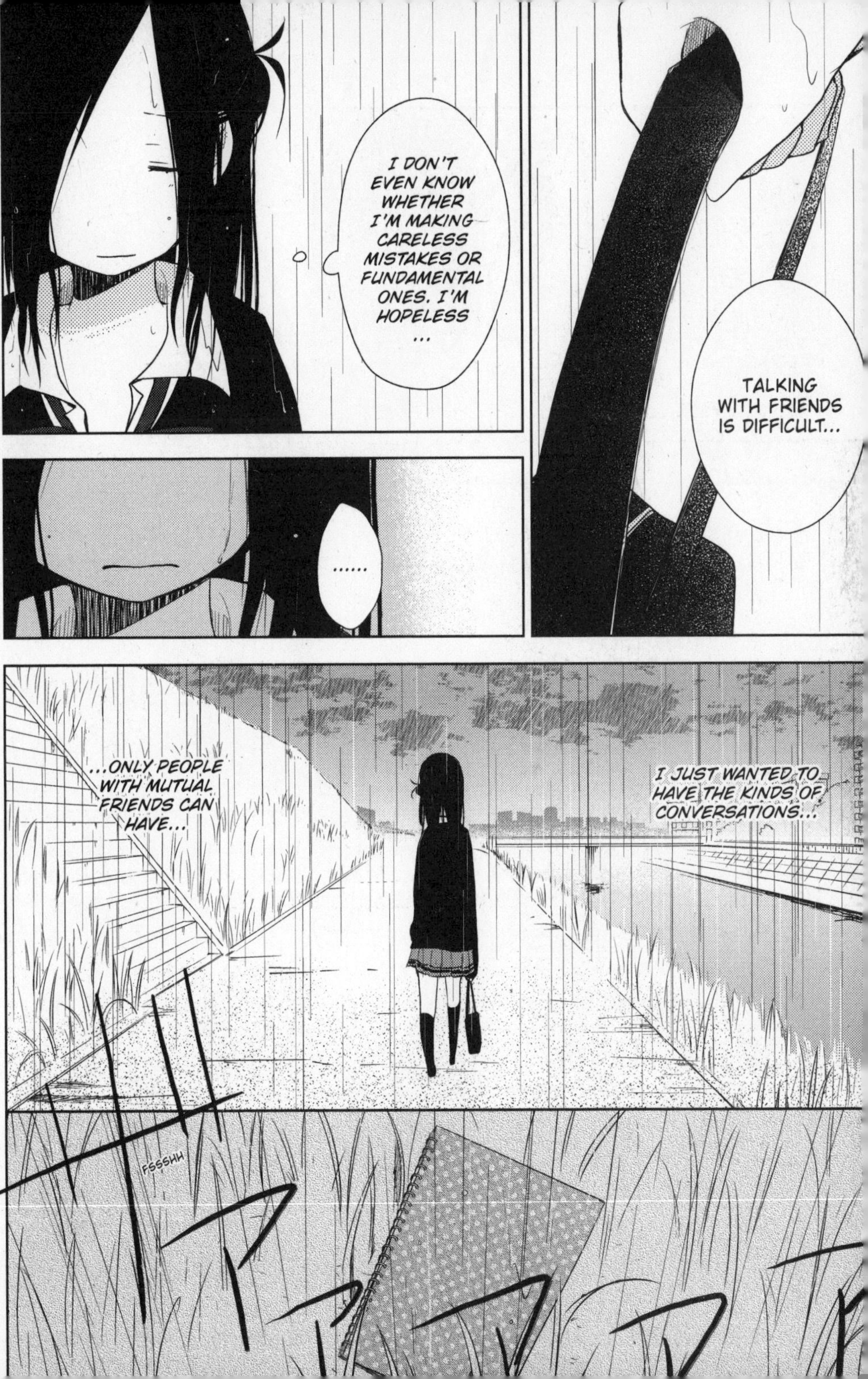
TALKING WITH FRIENDS IS DIFFICULT...
I DON'T EVEN KNOW WHETHER I'M MAKING CARELESS MISTAKES OR FUNDAMENTAL ONES. I'M HOPELESS ...
......
I JUST WANTED TO HAVE THE KINDS OF CONVERSATIONS...
...ONLY PEOPLE WITH MUTUAL FRIENDS CAN HAVE...
FSSSHH

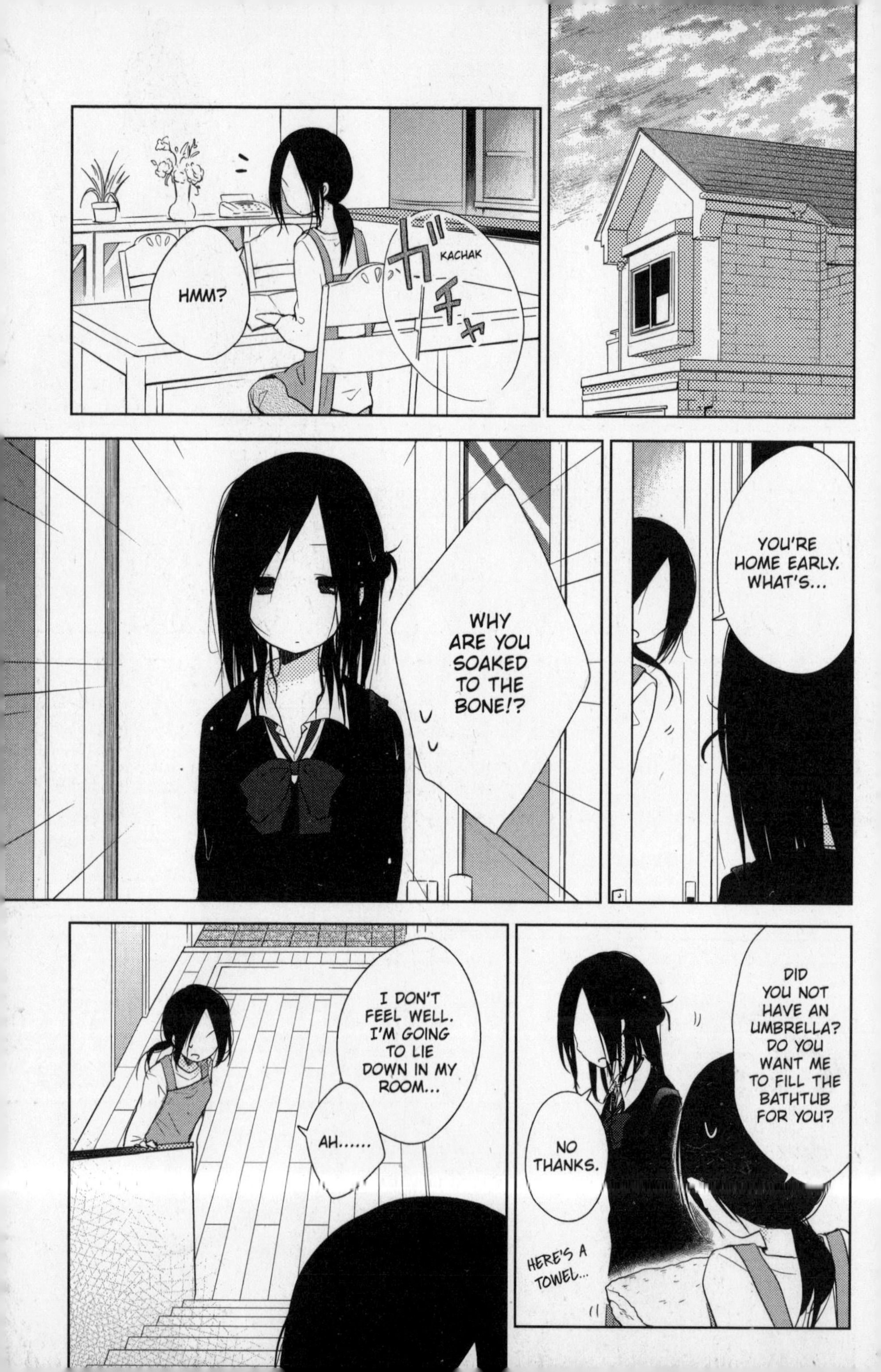
ガチャ
KACHAK
HMM?
YOU'RE HOME EARLY. WHAT'S...
WHY ARE YOU SOAKED TO THE BONE!?
DID YOU NOT HAVE AN UMBRELLA? DO YOU WANT ME TO FILL THE BATHTUB FOR YOU?
NO THANKS.
HERE'S A TOWEL...
I DON'T FEEL WELL. I'M GOING TO LIE DOWN IN MY ROOM...
AH......

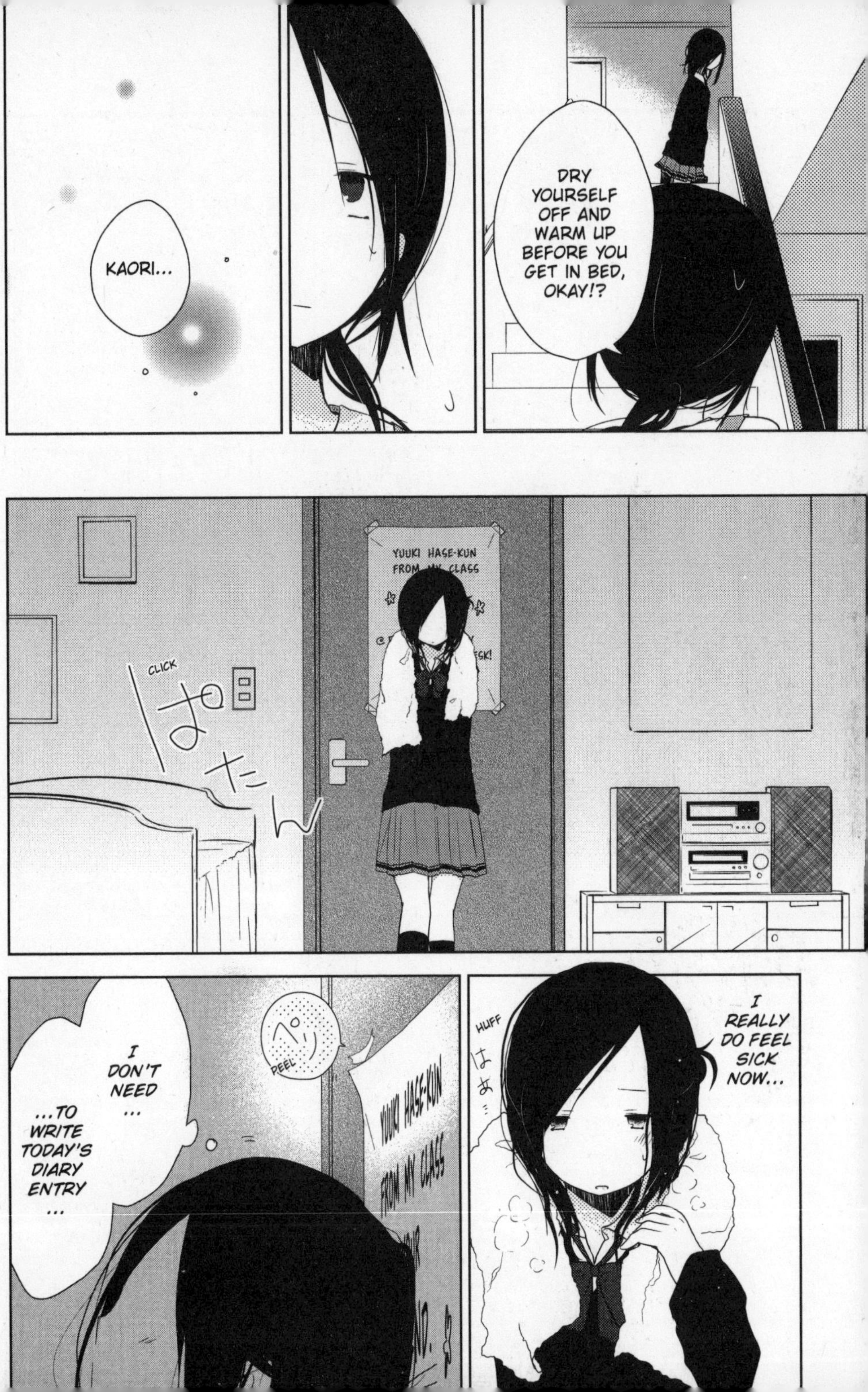
DRY YOURSELF OFF AND WARM UP BEFORE YOU GET IN BED, OKAY!?
KAORI...
YUUKI HASE-KUN FROM MY CLASS
CLICK
はたん
HUFF
はぁ
I REALLY DO FEEL SICK NOW...
ペリ
PEEL
I DON'T NEED ...
...TO WRITE TODAY'S DIARY ENTRY ...
YUUKI HASE-KUN FROM MY CLASS

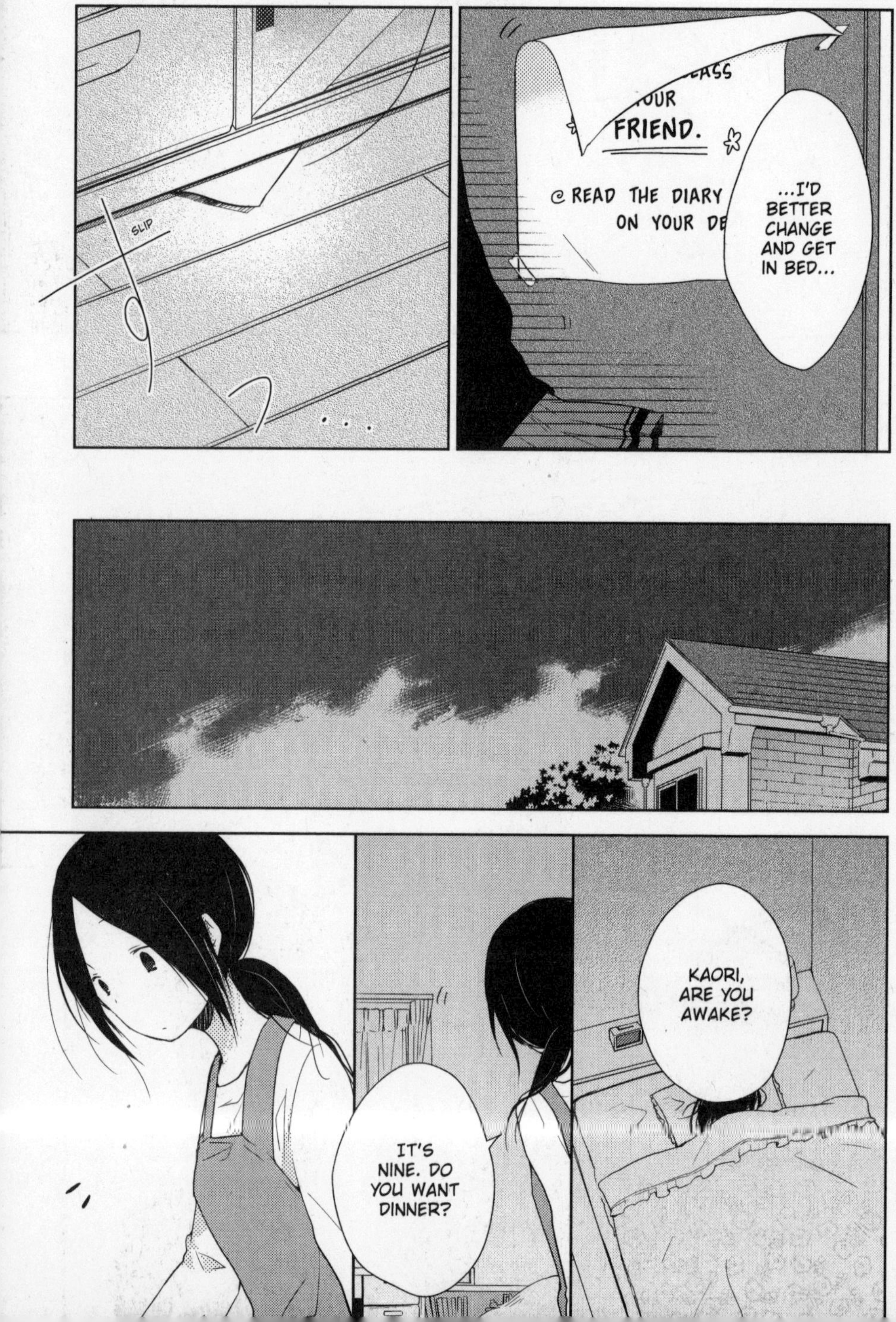
FRIEND.
READ THE DIARY
ON YOUR
...I'D BETTER CHANGE AND GET IN BED...
SLIP
...
KAORI, ARE YOU AWAKE?
IT'S NINE. DO YOU WANT DINNER?

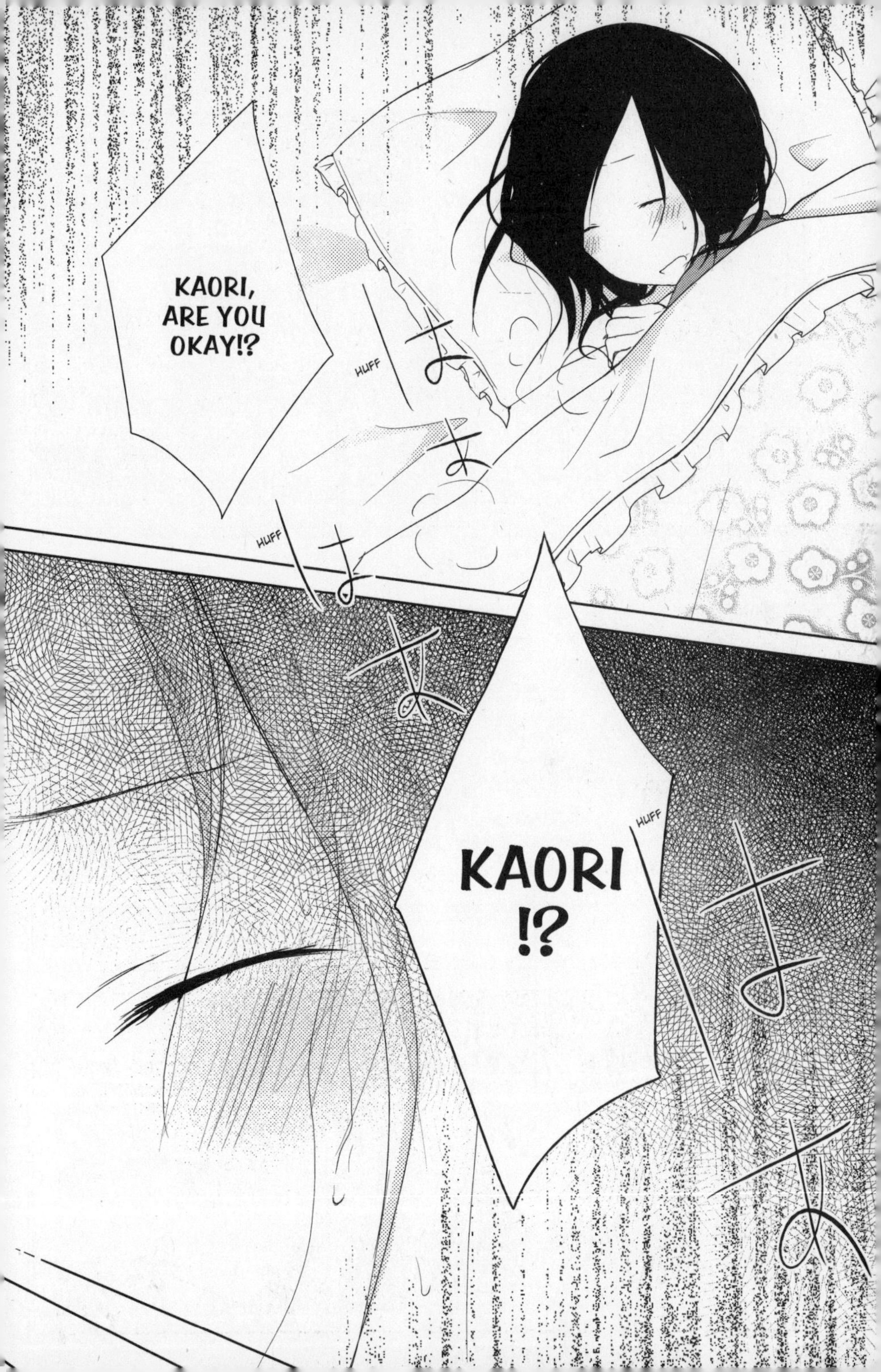
KAORI, ARE YOU OKAY!?
HUFF
HUFF
HUFF
KAORI !?

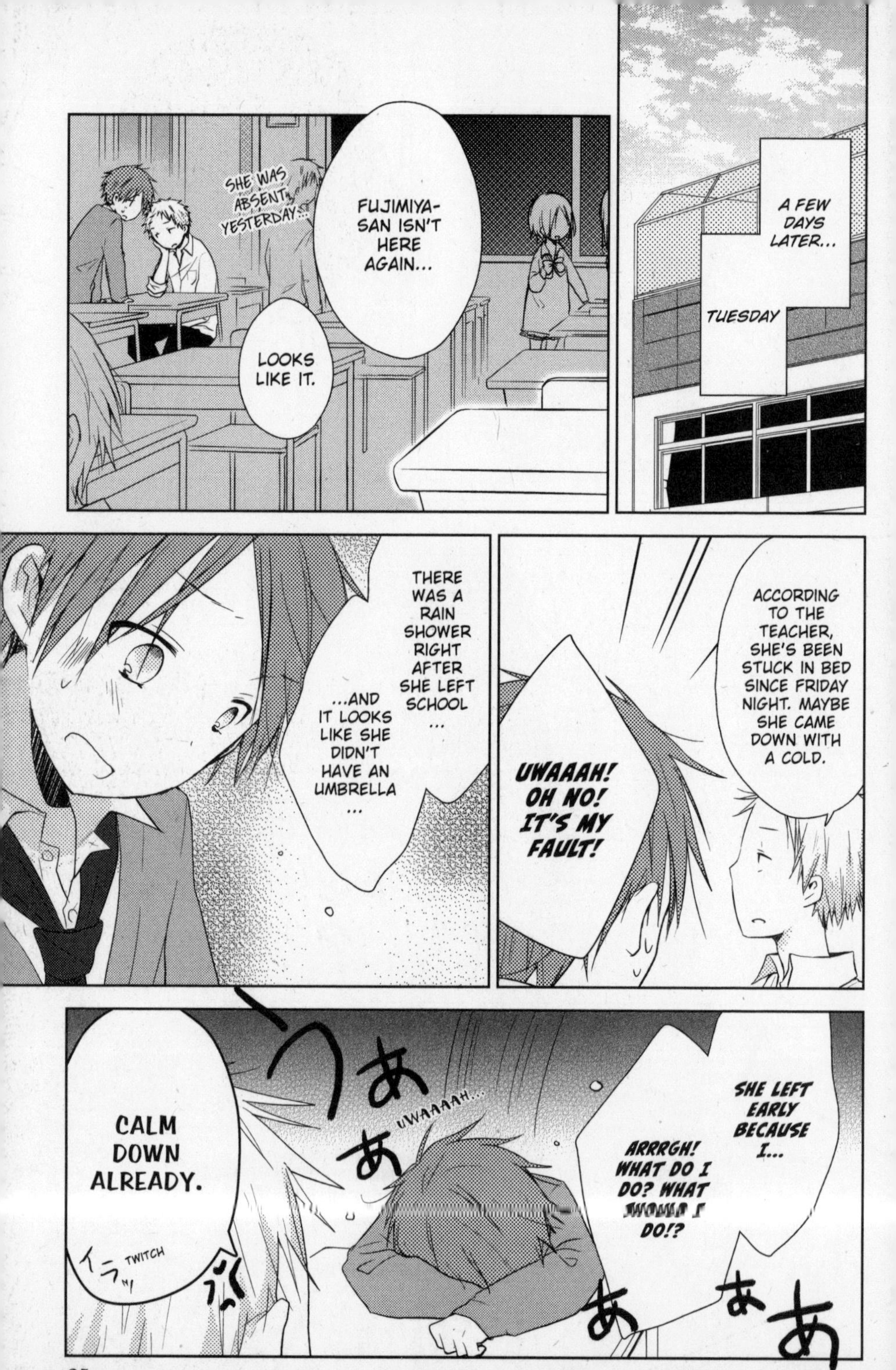
A FEW DAYS LATER...
TUESDAY
FUJIMIYA-SAN ISN'T HERE AGAIN...
SHE WAS ABSENT YESTERDAY...
LOOKS LIKE IT.
ACCORDING TO THE TEACHER, SHE'S BEEN STUCK IN BED SINCE FRIDAY NIGHT. MAYBE SHE CAME DOWN WITH A COLD.
UWAAAH! OH NO! IT'S MY FAULT!
THERE WAS A RAIN SHOWER RIGHT AFTER SHE LEFT SCHOOL...
...AND IT LOOKS LIKE SHE DIDN'T HAVE AN UMBRELLA...
SHE LEFT EARLY BECAUSE I...
ARRRGH! WHAT DO I DO? WHAT
DO!?
うああ
UWAAAAH...
CALM DOWN ALREADY.
イラッ
TWITCH

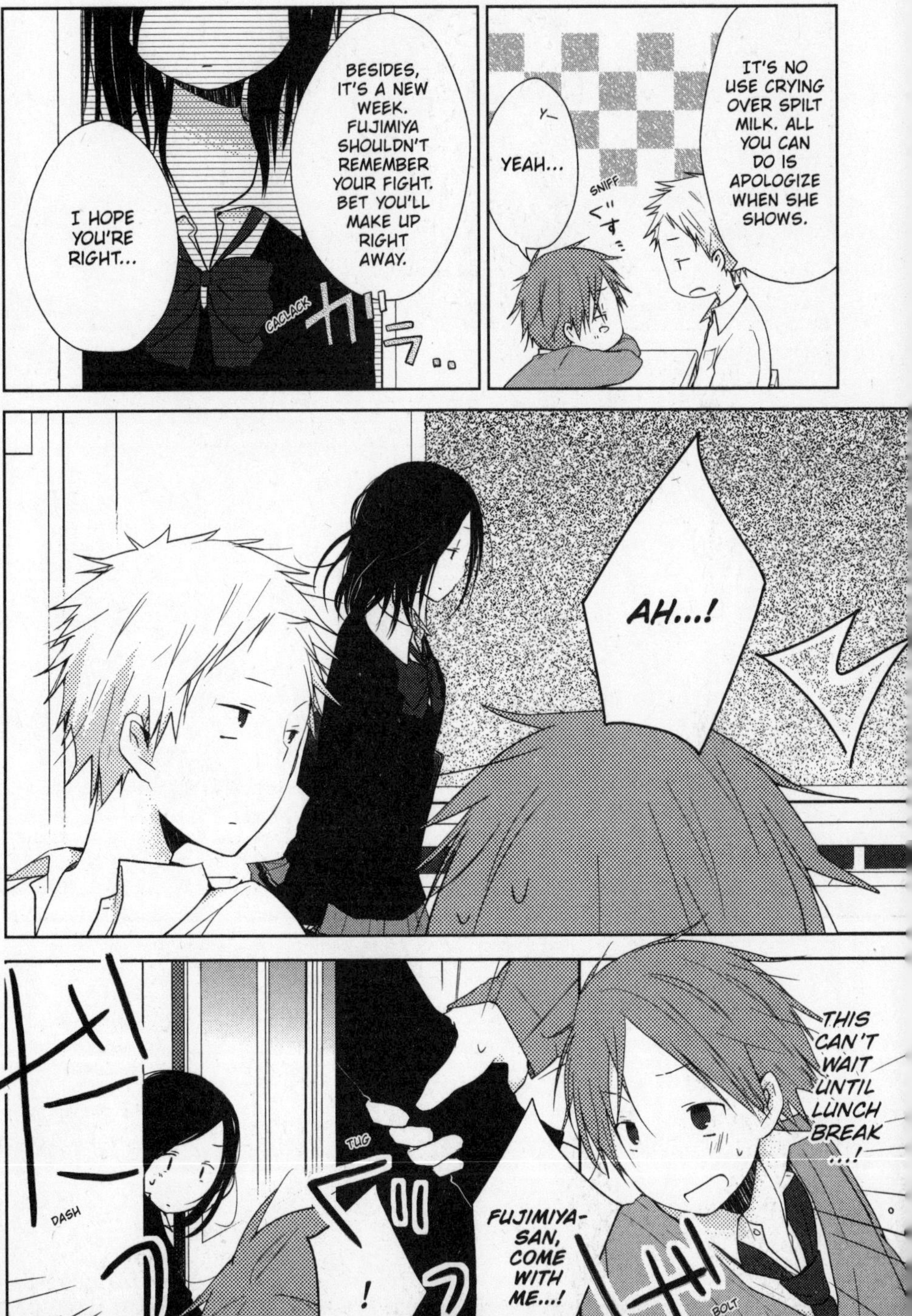
IT'S NO USE CRYING OVER SPILT MILK. ALL YOU CAN DO IS APOLOGIZE WHEN SHE SHOWS.
Y—
YEAH...
SNIFF
BESIDES, IT'S A NEW WEEK. FUJIMIYA SHOULDN'T REMEMBER YOUR FIGHT. BET YOU'LL MAKE UP RIGHT AWAY.
I HOPE YOU'RE RIGHT...
CACLACK
AH...!
THIS CAN'T WAIT UNTIL LUNCH BREAK ...!
BOLT
FUJIMIYA-SAN, COME WITH ME...!
TUG
DASH

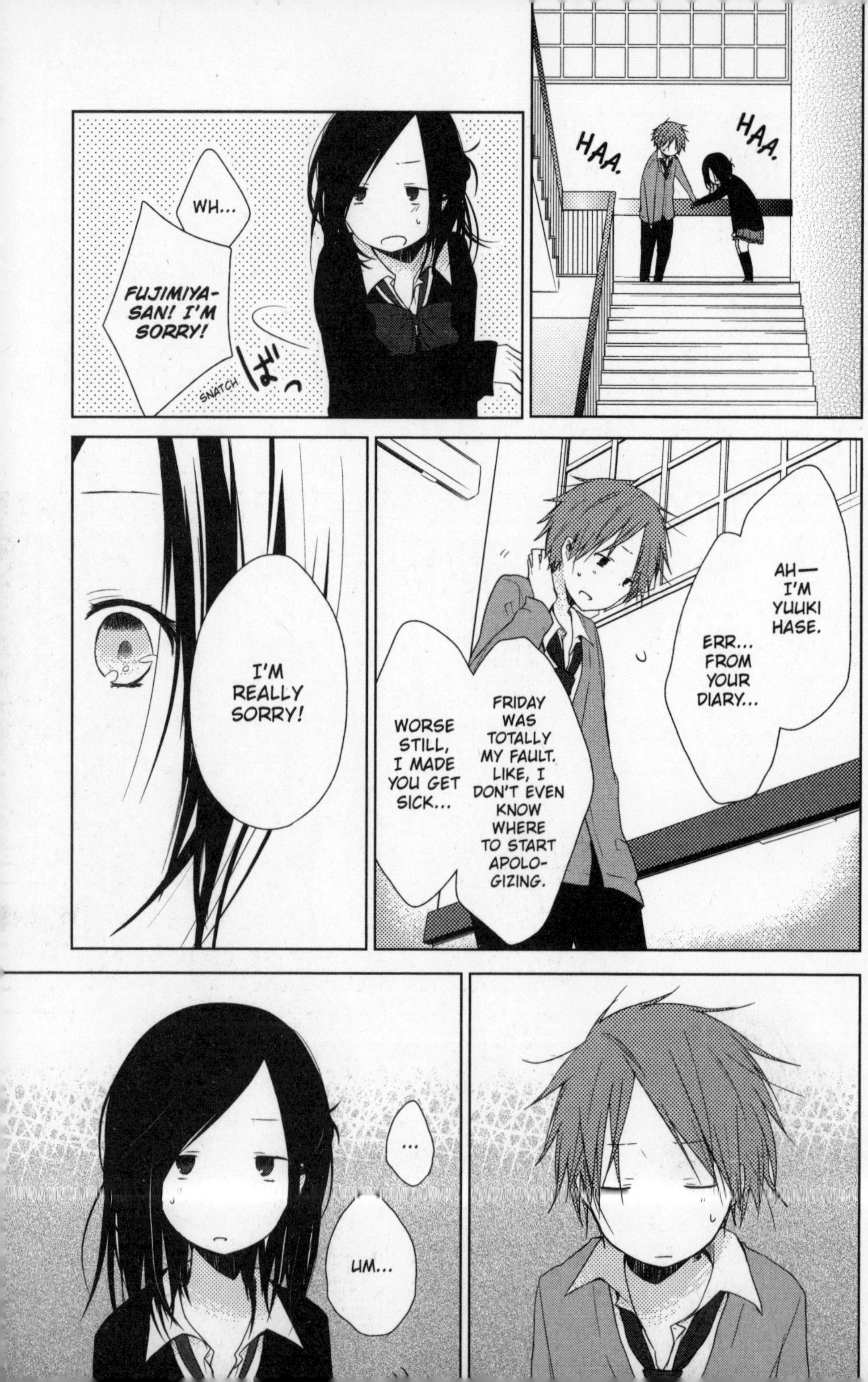
HAA.
HAA.
WH...
FUJIMIYA-SAN! I'M SORRY!
SNATCH
ばっ
AH— I'M YUUKI HASE.
ERR... FROM YOUR DIARY...
FRIDAY WAS TOTALLY MY FAULT. LIKE, I DON'T EVEN KNOW WHERE TO START APOLOGIZING.
WORSE STILL, I MADE YOU GET SICK...
I'M REALLY SORRY!
...
UM...

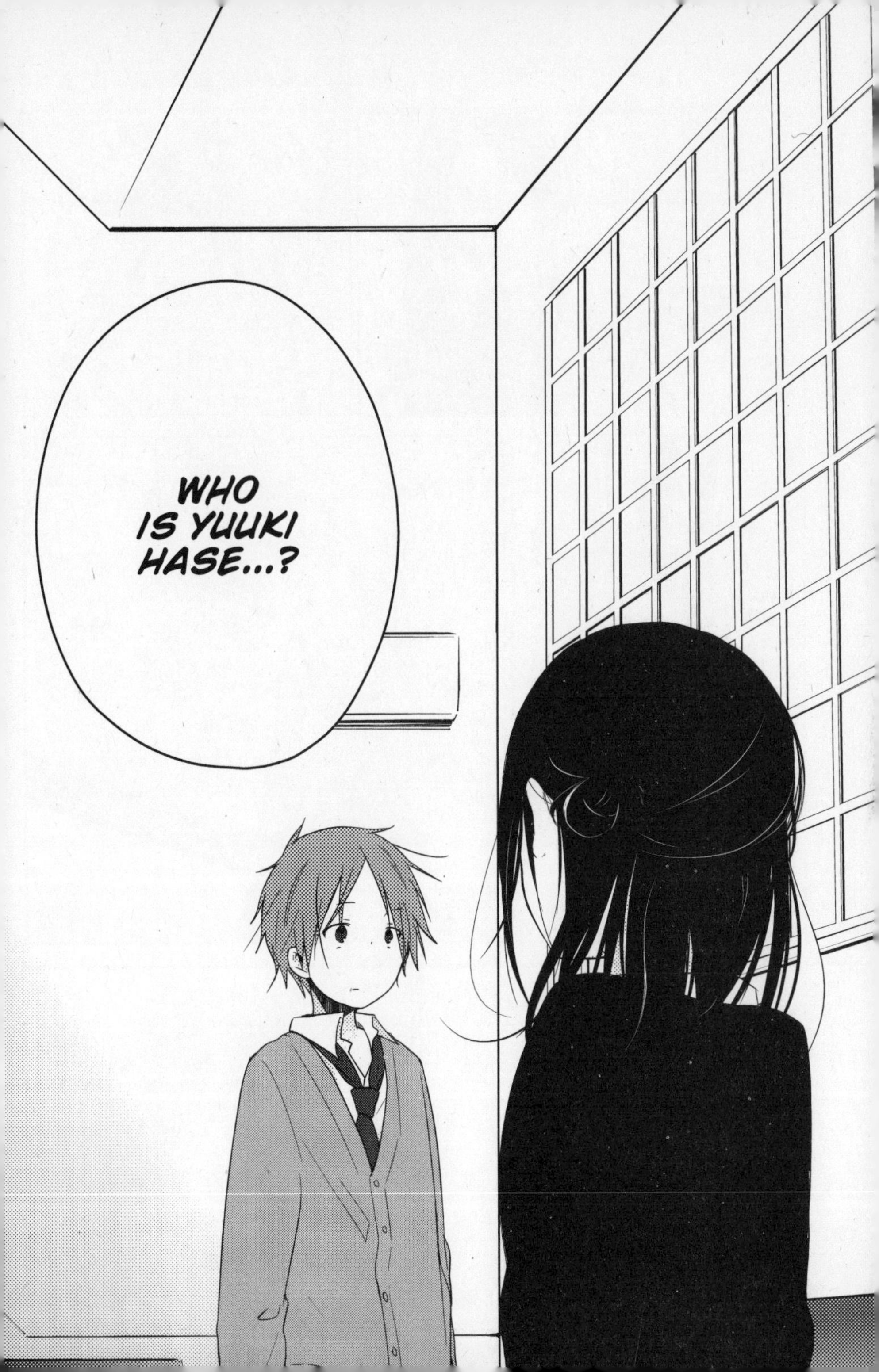
WHO IS YUUKI HASE...?

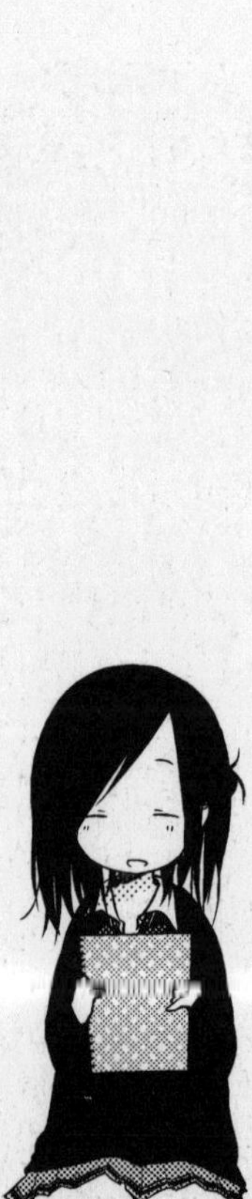

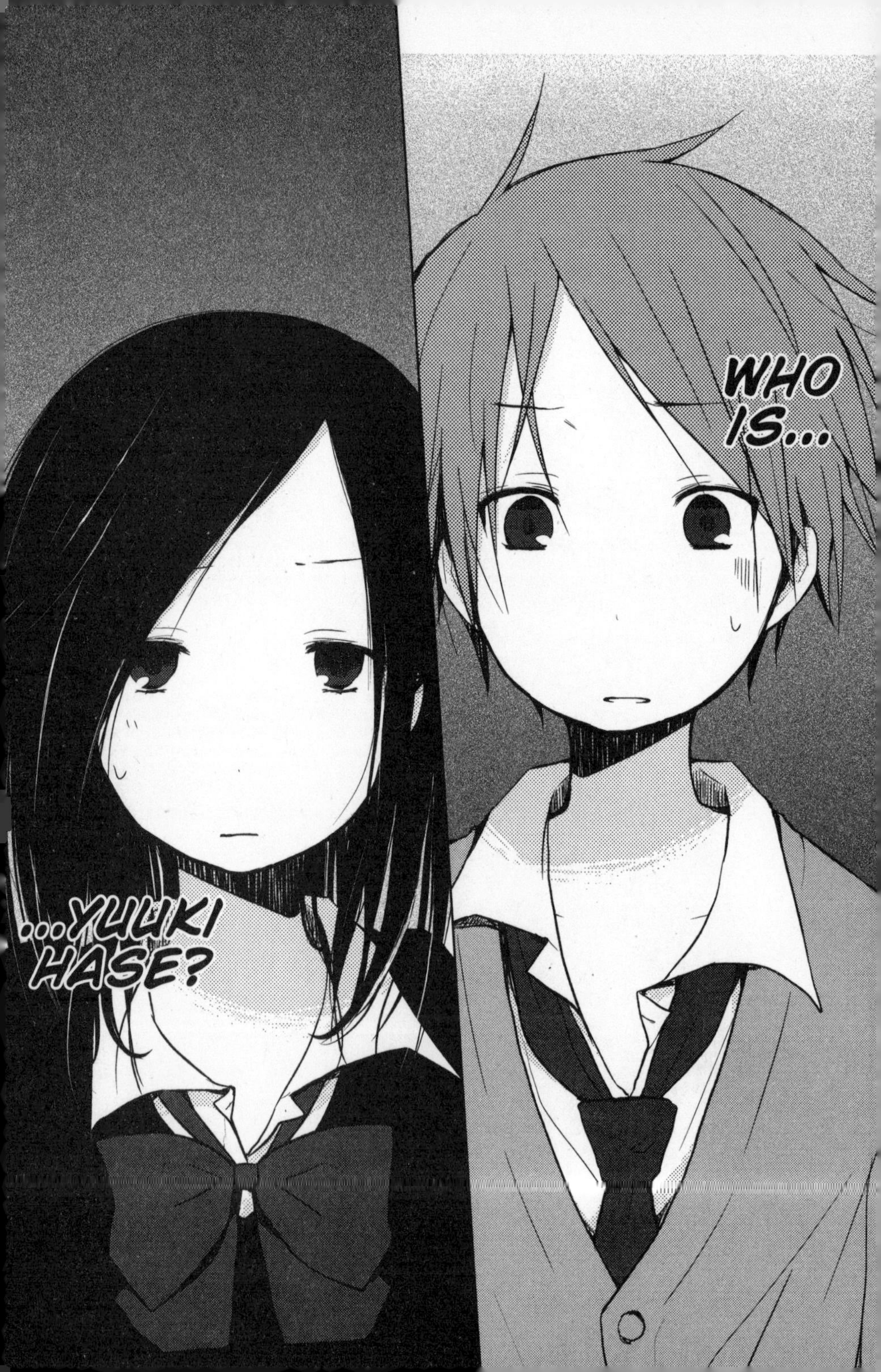
WHO IS...
...YUUKI HASE?

CHAPTER 5
FRIEND WHO?

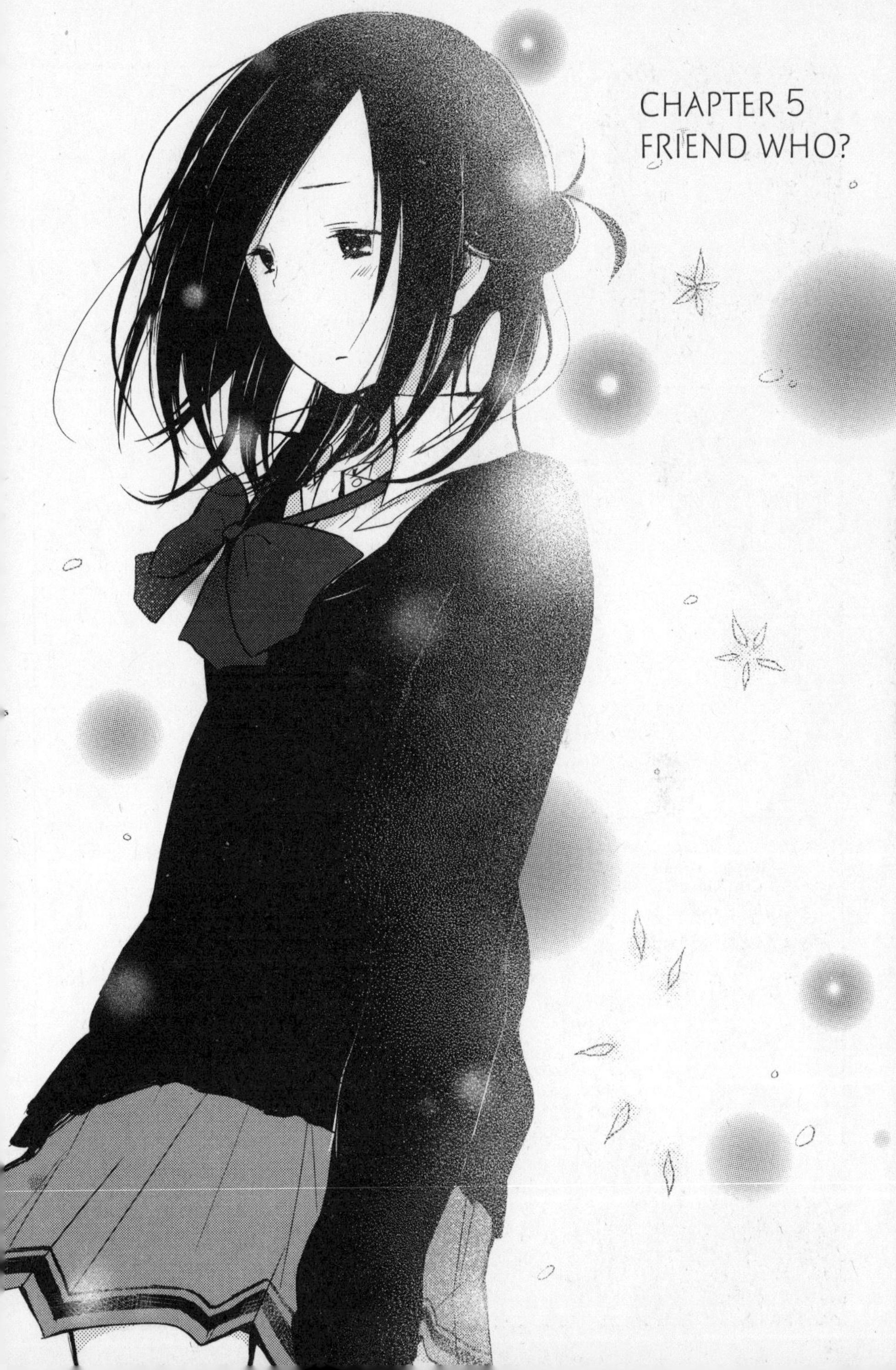

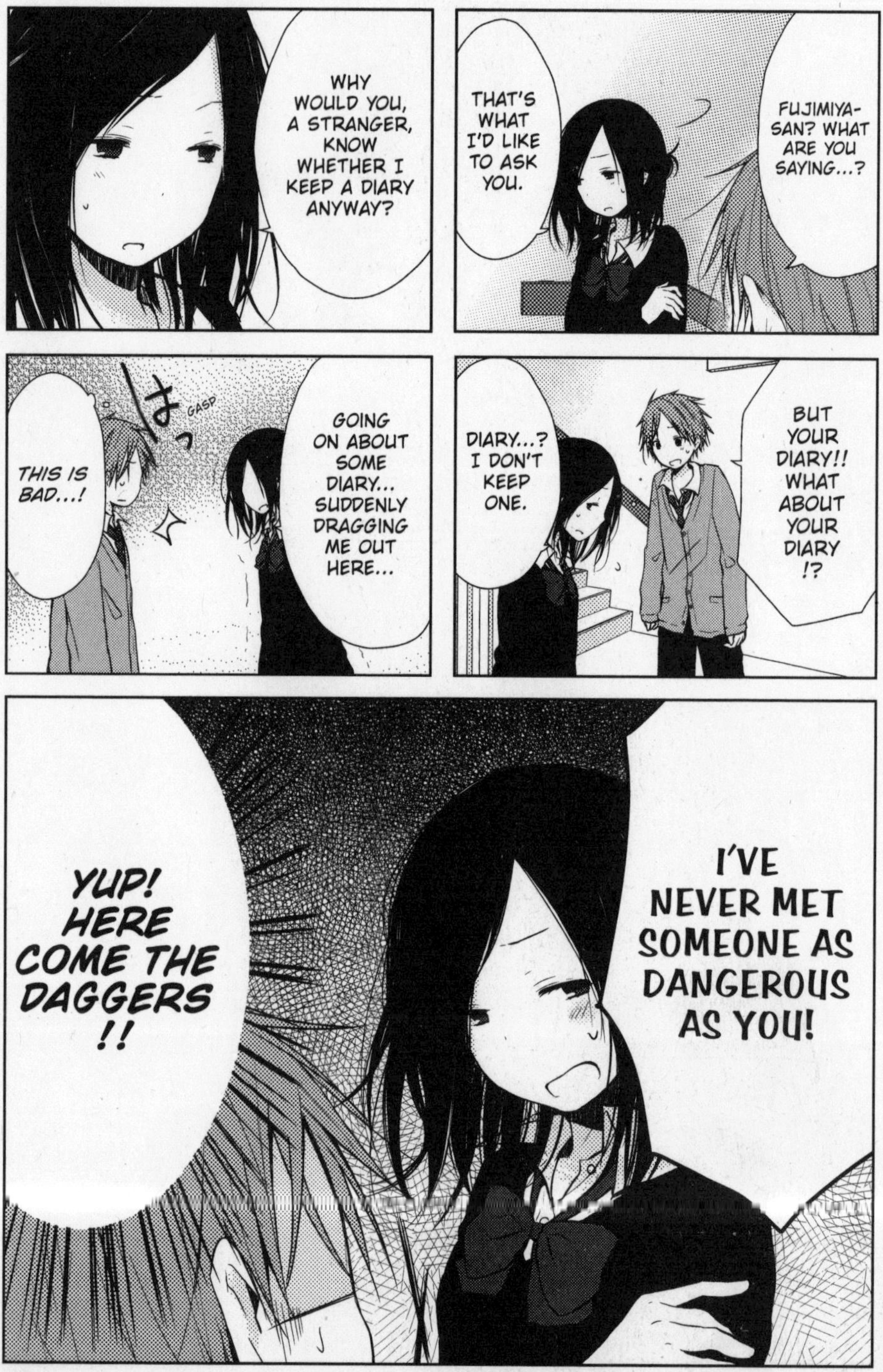
FUJIMIYA-SAN? WHAT ARE YOU SAYING...?
THAT'S WHAT I'D LIKE TO ASK YOU.
WHY WOULD YOU, A STRANGER, KNOW WHETHER I KEEP A DIARY ANYWAY?
BUT YOUR DIARY!! WHAT ABOUT YOUR DIARY!?
DIARY...? I DON'T KEEP ONE.
GOING ON ABOUT SOME DIARY... SUDDENLY DRAGGING ME OUT HERE...
はっ
GASP
THIS IS BAD...!
I'VE NEVER MET SOMEONE AS DANGEROUS AS YOU!
YUP! HERE COME THE DAGGERS!!

THE FINAL BLOW

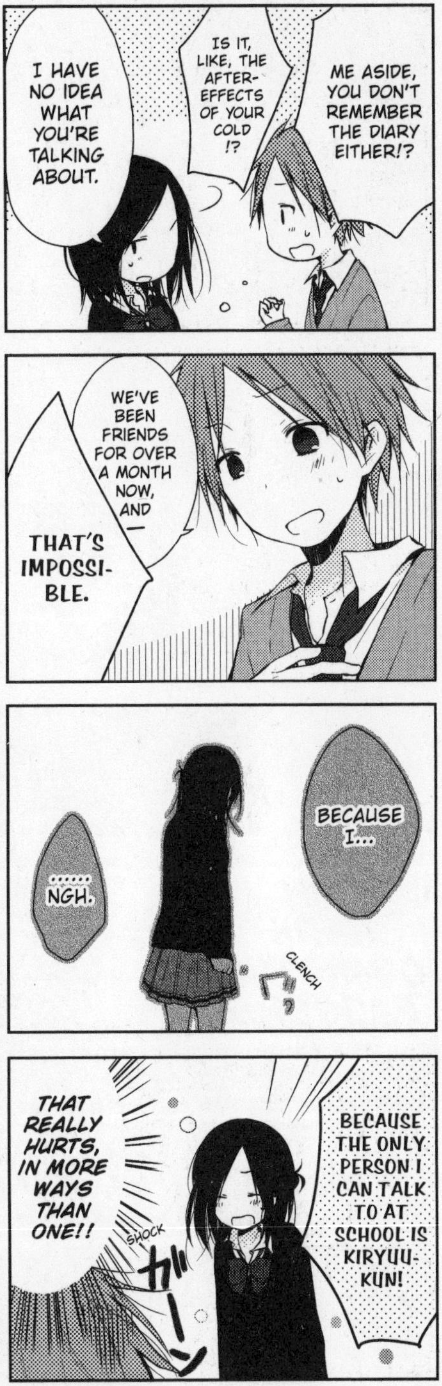
ME ASIDE, YOU DON'T REMEMBER THE DIARY EITHER!?
IS IT, LIKE, THE AFTER-EFFECTS OF YOUR COLD !?
I HAVE NO IDEA WHAT YOU'RE TALKING ABOUT.
WE'VE BEEN FRIENDS FOR OVER A MONTH NOW, AND —
THAT'S IMPOSSIBLE.
BECAUSE I...
...... NGH.
CLENCH
BECAUSE THE ONLY PERSON I CAN TALK TO AT SCHOOL IS KIRYUU-KUN!
THAT REALLY HURTS, IN MORE WAYS THAN ONE!!
SHOCK

SHOCK

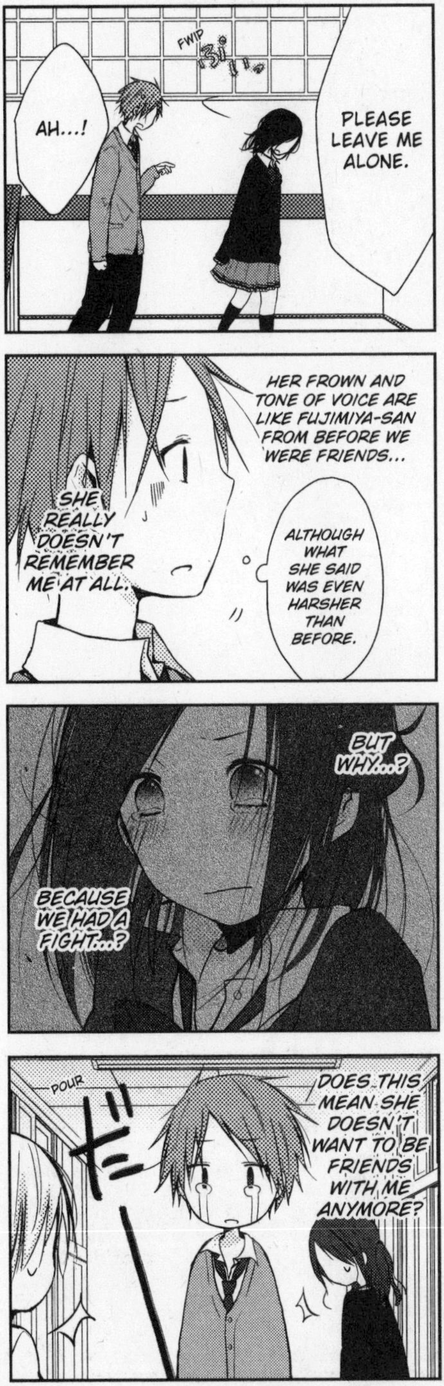
PLEASE LEAVE ME ALONE.
FWIP
AH...!
HER FROWN AND TONE OF VOICE ARE LIKE FUJIMIYA-SAN FROM BEFORE WE WERE FRIENDS...
ALTHOUGH WHAT SHE SAID WAS EVEN HARSHER THAN BEFORE.
SHE REALLY DOESN'T REMEMBER ME AT ALL.
BUT WHY...?
BECAUSE WE HAD A FIGHT...?
DOES THIS MEAN SHE DOESN'T WANT TO BE FRIENDS WITH ME ANYMORE?
POUR

FELT IT

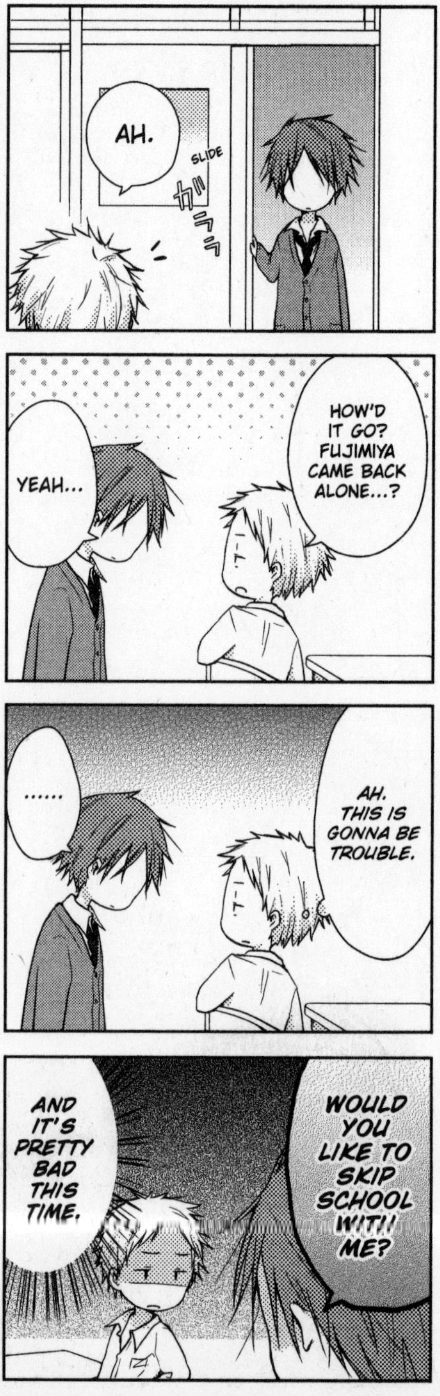
AH.
SLIDE
HOW'D IT GO? FUJIMIYA CAME BACK ALONE...?
YEAH...
AH. THIS IS GONNA BE TROUBLE.
......
WOULD YOU LIKE TO SKIP SCHOOL WITH ME?
AND IT'S PRETTY BAD THIS TIME.

POOR THING

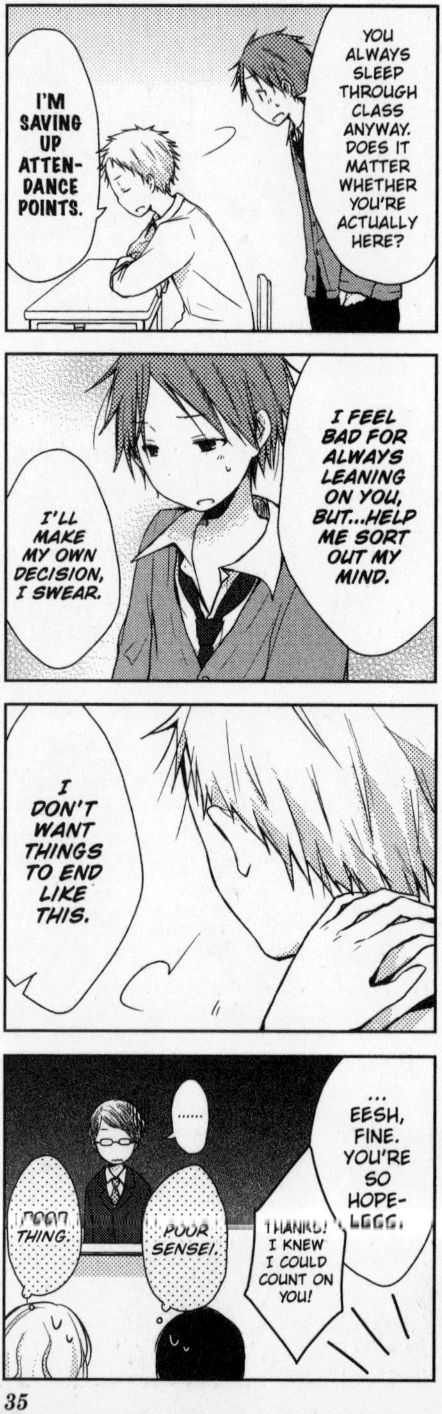
YOU ALWAYS SLEEP THROUGH CLASS ANYWAY. DOES IT MATTER WHETHER YOU'RE ACTUALLY HERE?
I'M SAVING UP ATTEN-DANCE POINTS.
I FEEL BAD FOR ALWAYS LEANING ON YOU, BUT...HELP ME SORT OUT MY MIND.
I'LL MAKE MY OWN DECISION, I SWEAR.
I DON'T WANT THINGS TO END LIKE THIS.
...EESH, FINE. YOU'RE SO HOPE-LESS.
......
THANKS! I KNEW I COULD COUNT ON YOU!
POOR SENSEI.
POOR THING.

SPECULATING

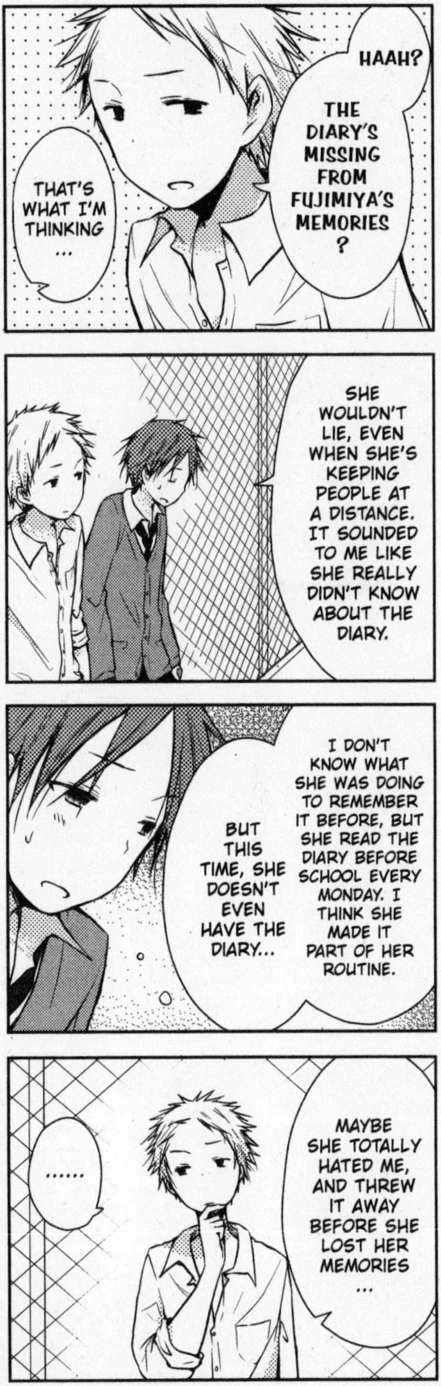
HAAH? THE DIARY'S MISSING FROM FUJIMIYA'S MEMORIES?
THAT'S WHAT I'M THINKING...
SHE WOULDN'T LIE, EVEN WHEN SHE'S KEEPING PEOPLE AT A DISTANCE. IT SOUNDED TO ME LIKE SHE REALLY DIDN'T KNOW ABOUT THE DIARY.
I DON'T KNOW WHAT SHE WAS DOING TO REMEMBER IT BEFORE, BUT SHE READ THE DIARY BEFORE SCHOOL EVERY MONDAY. I THINK SHE MADE IT PART OF HER ROUTINE.
BUT THIS TIME, SHE DOESN'T EVEN HAVE THE DIARY...
MAYBE SHE TOTALLY HATED ME, AND THREW IT AWAY BEFORE SHE LOST HER MEMORIES...
......

CAN'T STAND IT

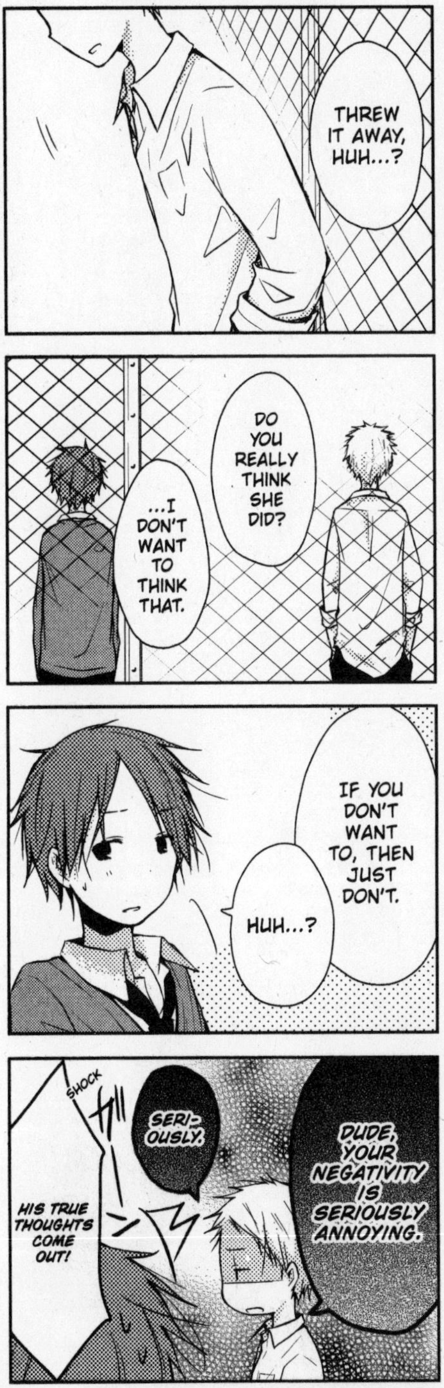
THREW IT AWAY, HUH...?
DO YOU REALLY THINK SHE DID?
...I DON'T WANT TO THINK THAT.
IF YOU DON'T WANT TO, THEN JUST DON'T.
HUH...?
DUDE, YOUR NEGATIVITY IS SERIOUSLY ANNOYING.
SERI-OUSLY.
SHOCK
HIS TRUE THOUGHTS COME OUT!

SERIOUS CONSIDERATION

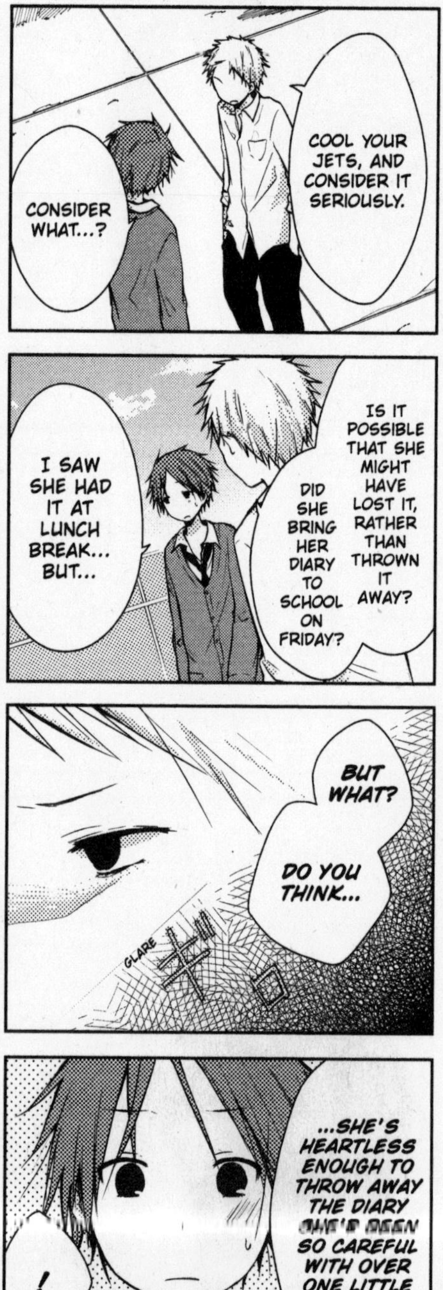
COOL YOUR JETS, AND CONSIDER IT SERIOUSLY.
CONSIDER WHAT...?
IS IT POSSIBLE THAT SHE MIGHT HAVE LOST IT, RATHER THAN THROWN IT AWAY?
DID SHE BRING HER DIARY TO SCHOOL ON FRIDAY?
I SAW SHE HAD IT AT LUNCH BREAK... BUT...
BUT WHAT?
DO YOU THINK...
GLARE
...SHE'S HEARTLESS ENOUGH TO THROW AWAY THE DIARY SHE'S BEEN SO CAREFUL WITH OVER ONE LITTLE FIGHT?
!

I...

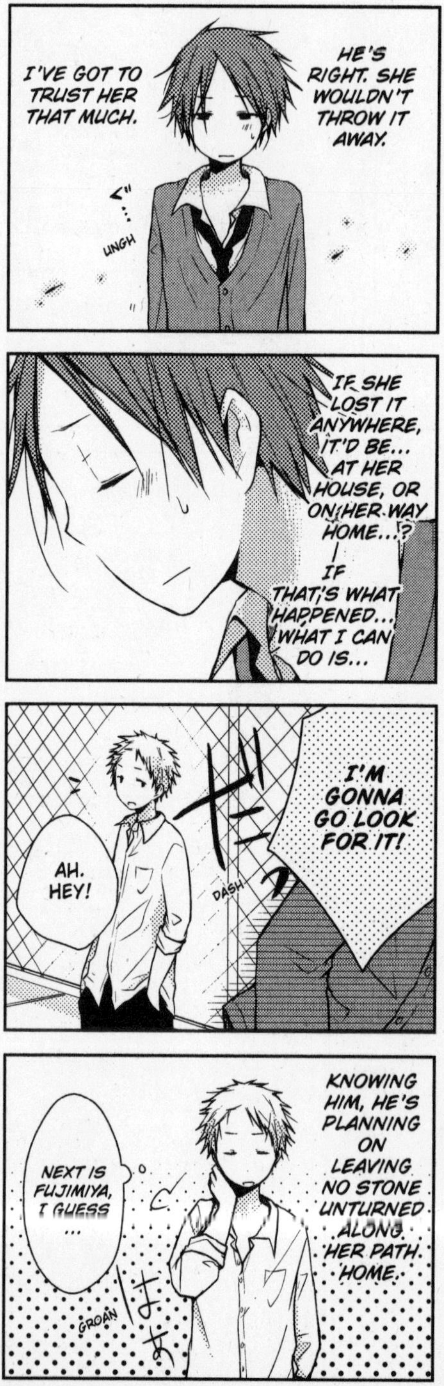
HE'S RIGHT. SHE WOULDN'T THROW IT AWAY.
I'VE GOT TO TRUST HER THAT MUCH.
UNGH
IF SHE LOST IT ANYWHERE, IT'D BE... AT HER HOUSE, OR ON HER WAY HOME...?
IF THAT'S WHAT HAPPENED... WHAT I CAN DO IS...
I'M GONNA GO LOOK FOR IT!
DASH
AH. HEY!
KNOWING HIM, HE'S PLANNING ON LEAVING NO STONE UNTURNED ALONG HER PATH HOME.
NEXT IS FUJIMIYA, I GUESS ...
GROAN
はぁ

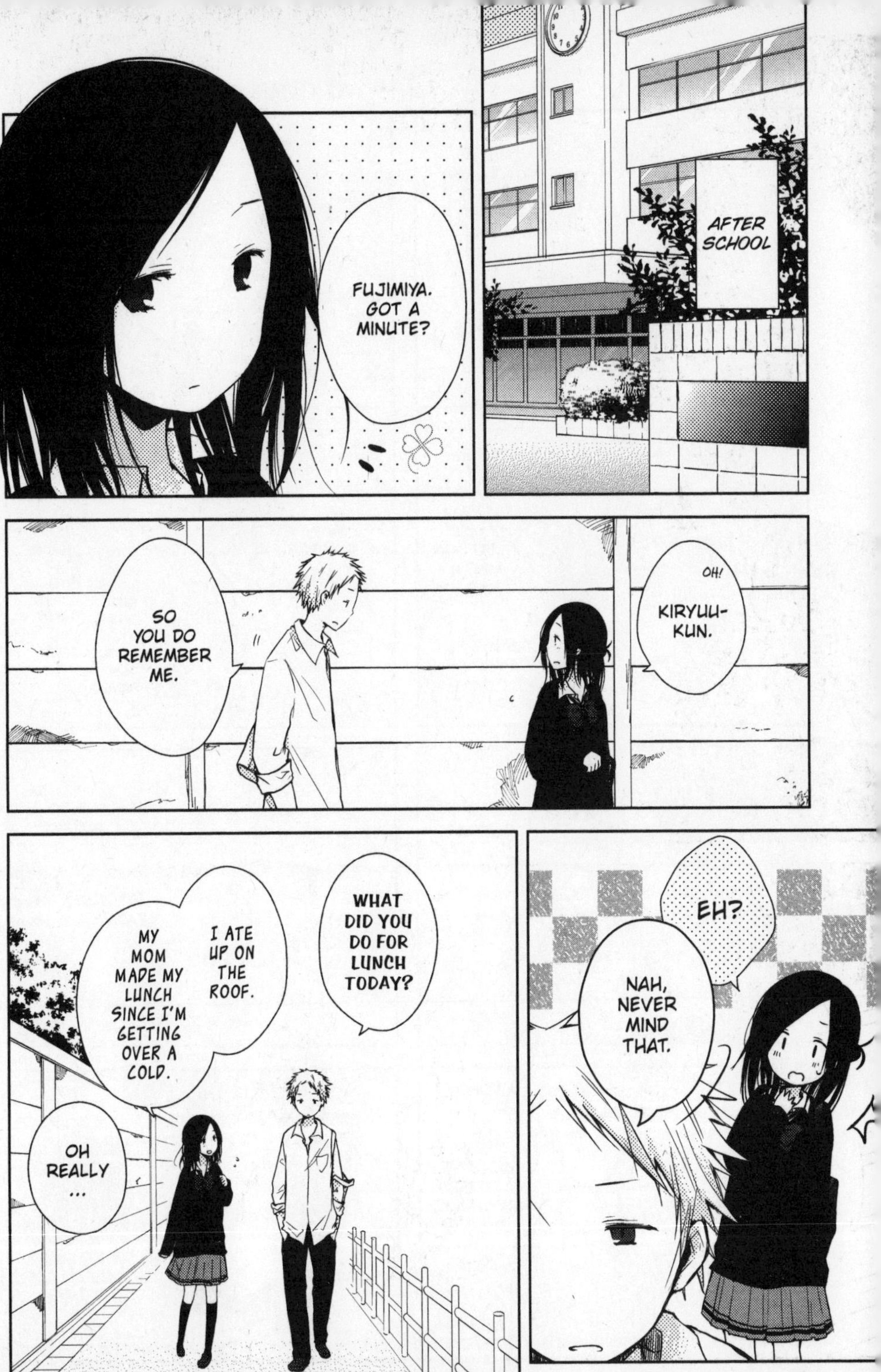
AFTER SCHOOL
FUJIMIYA. GOT A MINUTE?
OH! KIRYUU-KUN.
SO YOU DO REMEMBER ME.
EH?
NAH, NEVER MIND THAT.
WHAT DID YOU DO FOR LUNCH TODAY?
I ATE UP ON THE ROOF.
MY MOM MADE MY LUNCH SINCE I'M GETTING OVER A COLD.
OH REALLY ...

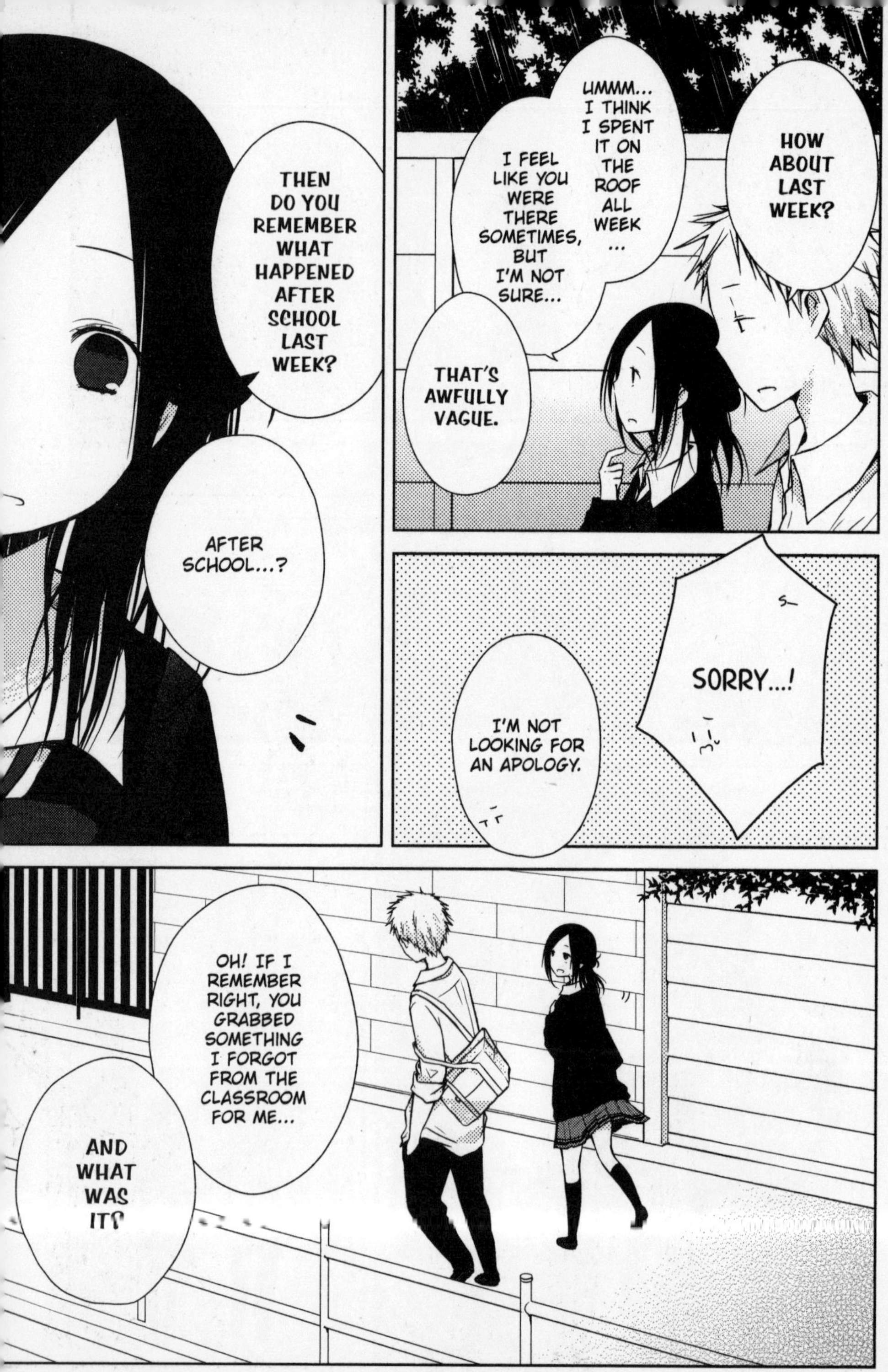
HOW ABOUT LAST WEEK?
UMMM... I THINK I SPENT IT ON THE ROOF ALL WEEK...
I FEEL LIKE YOU WERE THERE SOMETIMES, BUT I'M NOT SURE...
THAT'S AWFULLY VAGUE.
SORRY...!
I'M NOT LOOKING FOR AN APOLOGY.
THEN DO YOU REMEMBER WHAT HAPPENED AFTER SCHOOL LAST WEEK?
AFTER SCHOOL...?
OH! IF I REMEMBER RIGHT, YOU GRABBED SOMETHING I FORGOT FROM THE CLASSROOM FOR ME...
AND WHAT WAS IT?

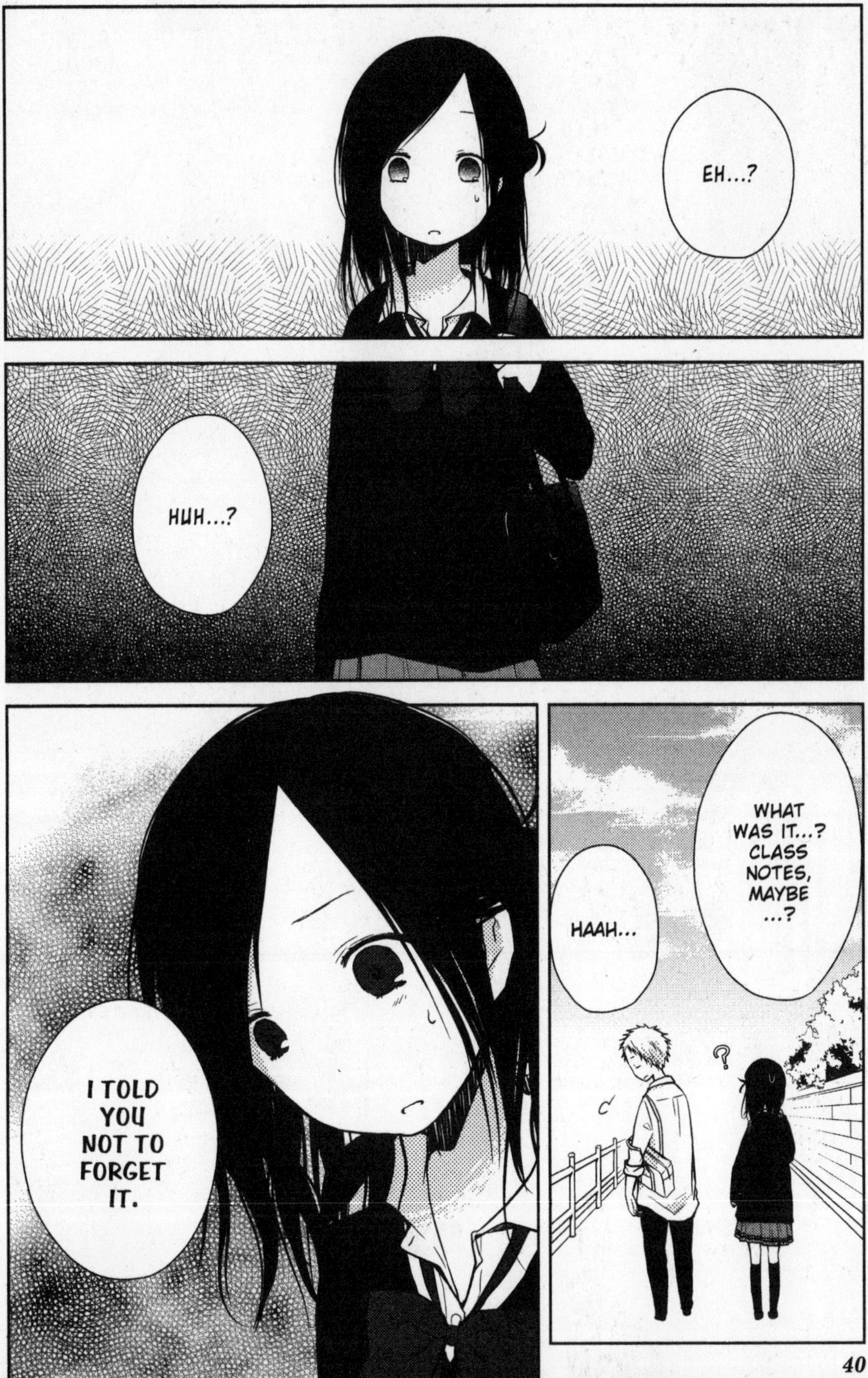
EH...?
HUH...?
WHAT WAS IT...? CLASS NOTES, MAYBE ...?
HAAH...
I TOLD YOU NOT TO FORGET IT.

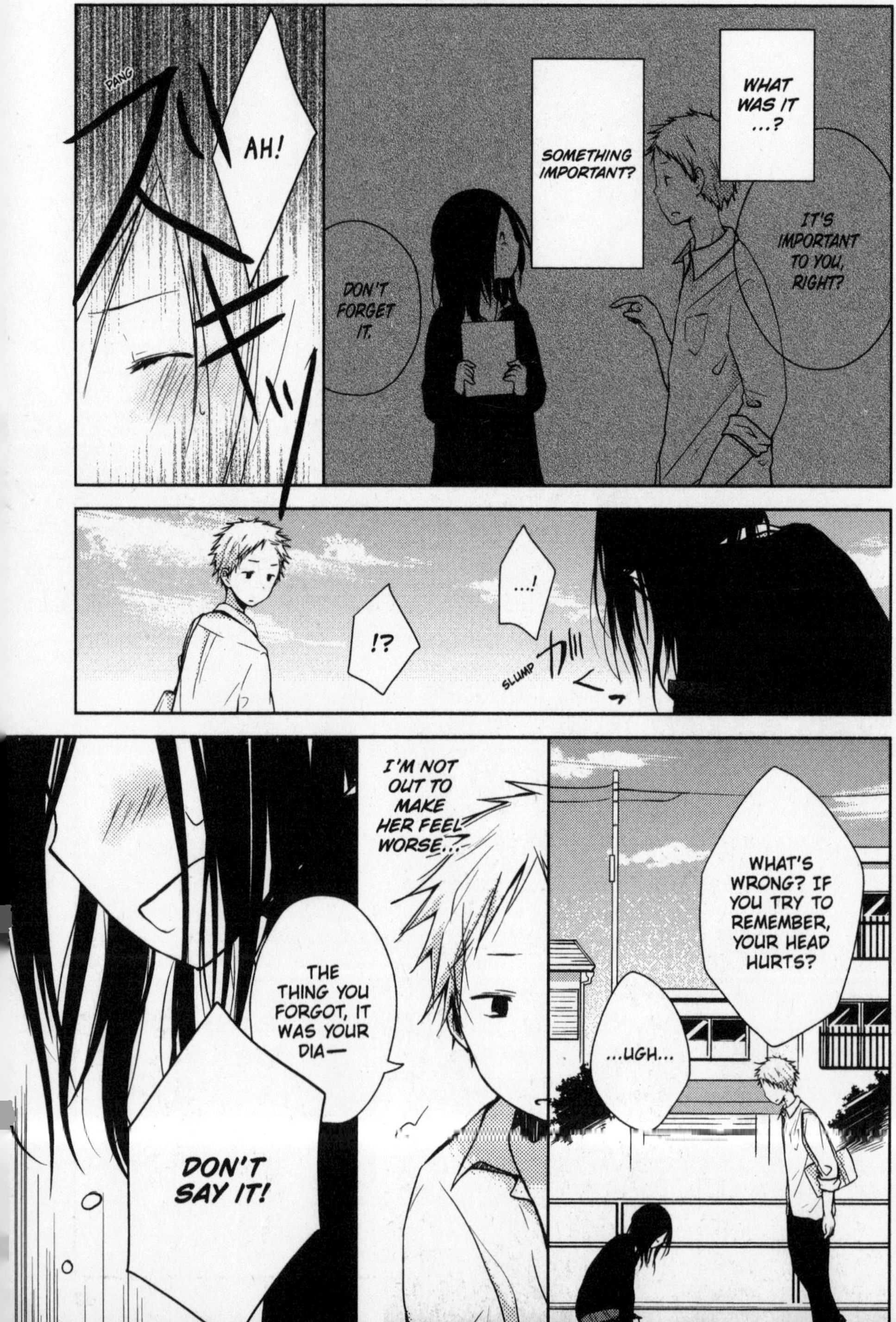
WHAT WAS IT ...?
IT'S IMPORTANT TO YOU, RIGHT?
SOMETHING IMPORTANT?
DON'T FORGET IT.
PANG
AH!
...!
SLUMP
!?
WHAT'S WRONG? IF YOU TRY TO REMEMBER, YOUR HEAD HURTS?
...UGH...
I'M NOT OUT TO MAKE HER FEEL WORSE...?
THE THING YOU FORGOT, IT WAS YOUR DIA—
DON'T SAY IT!

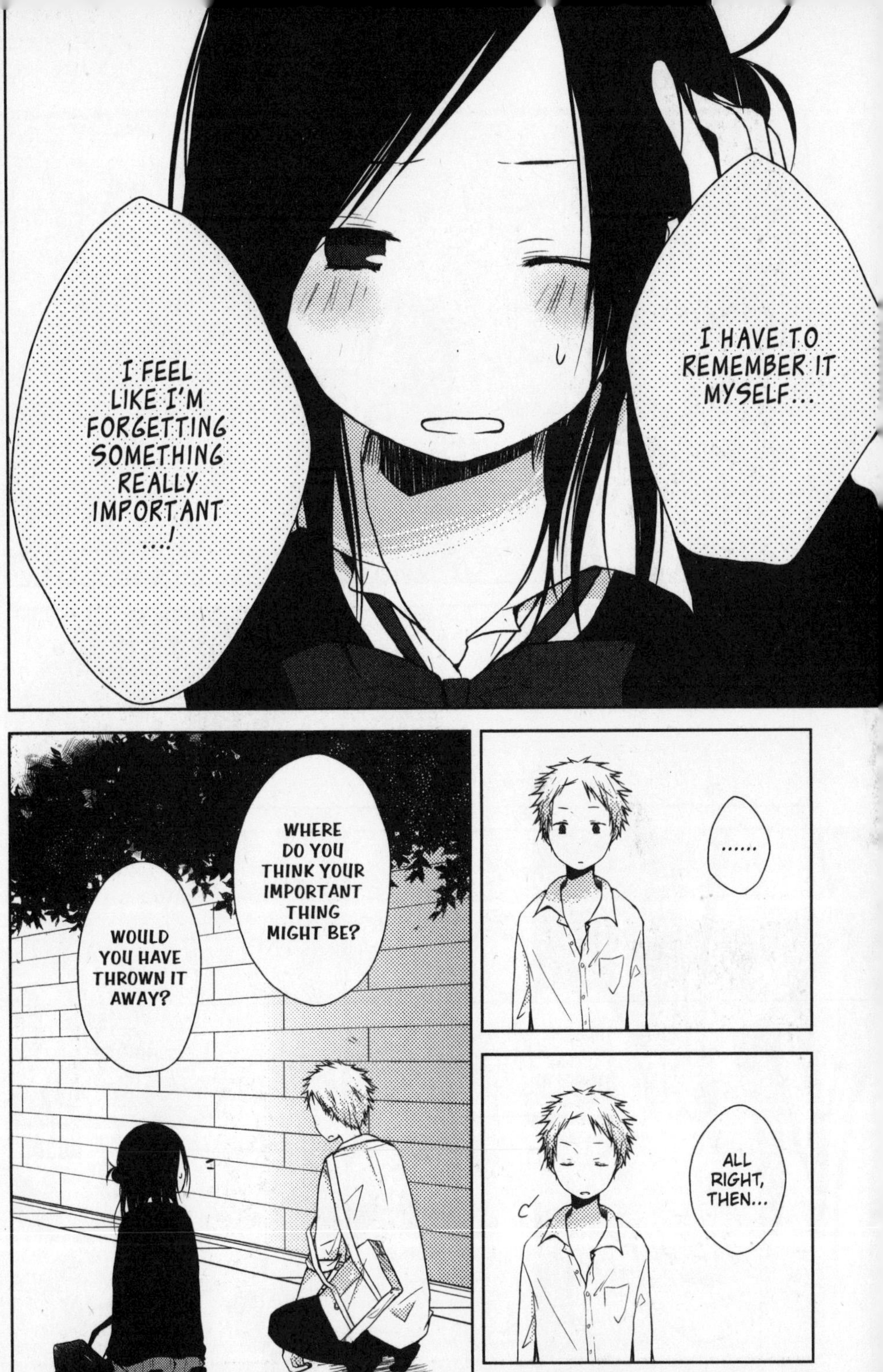
I HAVE TO REMEMBER IT MYSELF...
I FEEL LIKE I'M FORGETTING SOMETHING REALLY IMPORTANT ...!
......
ALL RIGHT, THEN...
WHERE DO YOU THINK YOUR IMPORTANT THING MIGHT BE?
WOULD YOU HAVE THROWN IT AWAY?

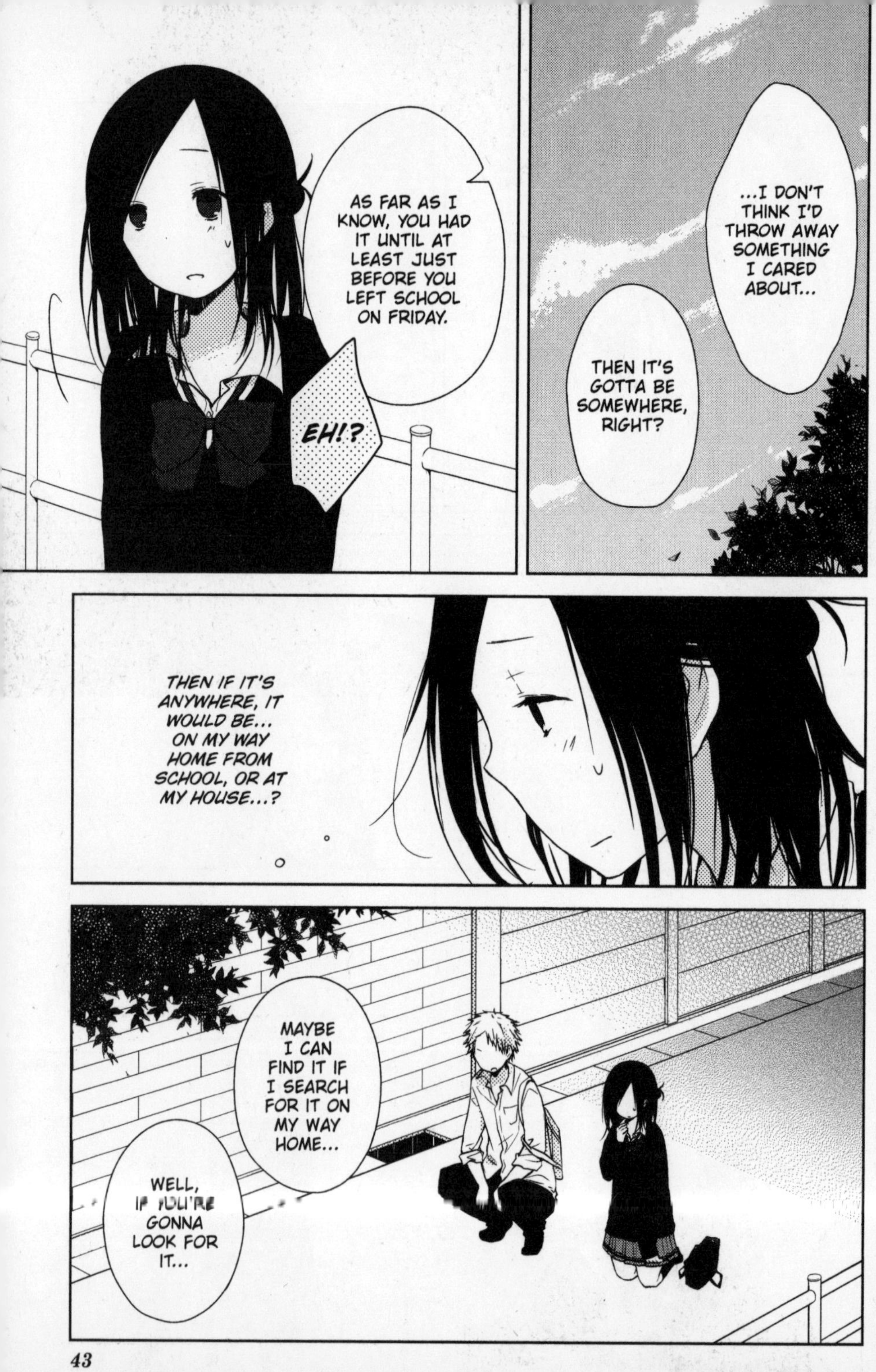
...I DON'T THINK I'D THROW AWAY SOMETHING I CARED ABOUT...
THEN IT'S GOTTA BE SOMEWHERE, RIGHT?
AS FAR AS I KNOW, YOU HAD IT UNTIL AT LEAST JUST BEFORE YOU LEFT SCHOOL ON FRIDAY.
EH!?
THEN IF IT'S ANYWHERE, IT WOULD BE... ON MY WAY HOME FROM SCHOOL, OR AT MY HOUSE...?
MAYBE I CAN FIND IT IF I SEARCH FOR IT ON MY WAY HOME...
WELL, IF YOU'RE GONNA LOOK FOR IT...

...I'VE GOT A FEELING YOU'LL RUN INTO THE GUY WHO DITCHED SCHOOL ALL DAY.
THE BOY FROM THIS MORNING ...?
IF YOU SAY SOMETHING WHEN YOU SEE HIM, I THINK HE'D BE REALLY HAPPY.
BUT...!
STARE
SHIVER
I'D APPRECIATE IT, FUJIMIYA.

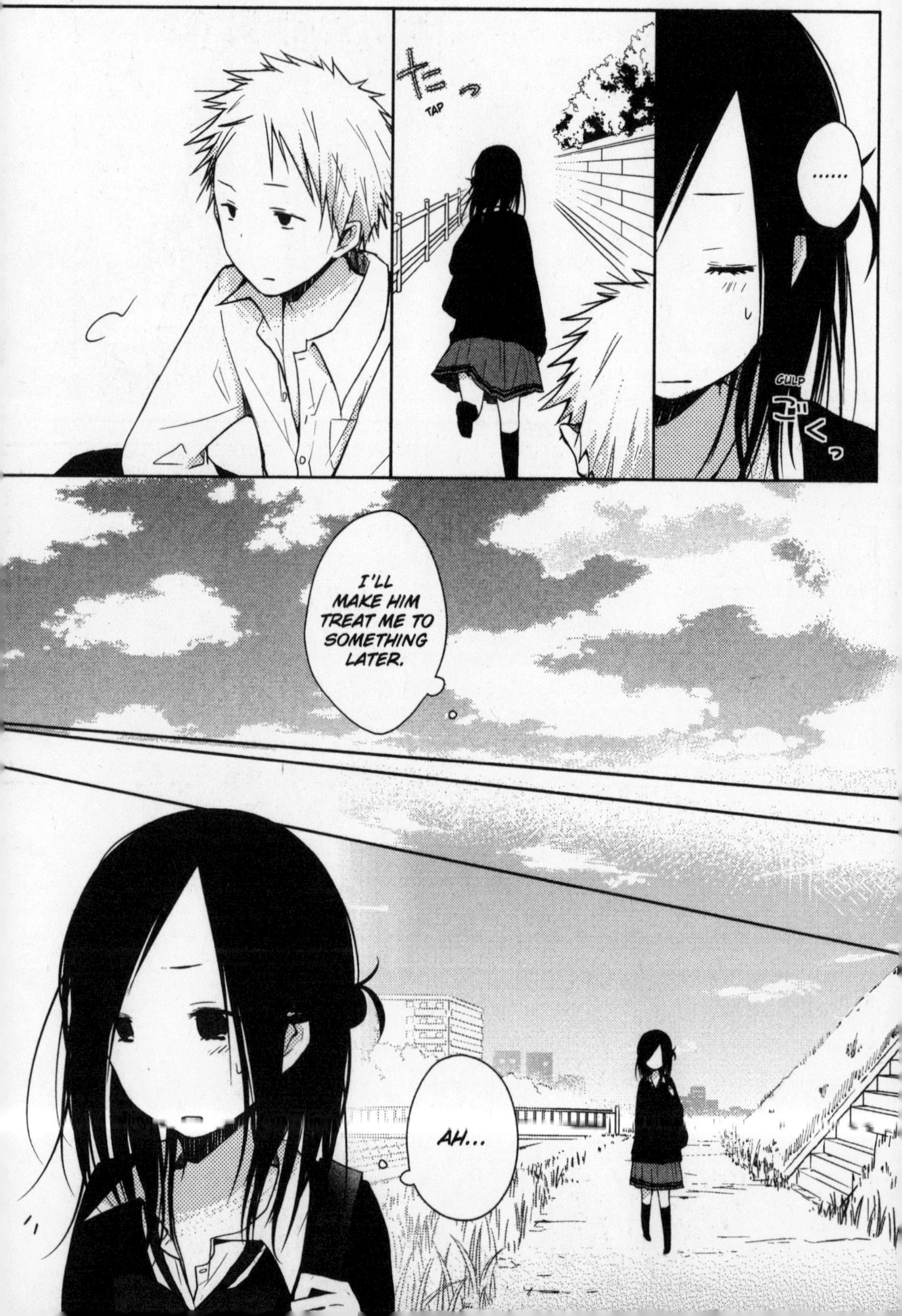
......
GULP
ごくっ
たっ
TAP
I'LL MAKE HIM TREAT ME TO SOMETHING LATER.
AH...

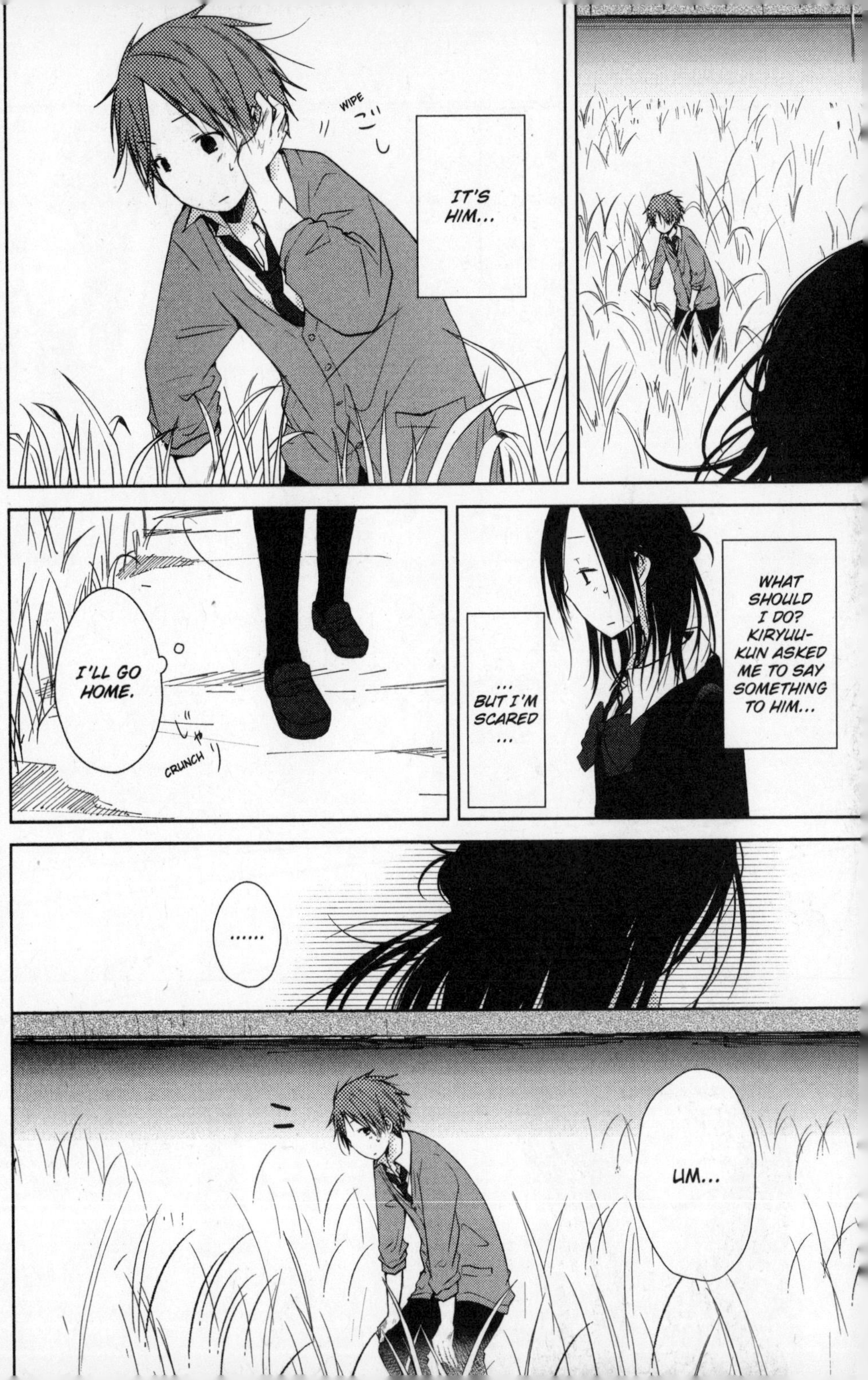
WIPE
IT'S HIM...
WHAT SHOULD I DO? KIRYUU-KUN ASKED ME TO SAY SOMETHING TO HIM...
... BUT I'M SCARED ...
I'LL GO HOME.
CRUNCH
......
UM...

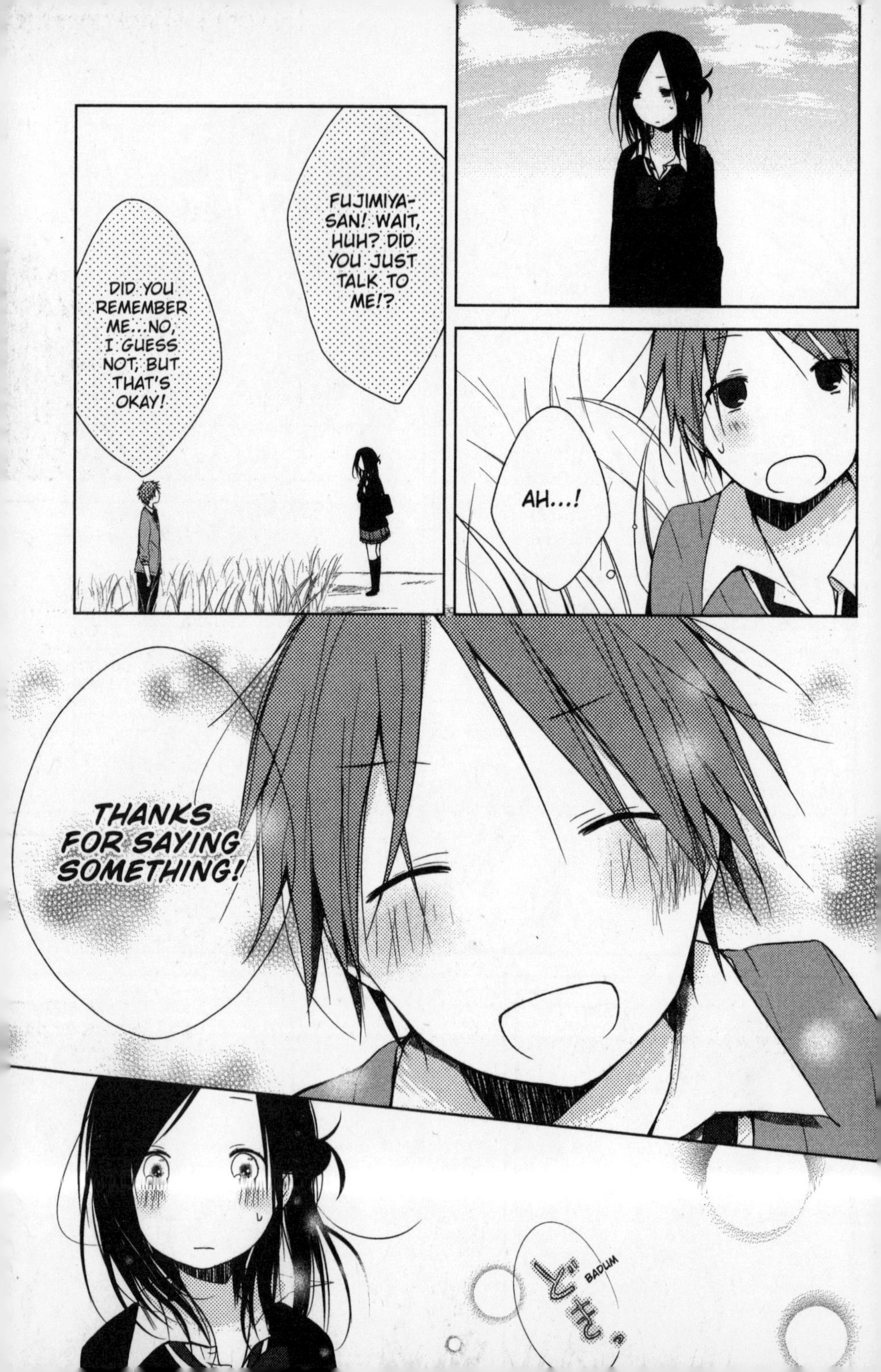
AH...!
FUJIMIYA-SAN! WAIT, HUH? DID YOU JUST TALK TO ME!?
DID YOU REMEMBER ME...NO, I GUESS NOT, BUT THAT'S OKAY!
THANKS FOR SAYING SOMETHING!
どきっ
BADUM

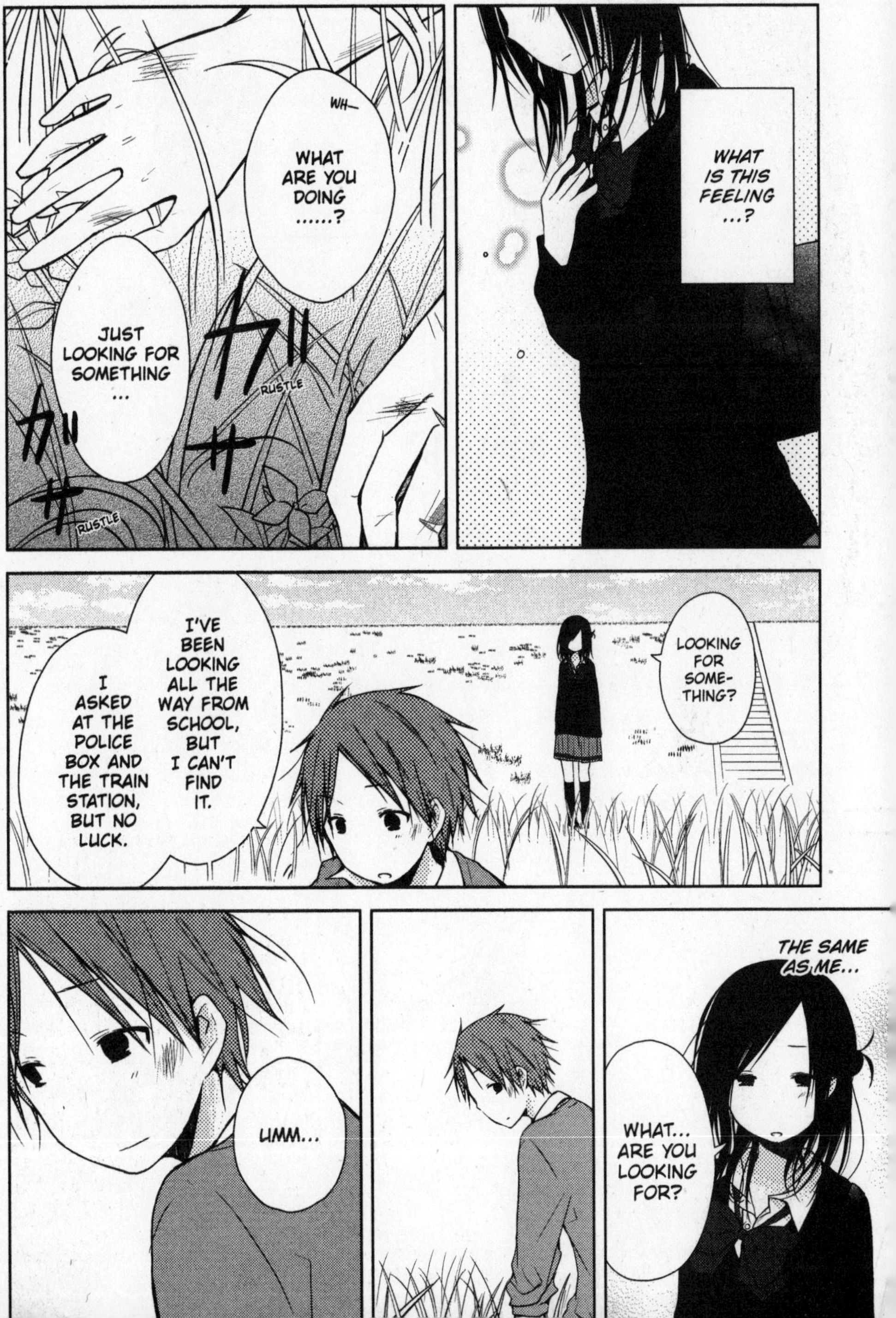
WHAT IS THIS FEELING ...?
WH—
WHAT ARE YOU DOING ......?
RUSTLE
JUST LOOKING FOR SOMETHING ...
RUSTLE
LOOKING FOR SOME-THING?
I'VE BEEN LOOKING ALL THE WAY FROM SCHOOL, BUT I CAN'T FIND IT.
I ASKED AT THE POLICE BOX AND THE TRAIN STATION, BUT NO LUCK.
THE SAME AS ME...
WHAT... ARE YOU LOOKING FOR?
UMM...

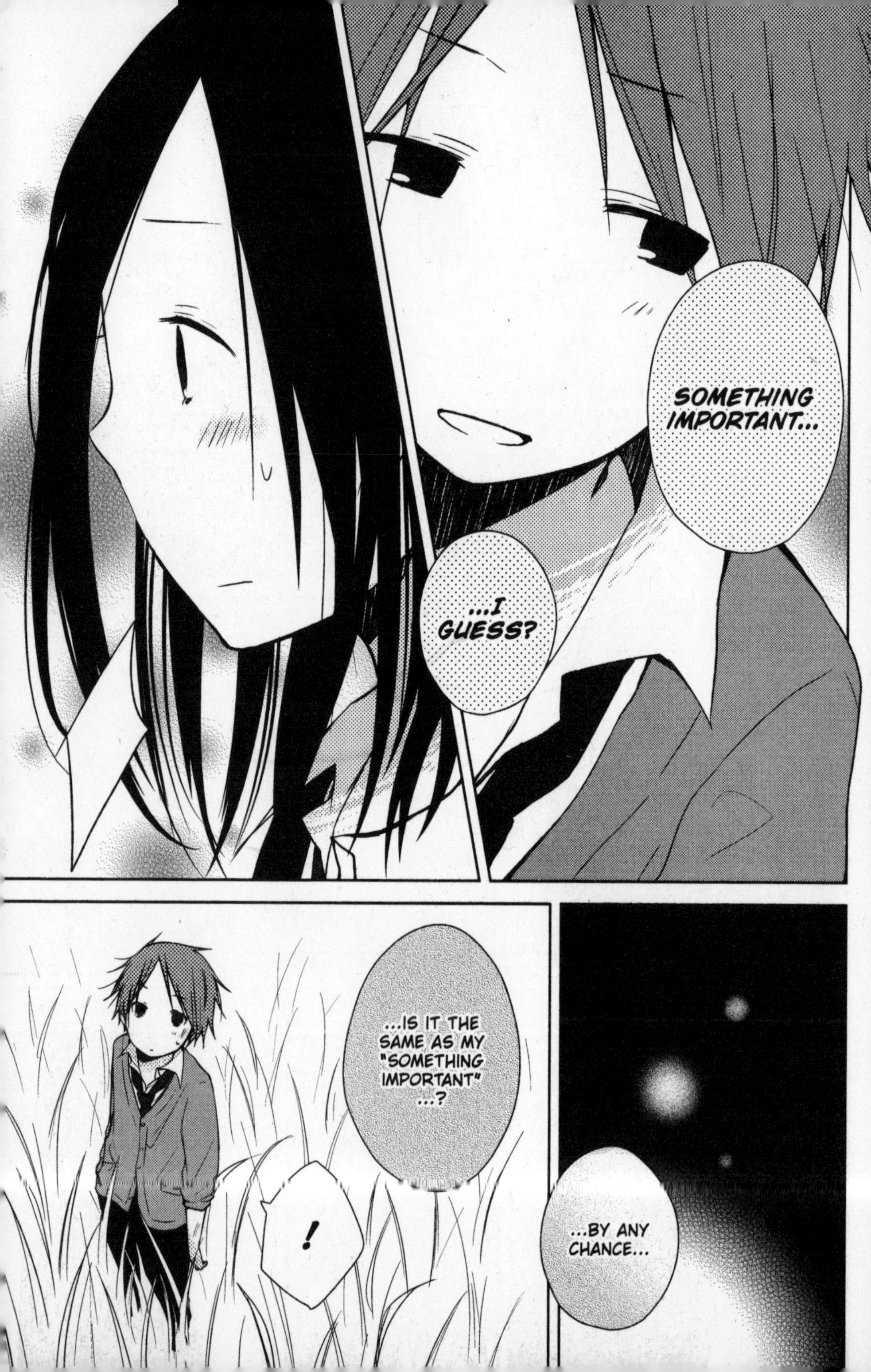
SOMETHING IMPORTANT...
...I GUESS?
...BY ANY CHANCE...
...IS IT THE SAME AS MY "SOMETHING IMPORTANT" ...?
!

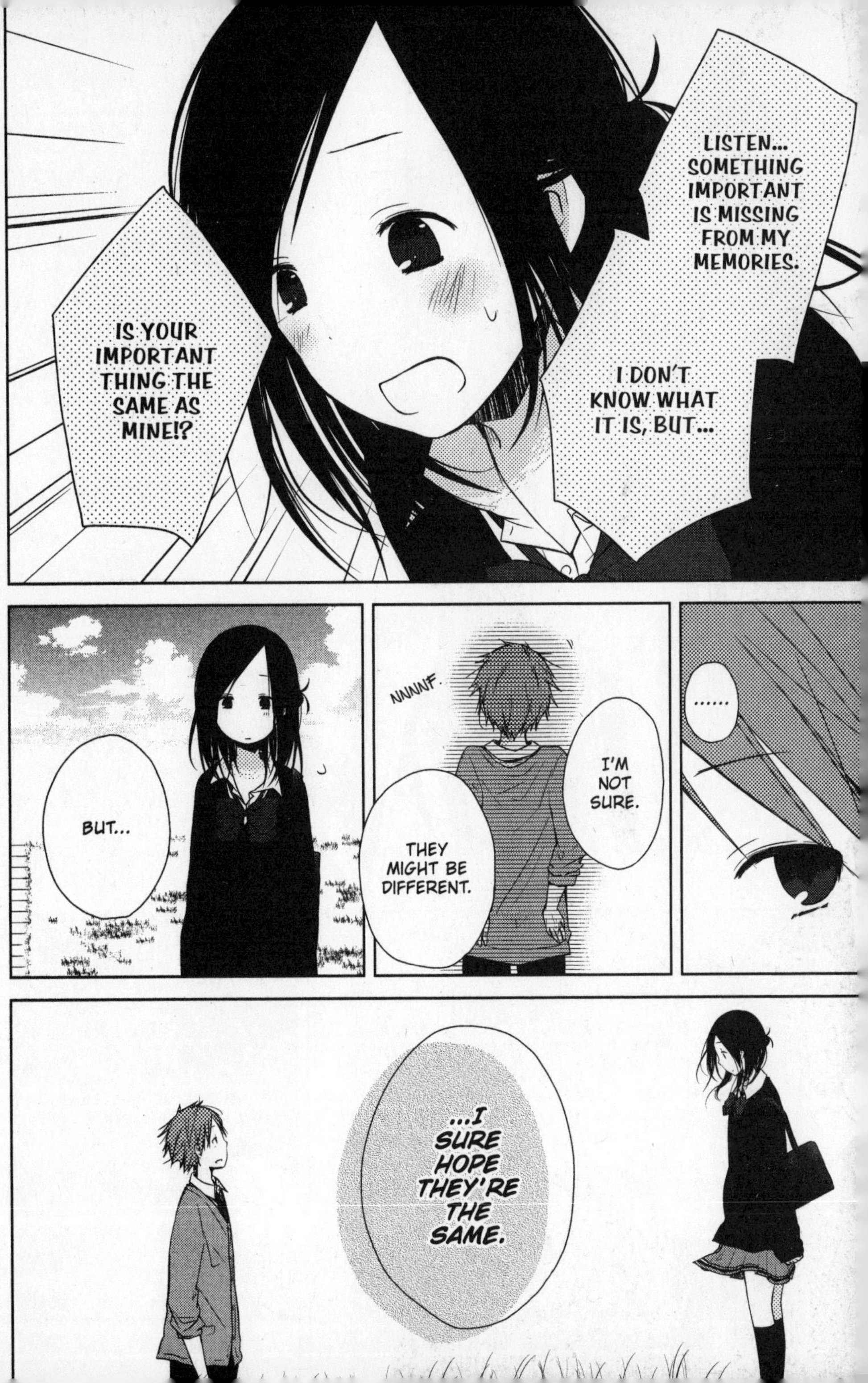
LISTEN... SOMETHING IMPORTANT IS MISSING FROM MY MEMORIES.
I DON'T KNOW WHAT IT IS, BUT...
IS YOUR IMPORTANT THING THE SAME AS MINE!?
......
I'M NOT SURE.
THEY MIGHT BE DIFFERENT.
NNNNF.
BUT...
...I SURE HOPE THEY'RE THE SAME.

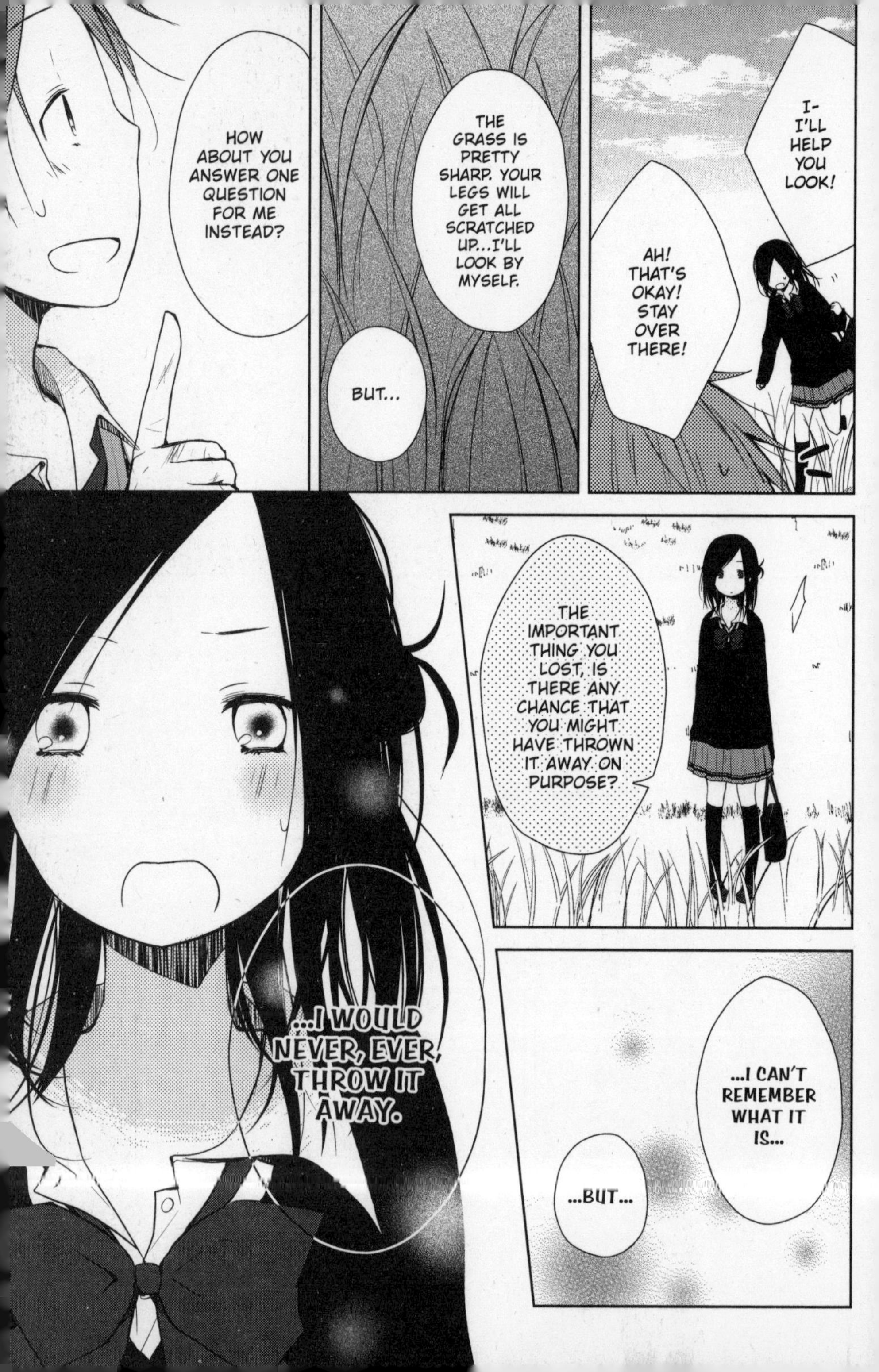
I- I'LL HELP YOU LOOK!
AH! THAT'S OKAY! STAY OVER THERE!
THE GRASS IS PRETTY SHARP. YOUR LEGS WILL GET ALL SCRATCHED UP...I'LL LOOK BY MYSELF.
BUT...
HOW ABOUT YOU ANSWER ONE QUESTION FOR ME INSTEAD?
THE IMPORTANT THING YOU LOST, IS THERE ANY CHANCE THAT YOU MIGHT HAVE THROWN IT AWAY ON PURPOSE?
...I CAN'T REMEMBER WHAT IT IS...
...BUT...
...I WOULD NEVER, EVER, THROW IT AWAY.

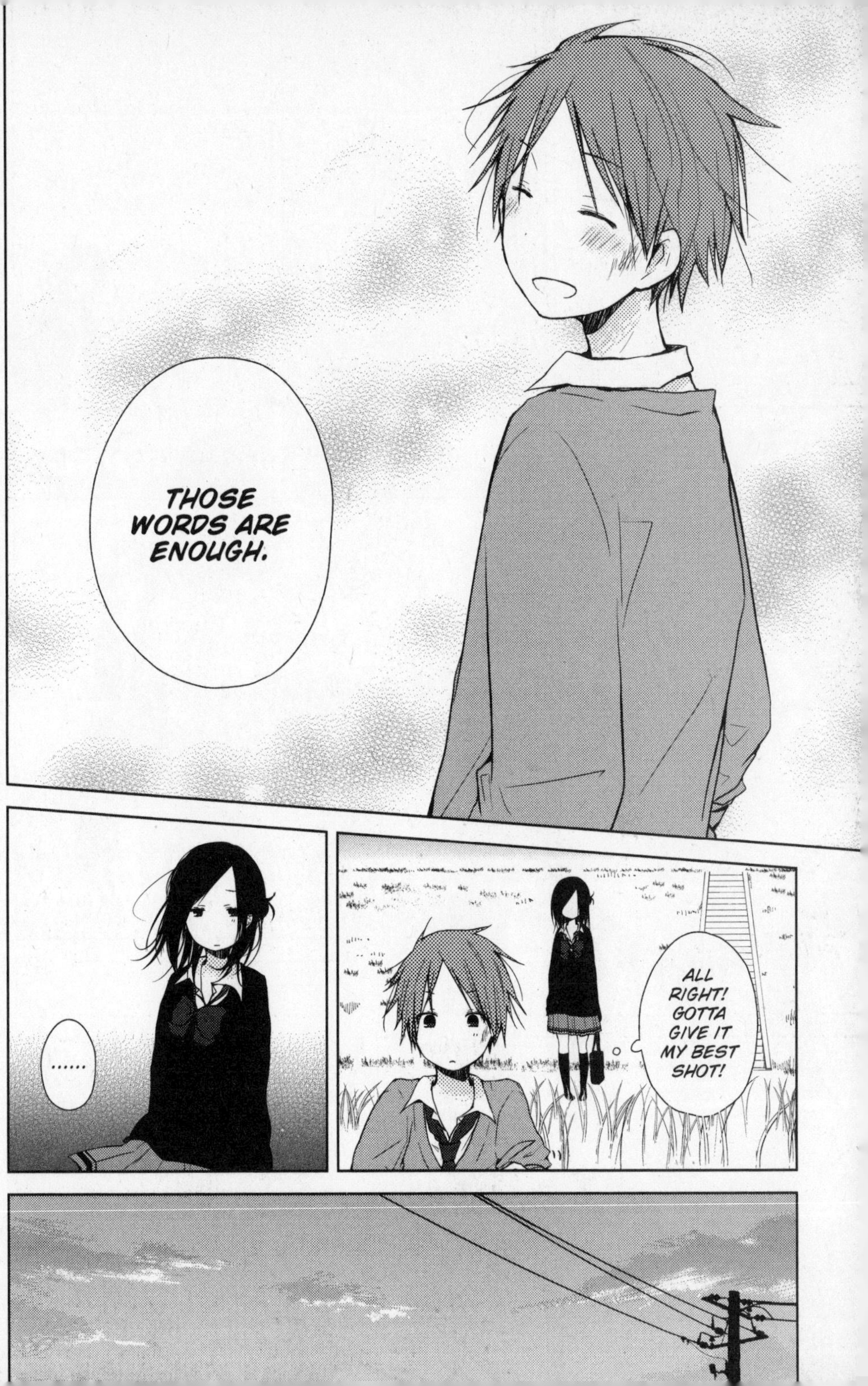
THOSE WORDS ARE ENOUGH.
ALL RIGHT! GOTTA GIVE IT MY BEST SHOT!
......

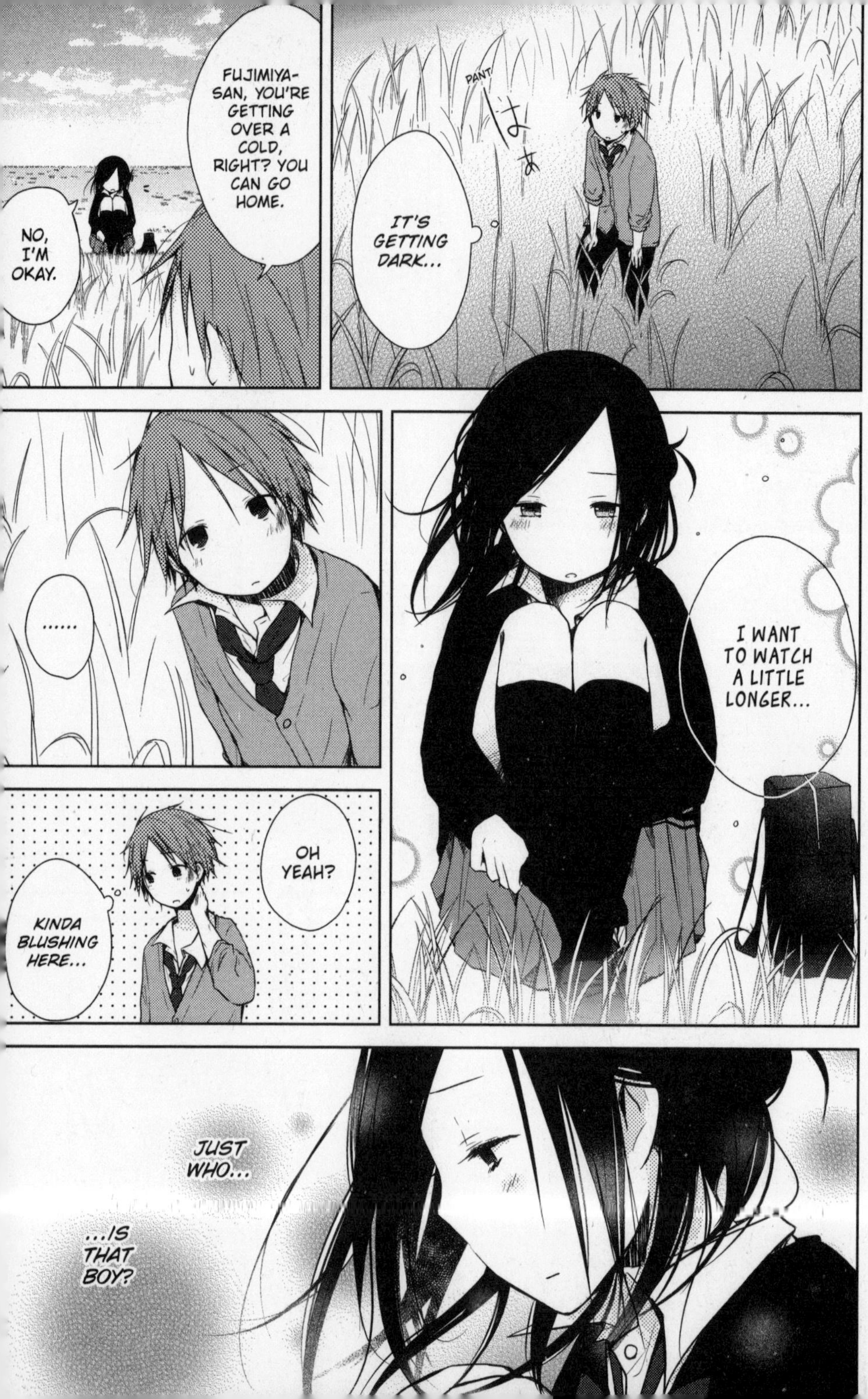
PANT
はぁ
IT'S GETTING DARK...
FUJIMIYA-SAN, YOU'RE GETTING OVER A COLD, RIGHT? YOU CAN GO HOME.
NO, I'M OKAY.
I WANT TO WATCH A LITTLE LONGER...
......
OH YEAH?
KINDA BLUSHING HERE...
JUST WHO...
...IS THAT BOY?

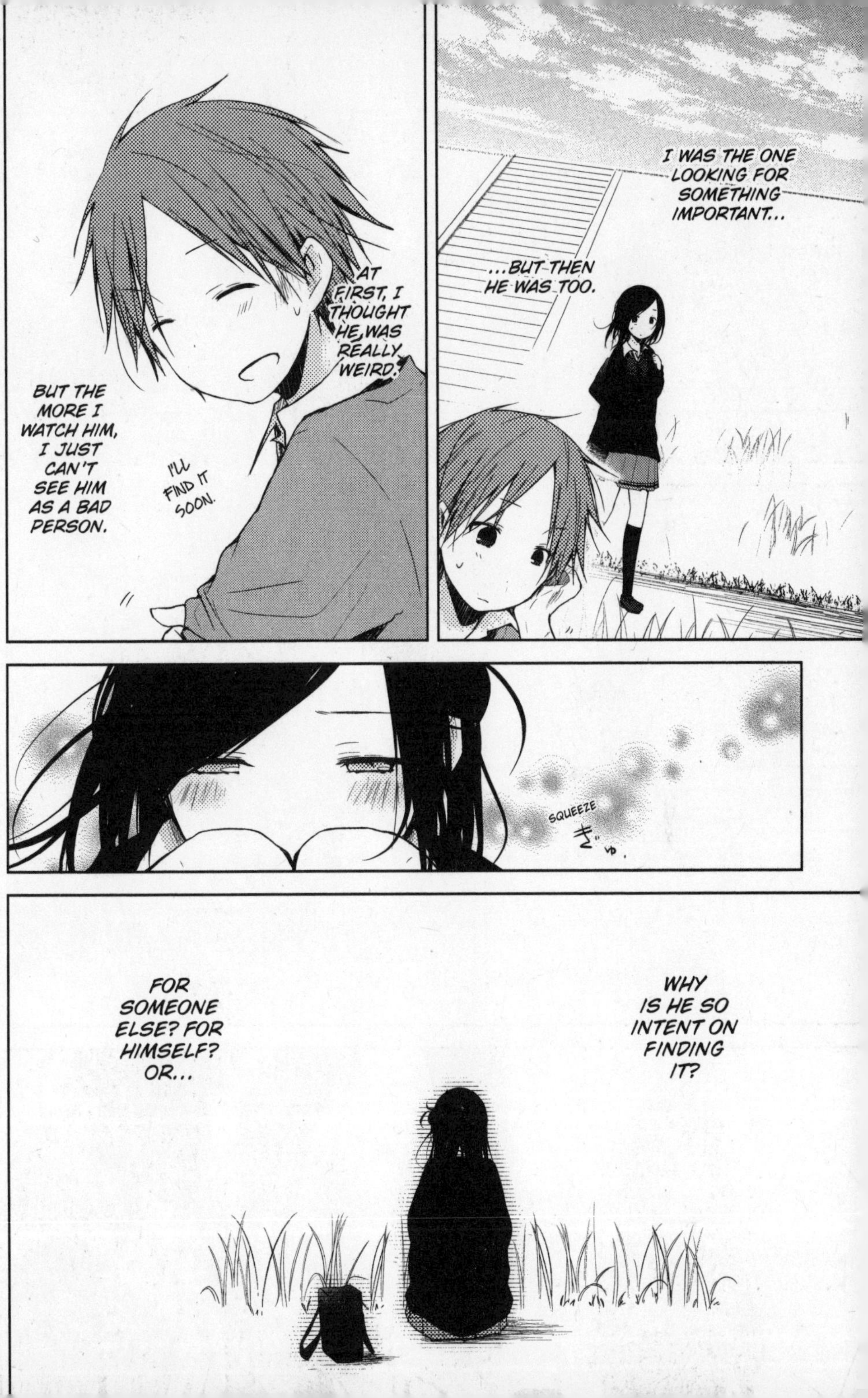
I WAS THE ONE LOOKING FOR SOMETHING IMPORTANT...
...BUT THEN HE WAS TOO.
AT FIRST, I THOUGHT HE WAS REALLY WEIRD.
BUT THE MORE I WATCH HIM, I JUST CAN'T SEE HIM AS A BAD PERSON.
I'LL FIND IT SOON.
SQUEEZE
ぎゅ
WHY IS HE SO INTENT ON FINDING IT?
FOR SOMEONE ELSE? FOR HIMSELF? OR...

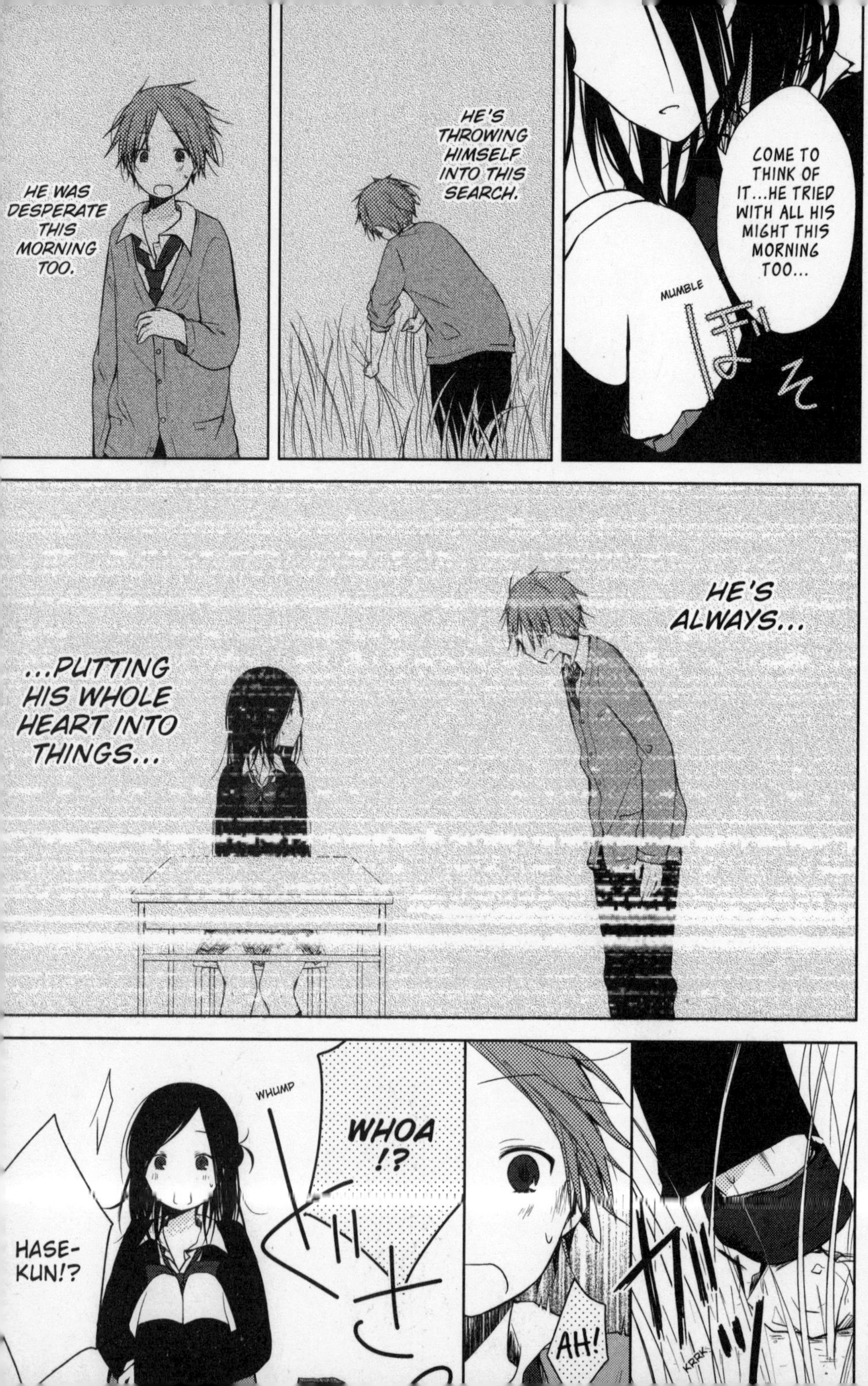
COME TO THINK OF IT...HE TRIED WITH ALL HIS MIGHT THIS MORNING TOO...
MUMBLE
HE'S THROWING HIMSELF INTO THIS SEARCH.
HE WAS DESPERATE THIS MORNING TOO.
HE'S ALWAYS...
...PUTTING HIS WHOLE HEART INTO THINGS...
KRRK
AH!
WHUMP
WHOA!?
HASE-KUN!?

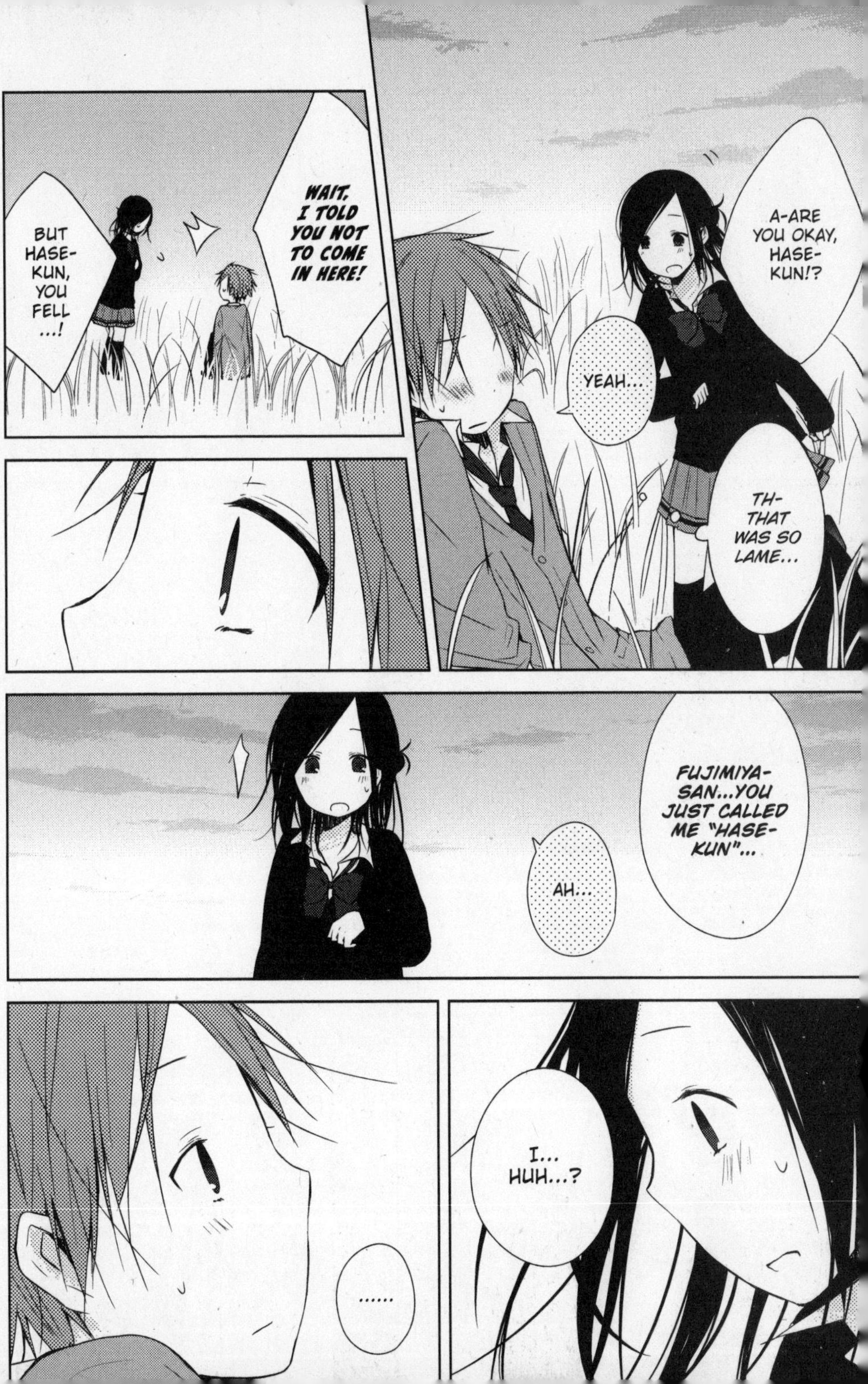
A-ARE YOU OKAY, HASE-KUN!?
YEAH...
TH-THAT WAS SO LAME...
WAIT, I TOLD YOU NOT TO COME IN HERE!
BUT HASE-KUN, YOU FELL...!
FUJIMIYA-SAN...YOU JUST CALLED ME "HASE-KUN"...
AH...
I... HUH...?
......

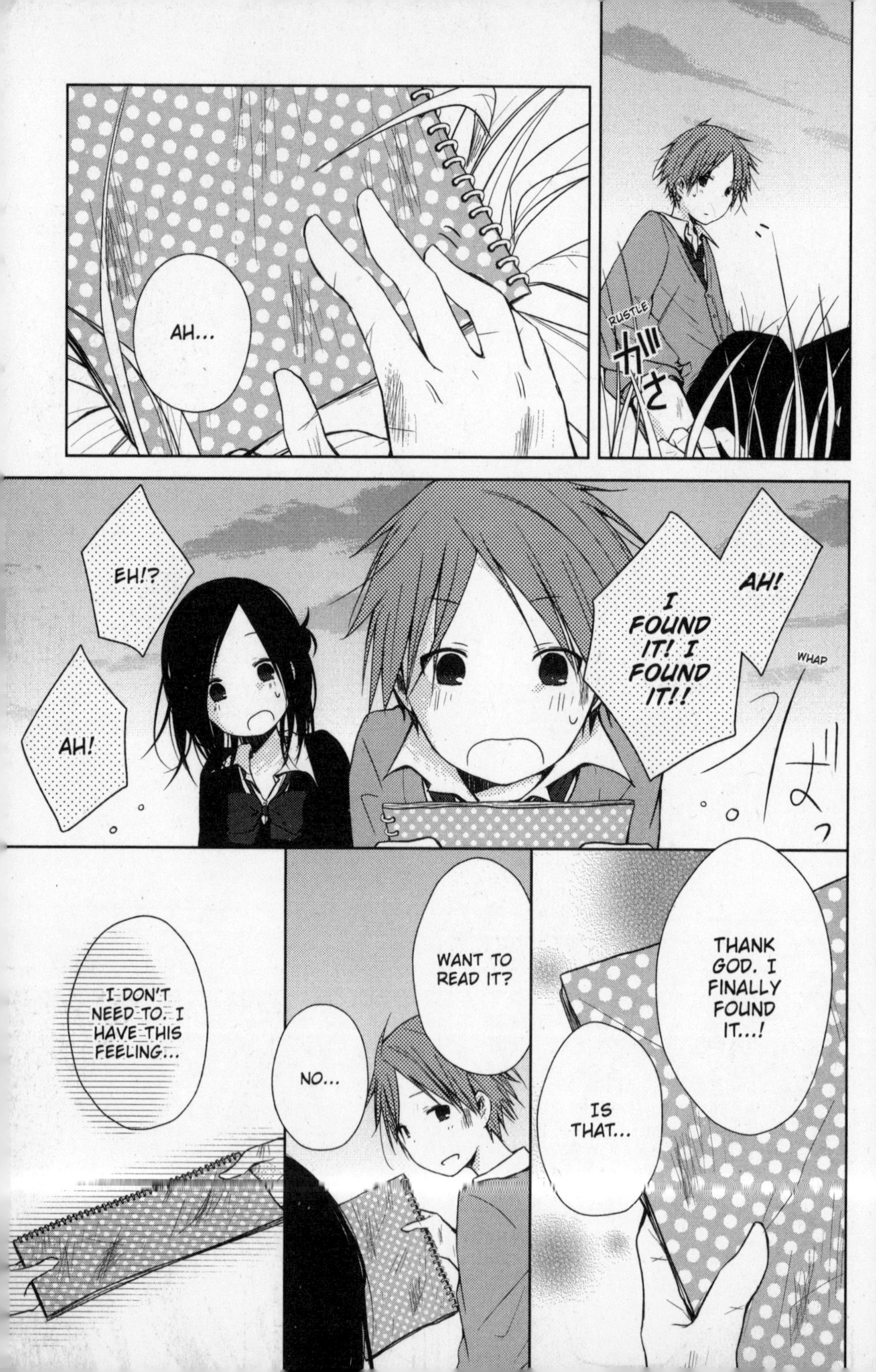
RUSTLE
がさ
AH...
AH! I FOUND IT! I FOUND IT!!
WHAP
ばっ
EH!?
AH!
THANK GOD. I FINALLY FOUND IT...!
IS THAT...
WANT TO READ IT?
NO...
I DON'T NEED TO. I HAVE THIS FEELING...

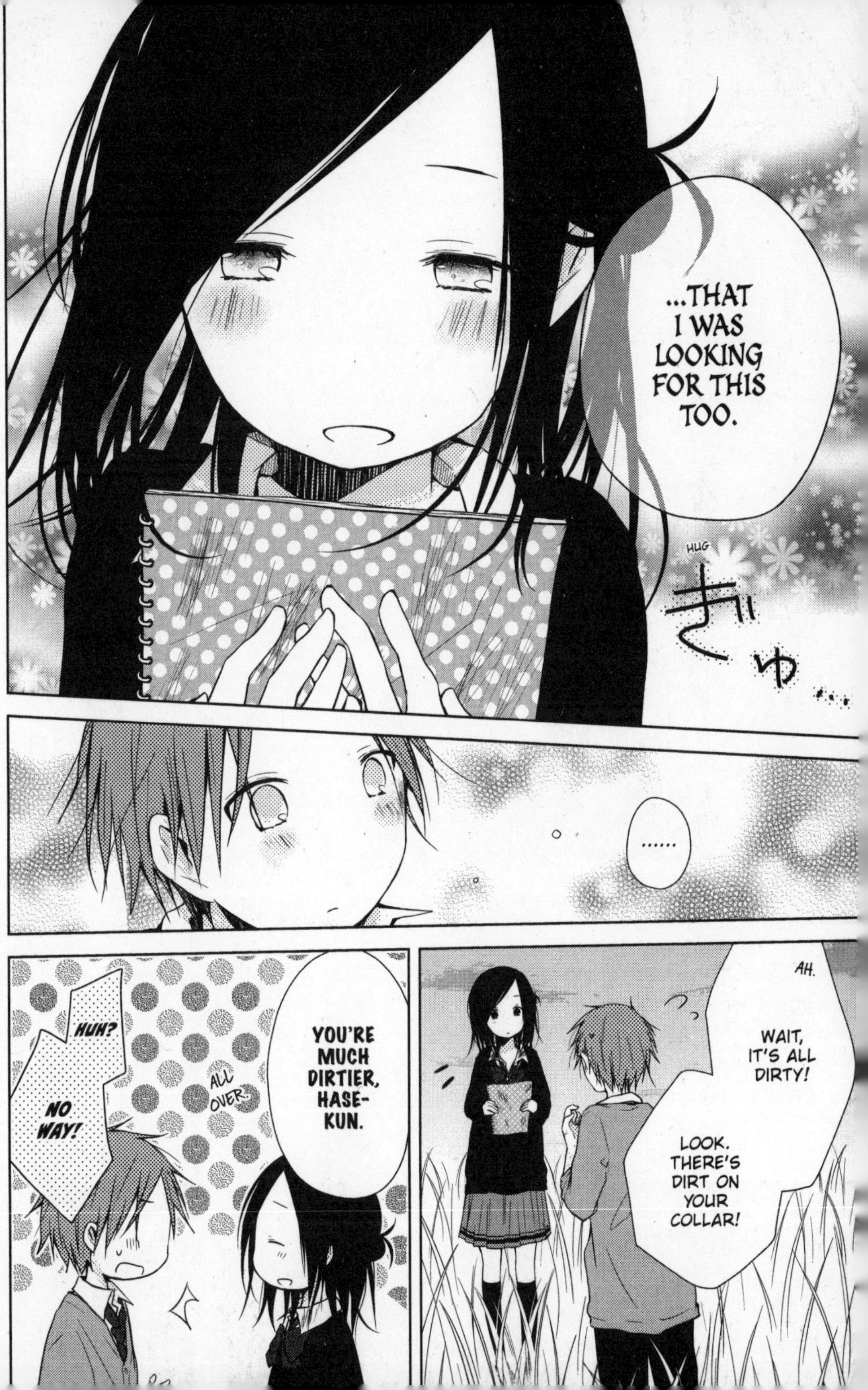
...THAT I WAS LOOKING FOR THIS TOO.
HUG
ぎゅ…
......
AH.
WAIT, IT'S ALL DIRTY!
LOOK. THERE'S DIRT ON YOUR COLLAR!
YOU'RE MUCH DIRTIER, HASE-KUN.
ALL OVER.
HUH?
NO WAY!

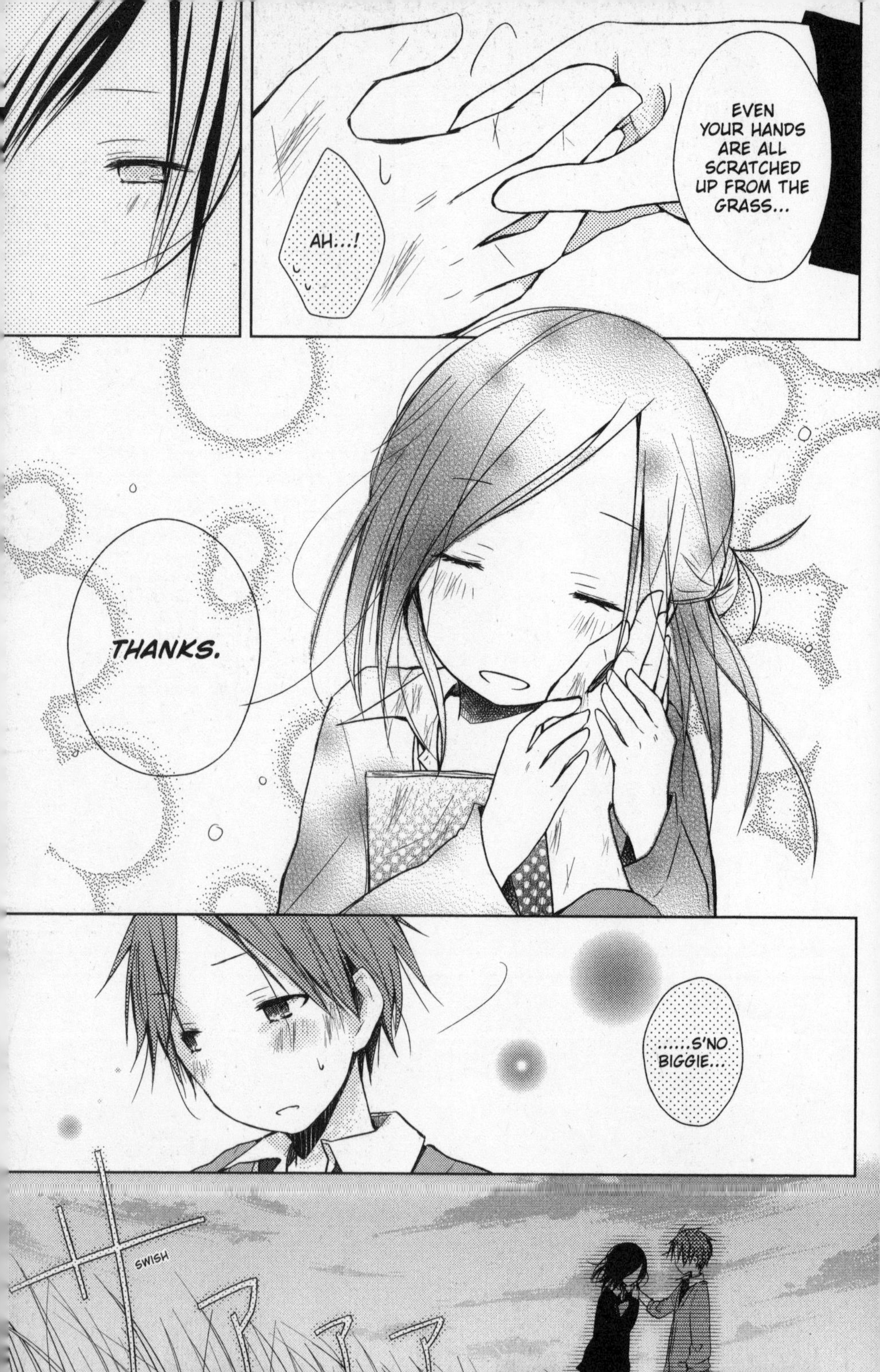
EVEN YOUR HANDS ARE ALL SCRATCHED UP FROM THE GRASS...
AH...!
THANKS.
......S'NO BIGGIE...
SWISH

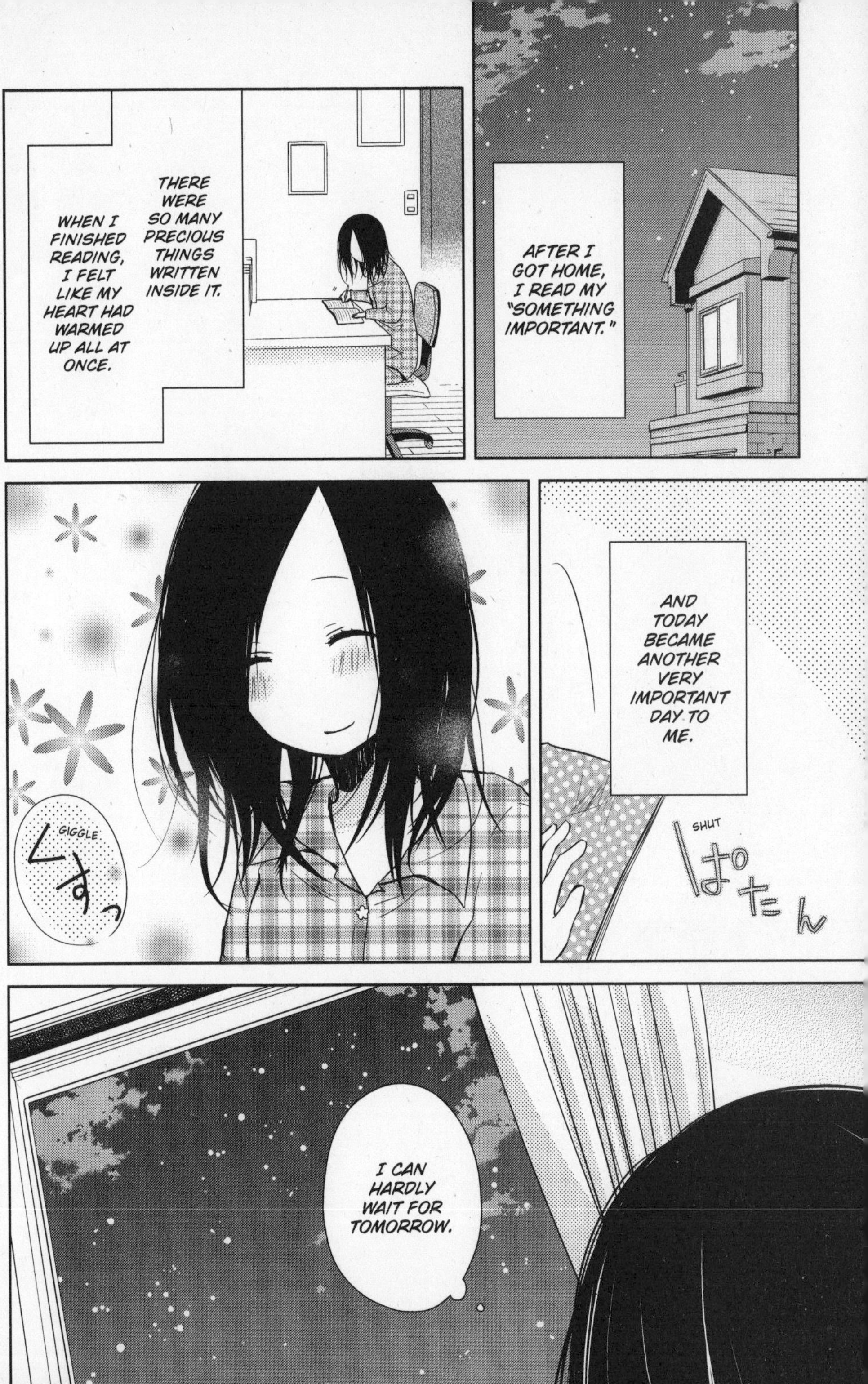
AFTER I GOT HOME, I READ MY "SOMETHING IMPORTANT."
THERE WERE SO MANY PRECIOUS THINGS WRITTEN INSIDE IT.
WHEN I FINISHED READING, I FELT LIKE MY HEART HAD WARMED UP ALL AT ONCE.
AND TODAY BECAME ANOTHER VERY IMPORTANT DAY TO ME.
SHUT
ぱたん
GIGGLE
くすっ
I CAN HARDLY WAIT FOR TOMORROW.

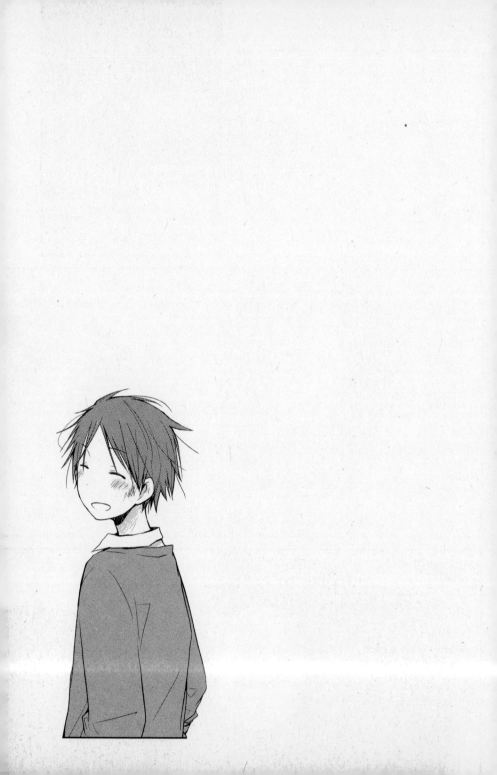

CHAPTER 6
HOME OF A FRIEND

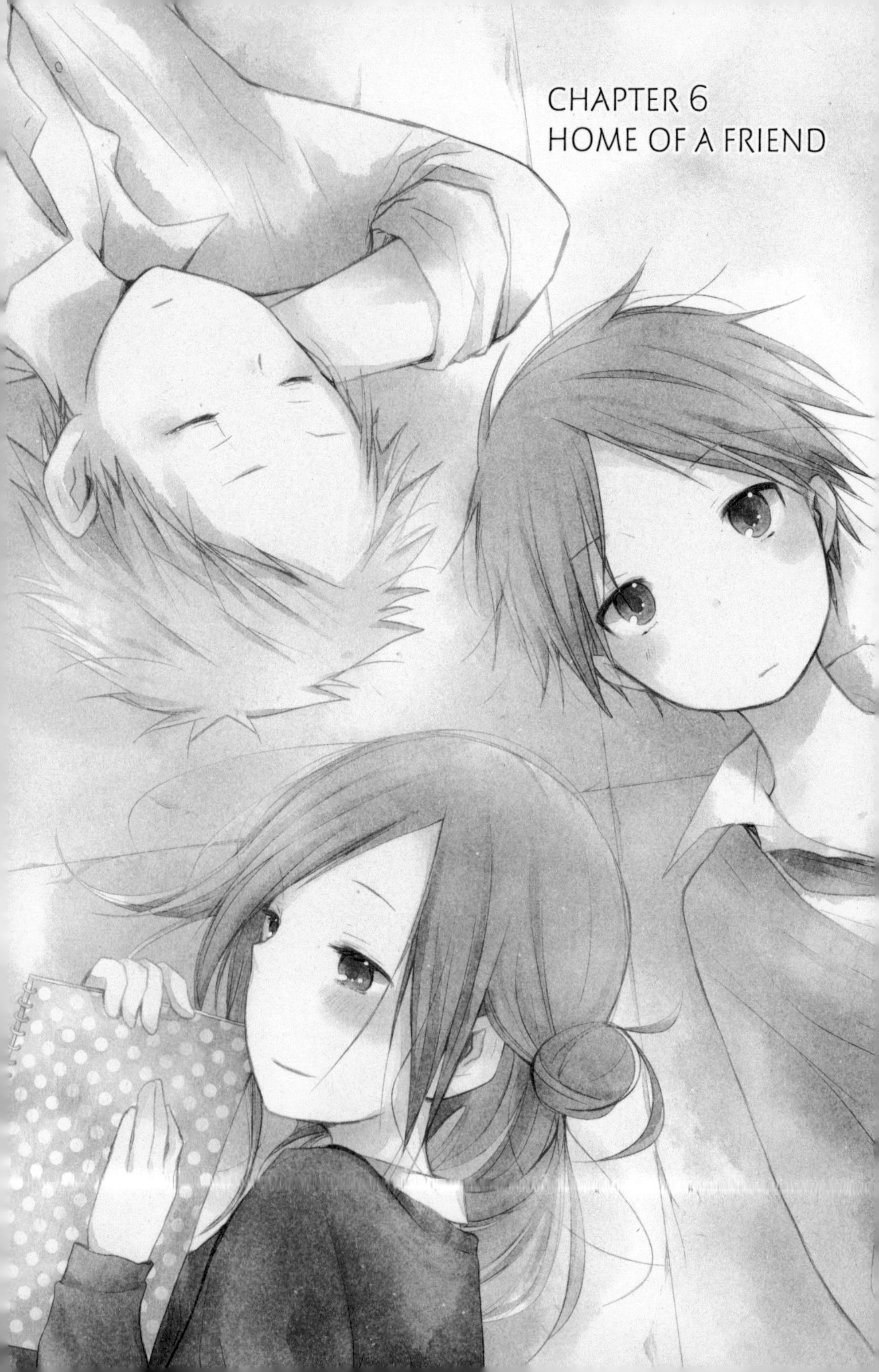

ONE
WEEK
FRIENDS

SURPRISE PREDICAMENT

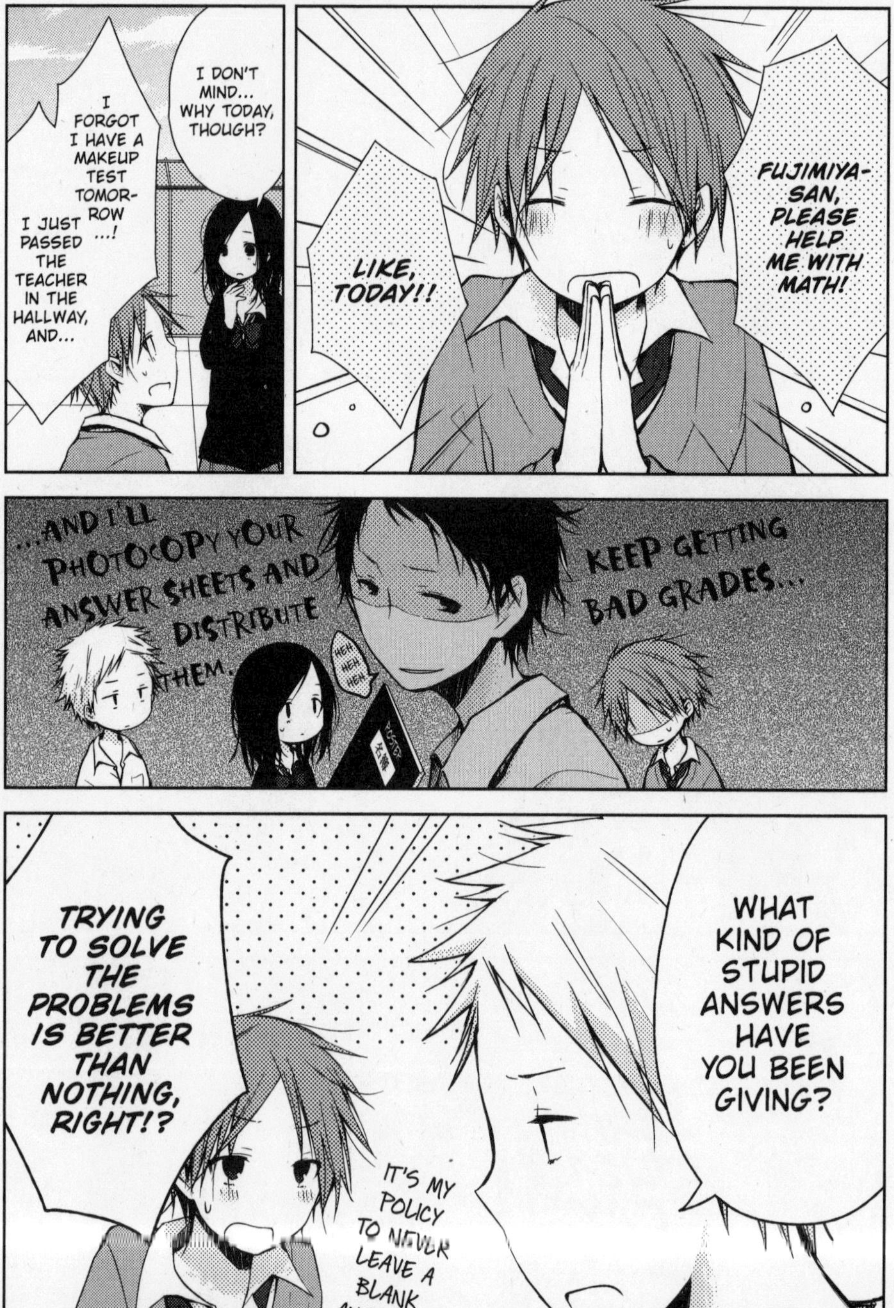
FUJIMIYA-SAN, PLEASE HELP ME WITH MATH!
LIKE, TODAY!!
I DON'T MIND... WHY TODAY, THOUGH?
I FORGOT I HAVE A MAKEUP TEST TOMORROW...!
I JUST PASSED THE TEACHER IN THE HALLWAY, AND...
KEEP GETTING BAD GRADES...
HEH HEH HEH
...AND I'LL PHOTOCOPY YOUR ANSWER SHEETS AND DISTRIBUTE THEM.
WHAT KIND OF STUPID ANSWERS HAVE YOU BEEN GIVING?
TRYING TO SOLVE THE PROBLEMS IS BETTER THAN NOTHING, RIGHT!?
IT'S MY POLICY TO NEVER LEAVE A BLANK ANSWER!

SUDDEN DEVELOPMENT

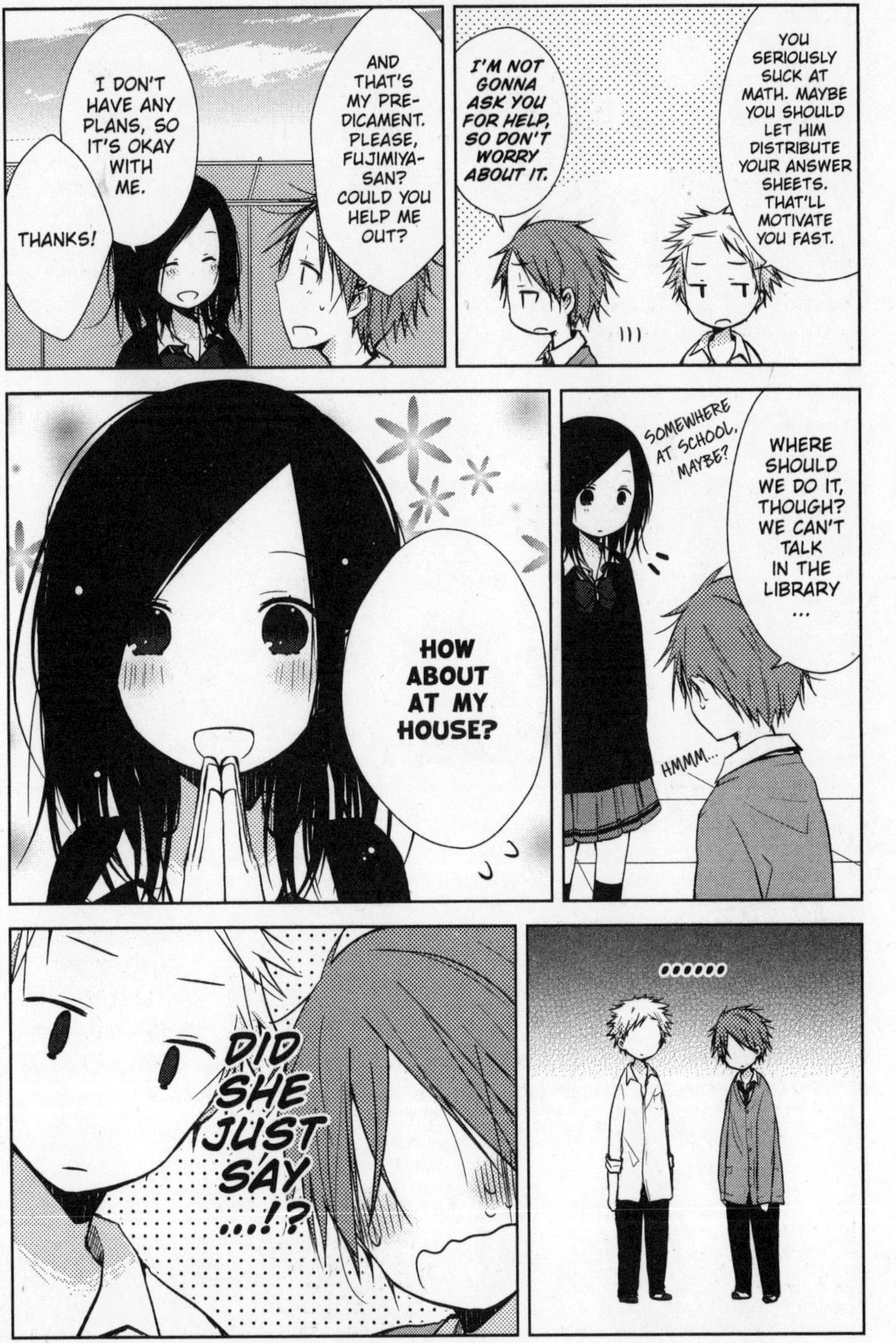
YOU SERIOUSLY SUCK AT MATH. MAYBE YOU SHOULD LET HIM DISTRIBUTE YOUR ANSWER SHEETS. THAT'LL MOTIVATE YOU FAST.
I'M NOT GONNA ASK YOU FOR HELP, SO DON'T WORRY ABOUT IT.
AND THAT'S MY PRE-DICAMENT. PLEASE, FUJIMIYA-SAN? COULD YOU HELP ME OUT?
I DON'T HAVE ANY PLANS, SO IT'S OKAY WITH ME.
THANKS!
WHERE SHOULD WE DO IT, THOUGH? WE CAN'T TALK IN THE LIBRARY ...
SOMEWHERE AT SCHOOL, MAYBE?
HMMM...
HOW ABOUT AT MY HOUSE?
......
DID SHE JUST SAY ...!?

NICE ASSIST?

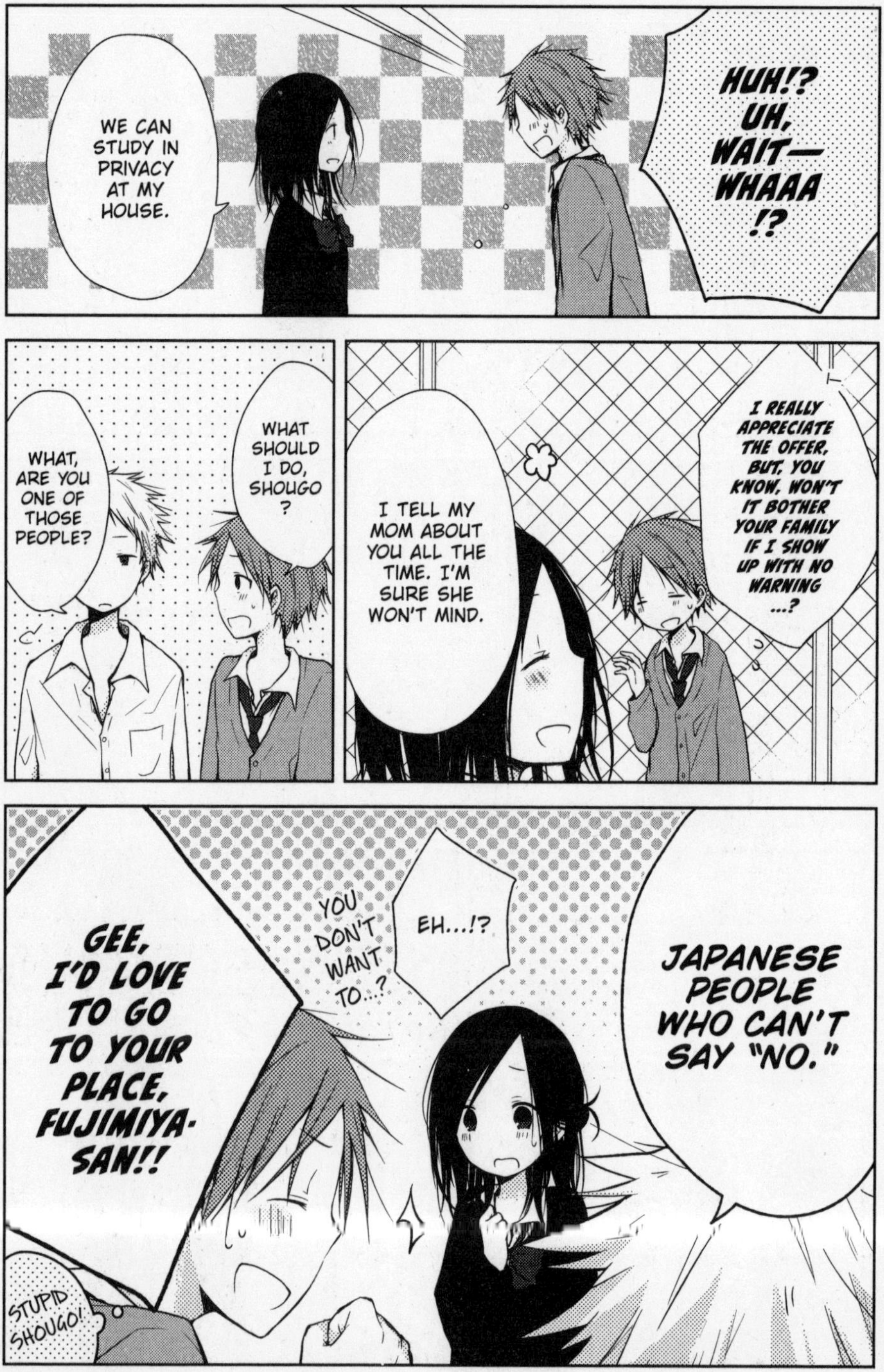
HUH!? UH, WAIT—WHAAA!?
WE CAN STUDY IN PRIVACY AT MY HOUSE.
I REALLY APPRECIATE THE OFFER, BUT, YOU KNOW, WON'T IT BOTHER YOUR FAMILY IF I SHOW UP WITH NO WARNING...?
I TELL MY MOM ABOUT YOU ALL THE TIME. I'M SURE SHE WON'T MIND.
WHAT SHOULD I DO, SHOUGO?
WHAT, ARE YOU ONE OF THOSE PEOPLE?
JAPANESE PEOPLE WHO CAN'T SAY "NO."
EH...!?
YOU DON'T WANT TO...?
GEE, I'D LOVE TO GO TO YOUR PLACE, FUJIMIYA-SAN!!
STUPID SHOUGO!

"THAT" KIND OF CONVO

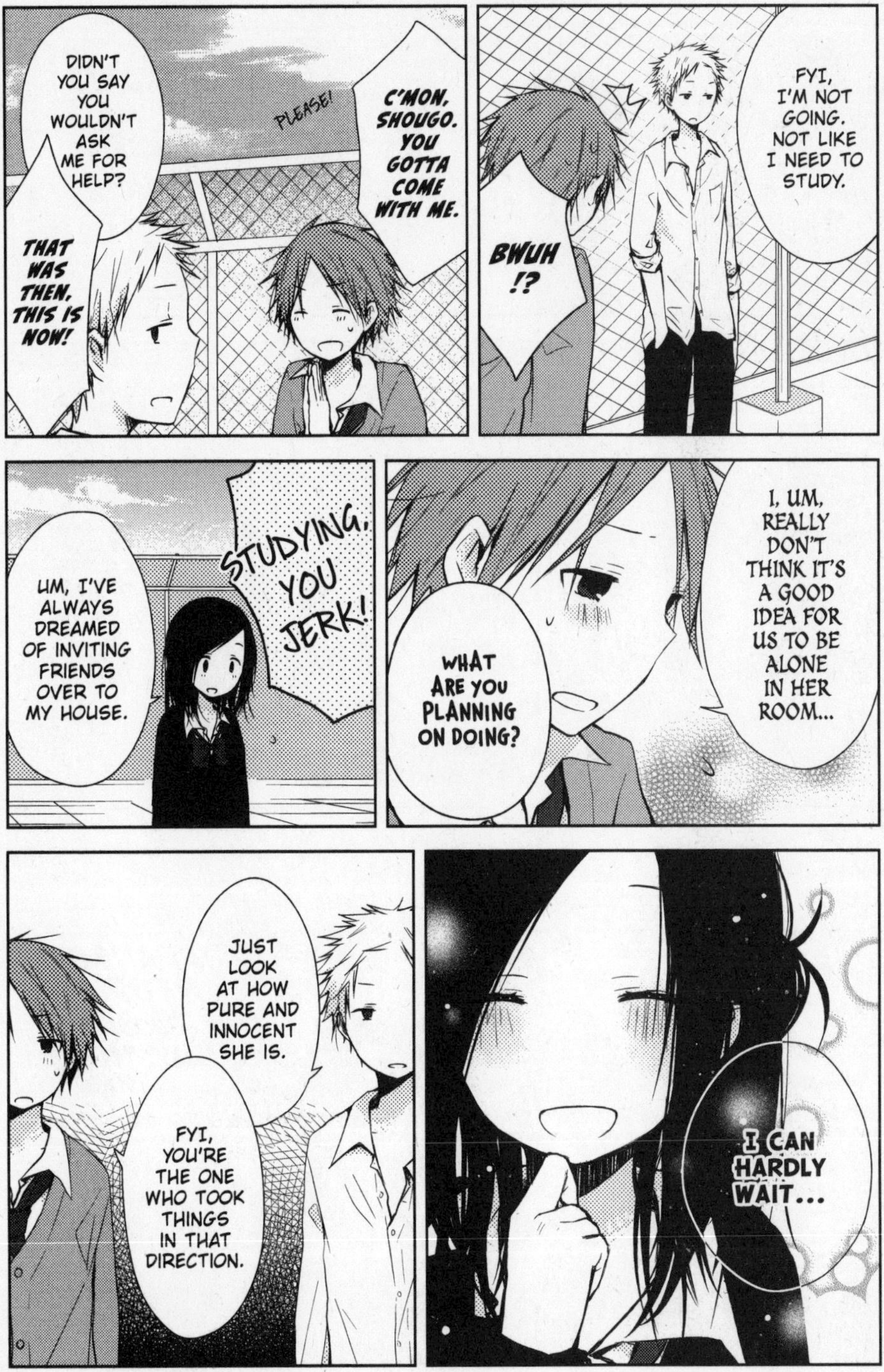
FYI, I'M NOT GOING. NOT LIKE I NEED TO STUDY.
BWUH !?
C'MON, SHOUGO. YOU GOTTA COME WITH ME.
PLEASE!
DIDN'T YOU SAY YOU WOULDN'T ASK ME FOR HELP?
THAT WAS THEN, THIS IS NOW!
I, UM, REALLY DON'T THINK IT'S A GOOD IDEA FOR US TO BE ALONE IN HER ROOM...
WHAT ARE YOU PLANNING ON DOING?
STUDYING, YOU JERK!
UM, I'VE ALWAYS DREAMED OF INVITING FRIENDS OVER TO MY HOUSE.
I CAN HARDLY WAIT...
JUST LOOK AT HOW PURE AND INNOCENT SHE IS.
FYI, YOU'RE THE ONE WHO TOOK THINGS IN THAT DIRECTION.

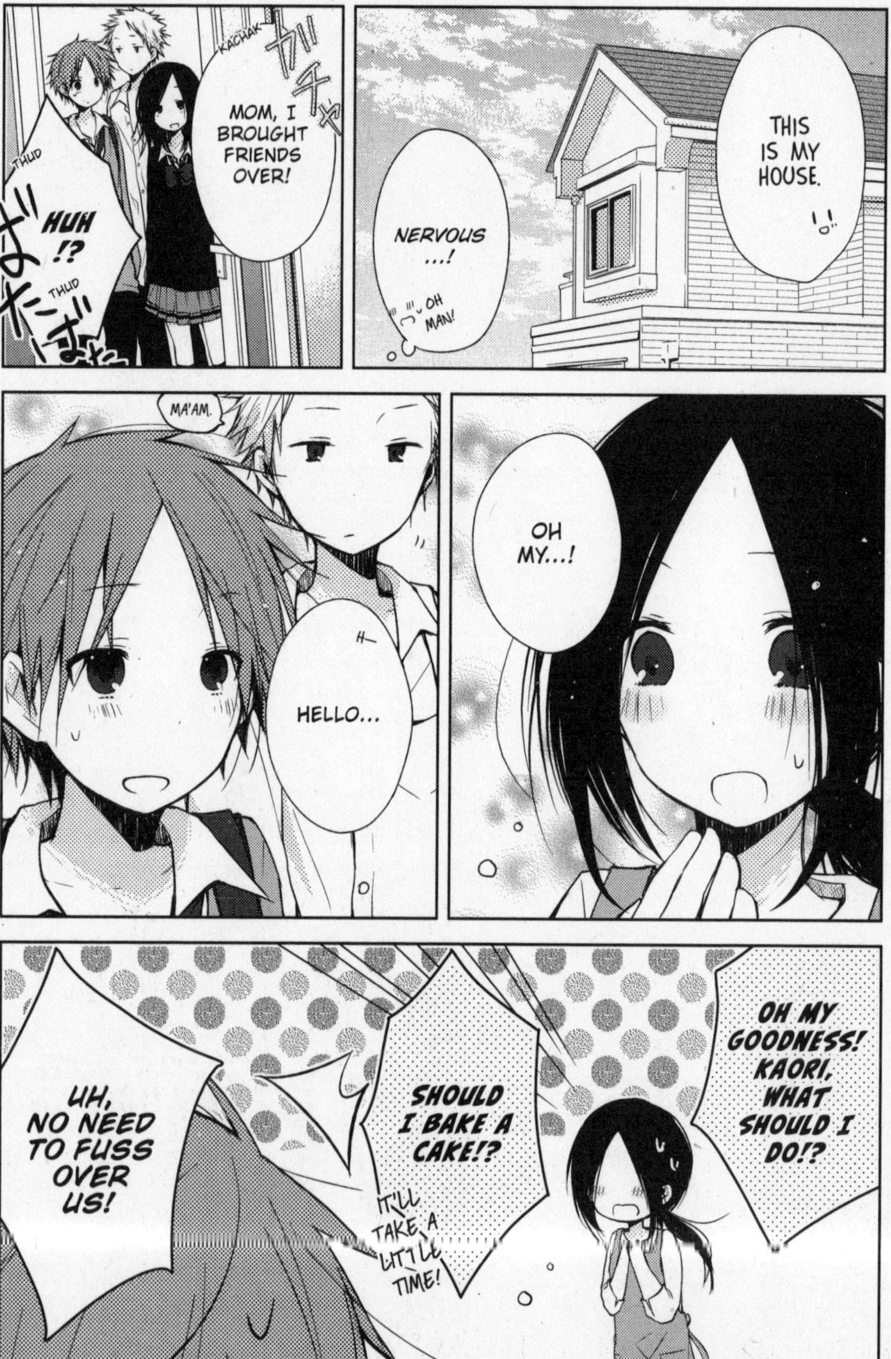
THIS IS MY HOUSE.
NERVOUS ...!
OH MAN!
KACHAK
MOM, I BROUGHT FRIENDS OVER!
THUD
HUH !?
THUD
OH MY...!
MA'AM.
H—
HELLO...
OH MY GOODNESS! KAORI, WHAT SHOULD I DO!?
SHOULD I BAKE A CAKE!?
IT'LL TAKE A LITTLE TIME!
UH, NO NEED TO FUSS OVER US!

DIFFERENCE IN REACTIONS

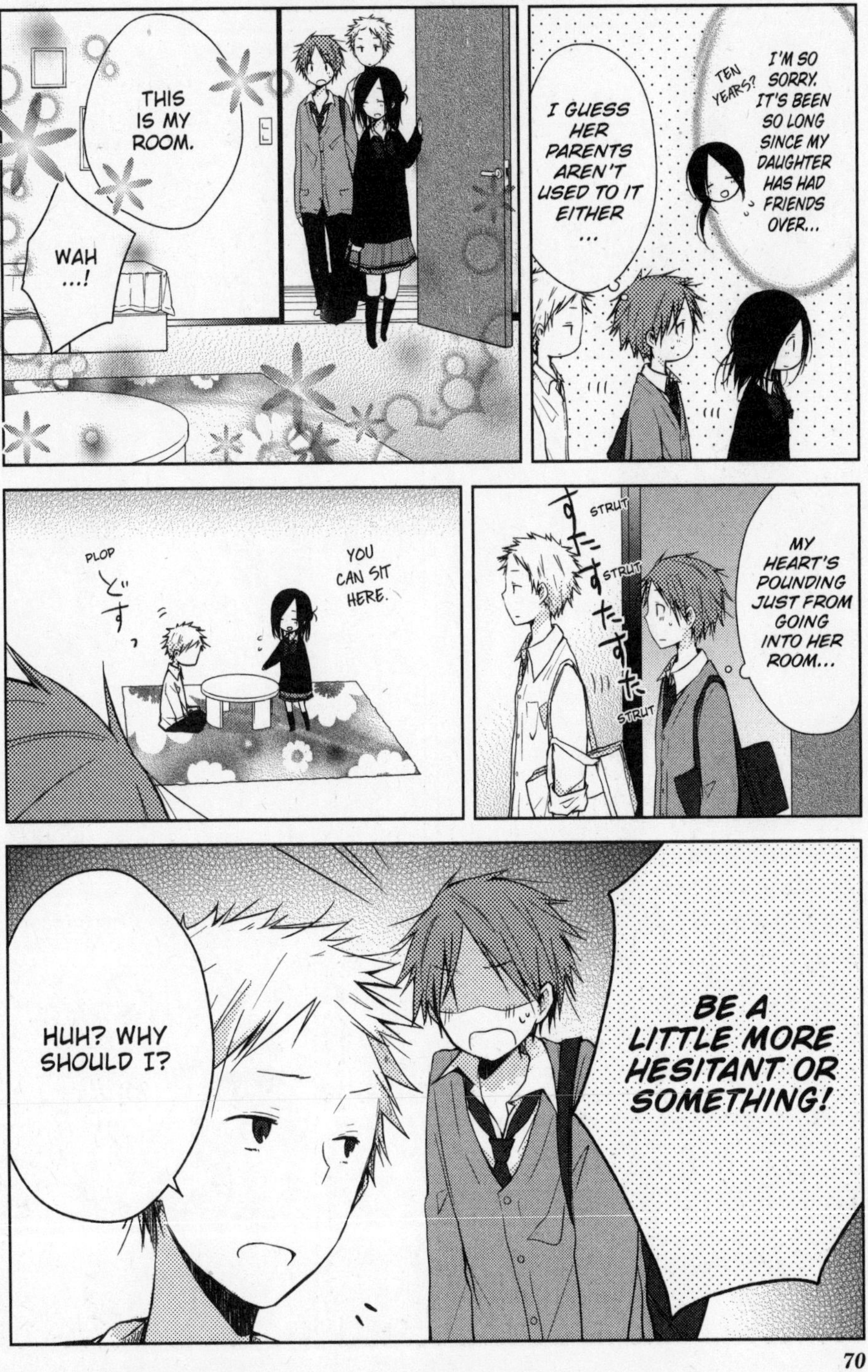
I'M SO SORRY. IT'S BEEN SO LONG SINCE MY DAUGHTER HAS HAD FRIENDS OVER...
TEN YEARS?
I GUESS HER PARENTS AREN'T USED TO IT EITHER...
THIS IS MY ROOM.
WAH...!
MY HEART'S POUNDING JUST FROM GOING INTO HER ROOM...
STRUT
すたすたすたすた
STRUT
STRUT
YOU CAN SIT HERE.
PLOP
どす
BE A LITTLE MORE HESITANT OR SOMETHING!
HUH? WHY SHOULD I?

REALLY THOUGHT IT

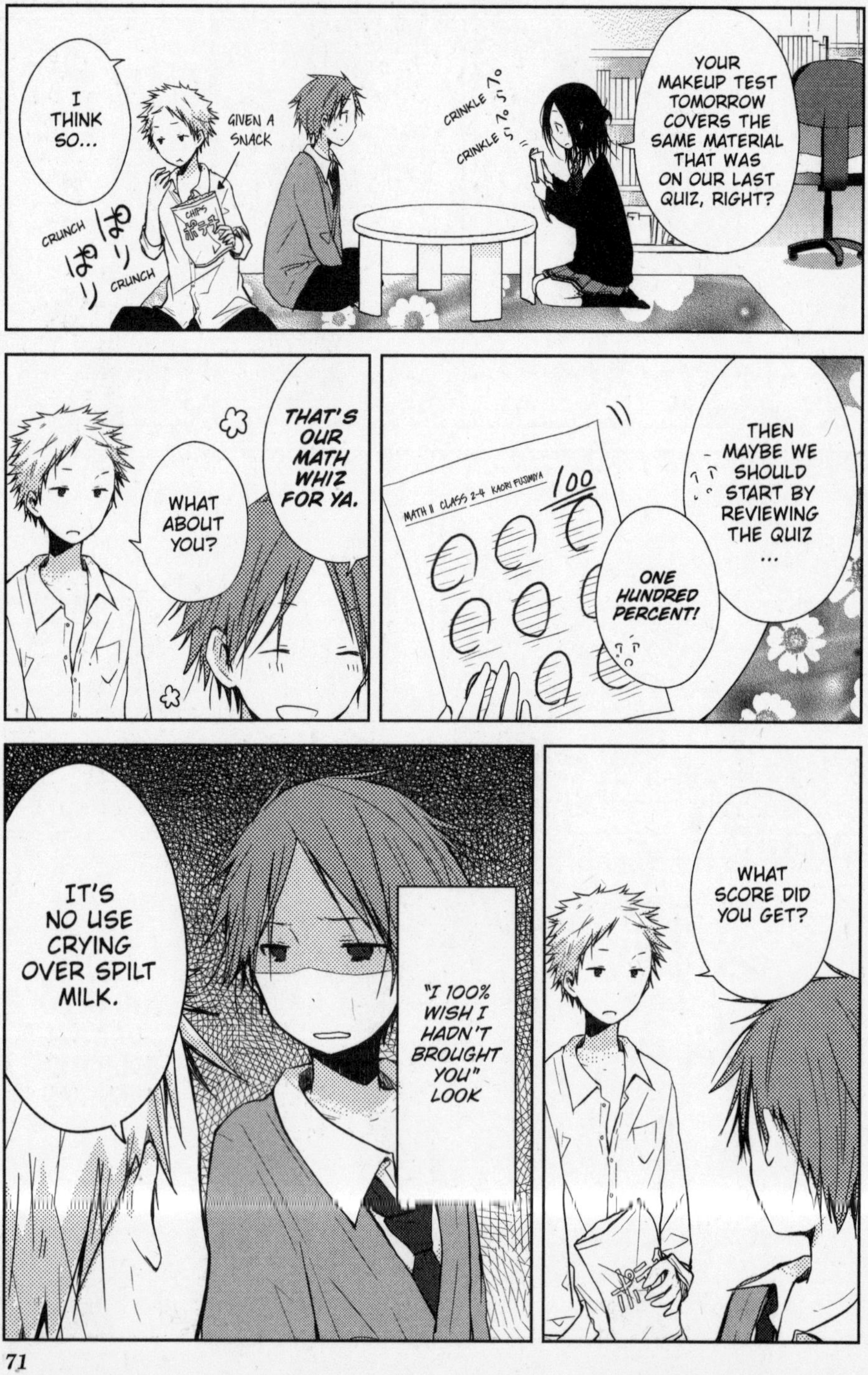
YOUR MAKEUP TEST TOMORROW COVERS THE SAME MATERIAL THAT WAS ON OUR LAST QUIZ, RIGHT?
CRINKLE
CRINKLE
I THINK SO...
GIVEN A SNACK
CHIPS
CRUNCH
CRUNCH
THEN MAYBE WE SHOULD START BY REVIEWING THE QUIZ ...
ONE HUNDRED PERCENT!
MATH II CLASS 2-4 KAORI FUJIMIYA
100
THAT'S OUR MATH WHIZ FOR YA.
WHAT ABOUT YOU?
WHAT SCORE DID YOU GET?
"I 100% WISH I HADN'T BROUGHT YOU" LOOK
IT'S NO USE CRYING OVER SPILT MILK.

AN INNOCENT QUESTION

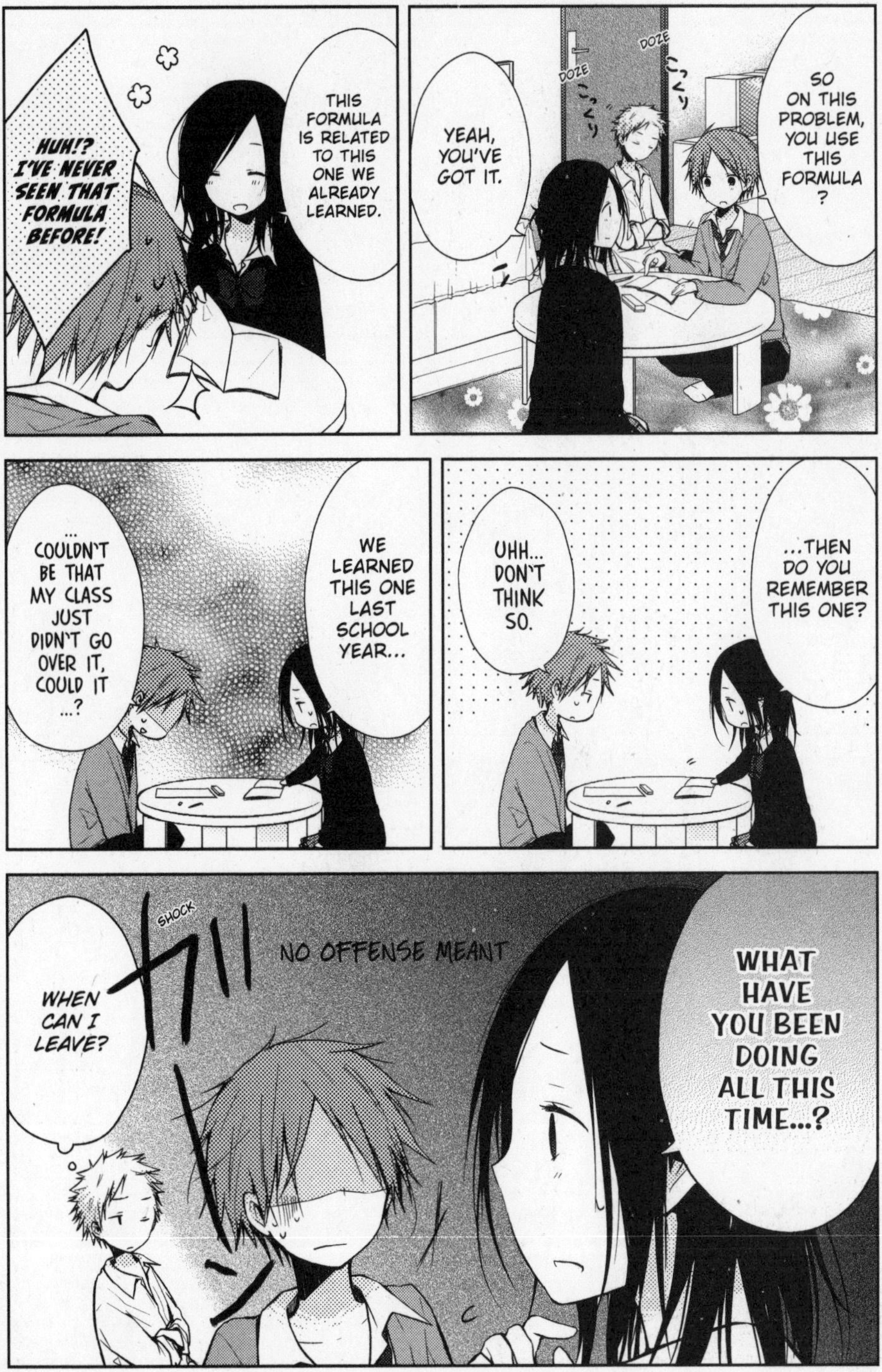

DOZE
こっくり
DOZE
こっくり
SO ON THIS PROBLEM, YOU USE THIS FORMULA?
YEAH, YOU'VE GOT IT.
THIS FORMULA IS RELATED TO THIS ONE WE ALREADY LEARNED.
HUH!? I'VE NEVER SEEN THAT FORMULA BEFORE!
...THEN DO YOU REMEMBER THIS ONE?
UHH... DON'T THINK SO.
WE LEARNED THIS ONE LAST SCHOOL YEAR...
...COULDN'T BE THAT MY CLASS JUST DIDN'T GO OVER IT, COULD IT...?
WHAT HAVE YOU BEEN DOING ALL THIS TIME...?
NO OFFENSE MEANT
SHOCK
WHEN CAN I LEAVE?

DON'T KNOW WHAT TO DO

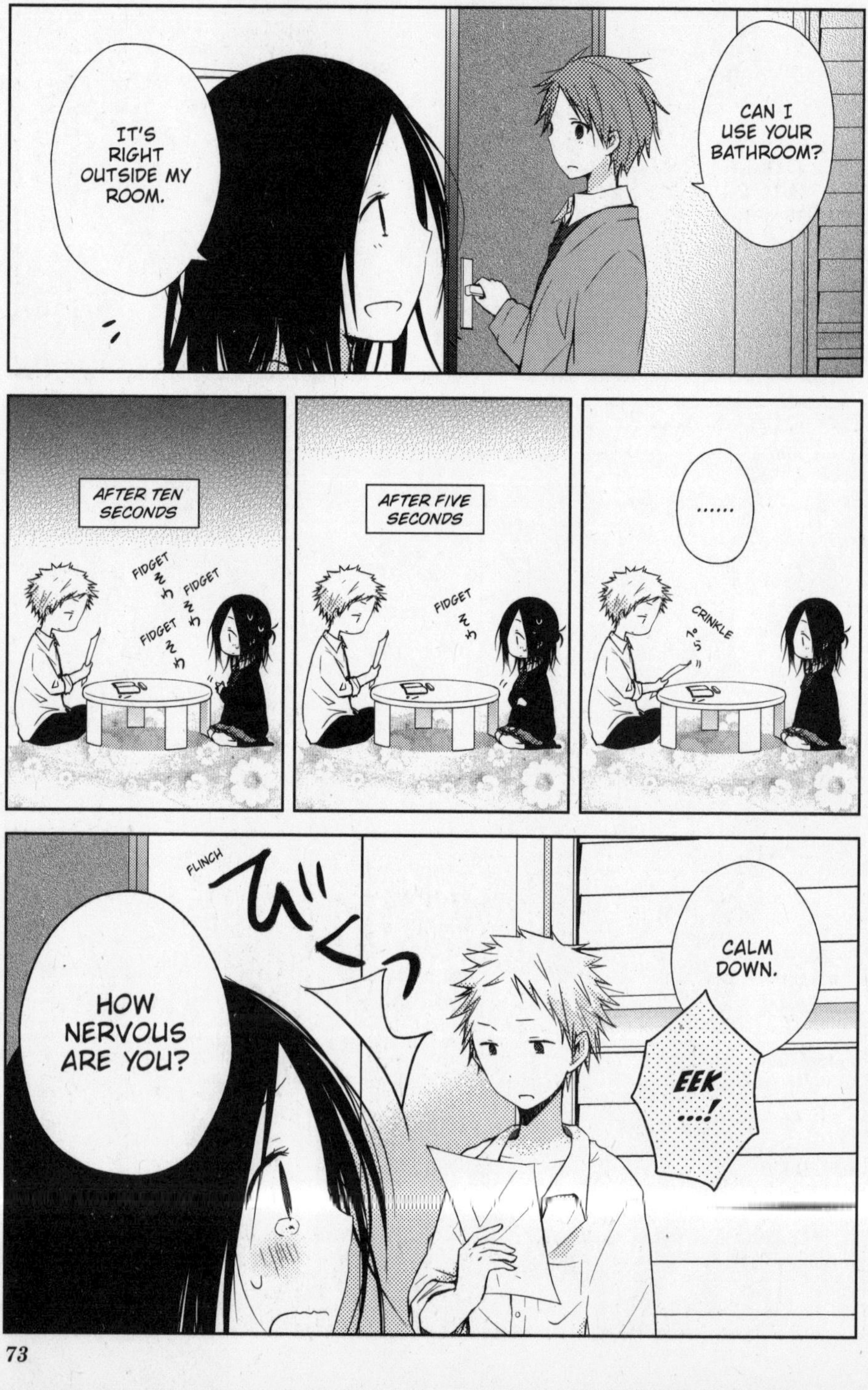
CAN I USE YOUR BATHROOM?
IT'S RIGHT OUTSIDE MY ROOM.
......
CRINKLE
AFTER FIVE SECONDS
FIDGET
AFTER TEN SECONDS
FIDGET
FIDGET
FIDGET
CALM DOWN.
EEK ...!
FLINCH
HOW NERVOUS ARE YOU?

DISTURBING CONVERSATION

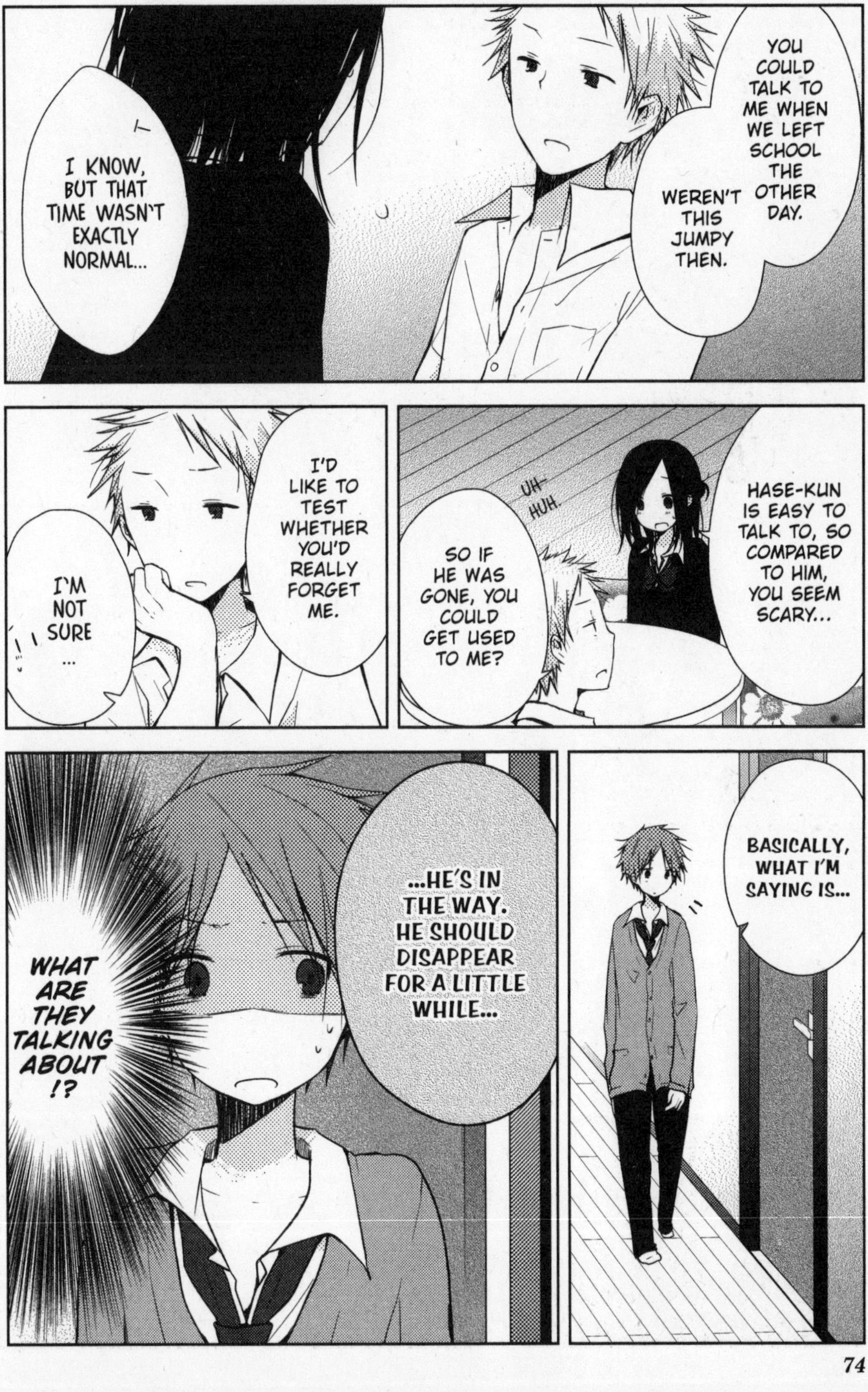
YOU COULD TALK TO ME WHEN WE LEFT SCHOOL THE OTHER DAY.
WEREN'T THIS JUMPY THEN.
I KNOW, BUT THAT TIME WASN'T EXACTLY NORMAL...
HASE-KUN IS EASY TO TALK TO, SO COMPARED TO HIM, YOU SEEM SCARY...
UH-HUH.
SO IF HE WAS GONE, YOU COULD GET USED TO ME?
I'D LIKE TO TEST WHETHER YOU'D REALLY FORGET ME.
I'M NOT SURE ...
BASICALLY, WHAT I'M SAYING IS...
...HE'S IN THE WAY. HE SHOULD DISAPPEAR FOR A LITTLE WHILE...
WHAT ARE THEY TALKING ABOUT !?

DIFFERENT TEMPERATURES

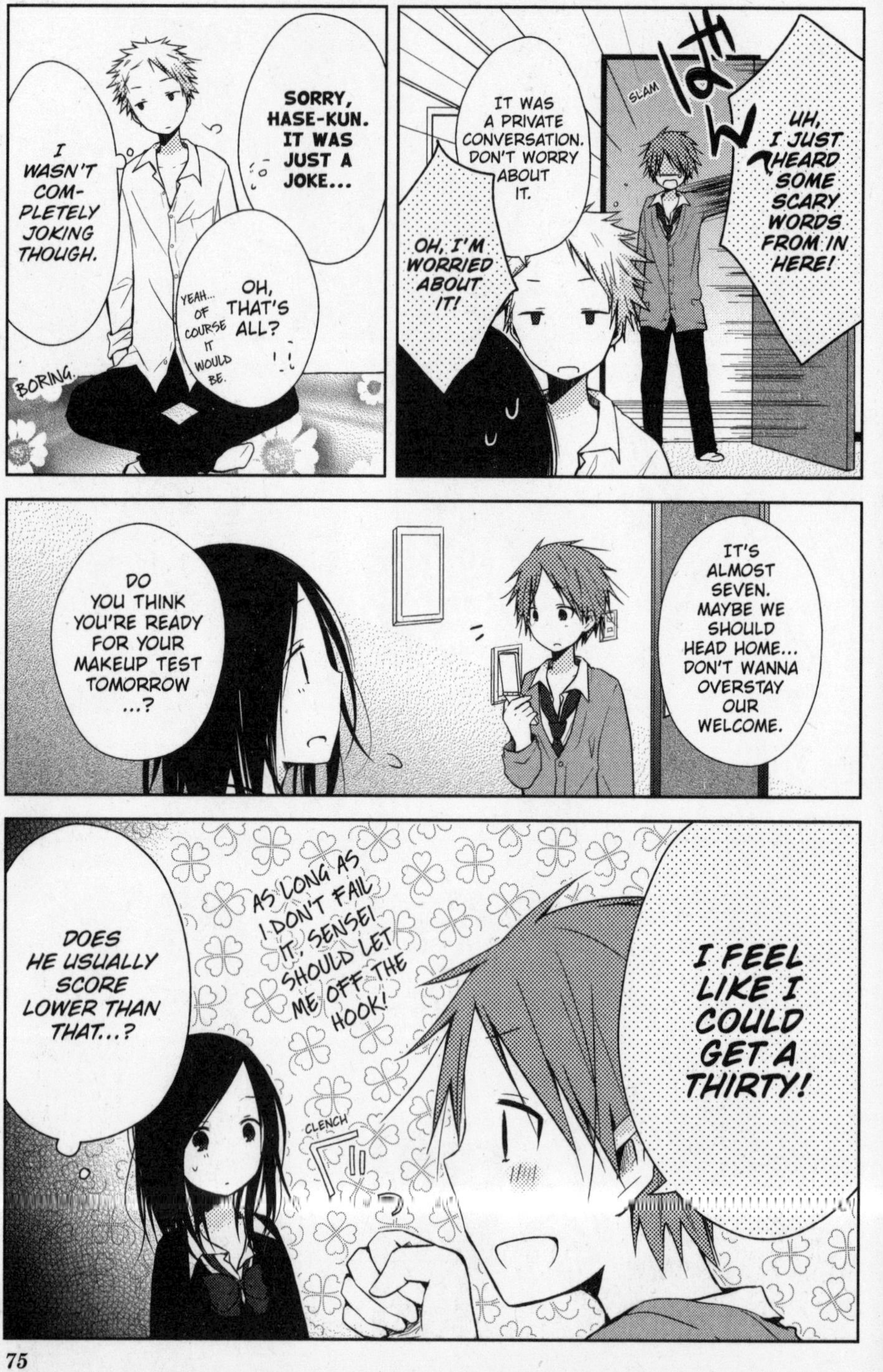
SLAM
ばん
UH, I JUST HEARD SOME SCARY WORDS FROM IN HERE!
IT WAS A PRIVATE CONVERSATION. DON'T WORRY ABOUT IT.
OH, I'M WORRIED ABOUT IT!
SORRY, HASE-KUN. IT WAS JUST A JOKE...
I WASN'T COMPLETELY JOKING THOUGH.
OH, THAT'S ALL?
YEAH... OF COURSE IT WOULD BE.
BORING.
IT'S ALMOST SEVEN. MAYBE WE SHOULD HEAD HOME... DON'T WANNA OVERSTAY OUR WELCOME.
DO YOU THINK YOU'RE READY FOR YOUR MAKEUP TEST TOMORROW ...?
I FEEL LIKE I COULD GET A THIRTY!
AS LONG AS I DON'T FAIL IT, SENSEI SHOULD LET ME OFF THE HOOK!
CLENCH
DOES HE USUALLY SCORE LOWER THAN THAT...?

SORT OF HAPPY, SORT OF SAD

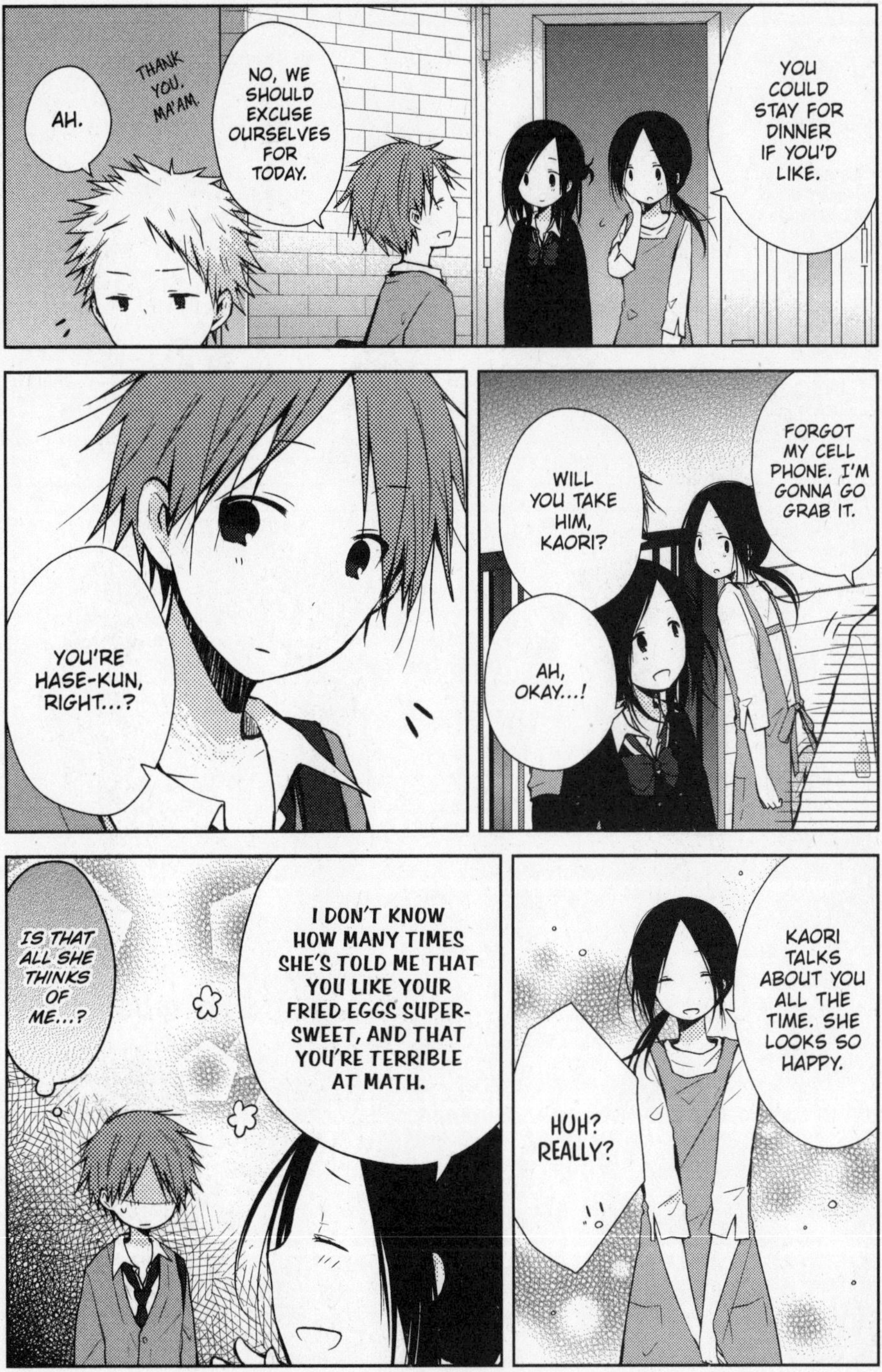

YOU COULD STAY FOR DINNER IF YOU'D LIKE.
NO, WE SHOULD EXCUSE OURSELVES FOR TODAY.
THANK YOU, MA'AM.
AH.
FORGOT MY CELL PHONE. I'M GONNA GO GRAB IT.
WILL YOU TAKE HIM, KAORI?
AH, OKAY...!
YOU'RE HASE-KUN, RIGHT...?
KAORI TALKS ABOUT YOU ALL THE TIME. SHE LOOKS SO HAPPY.
HUH? REALLY?
I DON'T KNOW HOW MANY TIMES SHE'S TOLD ME THAT YOU LIKE YOUR FRIED EGGS SUPER-SWEET, AND THAT YOU'RE TERRIBLE AT MATH.
IS THAT ALL SHE THINKS OF ME...?

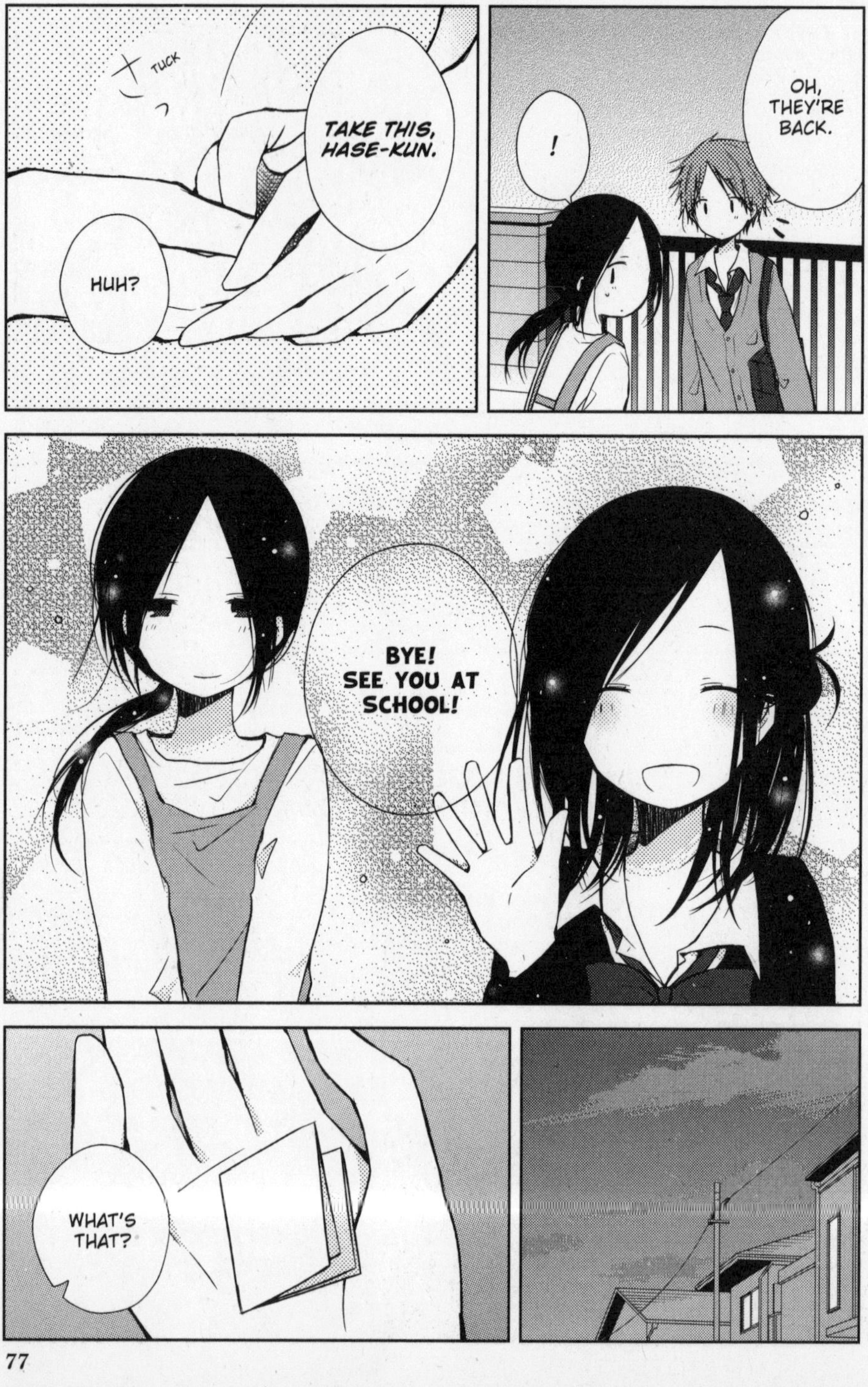
OH, THEY'RE BACK.
!
TAKE THIS, HASE-KUN.
TUCK
HUH?
BYE! SEE YOU AT SCHOOL!
WHAT'S THAT?

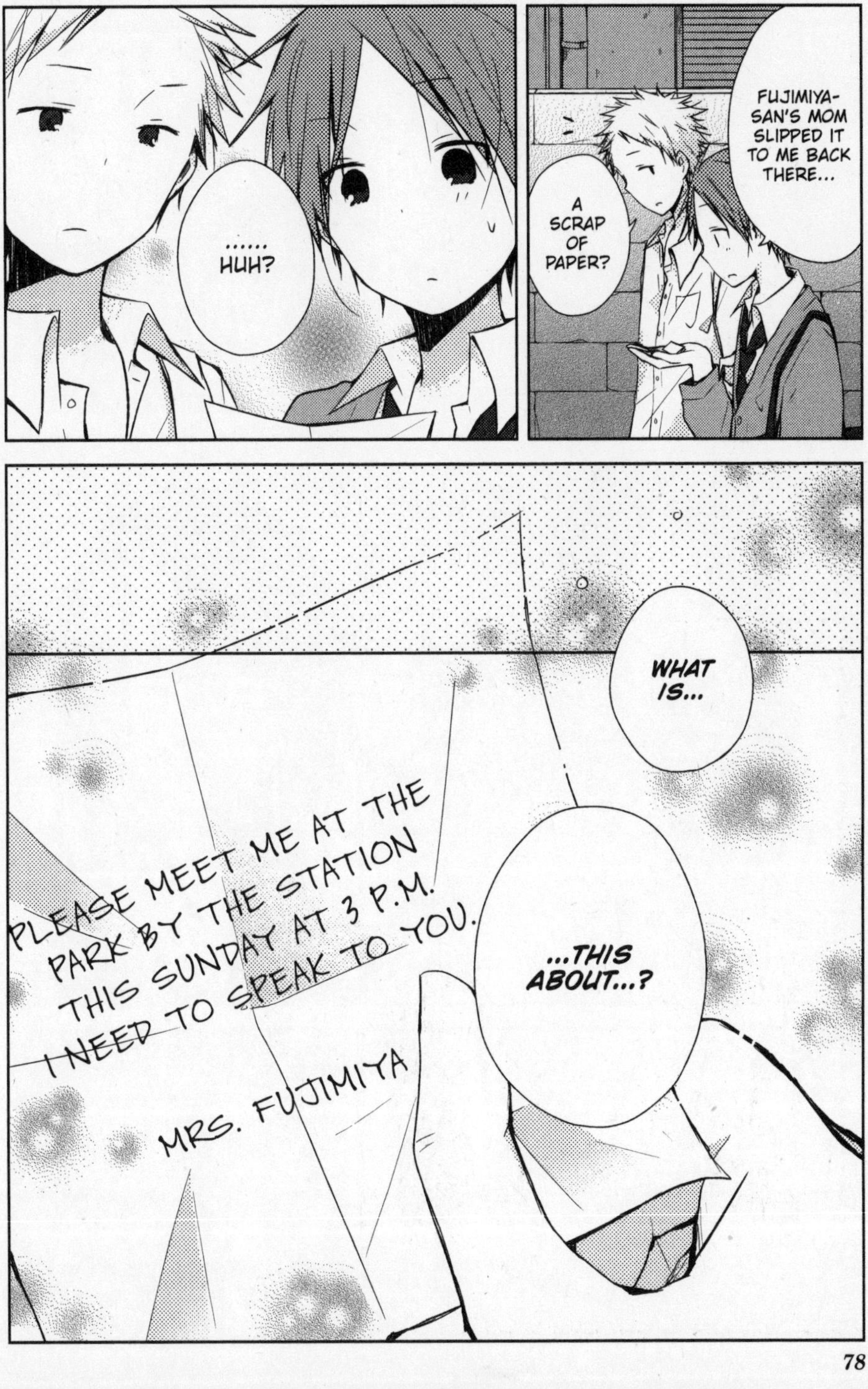
FUJIMIYA-SAN'S MOM SLIPPED IT TO ME BACK THERE...
A SCRAP OF PAPER?
......HUH?
WHAT IS...
...THIS ABOUT...?
PLEASE MEET ME AT THE PARK BY THE STATION THIS SUNDAY AT 3 P.M. I NEED TO SPEAK TO YOU.
MRS. FUJIMIYA

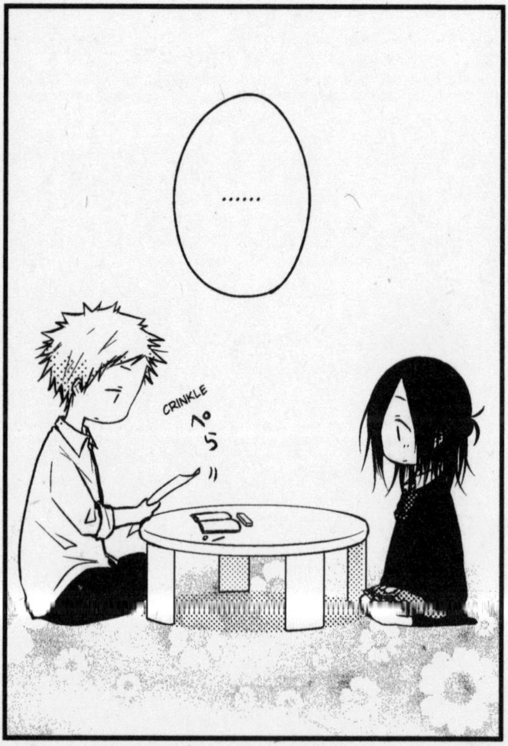
......
CRINKLE
へら

SIDE STORY: A CERTAIN WEEK OF ONE-WEEK FRIENDS

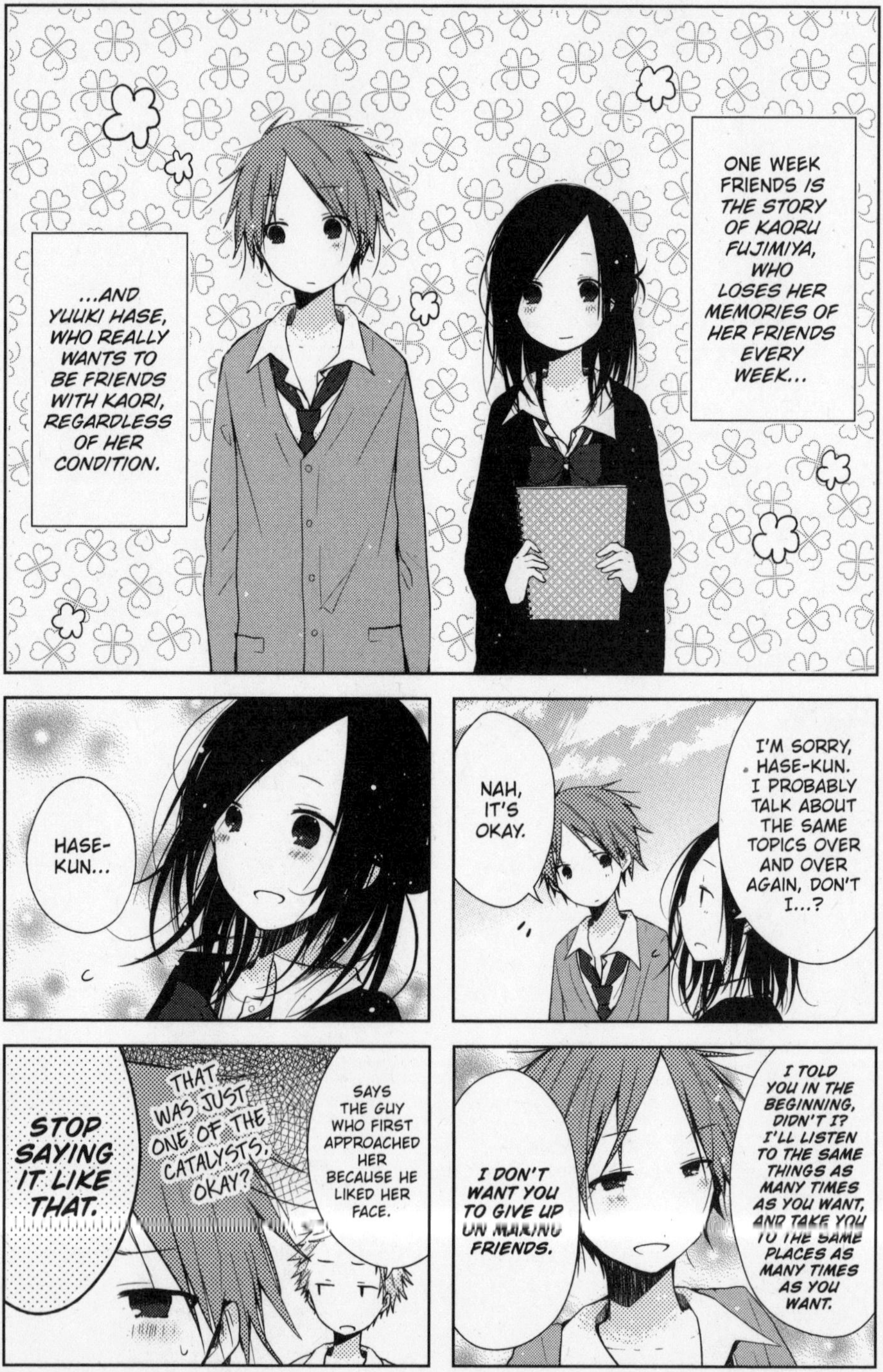
ONE WEEK FRIENDS IS THE STORY OF KAORU FUJIMIYA, WHO LOSES HER MEMORIES OF HER FRIENDS EVERY WEEK...
...AND YUUKI HASE, WHO REALLY WANTS TO BE FRIENDS WITH KAORI, REGARDLESS OF HER CONDITION.
I'M SORRY, HASE-KUN. I PROBABLY TALK ABOUT THE SAME TOPICS OVER AND OVER AGAIN, DON'T I...?
NAH, IT'S OKAY.
HASE-KUN...
I TOLD YOU IN THE BEGINNING, DIDN'T I? I'LL LISTEN TO THE SAME THINGS AS MANY TIMES AS YOU WANT, AND TAKE YOU TO THE SAME PLACES AS MANY TIMES AS YOU WANT.
I DON'T WANT YOU TO GIVE UP ON MAKING FRIENDS.
SAYS THE GUY WHO FIRST APPROACHED HER BECAUSE HE LIKED HER FACE.
THAT WAS JUST ONE OF THE CATALYSTS, OKAY?
STOP SAYING IT LIKE THAT.

IN THE CLASSROOM

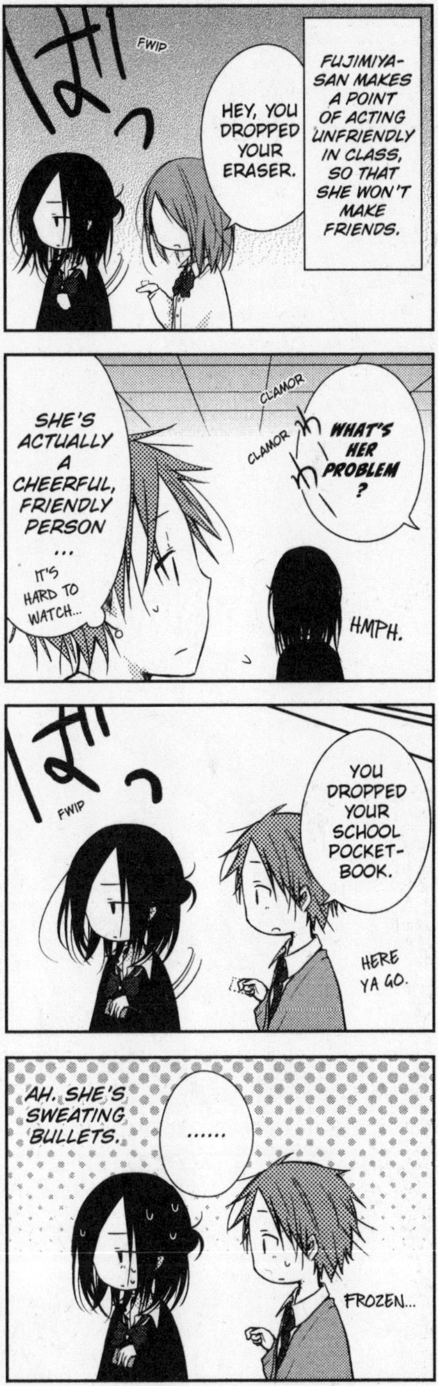
FUJIMIYA-SAN MAKES A POINT OF ACTING UNFRIENDLY IN CLASS, SO THAT SHE WON'T MAKE FRIENDS.
HEY, YOU DROPPED YOUR ERASER.
FWIP
WHAT'S HER PROBLEM?
CLAMOR
CLAMOR
SHE'S ACTUALLY A CHEERFUL, FRIENDLY PERSON...
IT'S HARD TO WATCH...
HMPH.
YOU DROPPED YOUR SCHOOL POCKET-BOOK.
FWIP
HERE YA GO.
AH. SHE'S SWEATING BULLETS.
......
FROZEN...

ON THE ROOF

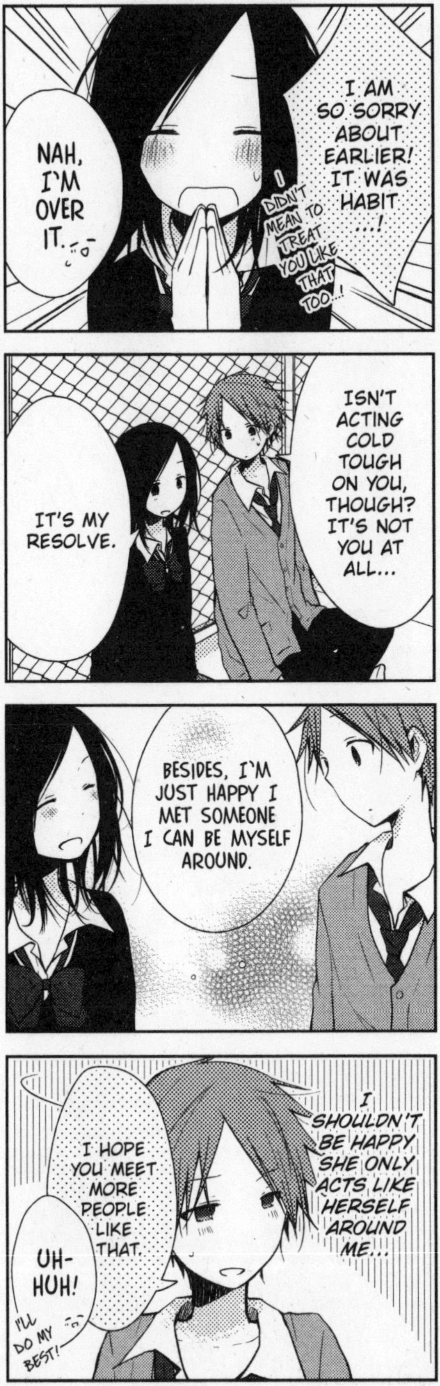
I AM SO SORRY ABOUT EARLIER! IT WAS HABIT...!
I DIDN'T MEAN TO TREAT YOU LIKE THAT TOO...!
NAH, I'M OVER IT.
ISN'T ACTING COLD TOUGH ON YOU, THOUGH? IT'S NOT YOU AT ALL...
IT'S MY RESOLVE.
BESIDES, I'M JUST HAPPY I MET SOMEONE I CAN BE MYSELF AROUND.
I SHOULDN'T BE HAPPY SHE ONLY ACTS LIKE HERSELF AROUND ME...
I HOPE YOU MEET MORE PEOPLE LIKE THAT.
UH-HUH!
I'LL DO MY BEST!

HASE'S FRIEND

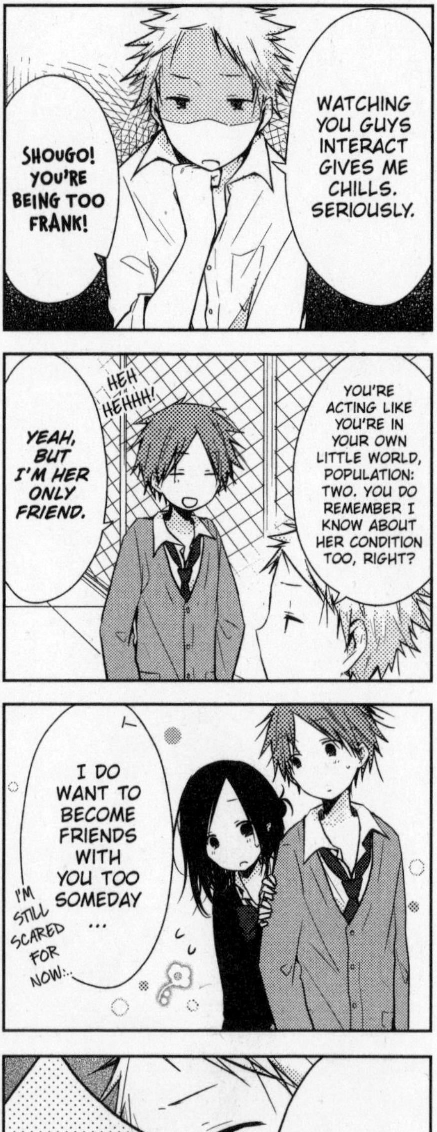
WATCHING YOU GUYS INTERACT GIVES ME CHILLS. SERIOUSLY.
SHOUGO! YOU'RE BEING TOO FRANK!
YOU'RE ACTING LIKE YOU'RE IN YOUR OWN LITTLE WORLD, POPULATION: TWO. YOU DO REMEMBER I KNOW ABOUT HER CONDITION TOO, RIGHT?
HEH HEHHH!
YEAH, BUT I'M HER ONLY FRIEND.
I DO WANT TO BECOME FRIENDS WITH YOU TOO SOMEDAY ...
I'M STILL SCARED FOR NOW...
I DON'T REALLY CARE EITHER WAY, THOUGH.
GIRLS ARE A PAIN.
THAT'S WHY SHE CAN'T OPEN UP TO YOU!
SHOCK

CLOSE

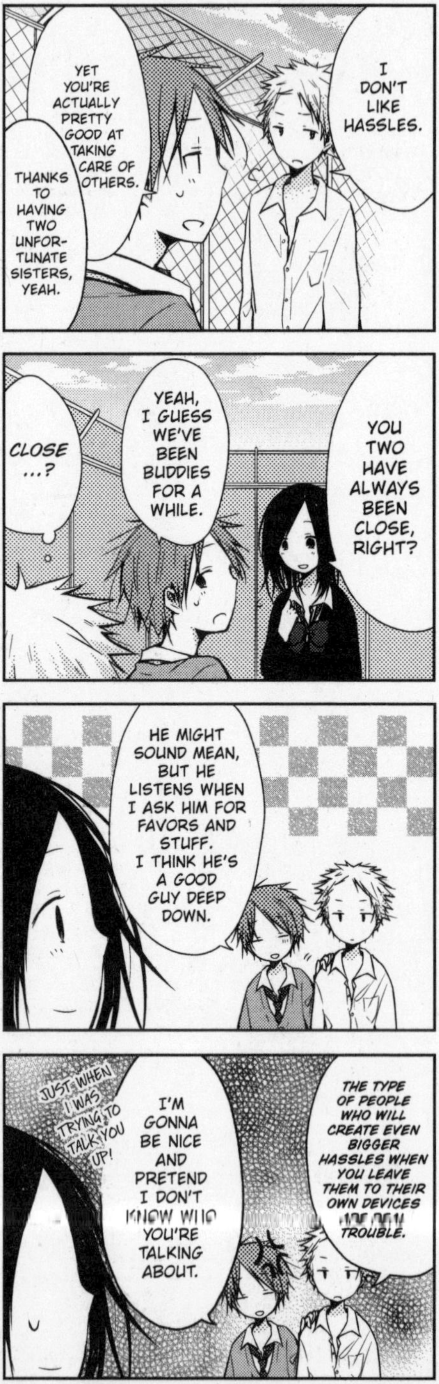
I DON'T LIKE HASSLES.
YET YOU'RE ACTUALLY PRETTY GOOD AT TAKING CARE OF OTHERS.
THANKS TO HAVING TWO UNFORTUNATE SISTERS, YEAH.
YOU TWO HAVE ALWAYS BEEN CLOSE, RIGHT?
YEAH, I GUESS WE'VE BEEN BUDDIES FOR A WHILE.
CLOSE ...?
HE MIGHT SOUND MEAN, BUT HE LISTENS WHEN I ASK HIM FOR FAVORS AND STUFF. I THINK HE'S A GOOD GUY DEEP DOWN.
THE TYPE OF PEOPLE WHO WILL CREATE EVEN BIGGER HASSLES WHEN YOU LEAVE THEM TO THEIR OWN DEVICES ARE REAL TROUBLE.
I'M GONNA BE NICE AND PRETEND I DON'T KNOW WHO YOU'RE TALKING ABOUT.
JUST WHEN I WAS TRYING TO TALK YOU UP!

THE DIARY ENTRIES

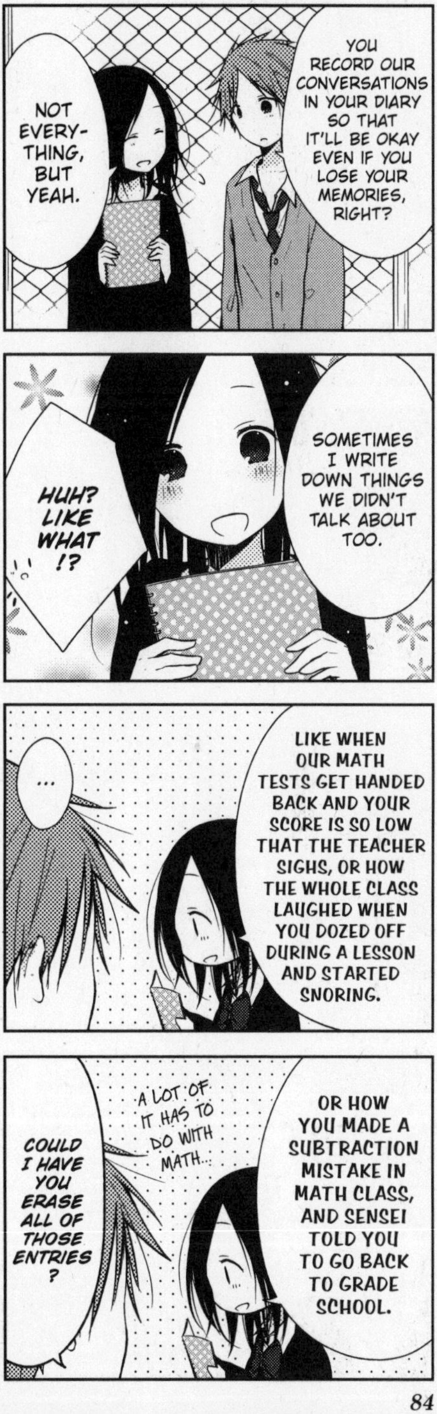
YOU RECORD OUR CONVERSATIONS IN YOUR DIARY SO THAT IT'LL BE OKAY EVEN IF YOU LOSE YOUR MEMORIES, RIGHT?
NOT EVERY-THING, BUT YEAH.
SOMETIMES I WRITE DOWN THINGS WE DIDN'T TALK ABOUT TOO.
HUH? LIKE WHAT !?
LIKE WHEN OUR MATH TESTS GET HANDED BACK AND YOUR SCORE IS SO LOW THAT THE TEACHER SIGHS, OR HOW THE WHOLE CLASS LAUGHED WHEN YOU DOZED OFF DURING A LESSON AND STARTED SNORING.
...
OR HOW YOU MADE A SUBTRACTION MISTAKE IN MATH CLASS, AND SENSEI TOLD YOU TO GO BACK TO GRADE SCHOOL.
A LOT OF IT HAS TO DO WITH MATH...
COULD I HAVE YOU ERASE ALL OF THOSE ENTRIES ?

BECAUSE IT'S FRIDAY

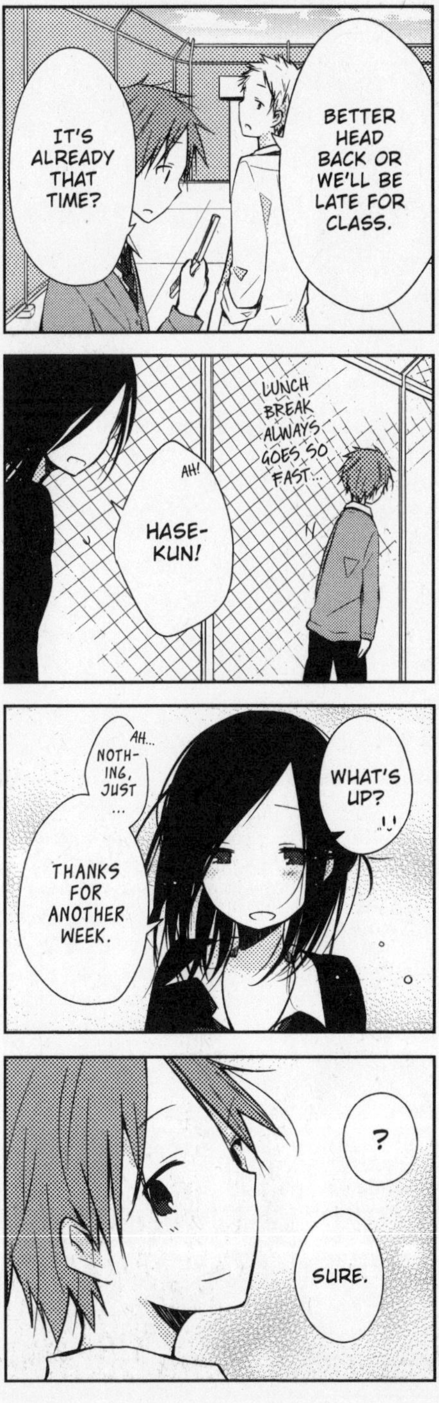
BETTER HEAD BACK OR WE'LL BE LATE FOR CLASS.
IT'S ALREADY THAT TIME?
LUNCH BREAK ALWAYS GOES SO FAST...
AH!
HASE-KUN!
WHAT'S UP?
AH... NOTHING, JUST ...
THANKS FOR ANOTHER WEEK.
?
SURE.

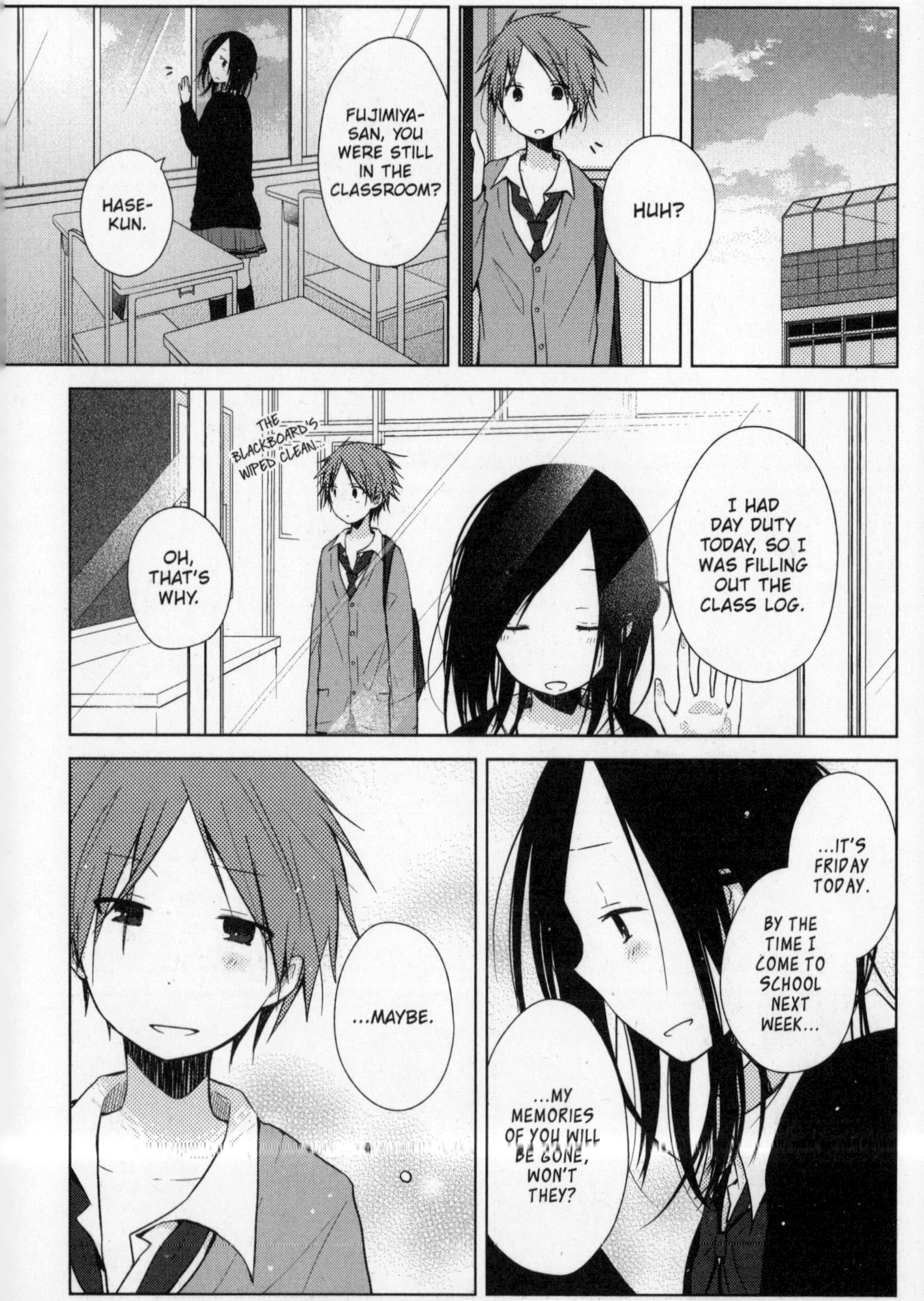
HUH?
FUJIMIYA-SAN, YOU WERE STILL IN THE CLASSROOM?
HASE-KUN.
I HAD DAY DUTY TODAY, SO I WAS FILLING OUT THE CLASS LOG.
THE BLACKBOARD'S WIPED CLEAN...
OH, THAT'S WHY.
...IT'S FRIDAY TODAY.
BY THE TIME I COME TO SCHOOL NEXT WEEK...
...MY MEMORIES OF YOU WILL BE GONE, WON'T THEY?
...MAYBE.

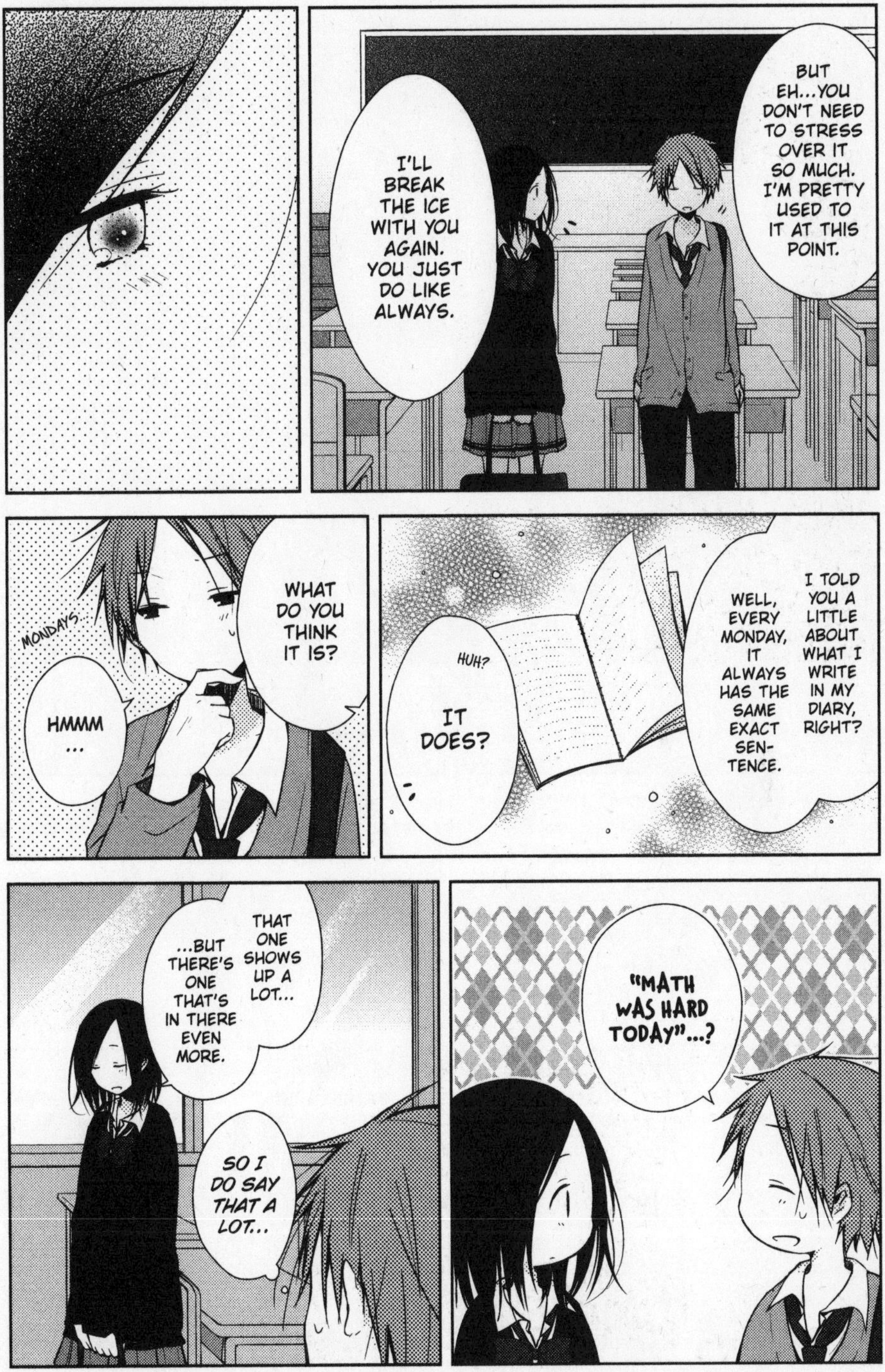
BUT EH...YOU DON'T NEED TO STRESS OVER IT SO MUCH. I'M PRETTY USED TO IT AT THIS POINT.
I'LL BREAK THE ICE WITH YOU AGAIN. YOU JUST DO LIKE ALWAYS.
I TOLD YOU A LITTLE ABOUT WHAT I WRITE IN MY DIARY, RIGHT?
WELL, EVERY MONDAY, IT ALWAYS HAS THE SAME EXACT SEN-TENCE.
HUH?
IT DOES?
WHAT DO YOU THINK IT IS?
MONDAYS...
HMMM ...
"MATH WAS HARD TODAY"...?
THAT ONE SHOWS UP A LOT...
...BUT THERE'S ONE THAT'S IN THERE EVEN MORE.
SO I DO SAY THAT A LOT...

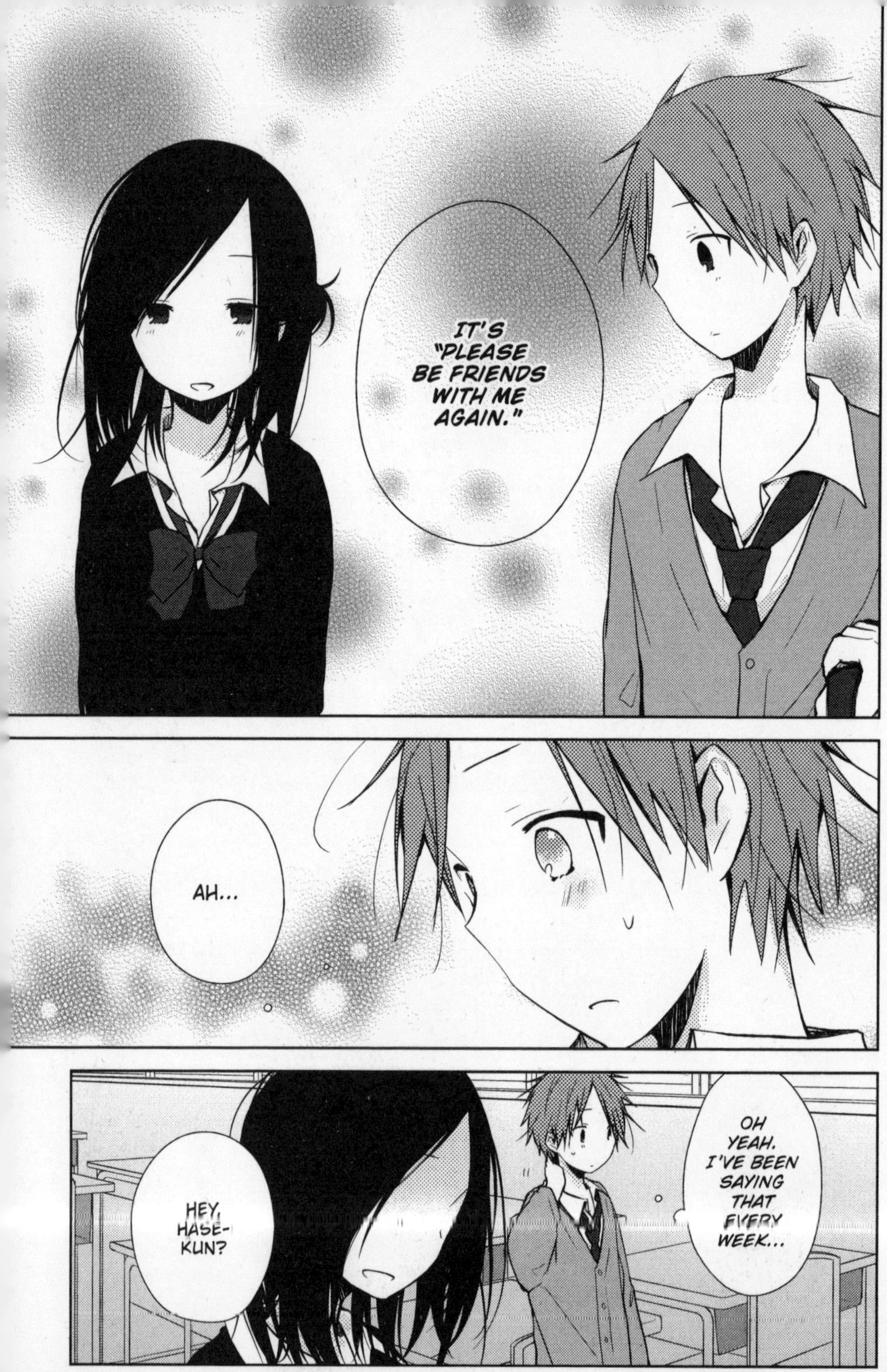
IT'S "PLEASE BE FRIENDS WITH ME AGAIN."
AH...
OH YEAH. I'VE BEEN SAYING THAT EVERY WEEK...
HEY, HASE-KUN?

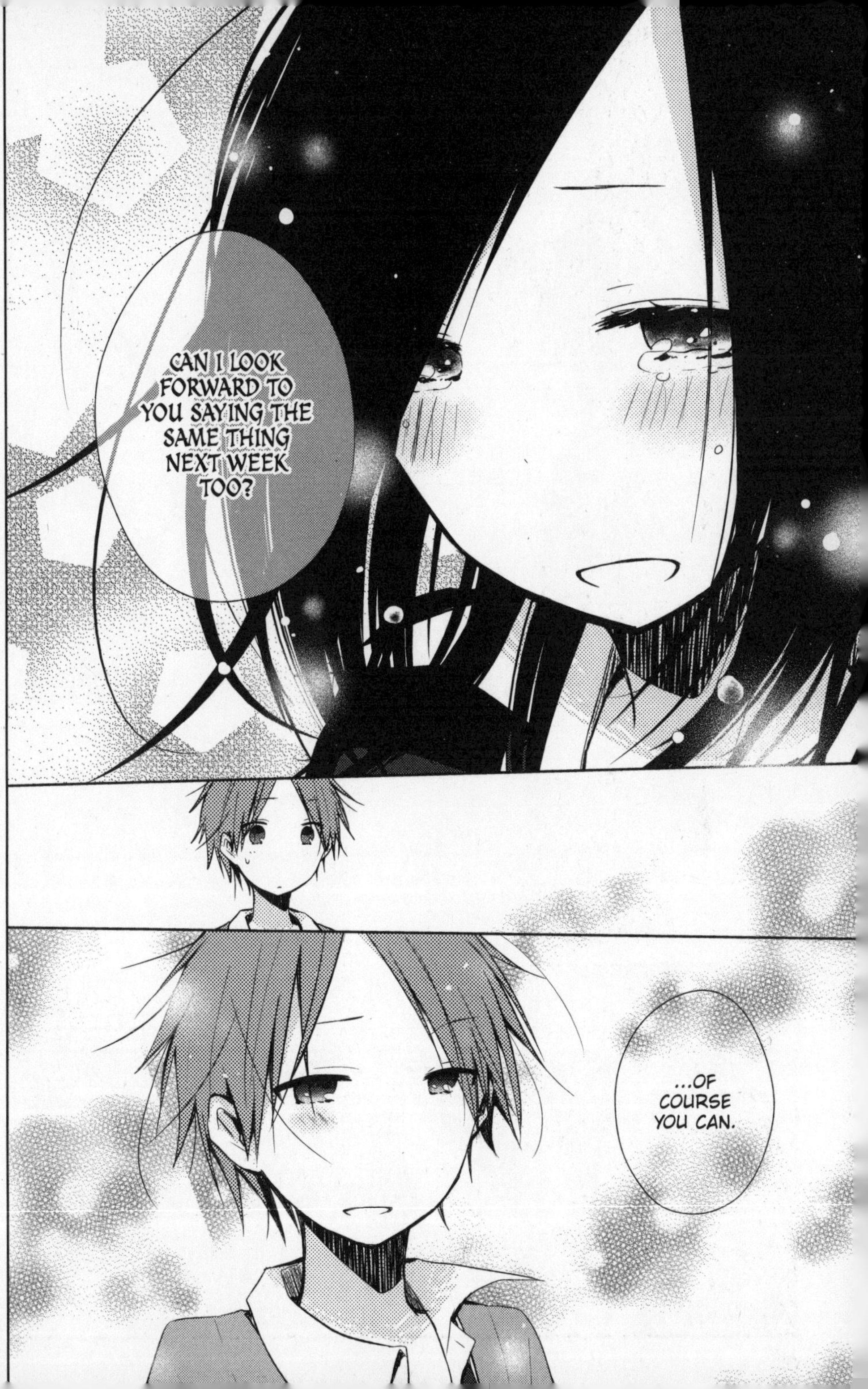
CAN I LOOK FORWARD TO YOU SAYING THE SAME THING NEXT WEEK TOO?
...OF COURSE YOU CAN.

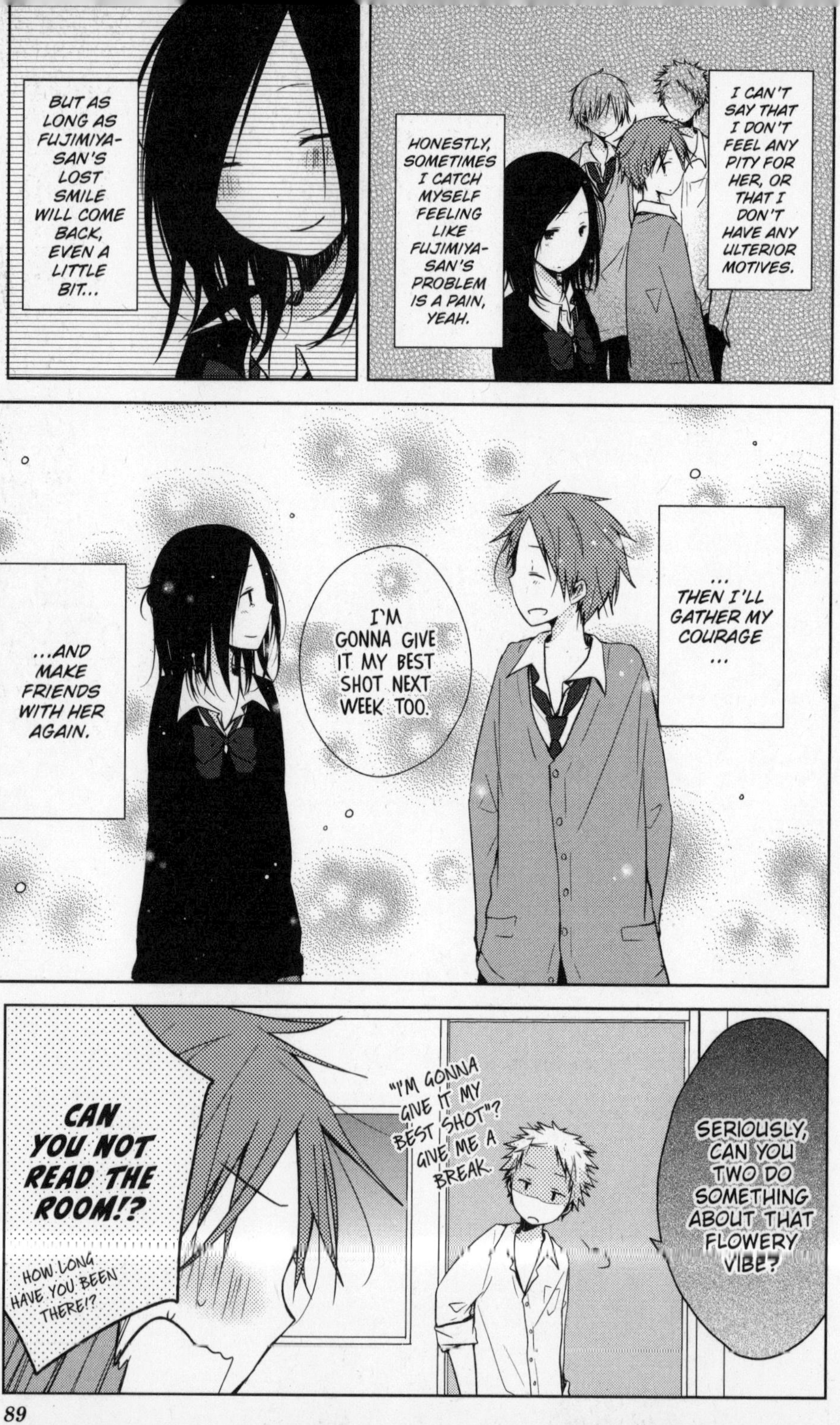
I CAN'T SAY THAT I DON'T FEEL ANY PITY FOR HER, OR THAT I DON'T HAVE ANY ULTERIOR MOTIVES.
HONESTLY, SOMETIMES I CATCH MYSELF FEELING LIKE FUJIMIYA-SAN'S PROBLEM IS A PAIN, YEAH.
BUT AS LONG AS FUJIMIYA-SAN'S LOST SMILE WILL COME BACK, EVEN A LITTLE BIT...
...THEN I'LL GATHER MY COURAGE...
I'M GONNA GIVE IT MY BEST SHOT NEXT WEEK TOO.
...AND MAKE FRIENDS WITH HER AGAIN.
SERIOUSLY, CAN YOU TWO DO SOMETHING ABOUT THAT FLOWERY VIBE?
"I'M GONNA GIVE IT MY BEST SHOT"? GIVE ME A BREAK.
CAN YOU NOT READ THE ROOM!?
HOW LONG HAVE YOU BEEN THERE!?

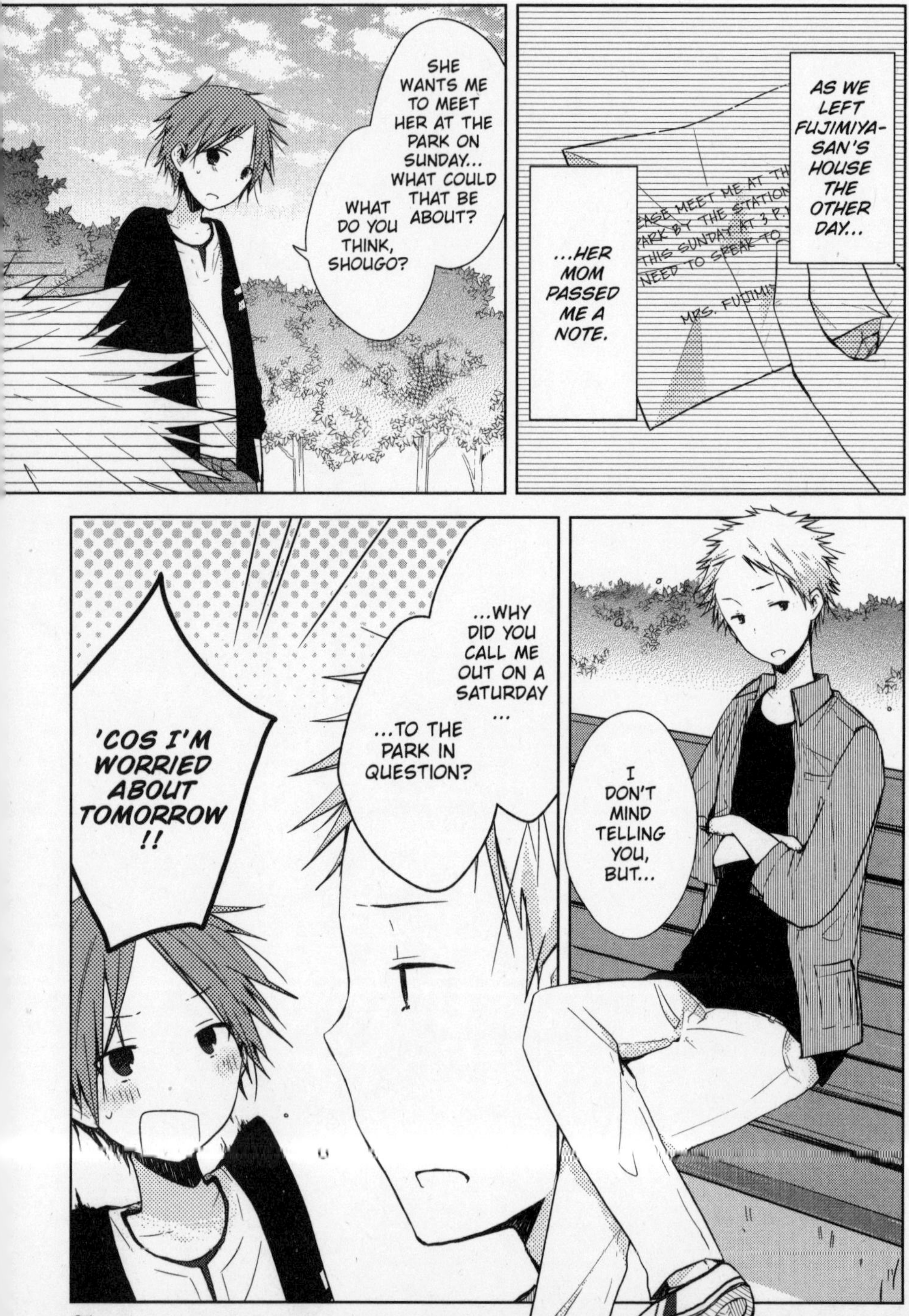
AS WE LEFT FUJIMIYA-SAN'S HOUSE THE OTHER DAY...
...HER MOM PASSED ME A NOTE.
SHE WANTS ME TO MEET HER AT THE PARK ON SUNDAY... WHAT COULD THAT BE ABOUT?
WHAT DO YOU THINK, SHOUGO?
I DON'T MIND TELLING YOU, BUT...
...WHY DID YOU CALL ME OUT ON A SATURDAY ...
...TO THE PARK IN QUESTION?
'COS I'M WORRIED ABOUT TOMORROW !!

CHAPTER 7
MOTHER OF A FRIEND

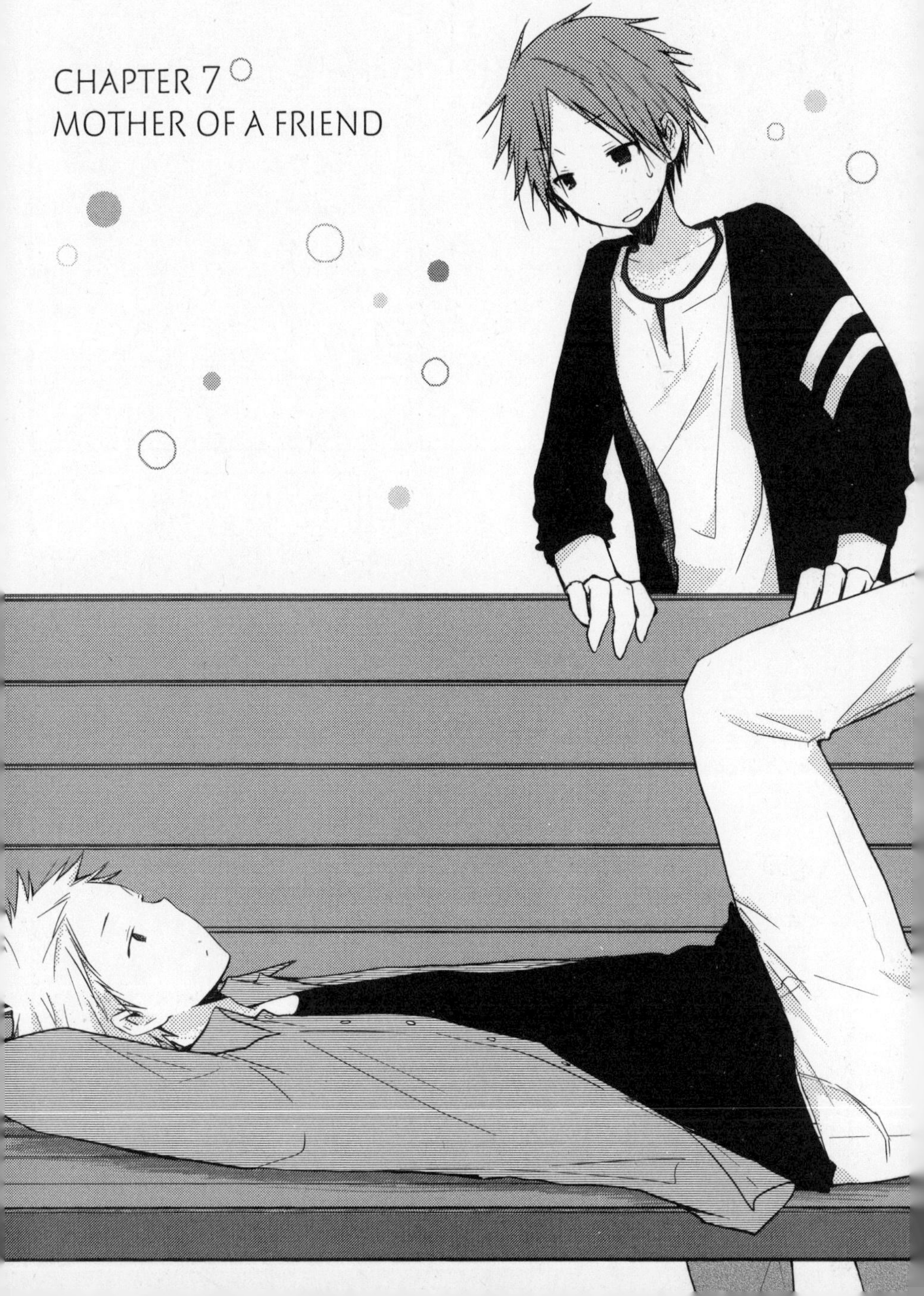

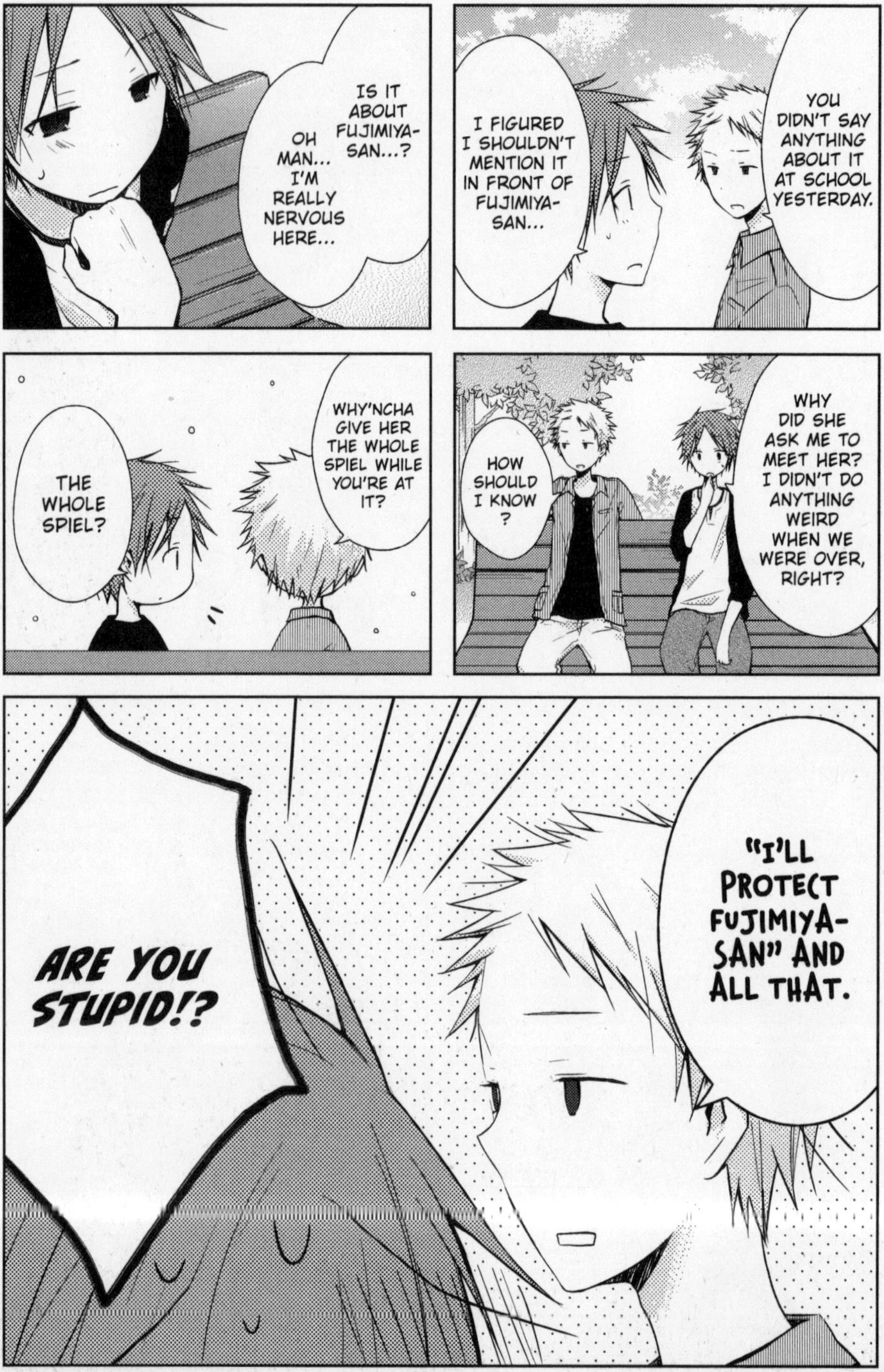
YOU DIDN'T SAY ANYTHING ABOUT IT AT SCHOOL YESTERDAY.
I FIGURED I SHOULDN'T MENTION IT IN FRONT OF FUJIMIYA-SAN...
IS IT ABOUT FUJIMIYA-SAN...?
OH MAN... I'M REALLY NERVOUS HERE...
WHY DID SHE ASK ME TO MEET HER? I DIDN'T DO ANYTHING WEIRD WHEN WE WERE OVER, RIGHT?
HOW SHOULD I KNOW?
WHY'NCHA GIVE HER THE WHOLE SPIEL WHILE YOU'RE AT IT?
THE WHOLE SPIEL?
"I'LL PROTECT FUJIMIYA-SAN" AND ALL THAT.
ARE YOU STUPID!?

NOW EVEN MORE SCARED

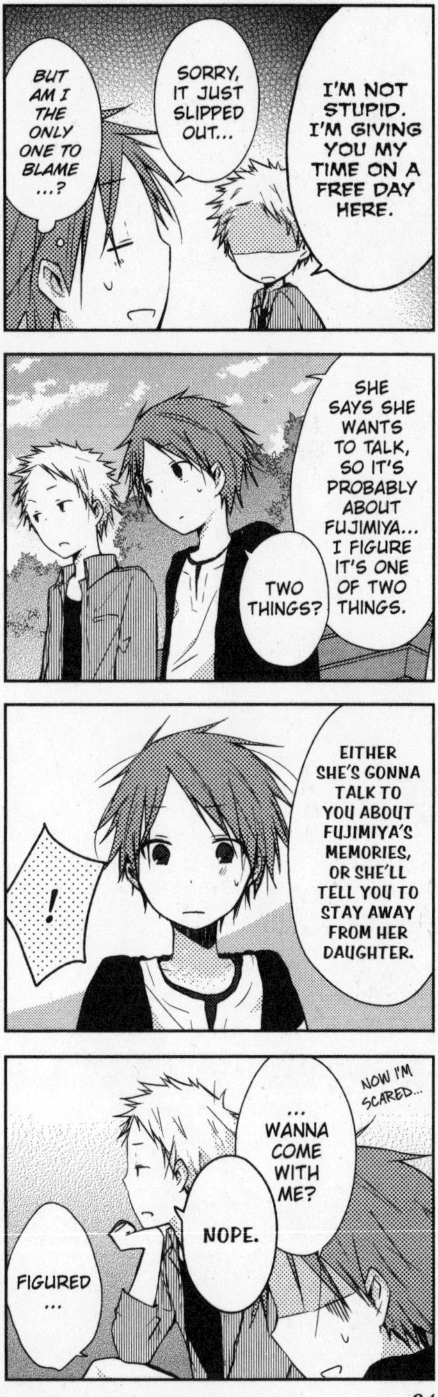
I'M NOT STUPID. I'M GIVING YOU MY TIME ON A FREE DAY HERE.
SORRY, IT JUST SLIPPED OUT...
BUT AM I THE ONLY ONE TO BLAME ...?
SHE SAYS SHE WANTS TO TALK, SO IT'S PROBABLY ABOUT FUJIMIYA... I FIGURE IT'S ONE OF TWO THINGS.
TWO THINGS?
EITHER SHE'S GONNA TALK TO YOU ABOUT FUJIMIYA'S MEMORIES, OR SHE'LL TELL YOU TO STAY AWAY FROM HER DAUGHTER.
!
NOW I'M SCARED...
... WANNA COME WITH ME?
NOPE.
FIGURED ...

HAND

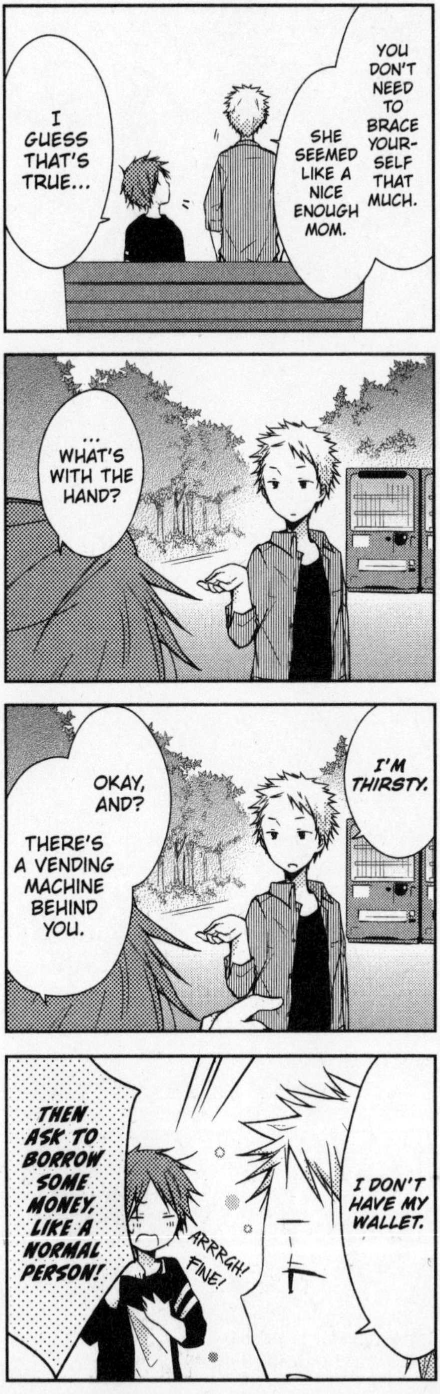
YOU DON'T NEED TO BRACE YOUR-SELF THAT MUCH.
SHE SEEMED LIKE A NICE ENOUGH MOM.
I GUESS THAT'S TRUE...
... WHAT'S WITH THE HAND?
I'M THIRSTY.
OKAY, AND?
THERE'S A VENDING MACHINE BEHIND YOU.
I DON'T HAVE MY WALLET.
THEN ASK TO BORROW SOME MONEY, LIKE A NORMAL PERSON!
ARRRGH! FINE!

THE REASON I CALLED YOU

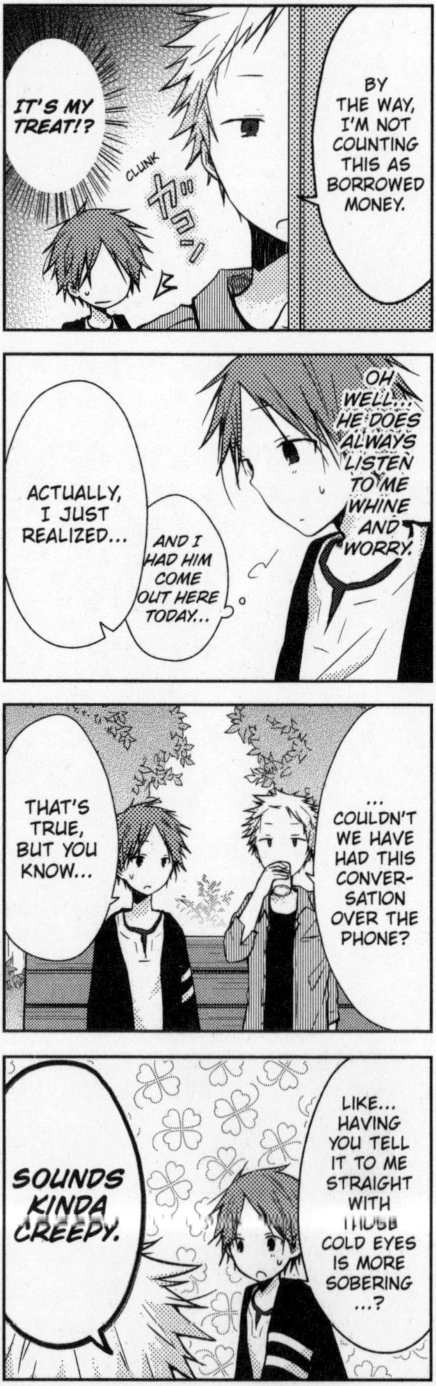
BY THE WAY, I'M NOT COUNTING THIS AS BORROWED MONEY.
IT'S MY TREAT!?
CLUNK
OH WELL... HE DOES ALWAYS LISTEN TO ME WHINE AND WORRY.
ACTUALLY, I JUST REALIZED...
AND I HAD HIM COME OUT HERE TODAY...
...COULDN'T WE HAVE HAD THIS CONVER-SATION OVER THE PHONE?
THAT'S TRUE, BUT YOU KNOW...
LIKE... HAVING YOU TELL IT TO ME STRAIGHT WITH THOSE COLD EYES IS MORE SOBERING ...?
SOUNDS KINDA CREEPY.

A LITTLE SYMPATHY

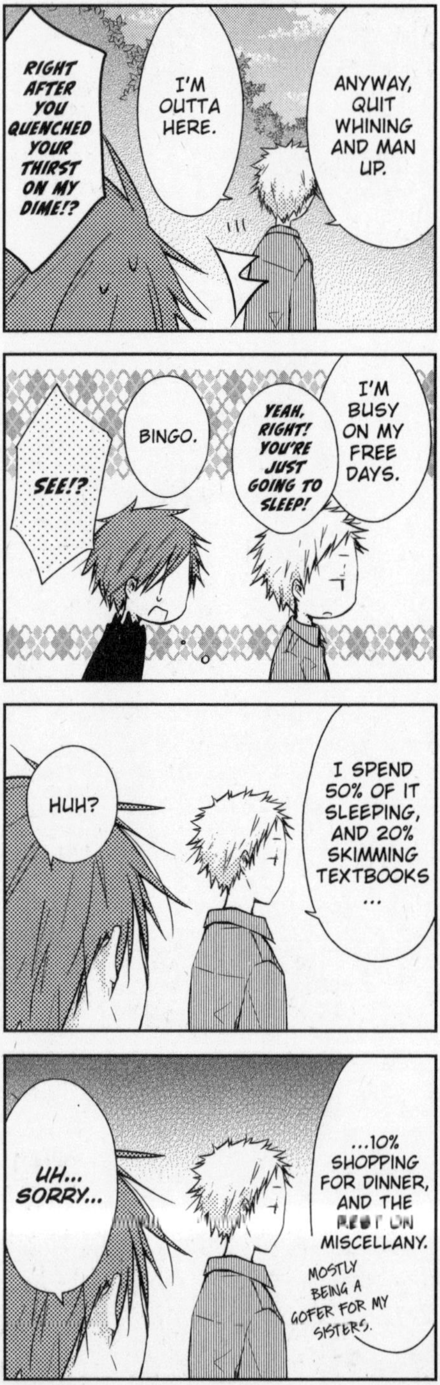
ANYWAY, QUIT WHINING AND MAN UP.
I'M OUTTA HERE.
RIGHT AFTER YOU QUENCHED YOUR THIRST ON MY DIME!?
I'M BUSY ON MY FREE DAYS.
YEAH, RIGHT! YOU'RE JUST GOING TO SLEEP!
BINGO.
SEE!?
I SPEND 50% OF IT SLEEPING, AND 20% SKIMMING TEXTBOOKS ...
HUH?
...10% SHOPPING FOR DINNER, AND THE REST ON MISCELLANY.
MOSTLY BEING A GOFER FOR MY SISTERS.
UH... SORRY...

MEETING

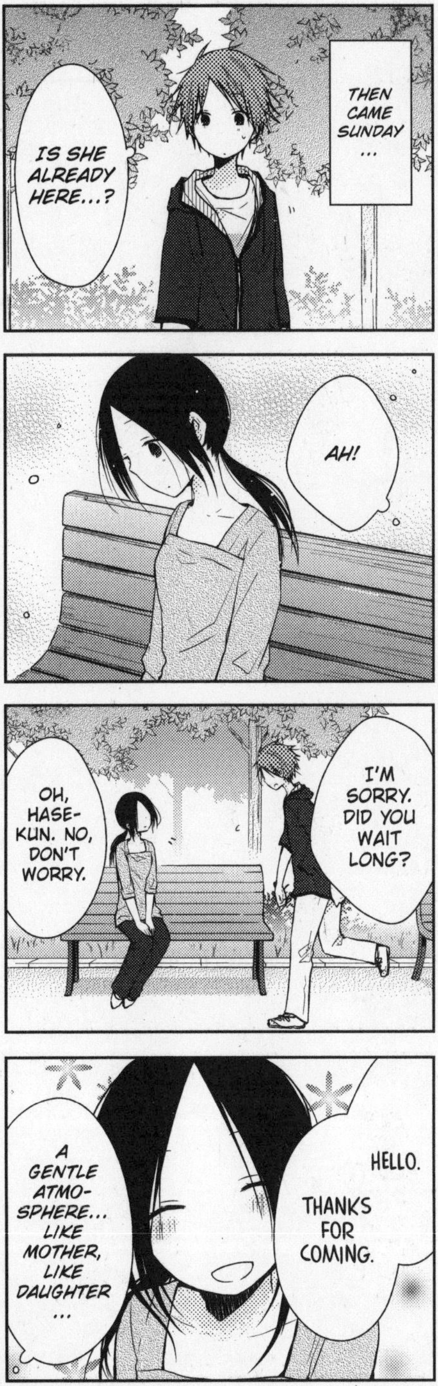
THEN CAME SUNDAY ...
IS SHE ALREADY HERE...?
AH!
I'M SORRY. DID YOU WAIT LONG?
OH, HASE-KUN. NO, DON'T WORRY.
HELLO.
THANKS FOR COMING.
A GENTLE ATMOSPHERE... LIKE MOTHER, LIKE DAUGHTER ...

UNEXPECTED REMARK

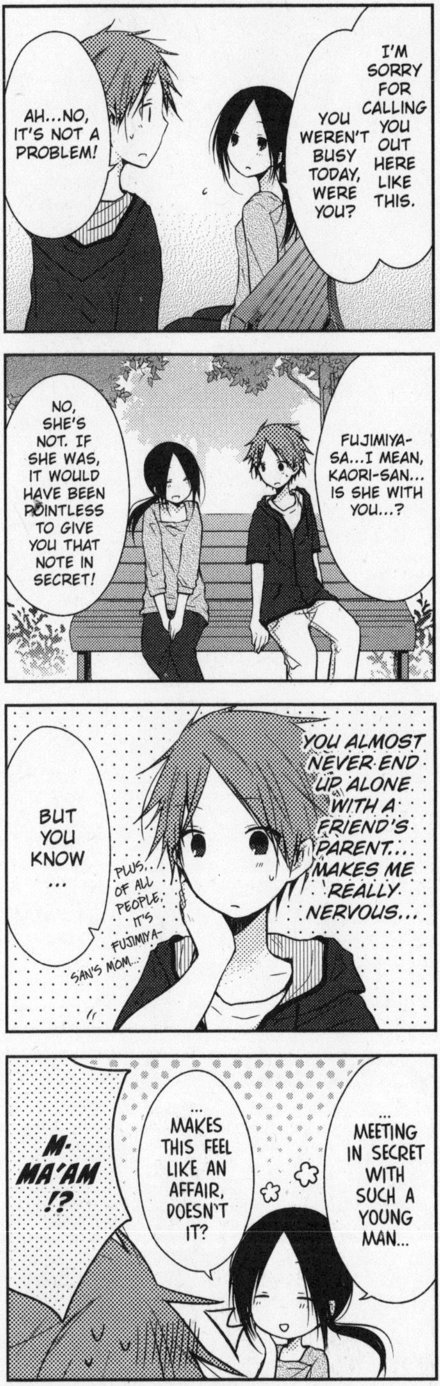
I'M SORRY FOR CALLING YOU OUT HERE LIKE THIS.
YOU WEREN'T BUSY TODAY, WERE YOU?
AH...NO, IT'S NOT A PROBLEM!
FUJIMIYA-SA...I MEAN, KAORI-SAN... IS SHE WITH YOU...?
NO, SHE'S NOT. IF SHE WAS, IT WOULD HAVE BEEN POINTLESS TO GIVE YOU THAT NOTE IN SECRET!
YOU ALMOST NEVER END UP ALONE WITH A FRIEND'S PARENT... MAKES ME REALLY NERVOUS...
PLUS, OF ALL PEOPLE, IT'S FUJIMIYA-SAN'S MOM...
BUT YOU KNOW ...
... MEETING IN SECRET WITH SUCH A YOUNG MAN...
... MAKES THIS FEEL LIKE AN AFFAIR, DOESN'T IT?
M-MA'AM !?

PRETTY SHARP

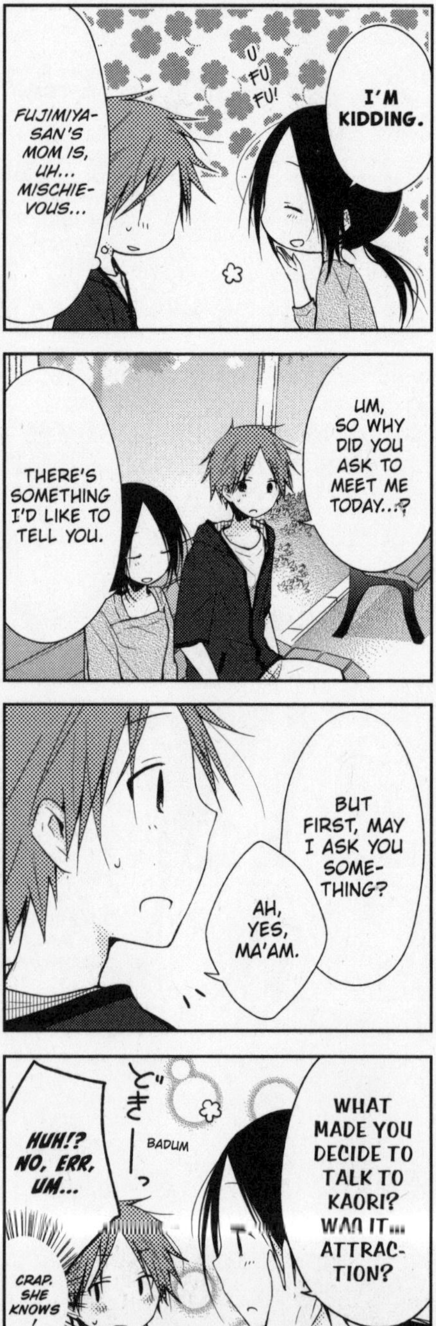
I'M KIDDING.
U FU FU!
FUJIMIYA-SAN'S MOM IS, UH... MISCHIEVOUS...
UM, SO WHY DID YOU ASK TO MEET ME TODAY...?
THERE'S SOMETHING I'D LIKE TO TELL YOU.
BUT FIRST, MAY I ASK YOU SOMETHING?
AH, YES, MA'AM.
WHAT MADE YOU DECIDE TO TALK TO KAORI? WAS IT... ATTRACTION?
どきーっ
BADUM
HUH!? NO, ERR, UM...
CRAP. SHE KNOWS!

PRETTY PERSISTENT

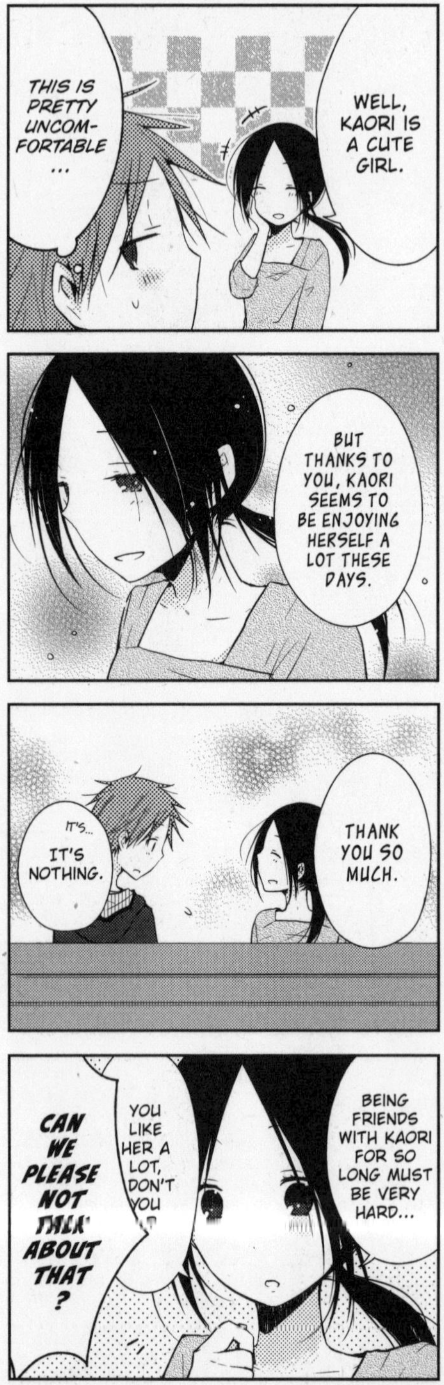
WELL, KAORI IS A CUTE GIRL.
THIS IS PRETTY UNCOMFORTABLE...
BUT THANKS TO YOU, KAORI SEEMS TO BE ENJOYING HERSELF A LOT THESE DAYS.
THANK YOU SO MUCH.
IT'S... IT'S NOTHING.
BEING FRIENDS WITH KAORI FOR SO LONG MUST BE VERY HARD...
YOU LIKE HER A LOT, DON'T YOU
CAN WE PLEASE NOT TALK ABOUT THAT?

ON THE DEFENSIVE

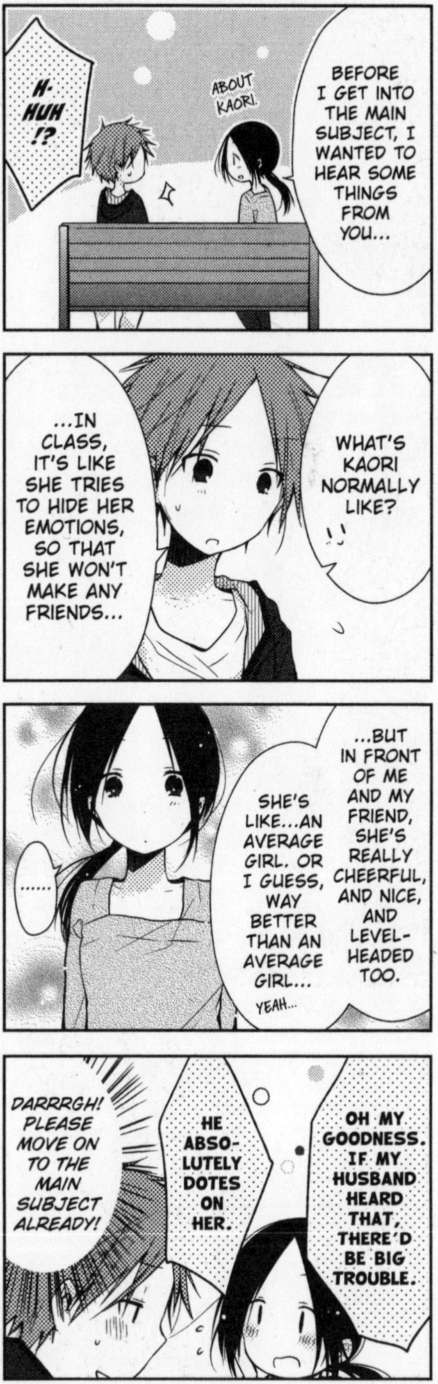
BEFORE I GET INTO THE MAIN SUBJECT, I WANTED TO HEAR SOME THINGS FROM YOU...
ABOUT KAORI.
H-HUH!?
WHAT'S KAORI NORMALLY LIKE?
...IN CLASS, IT'S LIKE SHE TRIES TO HIDE HER EMOTIONS, SO THAT SHE WON'T MAKE ANY FRIENDS...
...BUT IN FRONT OF ME AND MY FRIEND, SHE'S REALLY CHEERFUL, AND NICE, AND LEVEL-HEADED TOO.
SHE'S LIKE...AN AVERAGE GIRL. OR I GUESS, WAY BETTER THAN AN AVERAGE GIRL...
YEAH...
......
OH MY GOODNESS. IF MY HUSBAND HEARD THAT, THERE'D BE BIG TROUBLE.
HE ABSOLUTELY DOTES ON HER.
DARRRGH! PLEASE MOVE ON TO THE MAIN SUBJECT ALREADY!

FINALLY, THE MAIN SUBJECT

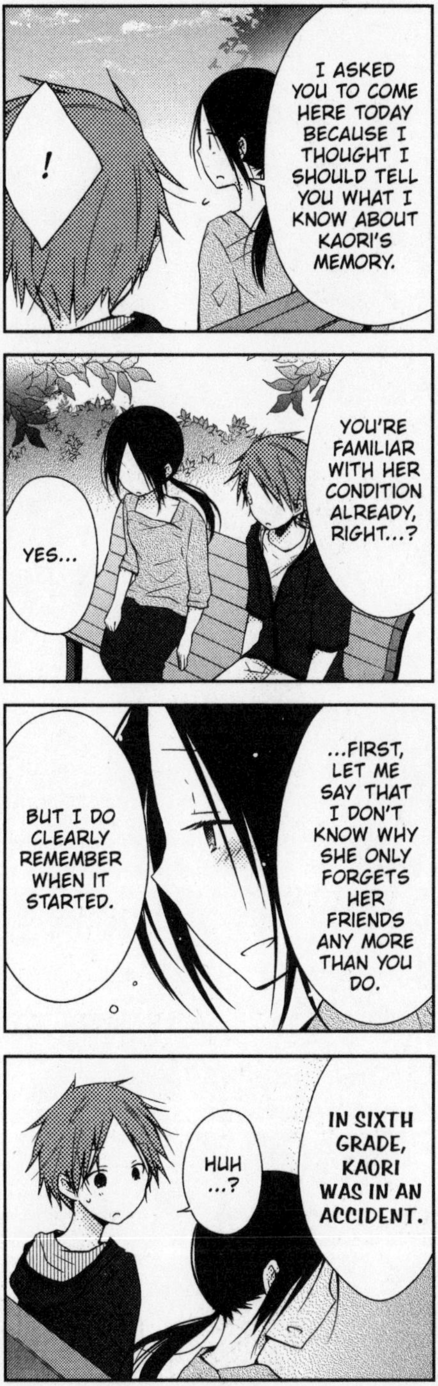
I ASKED YOU TO COME HERE TODAY BECAUSE I THOUGHT I SHOULD TELL YOU WHAT I KNOW ABOUT KAORI'S MEMORY.
!
YOU'RE FAMILIAR WITH HER CONDITION ALREADY, RIGHT...?
YES...
...FIRST, LET ME SAY THAT I DON'T KNOW WHY SHE ONLY FORGETS HER FRIENDS ANY MORE THAN YOU DO.
BUT I DO CLEARLY REMEMBER WHEN IT STARTED.
IN SIXTH GRADE, KAORI WAS IN AN ACCIDENT.
HUH...?

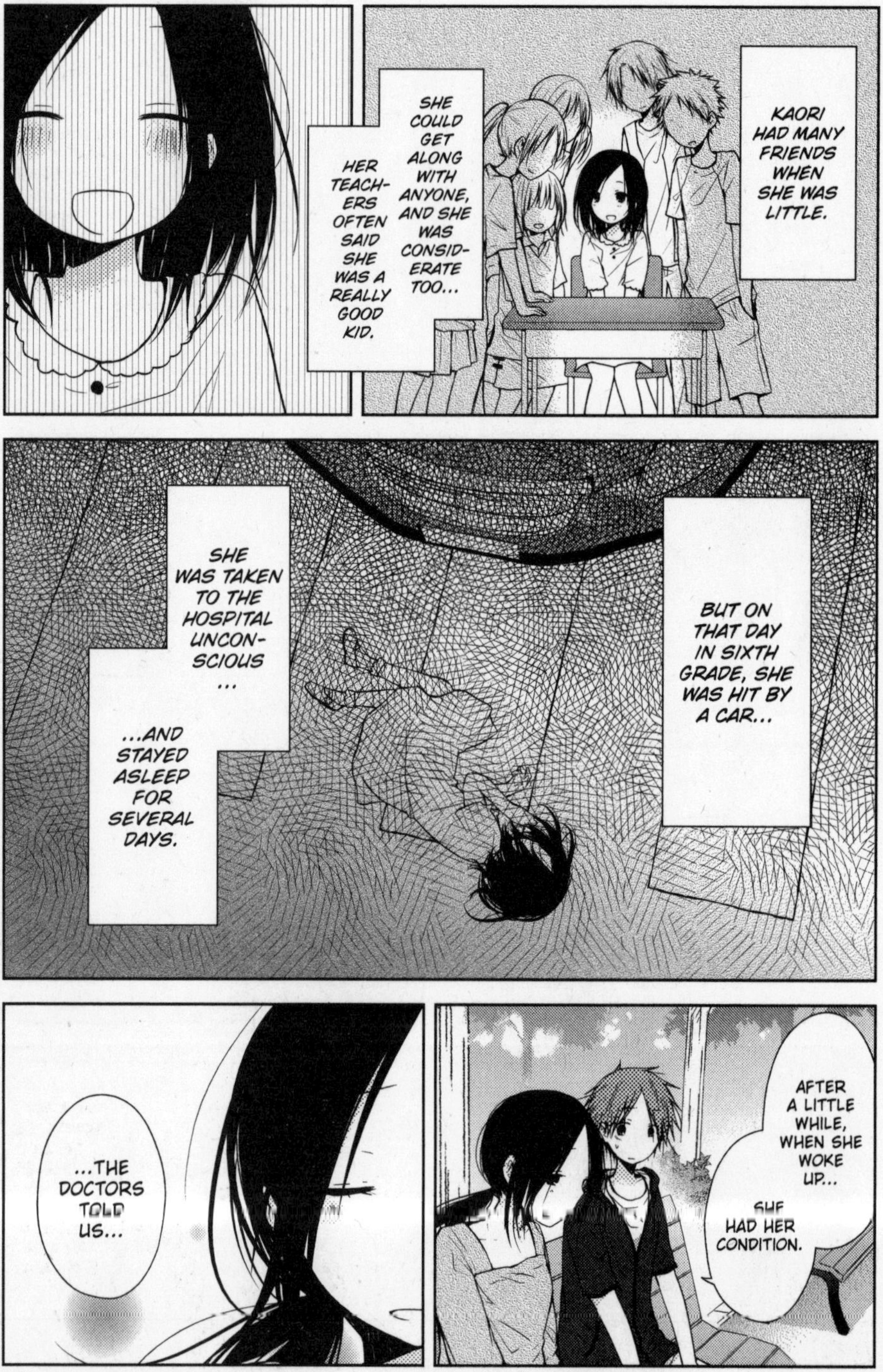
KAORI HAD MANY FRIENDS WHEN SHE WAS LITTLE.
SHE COULD GET ALONG WITH ANYONE, AND SHE WAS CONSID-ERATE TOO...
HER TEACH-ERS OFTEN SAID SHE WAS A REALLY GOOD KID.
BUT ON THAT DAY IN SIXTH GRADE, SHE WAS HIT BY A CAR...
SHE WAS TAKEN TO THE HOSPITAL UNCON-SCIOUS...
...AND STAYED ASLEEP FOR SEVERAL DAYS.
AFTER A LITTLE WHILE, WHEN SHE WOKE UP...
SHE HAD HER CONDITION.
...THE DOCTORS TOLD US...

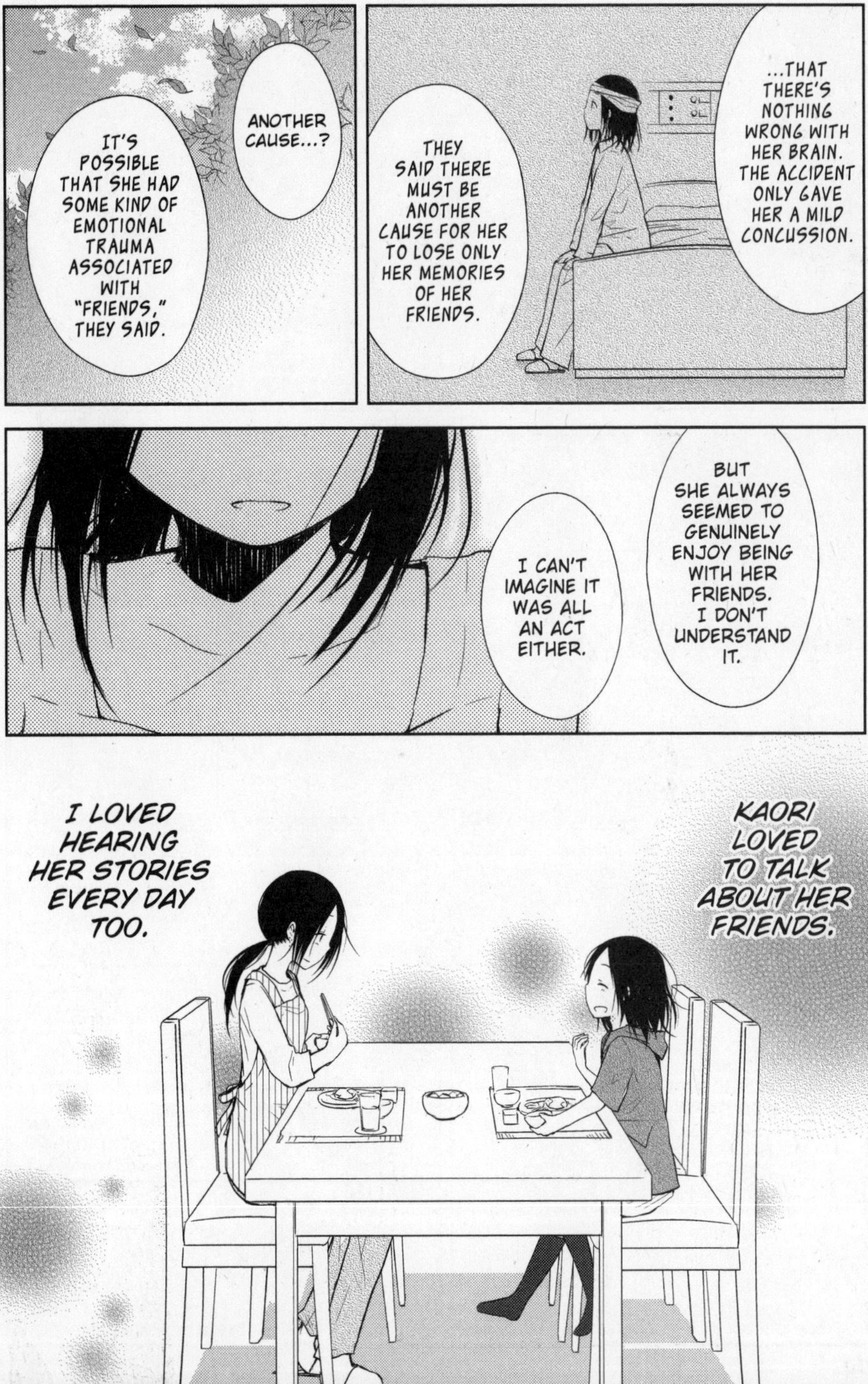
...THAT THERE'S NOTHING WRONG WITH HER BRAIN. THE ACCIDENT ONLY GAVE HER A MILD CONCUSSION.
THEY SAID THERE MUST BE ANOTHER CAUSE FOR HER TO LOSE ONLY HER MEMORIES OF HER FRIENDS.
ANOTHER CAUSE...?
IT'S POSSIBLE THAT SHE HAD SOME KIND OF EMOTIONAL TRAUMA ASSOCIATED WITH "FRIENDS," THEY SAID.
BUT SHE ALWAYS SEEMED TO GENUINELY ENJOY BEING WITH HER FRIENDS. I DON'T UNDERSTAND IT.
I CAN'T IMAGINE IT WAS ALL AN ACT EITHER.
KAORI LOVED TO TALK ABOUT HER FRIENDS.
I LOVED HEARING HER STORIES EVERY DAY TOO.

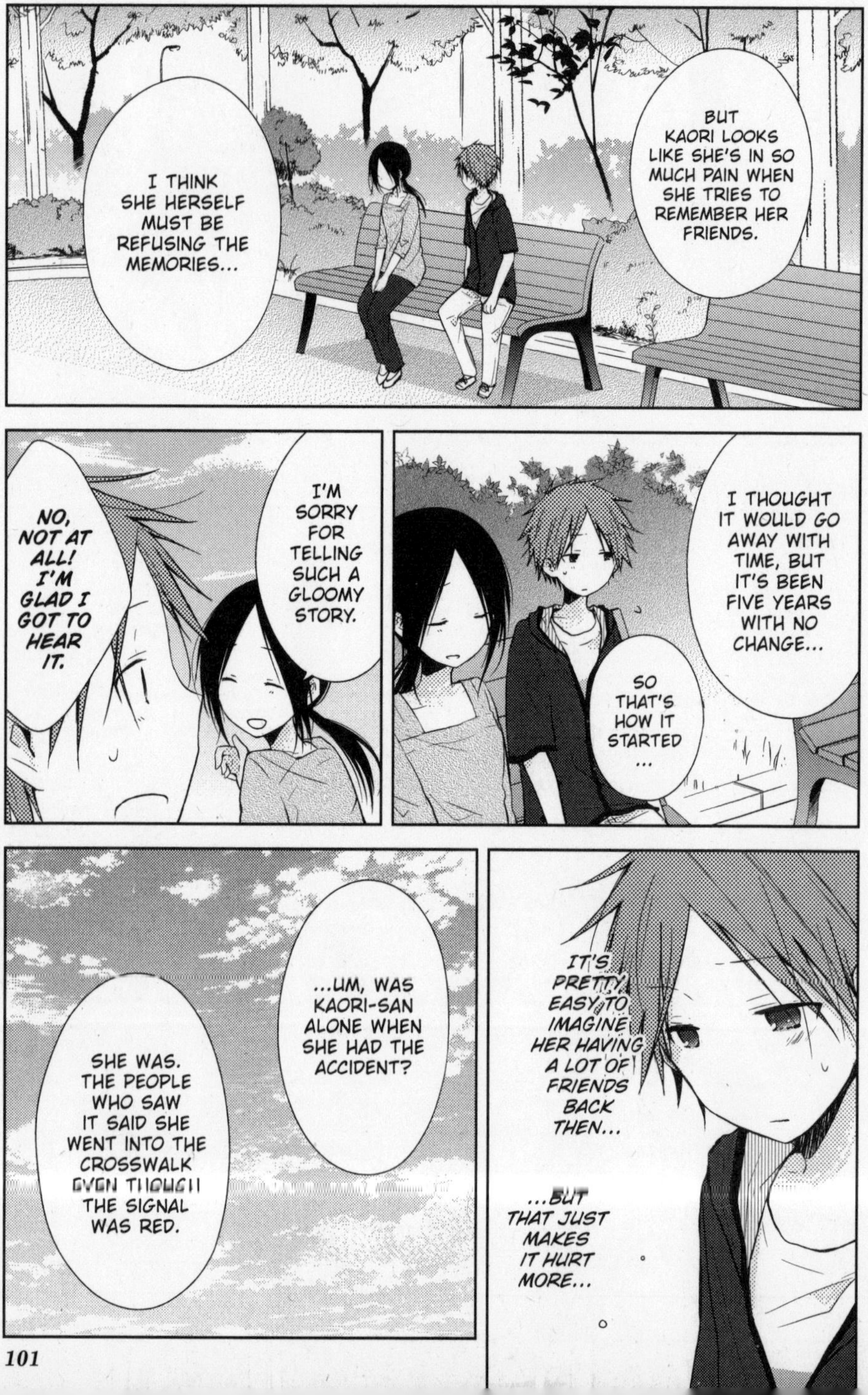
BUT KAORI LOOKS LIKE SHE'S IN SO MUCH PAIN WHEN SHE TRIES TO REMEMBER HER FRIENDS.
I THINK SHE HERSELF MUST BE REFUSING THE MEMORIES...
I THOUGHT IT WOULD GO AWAY WITH TIME, BUT IT'S BEEN FIVE YEARS WITH NO CHANGE...
SO THAT'S HOW IT STARTED...
I'M SORRY FOR TELLING SUCH A GLOOMY STORY.
NO, NOT AT ALL! I'M GLAD I GOT TO HEAR IT.
IT'S PRETTY EASY TO IMAGINE HER HAVING A LOT OF FRIENDS BACK THEN...
...BUT THAT JUST MAKES IT HURT MORE...
...UM, WAS KAORI-SAN ALONE WHEN SHE HAD THE ACCIDENT?
SHE WAS. THE PEOPLE WHO SAW IT SAID SHE WENT INTO THE CROSSWALK EVEN THOUGH THE SIGNAL WAS RED.

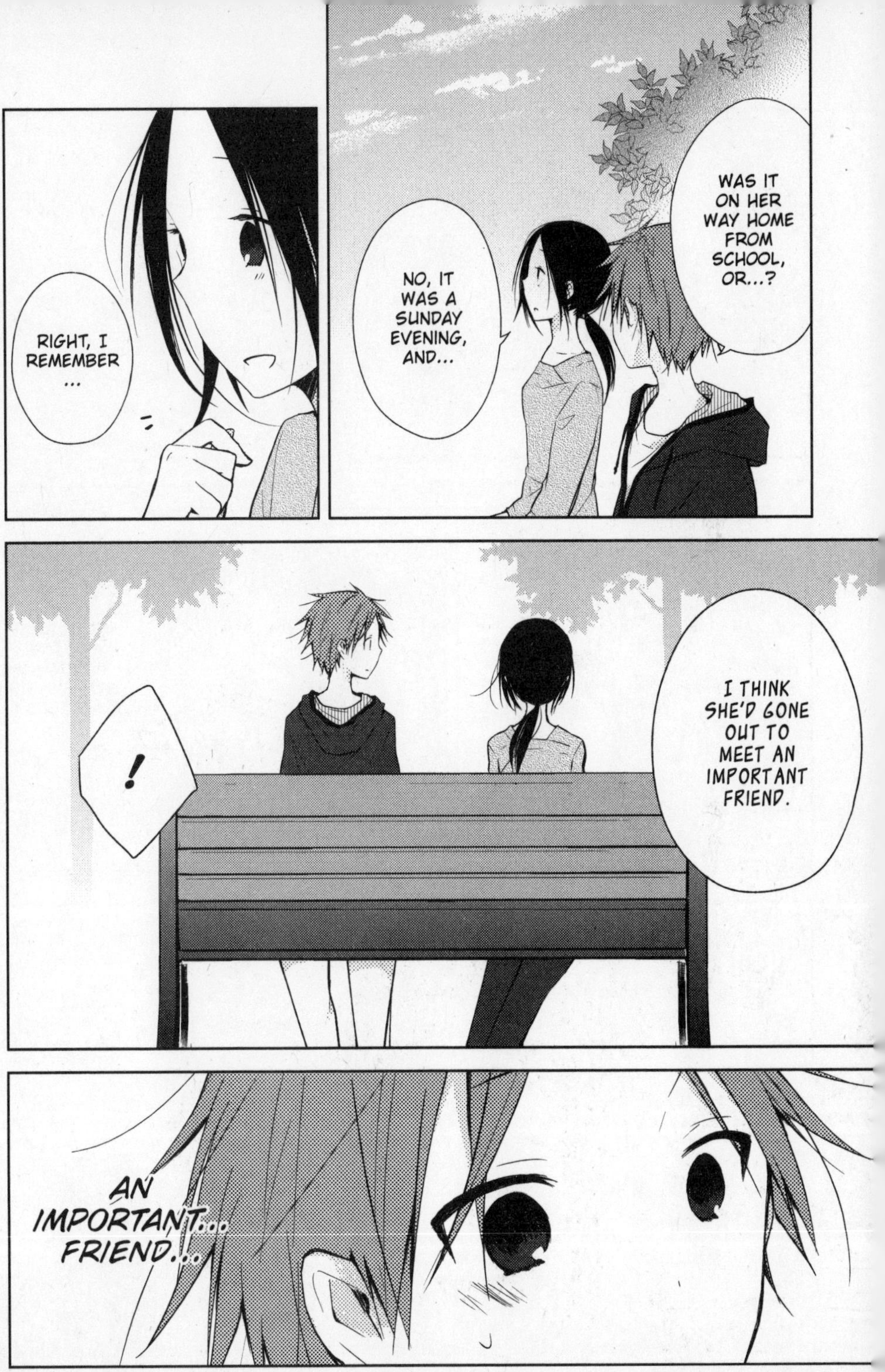
WAS IT ON HER WAY HOME FROM SCHOOL, OR...?
NO, IT WAS A SUNDAY EVENING, AND...
RIGHT, I REMEMBER ...
I THINK SHE'D GONE OUT TO MEET AN IMPORTANT FRIEND.
!
AN IMPORTANT... FRIEND...

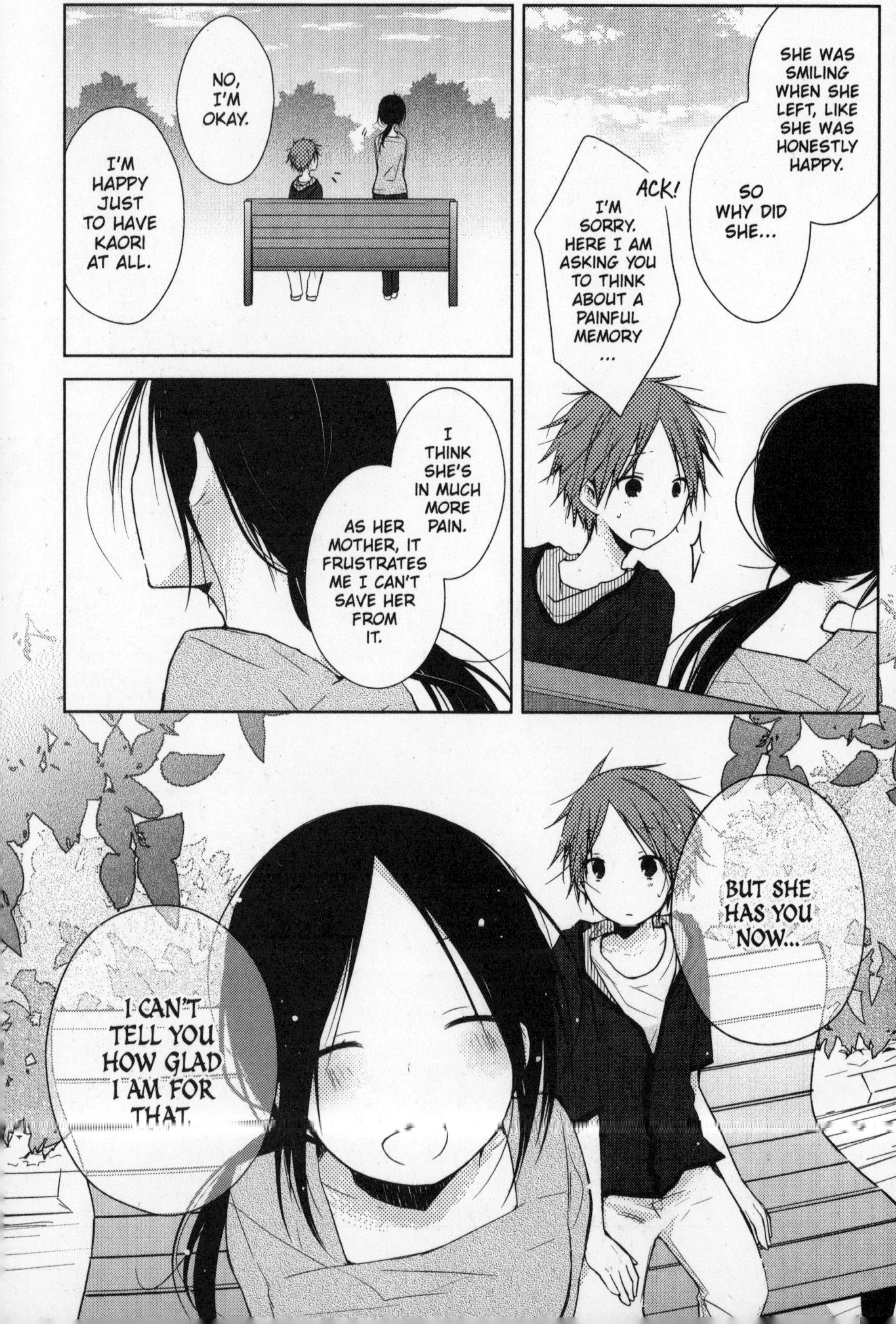
SHE WAS SMILING WHEN SHE LEFT, LIKE SHE WAS HONESTLY HAPPY.
SO WHY DID SHE...
ACK!
I'M SORRY. HERE I AM ASKING YOU TO THINK ABOUT A PAINFUL MEMORY ...
NO, I'M OKAY.
I'M HAPPY JUST TO HAVE KAORI AT ALL.
I THINK SHE'S IN MUCH MORE PAIN.
AS HER MOTHER, IT FRUSTRATES ME I CAN'T SAVE HER FROM IT.
BUT SHE HAS YOU NOW...
I CAN'T TELL YOU HOW GLAD I AM FOR THAT.

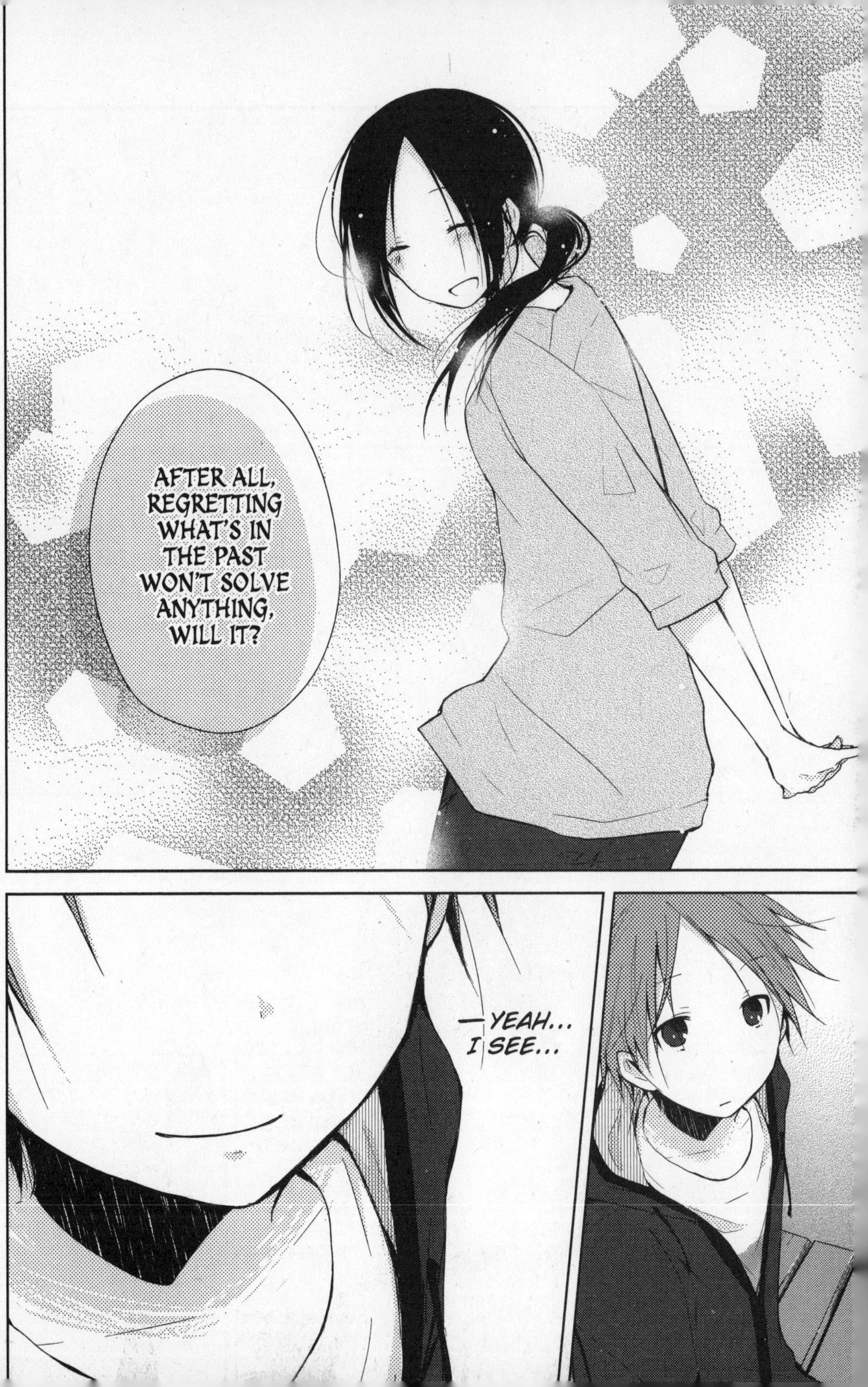
AFTER ALL, REGRETTING WHAT'S IN THE PAST WON'T SOLVE ANYTHING, WILL IT?
—YEAH... I SEE...

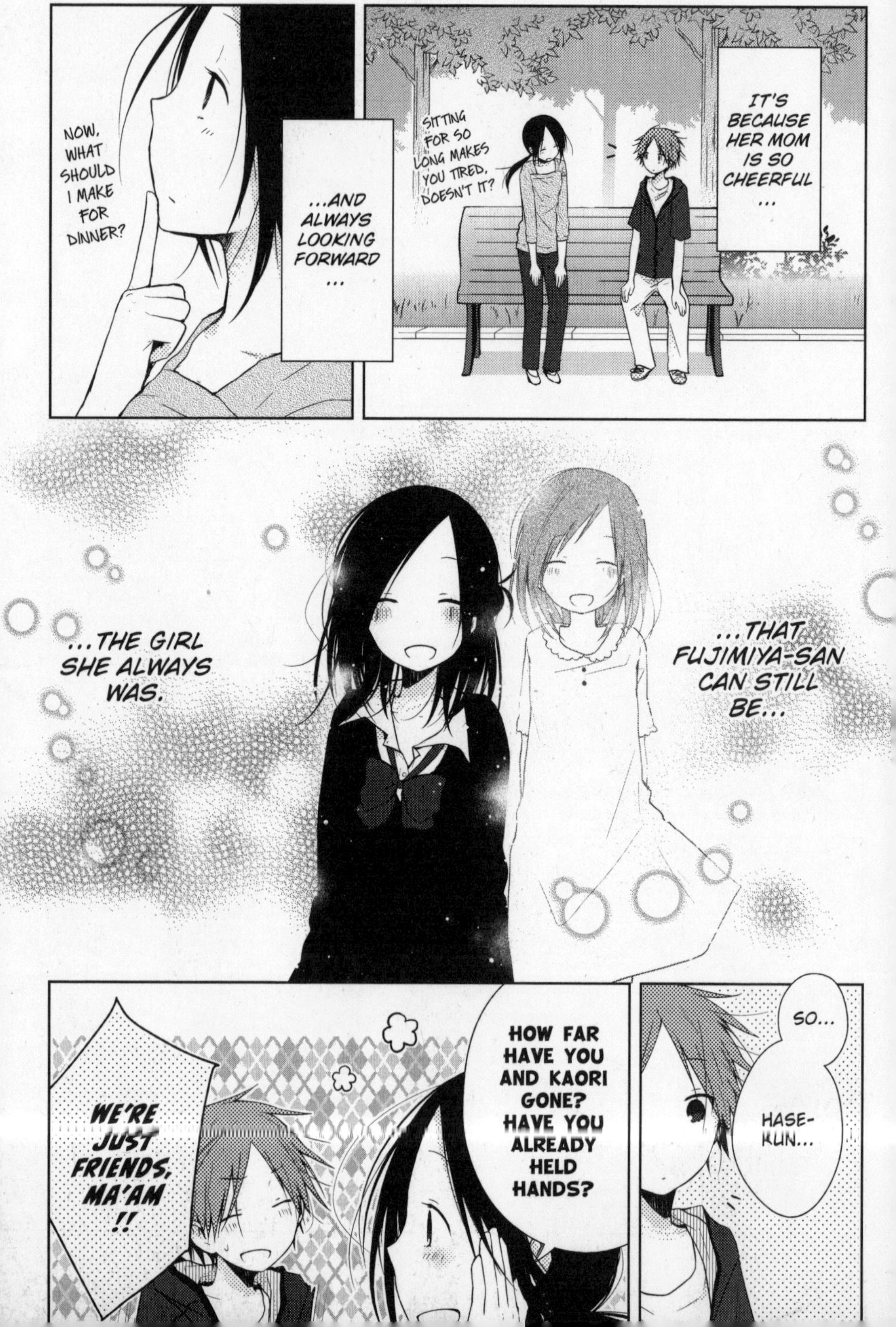
IT'S BECAUSE HER MOM IS SO CHEERFUL...
SITTING FOR SO LONG MAKES YOU TIRED, DOESN'T IT?
...AND ALWAYS LOOKING FORWARD...
NOW, WHAT SHOULD I MAKE FOR DINNER?
...THAT FUJIMIYA-SAN CAN STILL BE...
...THE GIRL SHE ALWAYS WAS.
SO... HASE-KUN...
HOW FAR HAVE YOU AND KAORI GONE? HAVE YOU ALREADY HELD HANDS?
WE'RE JUST FRIENDS, MA'AM!!

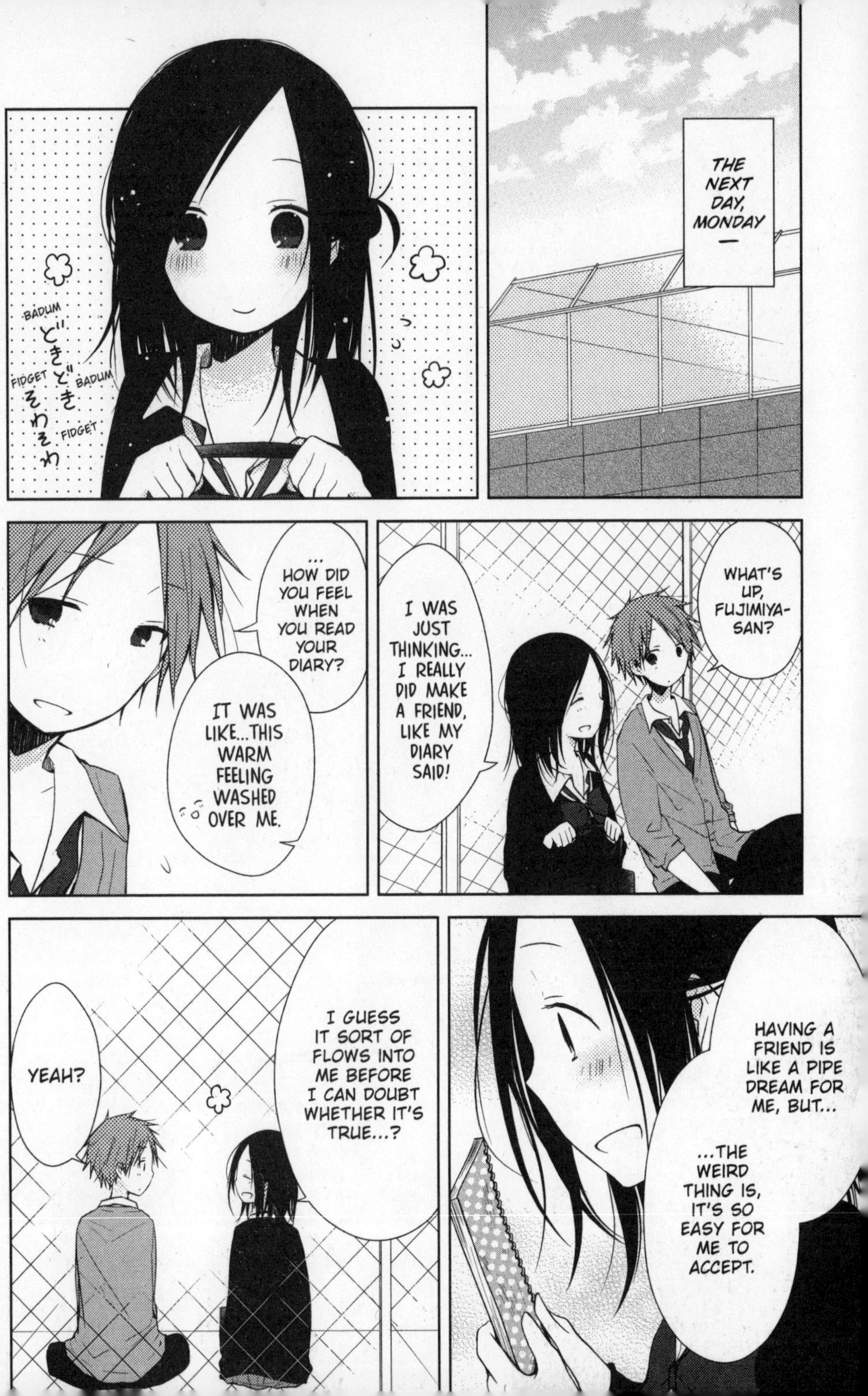
THE NEXT DAY, MONDAY —
BADUM どきどき BADUM
FIDGET そわそわ FIDGET
WHAT'S UP, FUJIMIYA-SAN?
I WAS JUST THINKING... I REALLY DID MAKE A FRIEND, LIKE MY DIARY SAID!
... HOW DID YOU FEEL WHEN YOU READ YOUR DIARY?
IT WAS LIKE...THIS WARM FEELING WASHED OVER ME.
HAVING A FRIEND IS LIKE A PIPE DREAM FOR ME, BUT...
...THE WEIRD THING IS, IT'S SO EASY FOR ME TO ACCEPT.
I GUESS IT SORT OF FLOWS INTO ME BEFORE I CAN DOUBT WHETHER IT'S TRUE...?
YEAH?

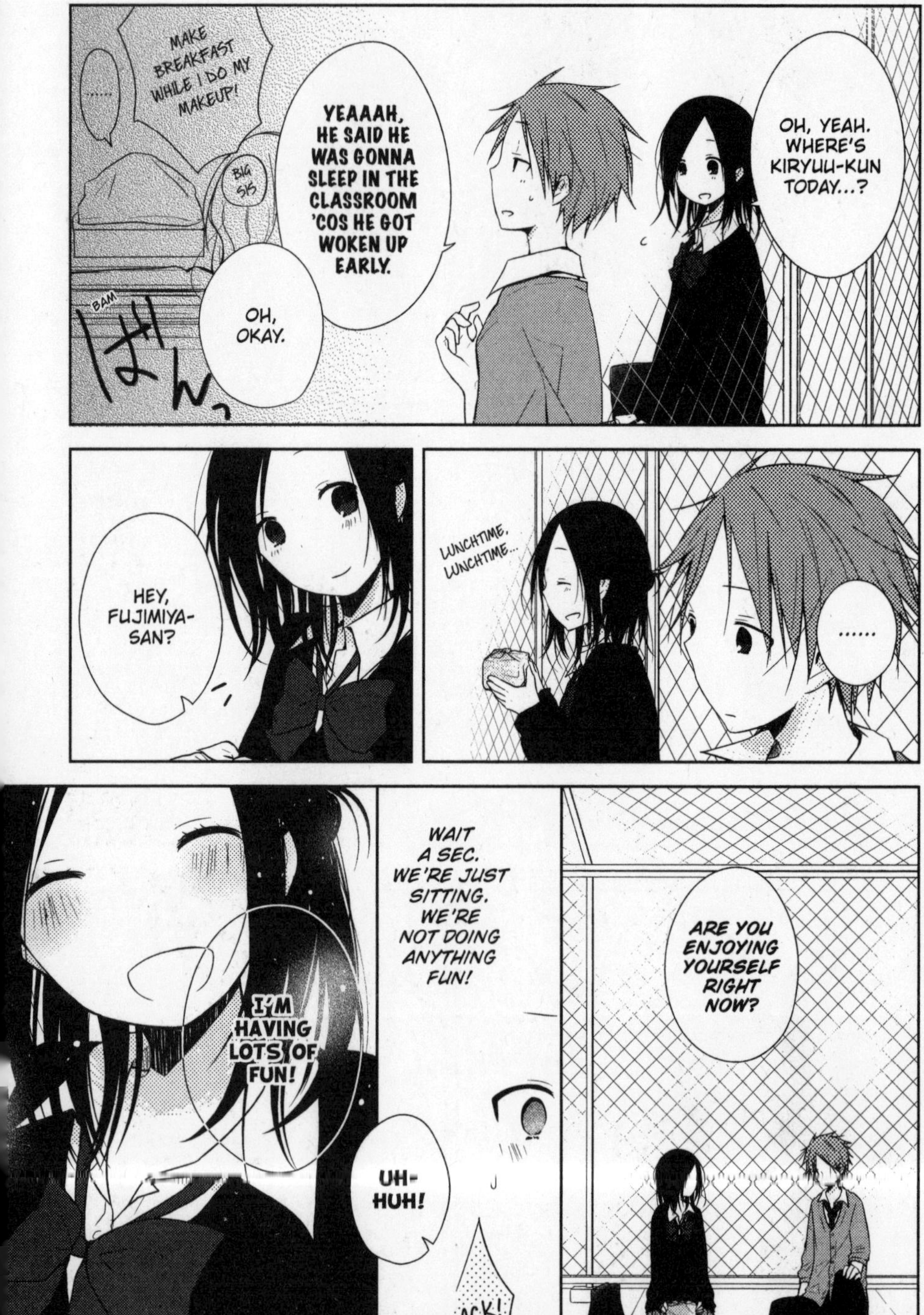
OH, YEAH. WHERE'S KIRYUU-KUN TODAY...?
YEAAAH, HE SAID HE WAS GONNA SLEEP IN THE CLASSROOM 'COS HE GOT WOKEN UP EARLY.
MAKE BREAKFAST WHILE I DO MY MAKEUP!
......
BIG SIS
BAM
OH, OKAY.
LUNCHTIME, LUNCHTIME...
......
HEY, FUJIMIYA-SAN?
ARE YOU ENJOYING YOURSELF RIGHT NOW?
UH-HUH!
WAIT A SEC. WE'RE JUST SITTING. WE'RE NOT DOING ANYTHING FUN!
ACK!
I'M HAVING LOTS OF FUN!

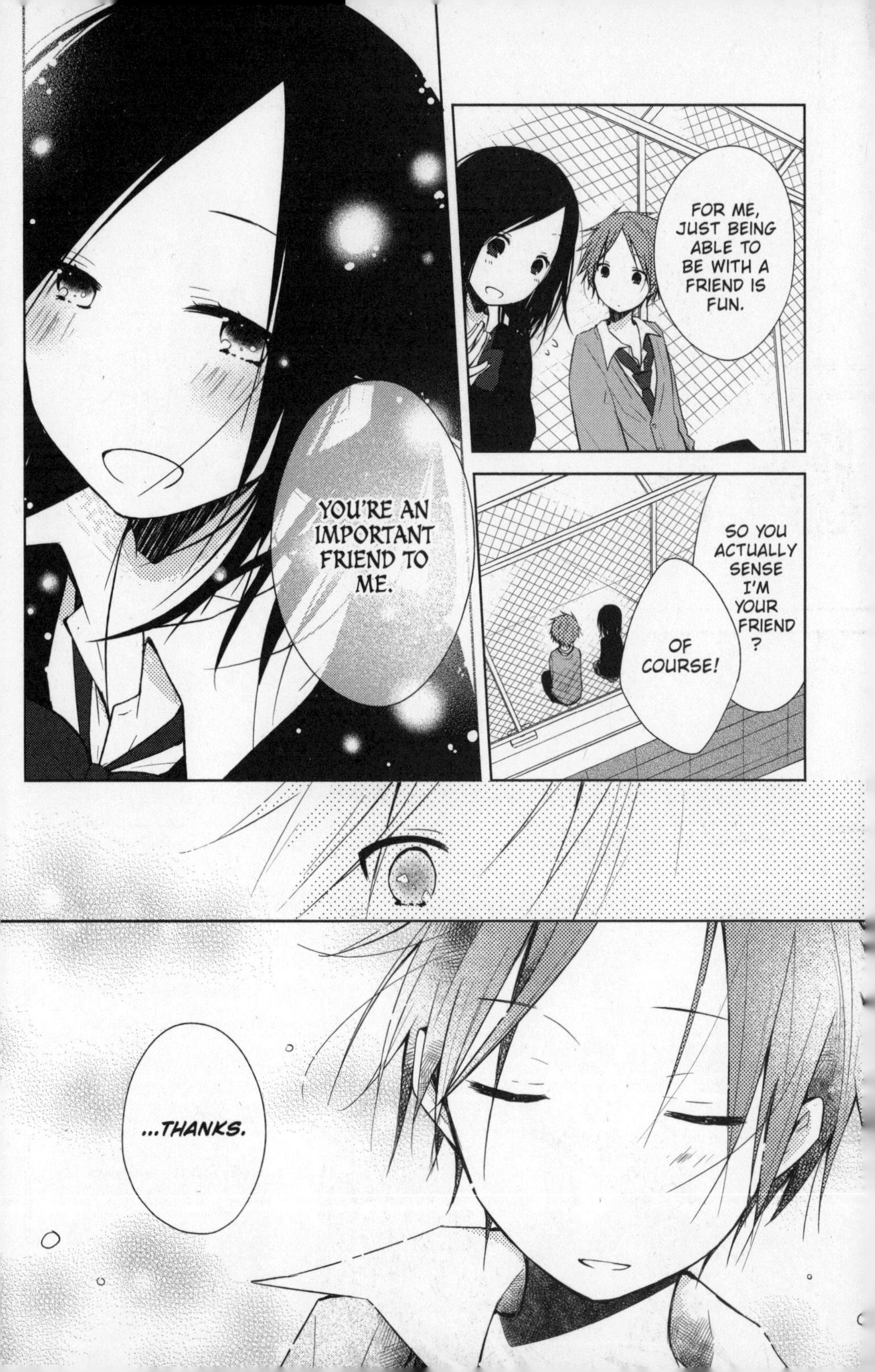
FOR ME, JUST BEING ABLE TO BE WITH A FRIEND IS FUN.
SO YOU ACTUALLY SENSE I'M YOUR FRIEND?
OF COURSE!
YOU'RE AN IMPORTANT FRIEND TO ME.
...THANKS.

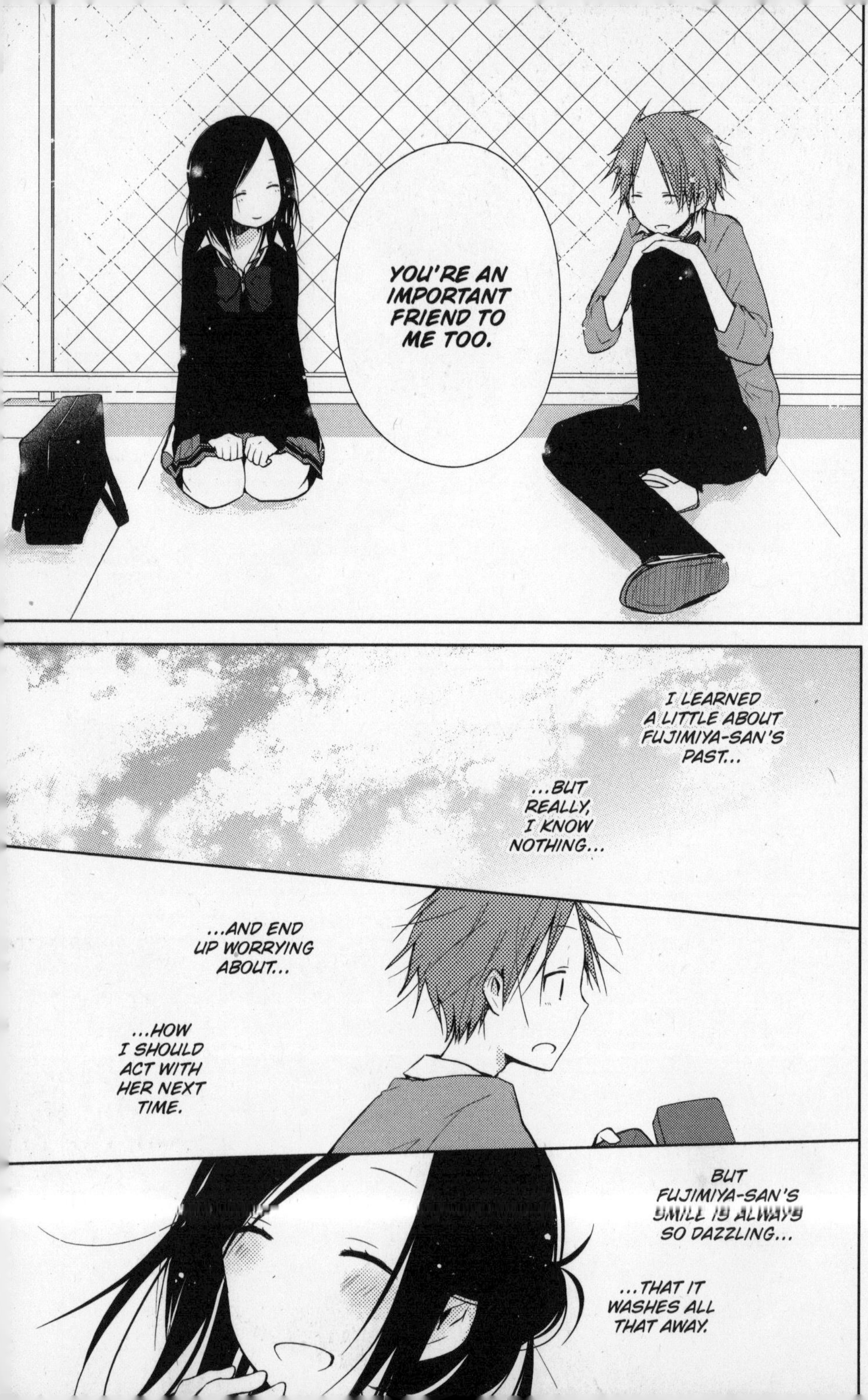
YOU'RE AN IMPORTANT FRIEND TO ME TOO.
I LEARNED A LITTLE ABOUT FUJIMIYA-SAN'S PAST...
...BUT REALLY, I KNOW NOTHING...
...AND END UP WORRYING ABOUT...
...HOW I SHOULD ACT WITH HER NEXT TIME.
BUT FUJIMIYA-SAN'S SMILE IS ALWAYS SO DAZZLING...
...THAT IT WASHES ALL THAT AWAY.

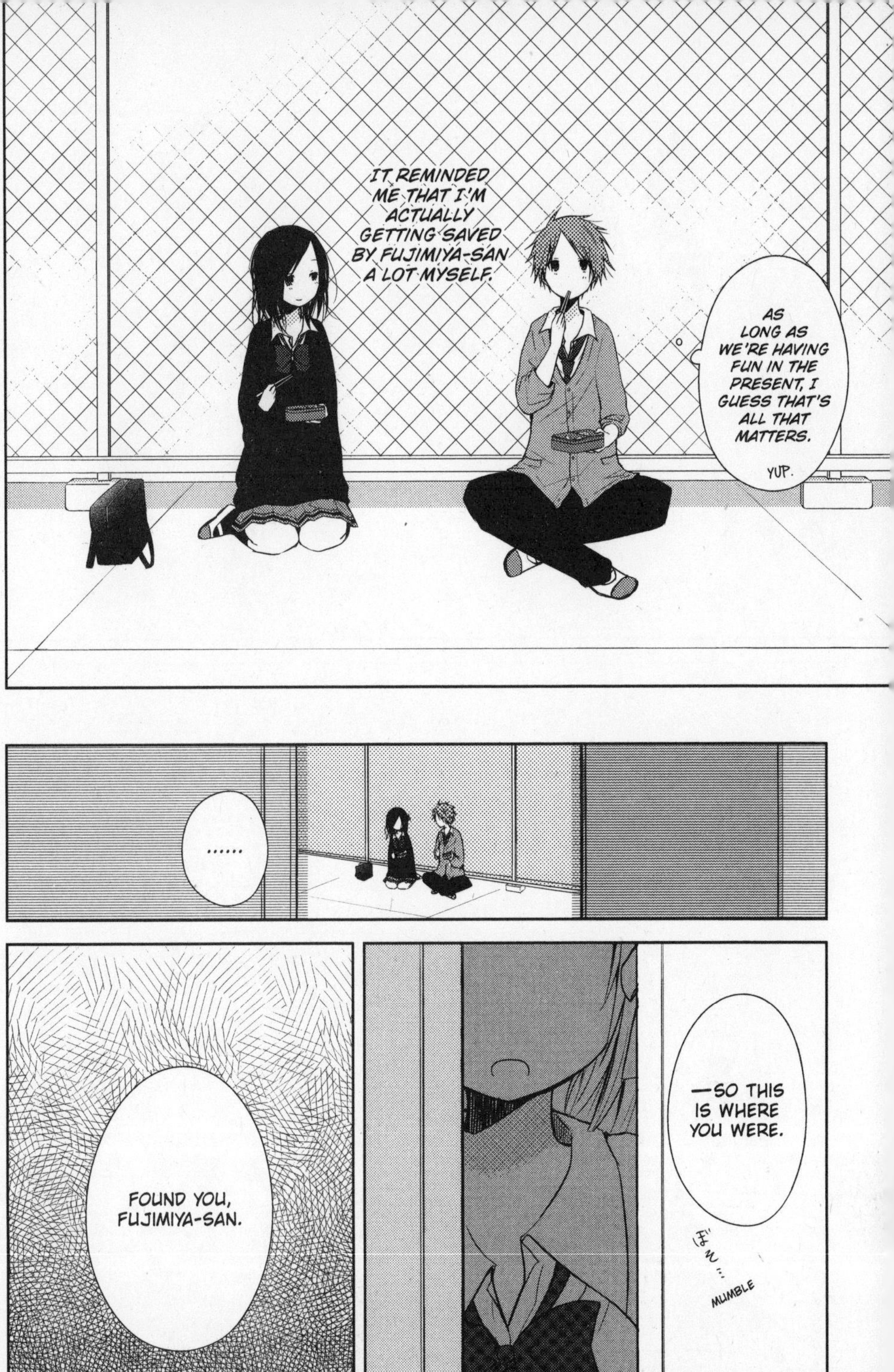
AS LONG AS WE'RE HAVING FUN IN THE PRESENT, I GUESS THAT'S ALL THAT MATTERS.
YUP.
IT REMINDED ME THAT I'M ACTUALLY GETTING SAVED BY FUJIMIYA-SAN A LOT MYSELF.
......
—SO THIS IS WHERE YOU WERE.
ぼそ…
MUMBLE
FOUND YOU, FUJIMIYA-SAN.

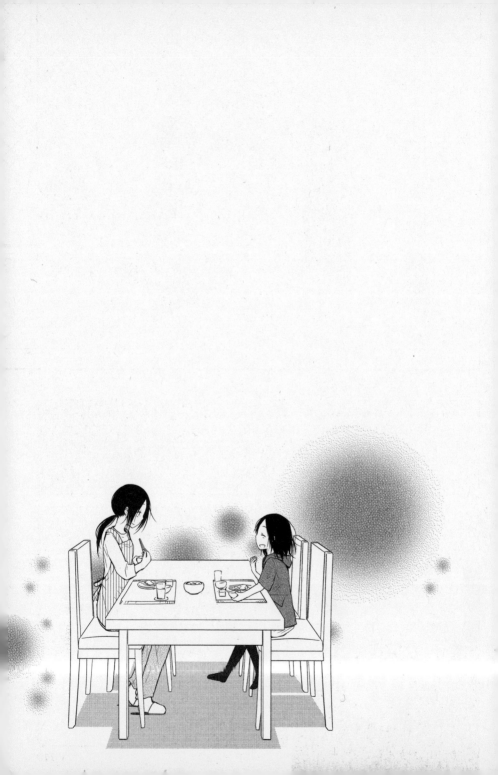

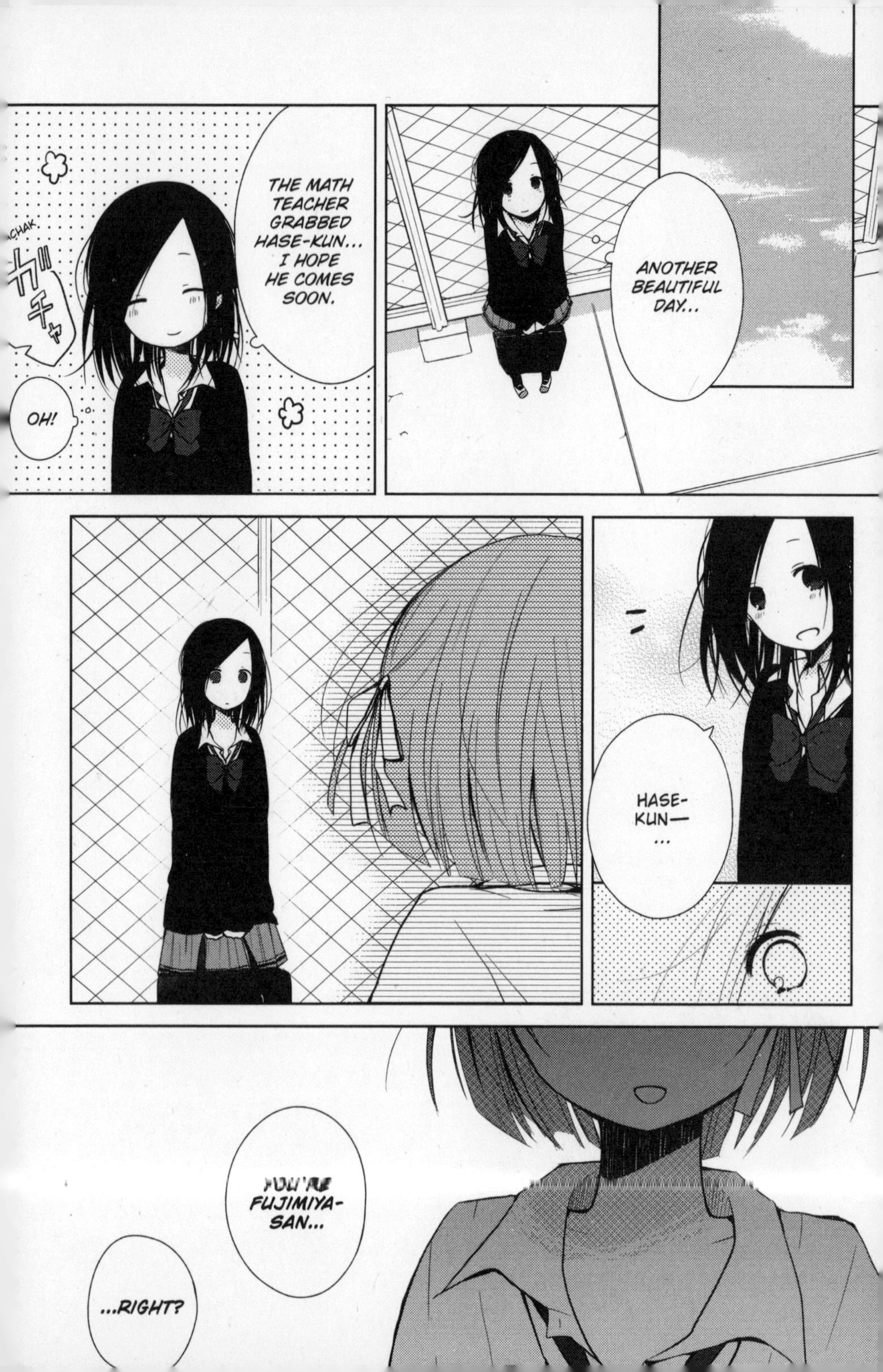
ANOTHER BEAUTIFUL DAY...
THE MATH TEACHER GRABBED HASE-KUN... I HOPE HE COMES SOON.
CHAK
ガチャ
OH!
HASE-KUN—...
YOU'RE FUJIMIYA-SAN...
...RIGHT?

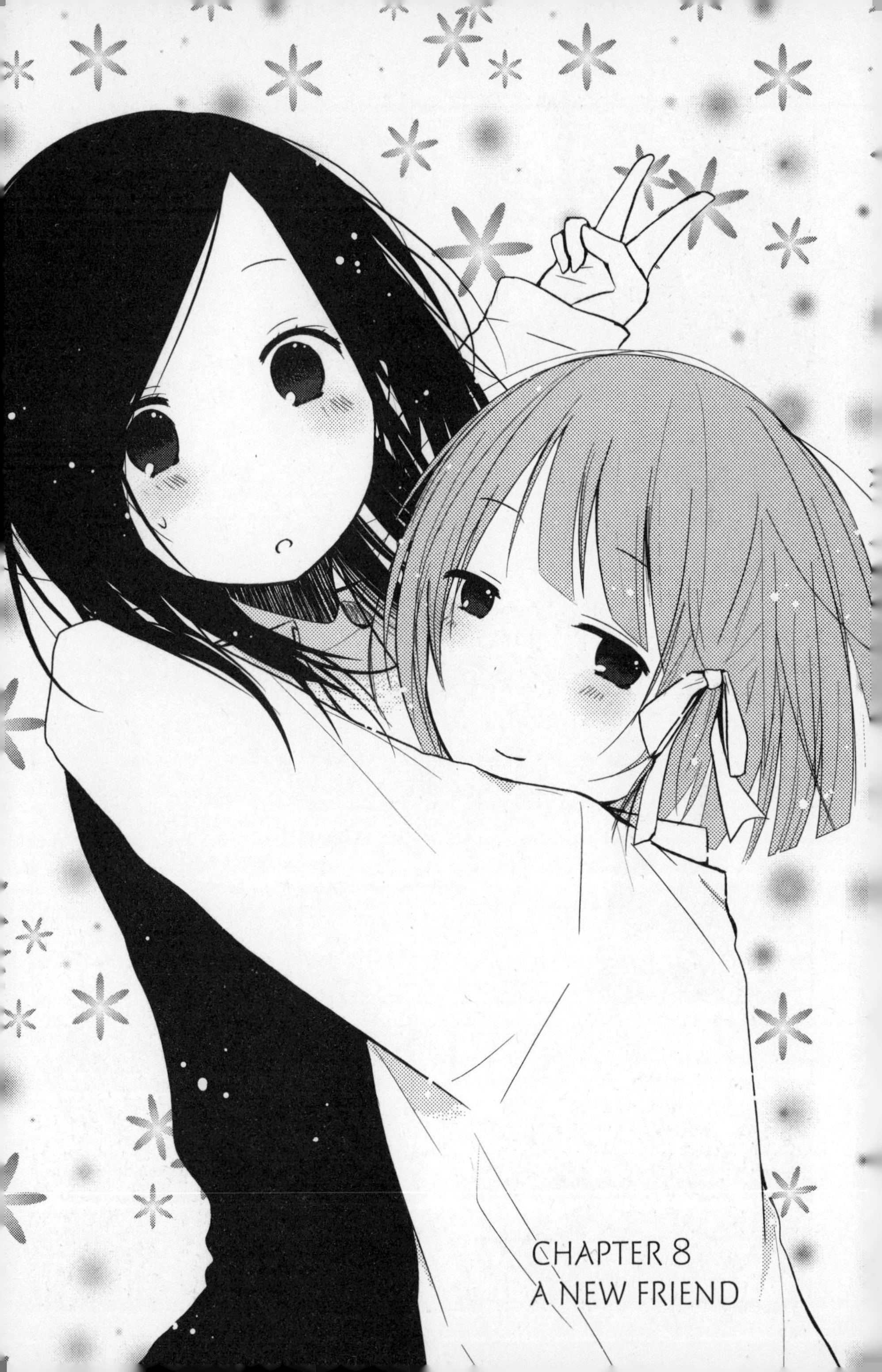
CHAPTER 8
A NEW FRIEND

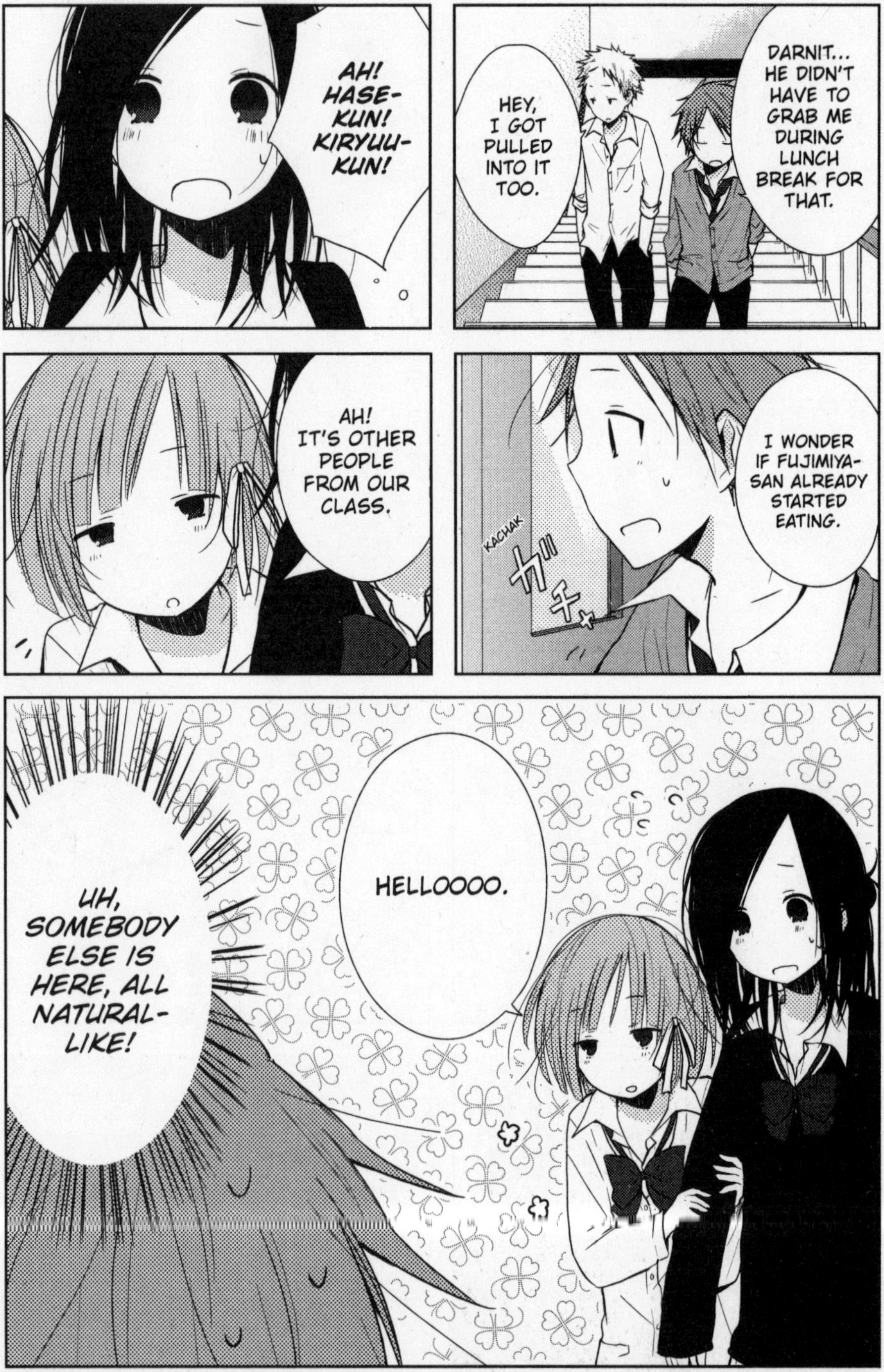
DARNIT... HE DIDN'T HAVE TO GRAB ME DURING LUNCH BREAK FOR THAT.
HEY, I GOT PULLED INTO IT TOO.
AH! HASE-KUN! KIRYUU-KUN!
I WONDER IF FUJIMIYA-SAN ALREADY STARTED EATING.
KACHAK
AH! IT'S OTHER PEOPLE FROM OUR CLASS.
HELLOOOO.
UH, SOMEBODY ELSE IS HERE, ALL NATURAL-LIKE!

SAKI YAMAGISHI

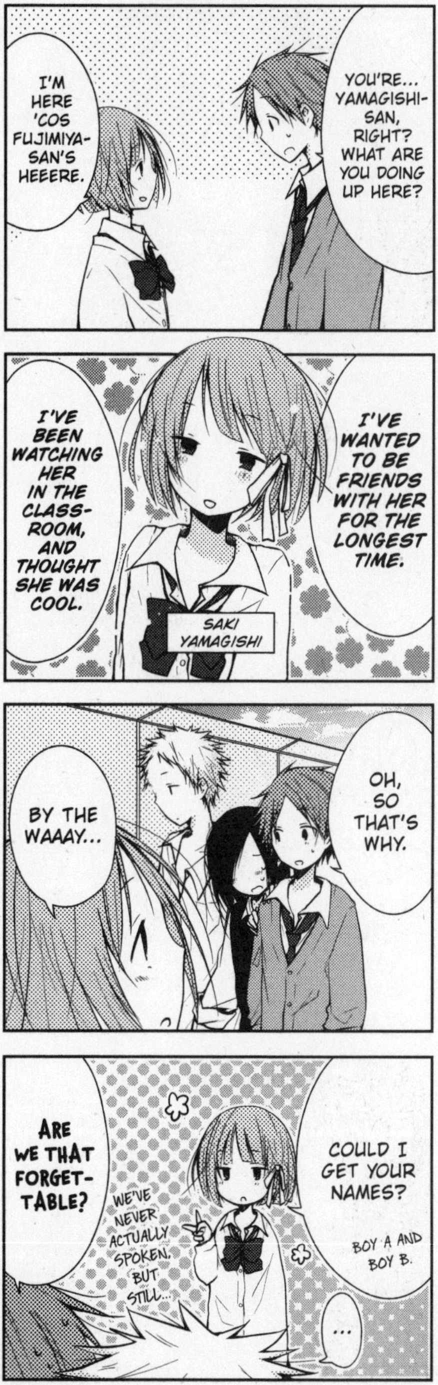
YOU'RE... YAMAGISHI-SAN, RIGHT? WHAT ARE YOU DOING UP HERE?
I'M HERE 'COS FUJIMIYA-SAN'S HEEERE.
I'VE WANTED TO BE FRIENDS WITH HER FOR THE LONGEST TIME.
I'VE BEEN WATCHING HER IN THE CLASSROOM, AND THOUGHT SHE WAS COOL.
SAKI YAMAGISHI
OH, SO THAT'S WHY.
BY THE WAAAY...
COULD I GET YOUR NAMES?
BOY A AND BOY B.
...
ARE WE THAT FORGETTABLE?
WE'VE NEVER ACTUALLY SPOKEN, BUT STILL...

RELAXED

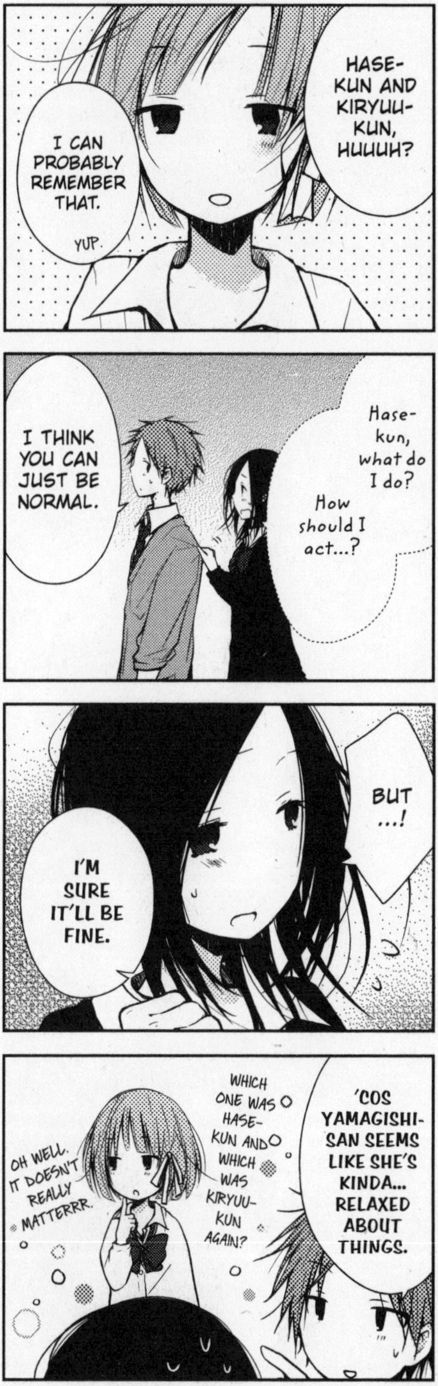
HASE-KUN AND KIRYUU-KUN, HUUUH?
I CAN PROBABLY REMEMBER THAT.
YUP.
Hase-kun, what do I do? How should I act...?
I THINK YOU CAN JUST BE NORMAL.
BUT ...!
I'M SURE IT'LL BE FINE.
'COS YAMAGISHI-SAN SEEMS LIKE SHE'S KINDA... RELAXED ABOUT THINGS.
WHICH ONE WAS HASE-KUN AND WHICH WAS KIRYUU-KUN AGAIN?
OH WELL. IT DOESN'T REALLY MATTERRR.

HONESTLY

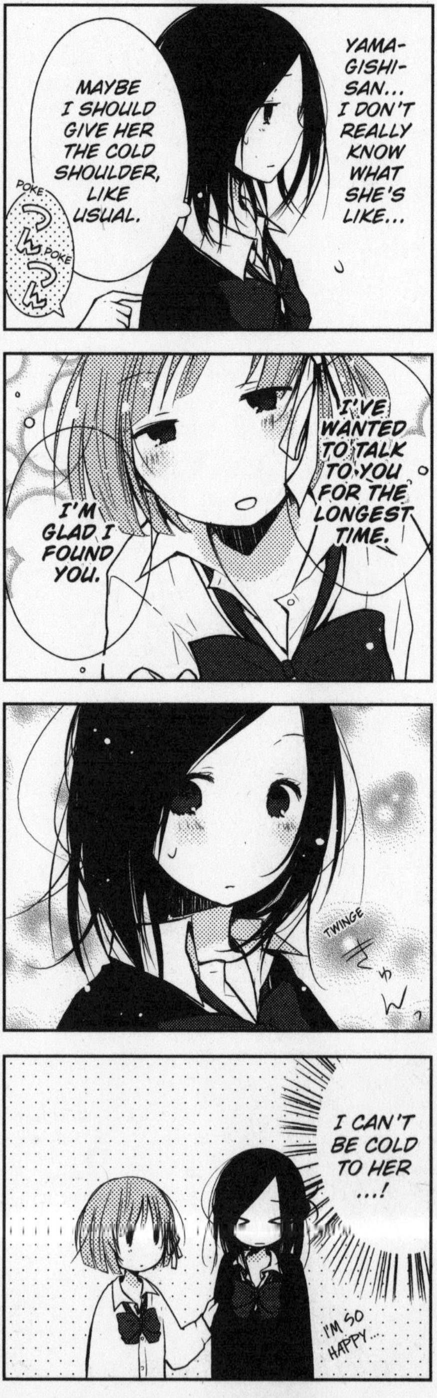
YAMA-GISHI-SAN... I DON'T REALLY KNOW WHAT SHE'S LIKE...
MAYBE I SHOULD GIVE HER THE COLD SHOULDER, LIKE USUAL.
POKE
POKE
I'VE WANTED TO TALK TO YOU FOR THE LONGEST TIME.
I'M GLAD I FOUND YOU.
TWINGE
I CAN'T BE COLD TO HER ...!
I'M SO HAPPY...

BREAKAWAY

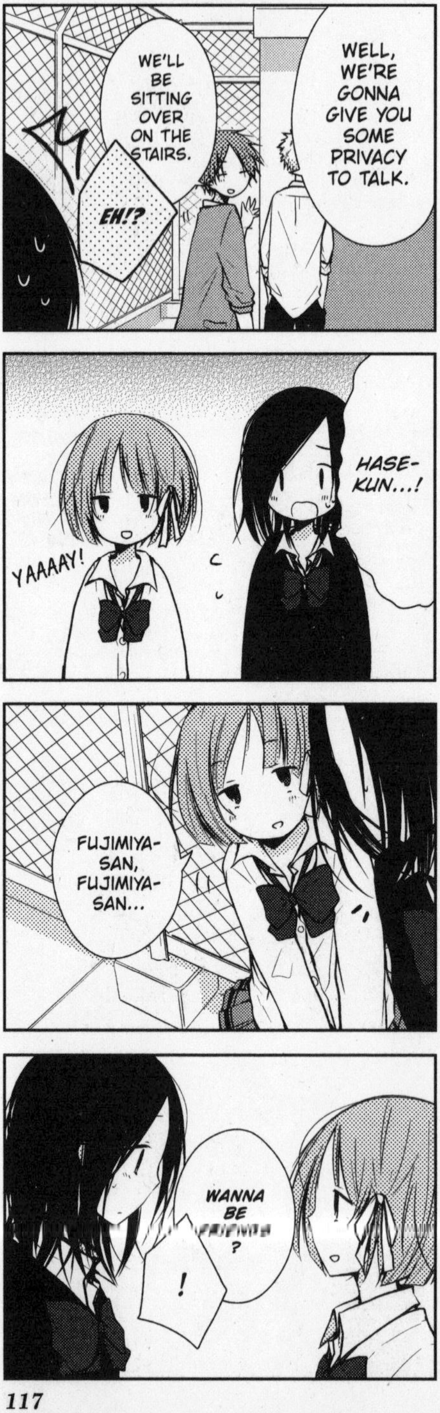
WELL, WE'RE GONNA GIVE YOU SOME PRIVACY TO TALK.
WE'LL BE SITTING OVER ON THE STAIRS.
EH!?
HASE-KUN...!
YAAAAY!
FUJIMIYA-SAN, FUJIMIYA-SAN...
WANNA BE ?
!

LOST FOR WORDS

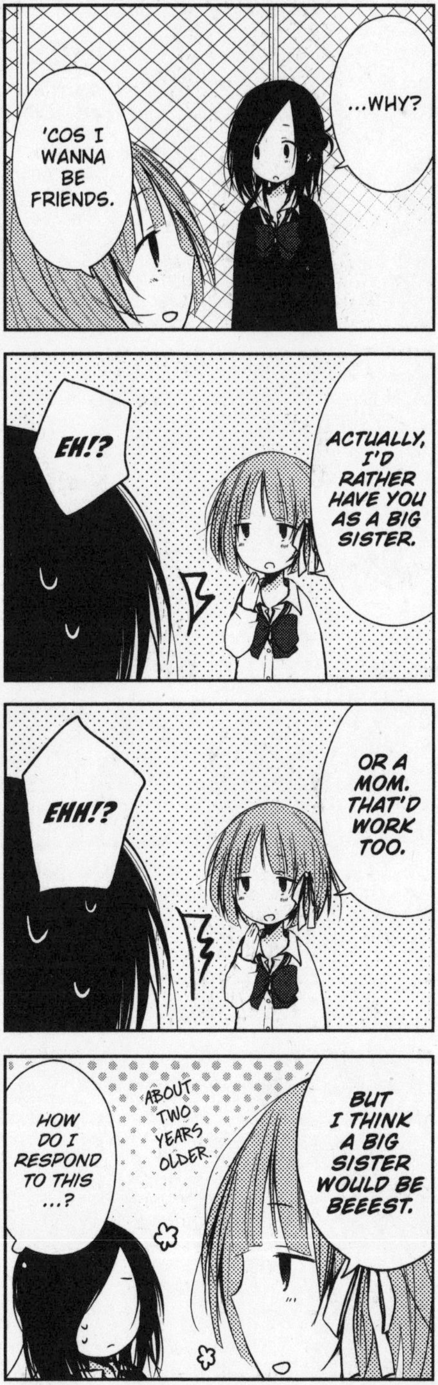
...WHY?
'COS I WANNA BE FRIENDS.
ACTUALLY, I'D RATHER HAVE YOU AS A BIG SISTER.
EH!?
OR A MOM. THAT'D WORK TOO.
EHH!?
BUT I THINK A BIG SISTER WOULD BE BEEEST.
ABOUT TWO YEARS OLDER.
HOW DO I RESPOND TO THIS ...?

GUILT

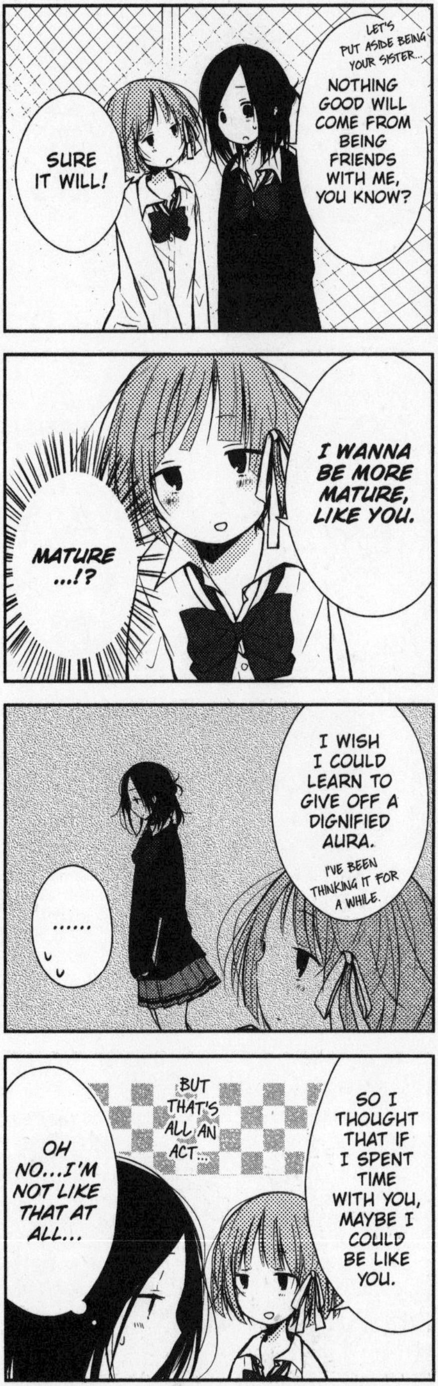
LET'S PUT ASIDE BEING YOUR SISTER...
NOTHING GOOD WILL COME FROM BEING FRIENDS WITH ME, YOU KNOW?
SURE IT WILL!
I WANNA BE MORE MATURE, LIKE YOU.
MATURE ...!?
I WISH I COULD LEARN TO GIVE OFF A DIGNIFIED AURA.
I'VE BEEN THINKING IT FOR A WHILE.
......
SO I THOUGHT THAT IF I SPENT TIME WITH YOU, MAYBE I COULD BE LIKE YOU.
BUT THAT'S ALL AN ACT...
OH NO...I'M NOT LIKE THAT AT ALL...

WHAT SHE MEANT

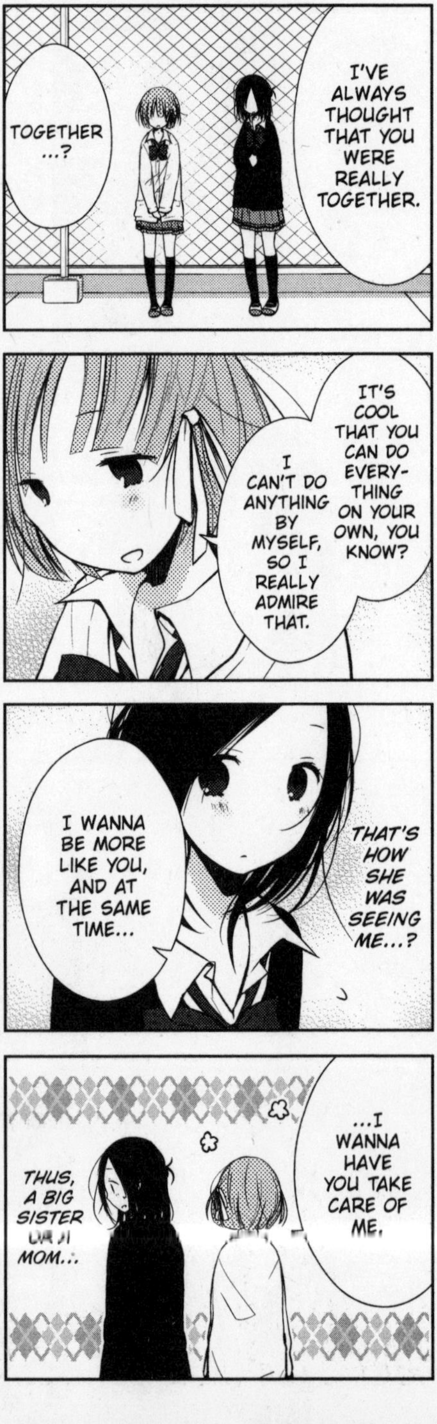
I'VE ALWAYS THOUGHT THAT YOU WERE REALLY TOGETHER.
TOGETHER ...?
IT'S COOL THAT YOU CAN DO EVERY-THING ON YOUR OWN, YOU KNOW?
I CAN'T DO ANYTHING BY MYSELF, SO I REALLY ADMIRE THAT.
THAT'S HOW SHE WAS SEEING ME...?
I WANNA BE MORE LIKE YOU, AND AT THE SAME TIME...
...I WANNA HAVE YOU TAKE CARE OF ME.
THUS, A BIG SISTER
MOM...

WORDS

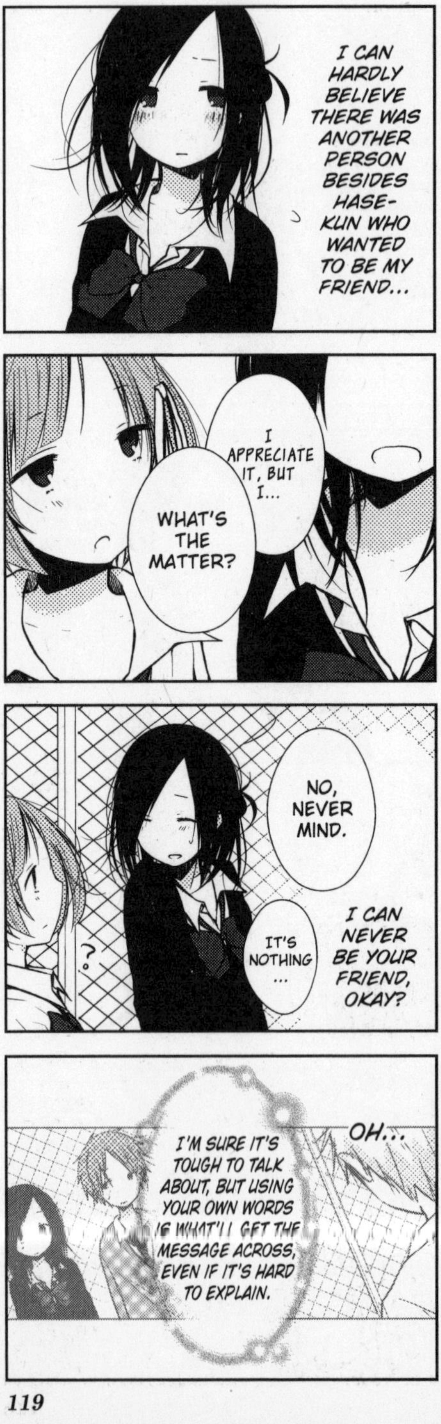
I CAN HARDLY BELIEVE THERE WAS ANOTHER PERSON BESIDES HASE-KUN WHO WANTED TO BE MY FRIEND...
I APPRECIATE IT, BUT I...
WHAT'S THE MATTER?
NO, NEVER MIND.
I CAN NEVER BE YOUR FRIEND, OKAY?
IT'S NOTHING ...
OH...
I'M SURE IT'S TOUGH TO TALK ABOUT, BUT USING YOUR OWN WORDS IS WHAT'LL GET THE MESSAGE ACROSS, EVEN IF IT'S HARD TO EXPLAIN.

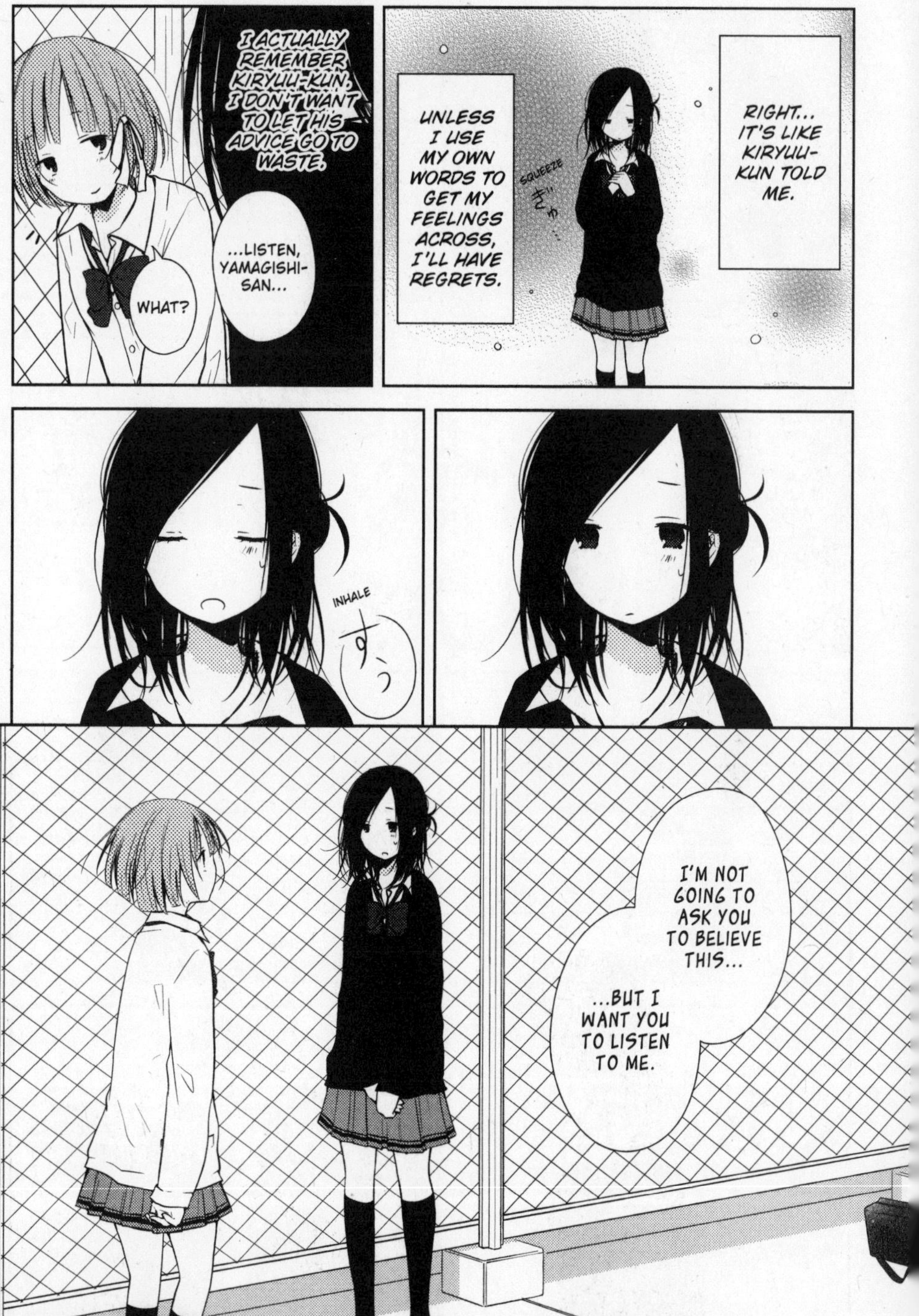
RIGHT... IT'S LIKE KIRYUU-KUN TOLD ME.
UNLESS I USE MY OWN WORDS TO GET MY FEELINGS ACROSS, I'LL HAVE REGRETS.
SQUEEZE
I ACTUALLY REMEMBER KIRYUU-KUN. I DON'T WANT TO LET HIS ADVICE GO TO WASTE.
...LISTEN, YAMAGISHI-SAN...
WHAT?
INHALE
I'M NOT GOING TO ASK YOU TO BELIEVE THIS...
...BUT I WANT YOU TO LISTEN TO ME.

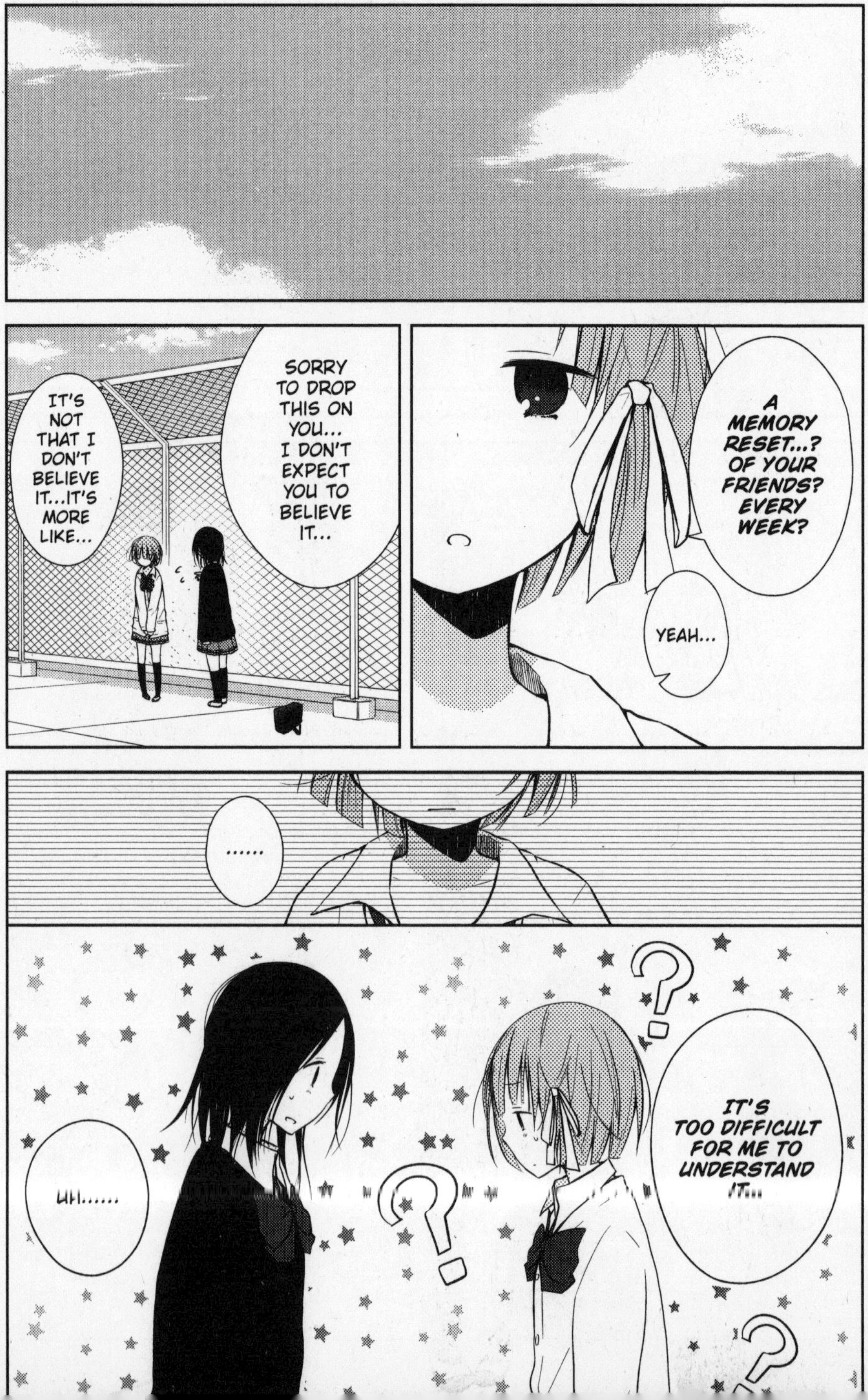
A MEMORY RESET...? OF YOUR FRIENDS? EVERY WEEK?
YEAH...
SORRY TO DROP THIS ON YOU... I DON'T EXPECT YOU TO BELIEVE IT...
IT'S NOT THAT I DON'T BELIEVE IT...IT'S MORE LIKE...
......
IT'S TOO DIFFICULT FOR ME TO UNDERSTAND IT...
UH......

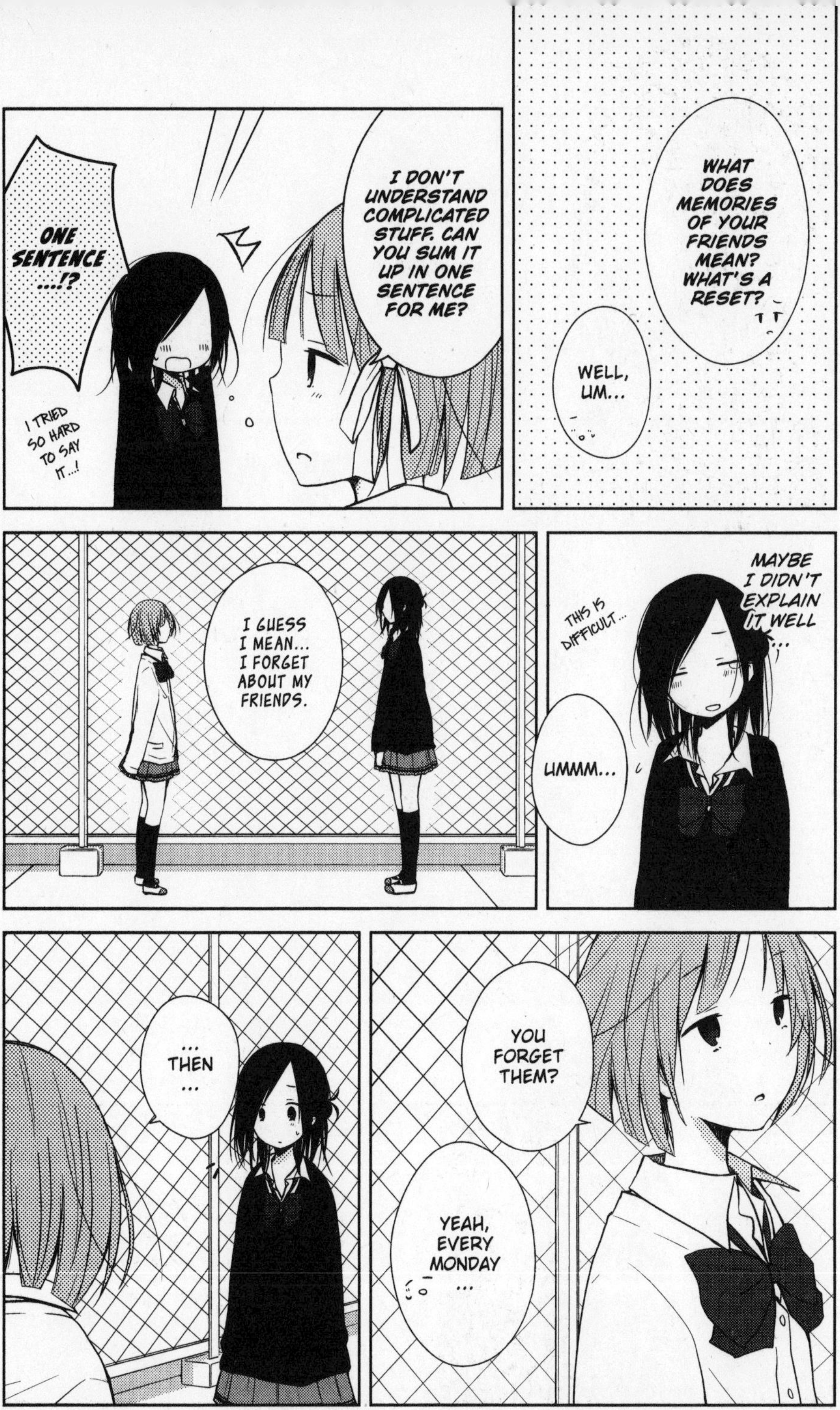
WHAT DOES MEMORIES OF YOUR FRIENDS MEAN? WHAT'S A RESET?
WELL, UM...
I DON'T UNDERSTAND COMPLICATED STUFF. CAN YOU SUM IT UP IN ONE SENTENCE FOR ME?
ONE SENTENCE ...!?
I TRIED SO HARD TO SAY IT...!
MAYBE I DIDN'T EXPLAIN IT WELL...
THIS IS DIFFICULT...
UMMM...
I GUESS I MEAN... I FORGET ABOUT MY FRIENDS.
YOU FORGET THEM?
YEAH, EVERY MONDAY ...
... THEN ...

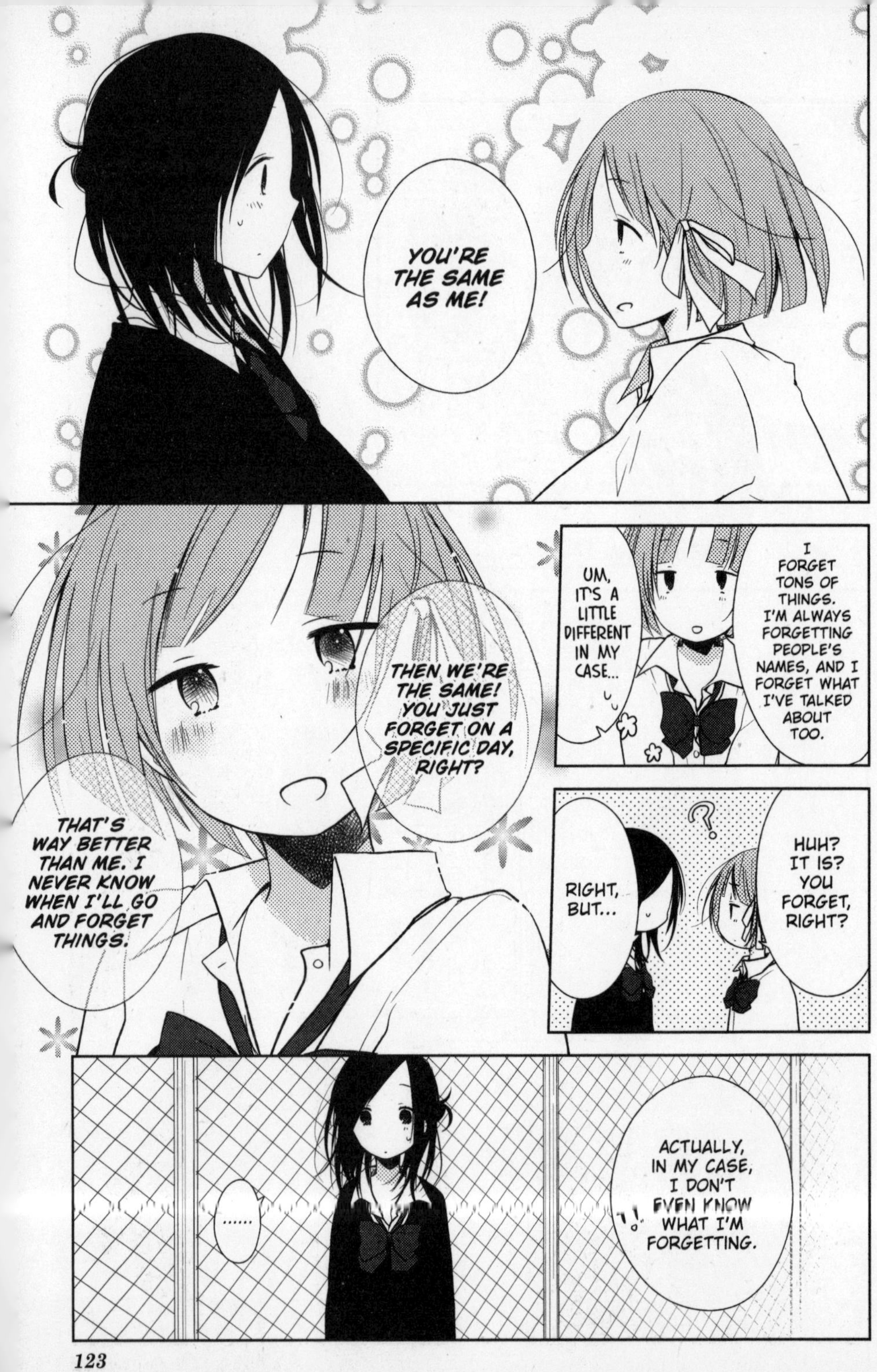
YOU'RE THE SAME AS ME!
I FORGET TONS OF THINGS. I'M ALWAYS FORGETTING PEOPLE'S NAMES, AND I FORGET WHAT I'VE TALKED ABOUT TOO.
UM, IT'S A LITTLE DIFFERENT IN MY CASE...
HUH? IT IS? YOU FORGET, RIGHT?
RIGHT, BUT...
THEN WE'RE THE SAME! YOU JUST FORGET ON A SPECIFIC DAY, RIGHT?
THAT'S WAY BETTER THAN ME. I NEVER KNOW WHEN I'LL GO AND FORGET THINGS.
ACTUALLY, IN MY CASE, I DON'T EVEN KNOW WHAT I'M FORGETTING.
!
......

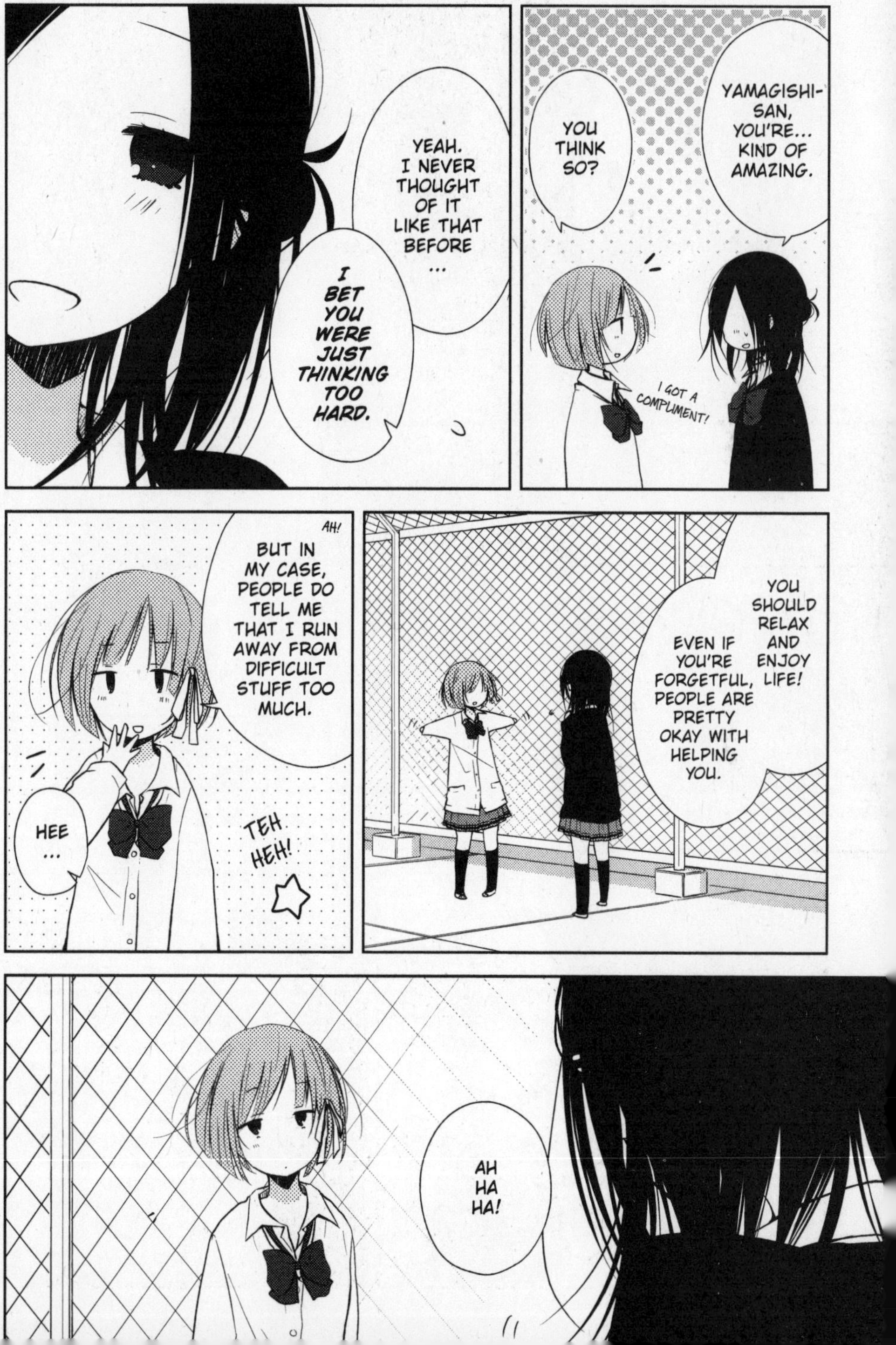
YAMAGISHI-SAN, YOU'RE... KIND OF AMAZING.
YOU THINK SO?
I GOT A COMPLIMENT!
YEAH. I NEVER THOUGHT OF IT LIKE THAT BEFORE...
I BET YOU WERE JUST THINKING TOO HARD.
YOU SHOULD RELAX AND ENJOY LIFE!
EVEN IF YOU'RE FORGETFUL, PEOPLE ARE PRETTY OKAY WITH HELPING YOU.
AH!
BUT IN MY CASE, PEOPLE DO TELL ME THAT I RUN AWAY FROM DIFFICULT STUFF TOO MUCH.
HEE...
TEH HEH!
AH HA HA!

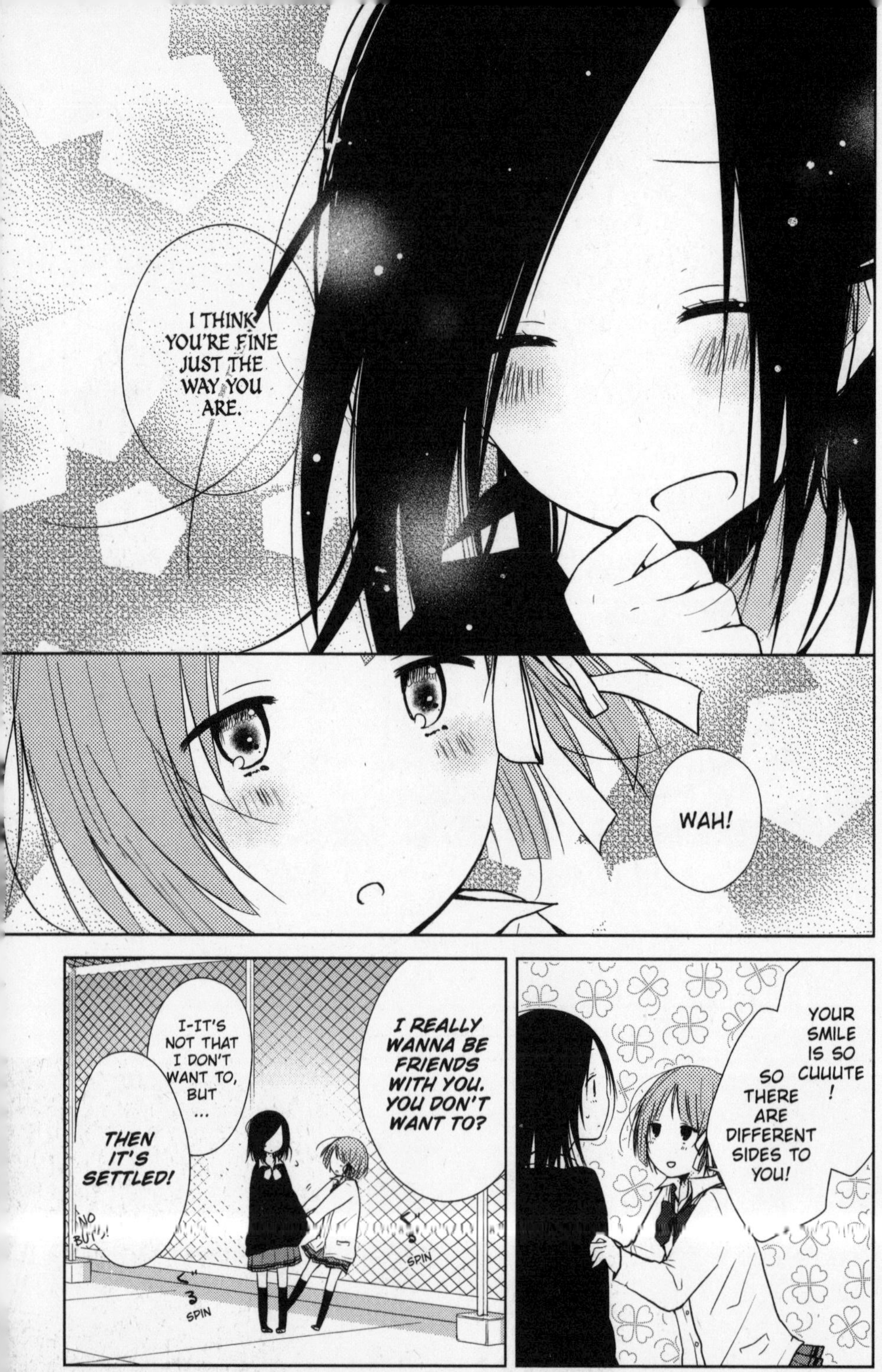
I THINK YOU'RE FINE JUST THE WAY YOU ARE.
WAH!
YOUR SMILE IS SO CUUUTE!
SO THERE ARE DIFFERENT SIDES TO YOU!
I REALLY WANNA BE FRIENDS WITH YOU. YOU DON'T WANT TO?
I-IT'S NOT THAT I DON'T WANT TO, BUT ...
THEN IT'S SETTLED!
SPIN
SPIN

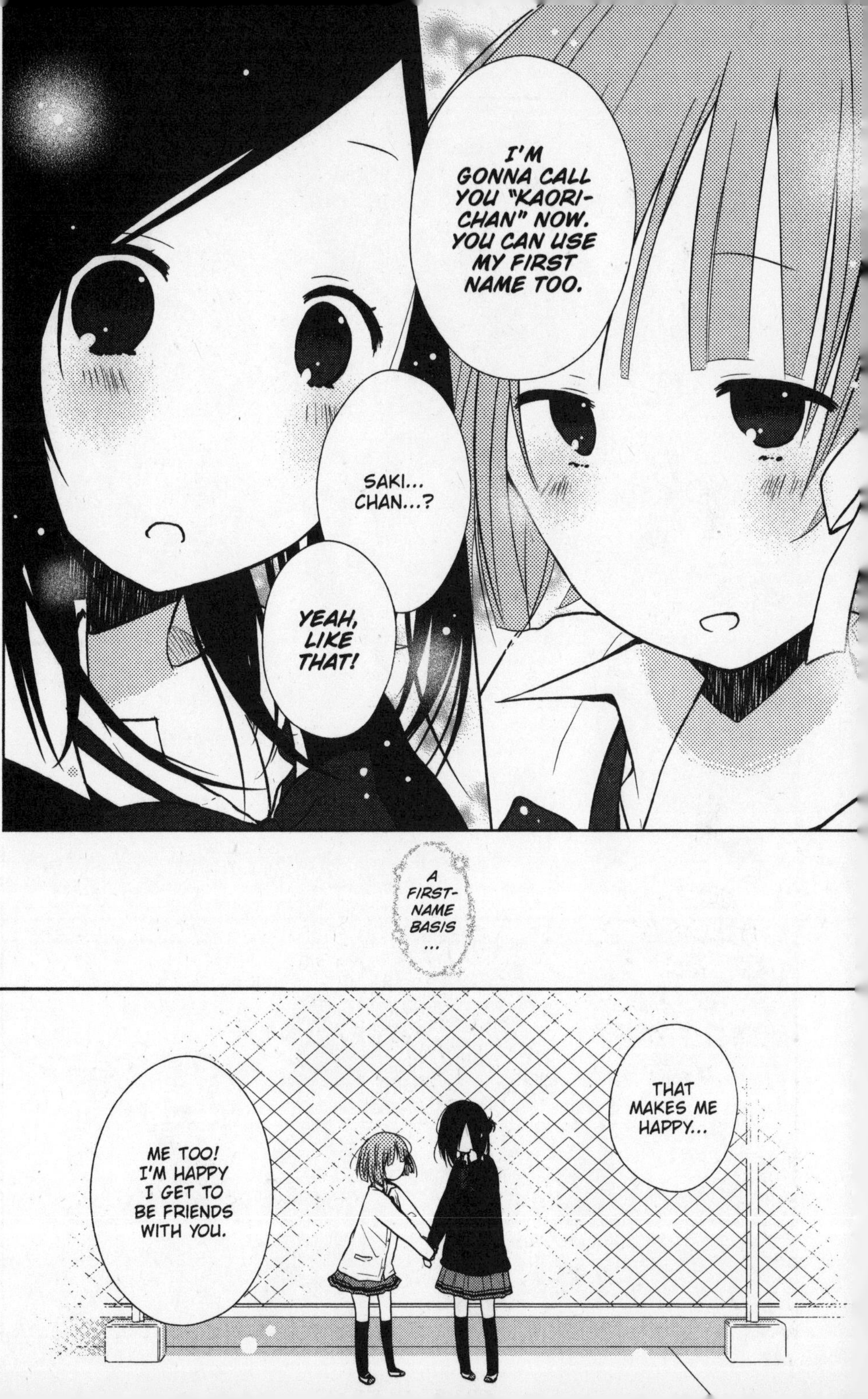
I'M GONNA CALL YOU "KAORI-CHAN" NOW. YOU CAN USE MY FIRST NAME TOO.
SAKI... CHAN...?
YEAH, LIKE THAT!
A FIRST-NAME BASIS...
THAT MAKES ME HAPPY...
ME TOO! I'M HAPPY I GET TO BE FRIENDS WITH YOU.

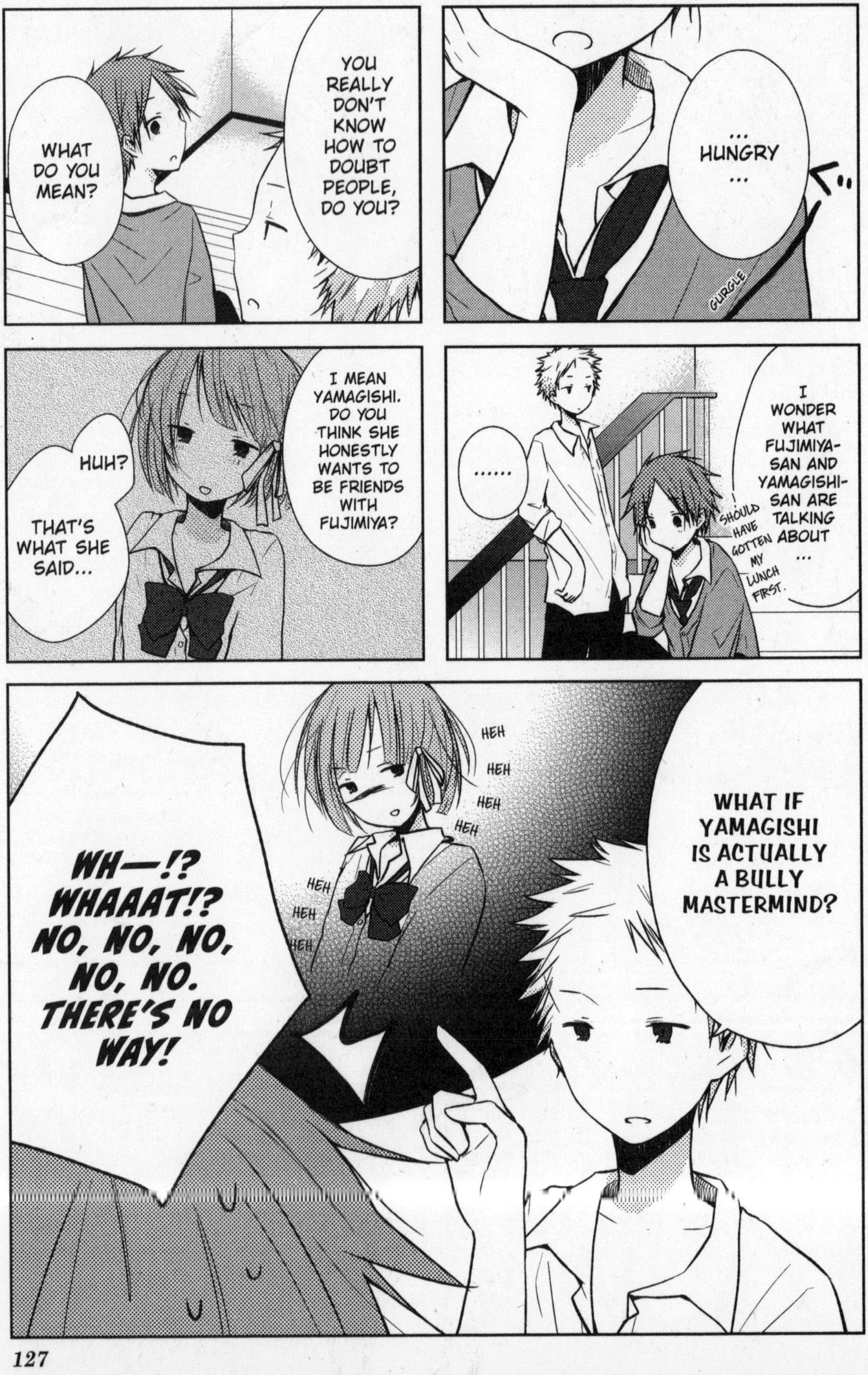
... HUNGRY ...
GURGLE
YOU REALLY DON'T KNOW HOW TO DOUBT PEOPLE, DO YOU?
WHAT DO YOU MEAN?
I WONDER WHAT FUJIMIYA-SAN AND YAMAGISHI-SAN ARE TALKING ABOUT ...
I SHOULD HAVE GOTTEN MY LUNCH FIRST.
......
I MEAN YAMAGISHI. DO YOU THINK SHE HONESTLY WANTS TO BE FRIENDS WITH FUJIMIYA?
HUH?
THAT'S WHAT SHE SAID...
WHAT IF YAMAGISHI IS ACTUALLY A BULLY MASTERMIND?
HEH
HEH
HEH
HEH
HEH
HEH
HEH
WH—!? WHAAAT!? NO, NO, NO, NO, NO. THERE'S NO WAY!

YAMAGISHI-SAN

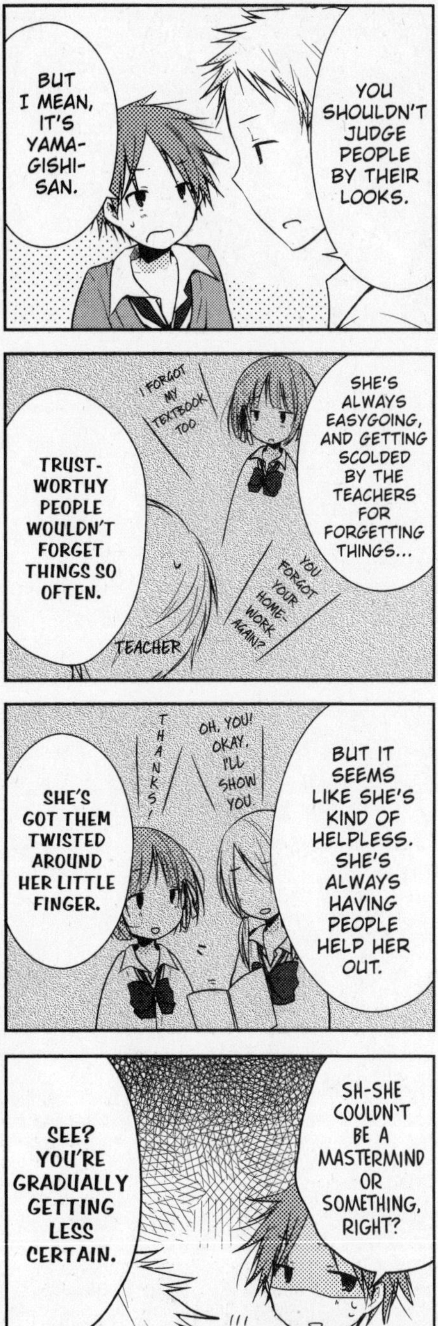
YOU SHOULDN'T JUDGE PEOPLE BY THEIR LOOKS.
BUT I MEAN, IT'S YAMAGISHI-SAN.
SHE'S ALWAYS EASYGOING, AND GETTING SCOLDED BY THE TEACHERS FOR FORGETTING THINGS...
I FORGOT MY TEXTBOOK TOO.
YOU FORGOT YOUR HOMEWORK AGAIN?
TRUSTWORTHY PEOPLE WOULDN'T FORGET THINGS SO OFTEN.
TEACHER
BUT IT SEEMS LIKE SHE'S KIND OF HELPLESS. SHE'S ALWAYS HAVING PEOPLE HELP HER OUT.
OH, YOU! OKAY, I'LL SHOW YOU.
THANKS!
SHE'S GOT THEM TWISTED AROUND HER LITTLE FINGER.
SH-SHE COULDN'T BE A MASTERMIND OR SOMETHING, RIGHT?
SEE? YOU'RE GRADUALLY GETTING LESS CERTAIN.

DEVIL'S WHISPERS

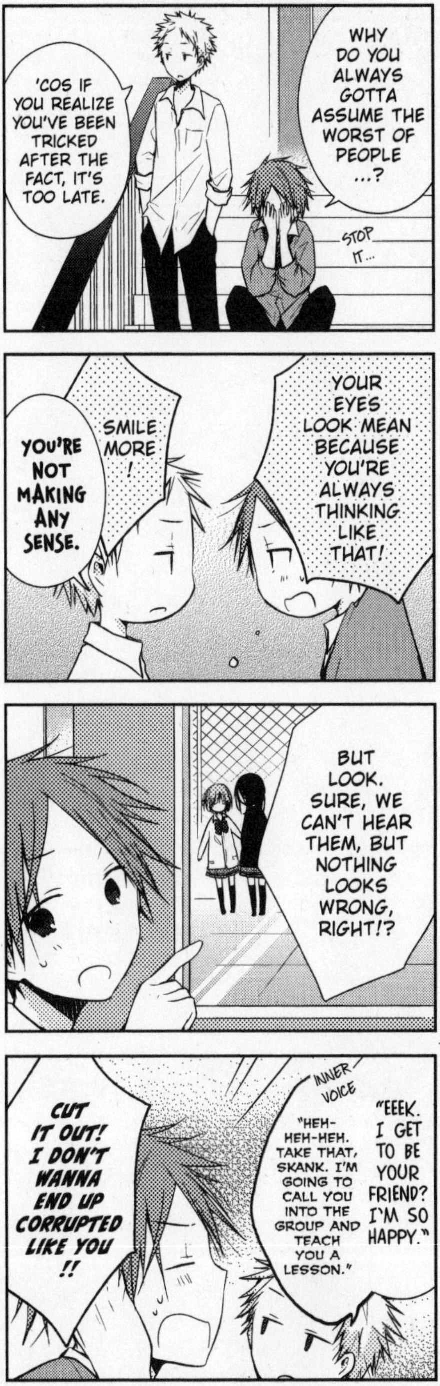
WHY DO YOU ALWAYS GOTTA ASSUME THE WORST OF PEOPLE ...?
STOP IT...
'COS IF YOU REALIZE YOU'VE BEEN TRICKED AFTER THE FACT, IT'S TOO LATE.
YOUR EYES LOOK MEAN BECAUSE YOU'RE ALWAYS THINKING LIKE THAT!
SMILE MORE!
YOU'RE NOT MAKING ANY SENSE.
BUT LOOK. SURE, WE CAN'T HEAR THEM, BUT NOTHING LOOKS WRONG, RIGHT!?
"EEEK. I GET TO BE YOUR FRIEND? I'M SO HAPPY."
INNER VOICE
"HEH-HEH-HEH. TAKE THAT, SKANK. I'M GOING TO CALL YOU INTO THE GROUP AND TEACH YOU A LESSON."
CUT IT OUT! I DON'T WANNA END UP CORRUPTED LIKE YOU!!

ACTUALLY

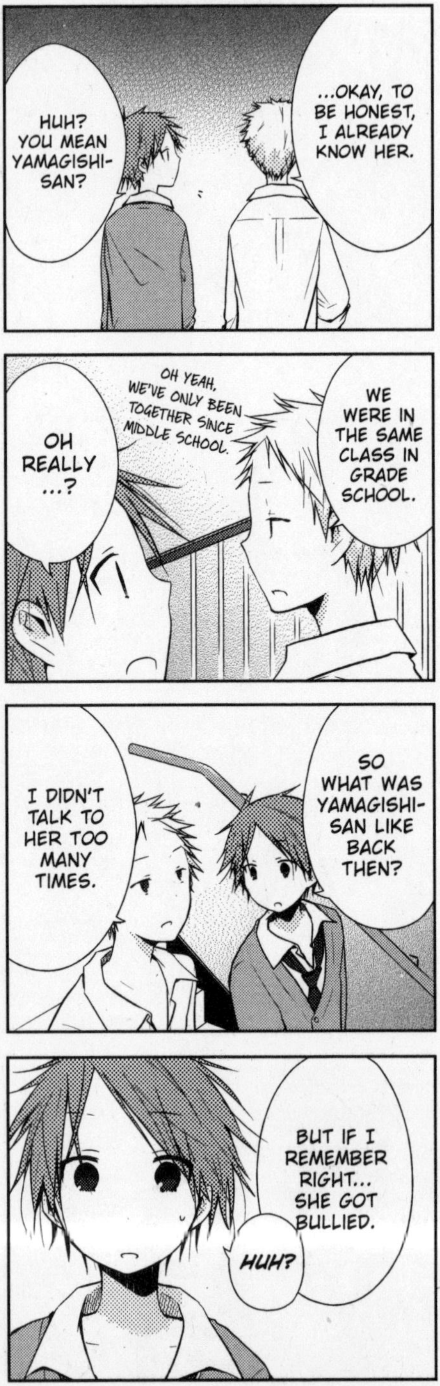
...OKAY, TO BE HONEST, I ALREADY KNOW HER.
HUH? YOU MEAN YAMAGISHI-SAN?
WE WERE IN THE SAME CLASS IN GRADE SCHOOL.
OH YEAH, WE'VE ONLY BEEN TOGETHER SINCE MIDDLE SCHOOL.
OH REALLY ...?
SO WHAT WAS YAMAGISHI-SAN LIKE BACK THEN?
I DIDN'T TALK TO HER TOO MANY TIMES.
BUT IF I REMEMBER RIGHT... SHE GOT BULLIED.
HUH?

THE PAST

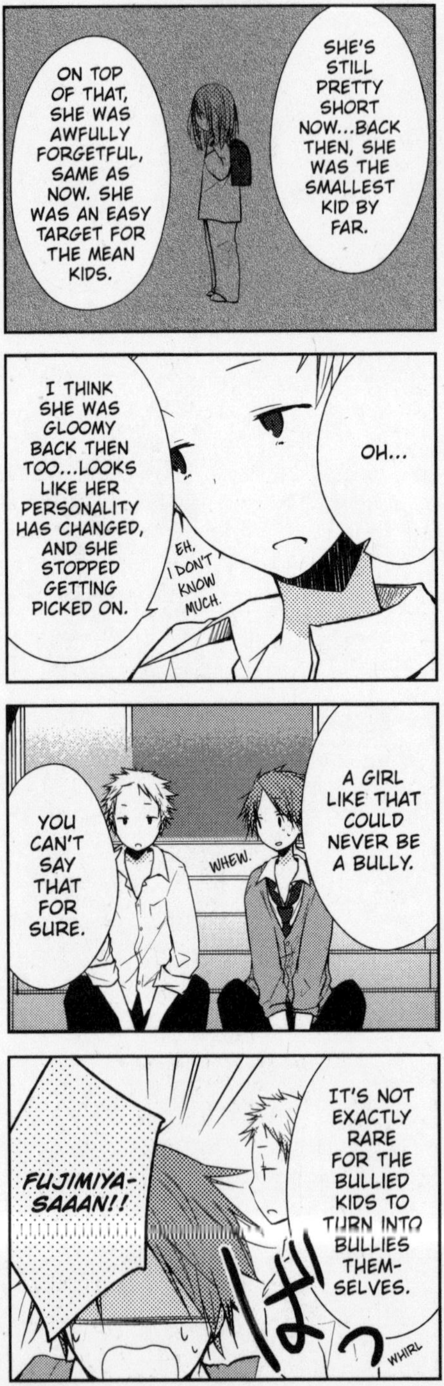
SHE'S STILL PRETTY SHORT NOW...BACK THEN, SHE WAS THE SMALLEST KID BY FAR.
ON TOP OF THAT, SHE WAS AWFULLY FORGETFUL, SAME AS NOW. SHE WAS AN EASY TARGET FOR THE MEAN KIDS.
OH...
I THINK SHE WAS GLOOMY BACK THEN TOO...LOOKS LIKE HER PERSONALITY HAS CHANGED, AND SHE STOPPED GETTING PICKED ON.
EH, I DON'T KNOW MUCH.
A GIRL LIKE THAT COULD NEVER BE A BULLY.
WHEW.
YOU CAN'T SAY THAT FOR SURE.
IT'S NOT EXACTLY RARE FOR THE BULLIED KIDS TO TURN INTO BULLIES THEM-SELVES.
FUJIMIYA-SAAAN!!
ぱっ
WHIRL

MY

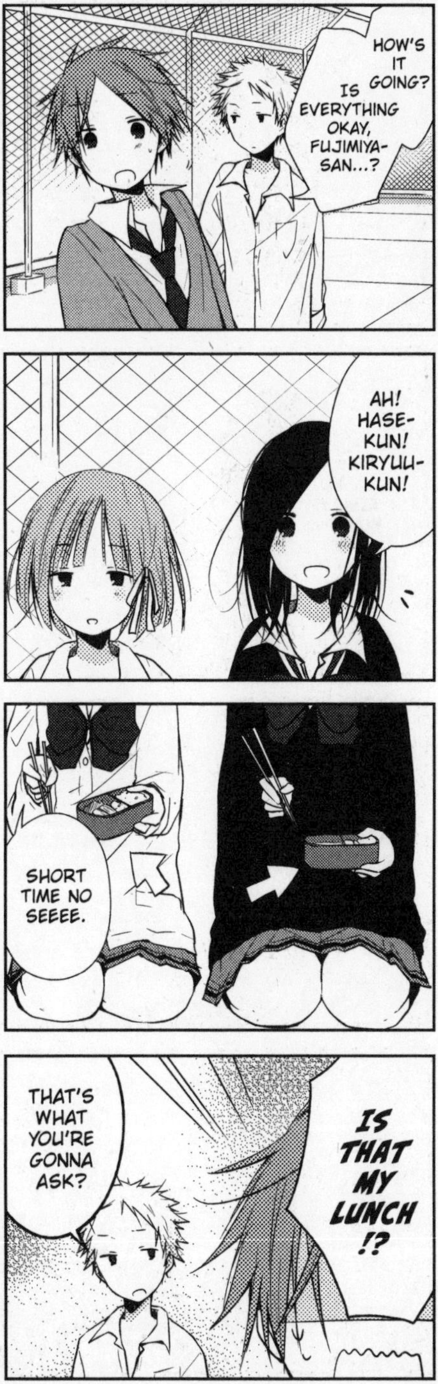
HOW'S IT GOING? IS EVERYTHING OKAY, FUJIMIYA-SAN...?
AH! HASE-KUN! KIRYUU-KUN!
SHORT TIME NO SEEEE.
IS THAT MY LUNCH!?
THAT'S WHAT YOU'RE GONNA ASK?

SINCE WE'RE FRIENDS NOW

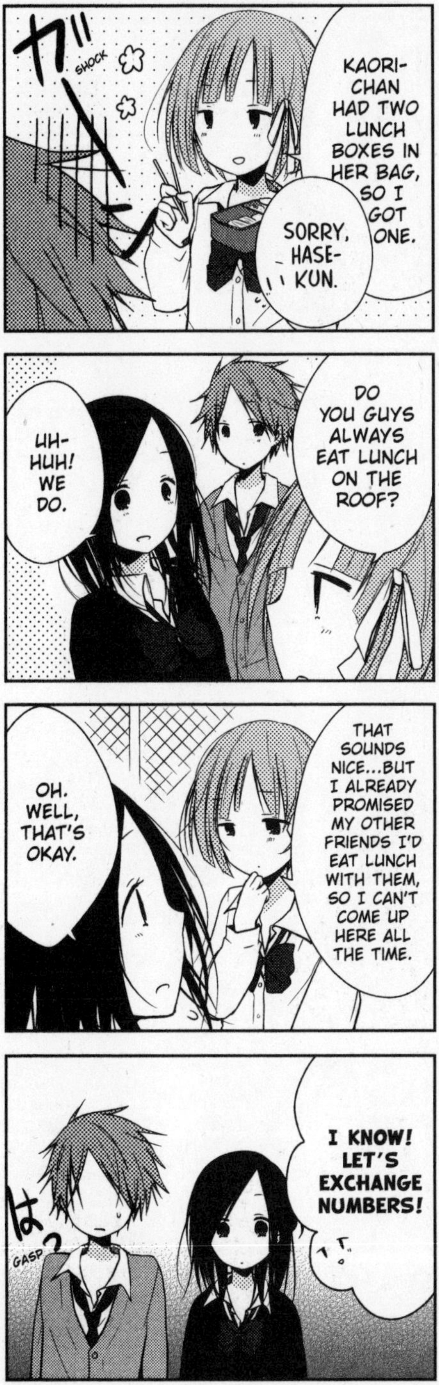
KAORI-CHAN HAD TWO LUNCH BOXES IN HER BAG, SO I GOT ONE.
SORRY, HASE-KUN.
SHOCK
DO YOU GUYS ALWAYS EAT LUNCH ON THE ROOF?
UH-HUH! WE DO.
THAT SOUNDS NICE...BUT I ALREADY PROMISED MY OTHER FRIENDS I'D EAT LUNCH WITH THEM, SO I CAN'T COME UP HERE ALL THE TIME.
OH. WELL, THAT'S OKAY.
I KNOW! LET'S EXCHANGE NUMBERS!
は
GASP

THE SAME?

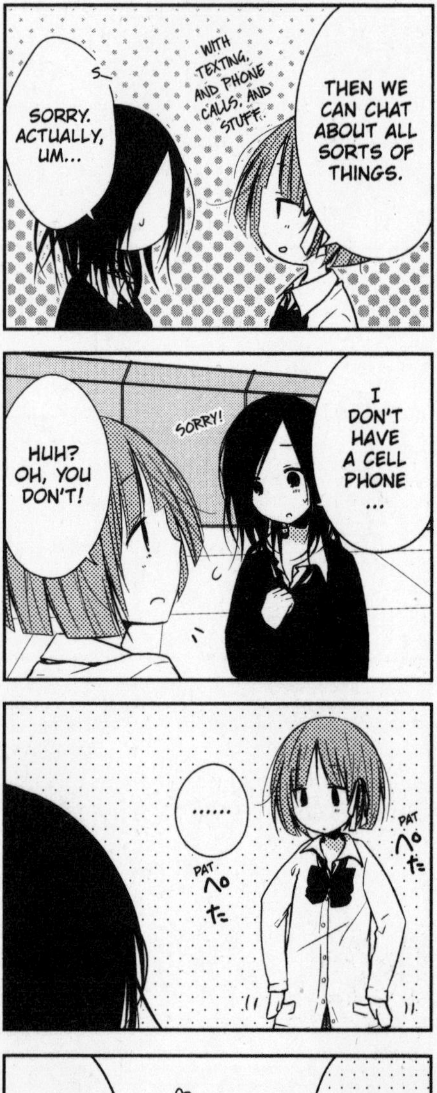
THEN WE CAN CHAT ABOUT ALL SORTS OF THINGS.
WITH TEXTING, AND PHONE CALLS, AND STUFF.
SORRY. ACTUALLY, UM...
I DON'T HAVE A CELL PHONE...
SORRY!
HUH? OH, YOU DON'T!
PAT
......
PAT
LOOKS LIKE I LEFT MY CELL PHONE AT HOME.
I DON'T HAVE ONE EITHER!
THAT'S AWFULLY CONVENIENT.

EASY TO READ

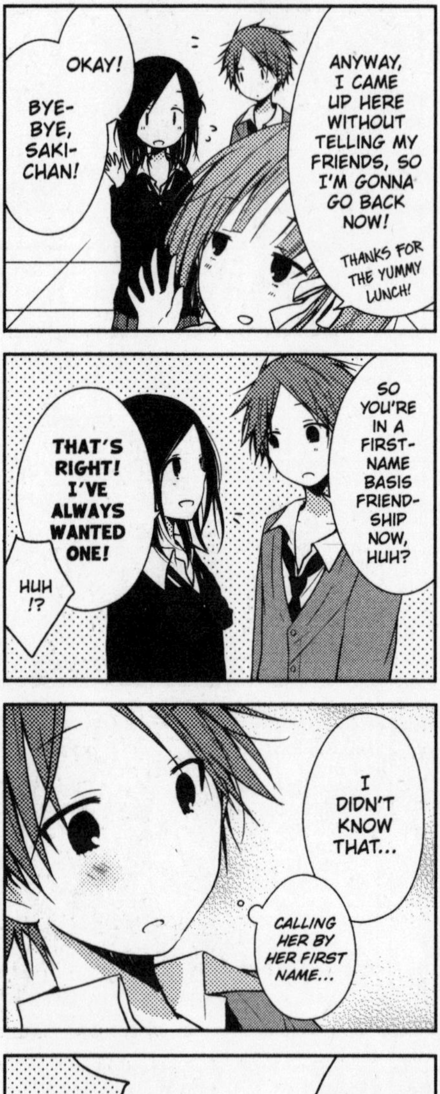
ANYWAY, I CAME UP HERE WITHOUT TELLING MY FRIENDS, SO I'M GONNA GO BACK NOW!
THANKS FOR THE YUMMY LUNCH!
OKAY!
BYE-BYE, SAKI-CHAN!
SO YOU'RE IN A FIRST-NAME BASIS FRIENDSHIP NOW, HUH?
THAT'S RIGHT! I'VE ALWAYS WANTED ONE!
HUH!?
I DIDN'T KNOW THAT...
CALLING HER BY HER FIRST NAME...
QUIT THAT HABIT OF JUMPING TO THOUGHTS LIKE THAT.
IT'S NOT A HABIT!
YOU QUIT READING MY

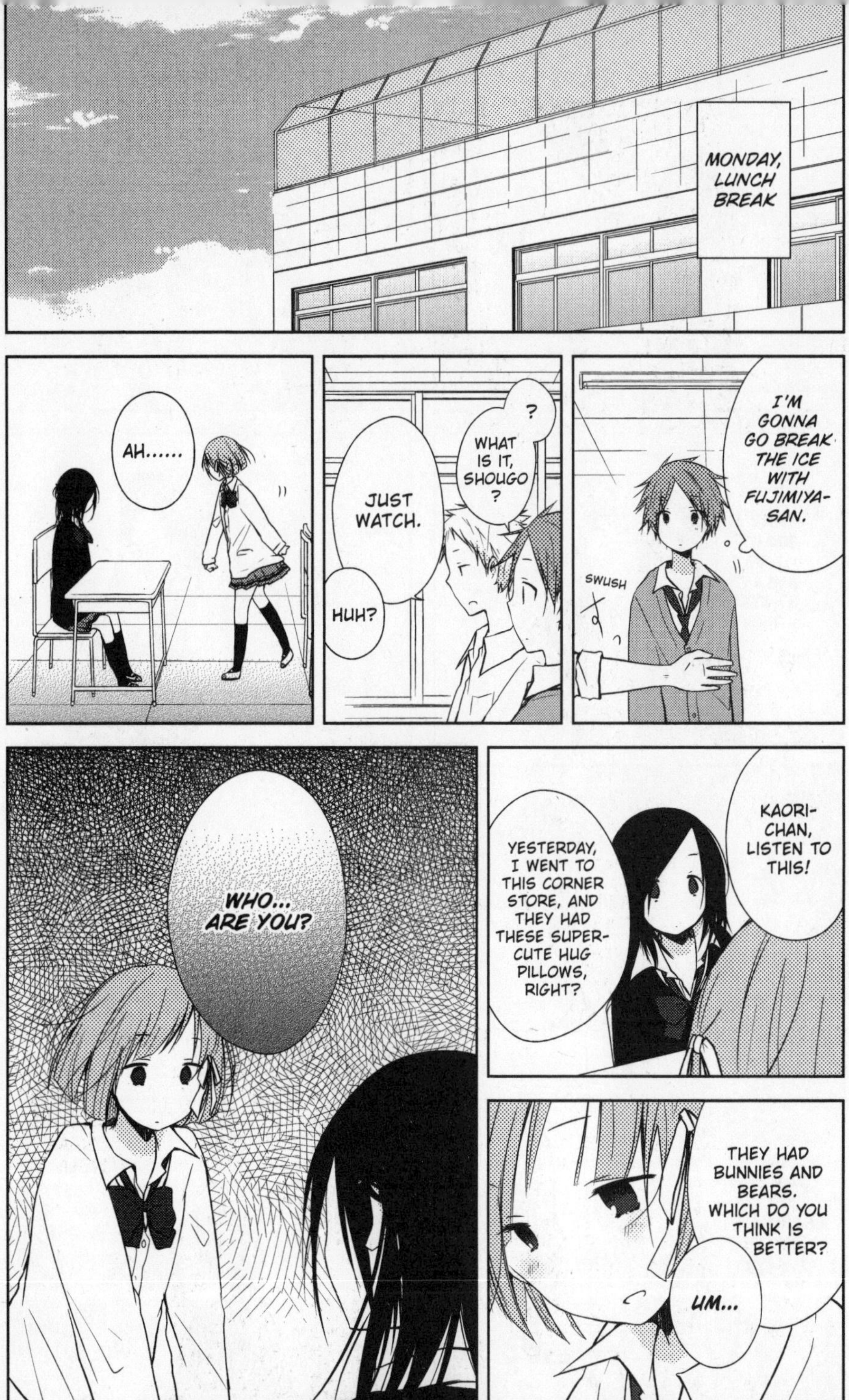
MONDAY, LUNCH BREAK
I'M GONNA GO BREAK THE ICE WITH FUJIMIYA-SAN.
SWUSH
?
WHAT IS IT, SHOUGO?
JUST WATCH.
HUH?
AH......
KAORI-CHAN, LISTEN TO THIS!
YESTERDAY, I WENT TO THIS CORNER STORE, AND THEY HAD THESE SUPER-CUTE HUG PILLOWS, RIGHT?
THEY HAD BUNNIES AND BEARS. WHICH DO YOU THINK IS BETTER?
UM...
WHO... ARE YOU?

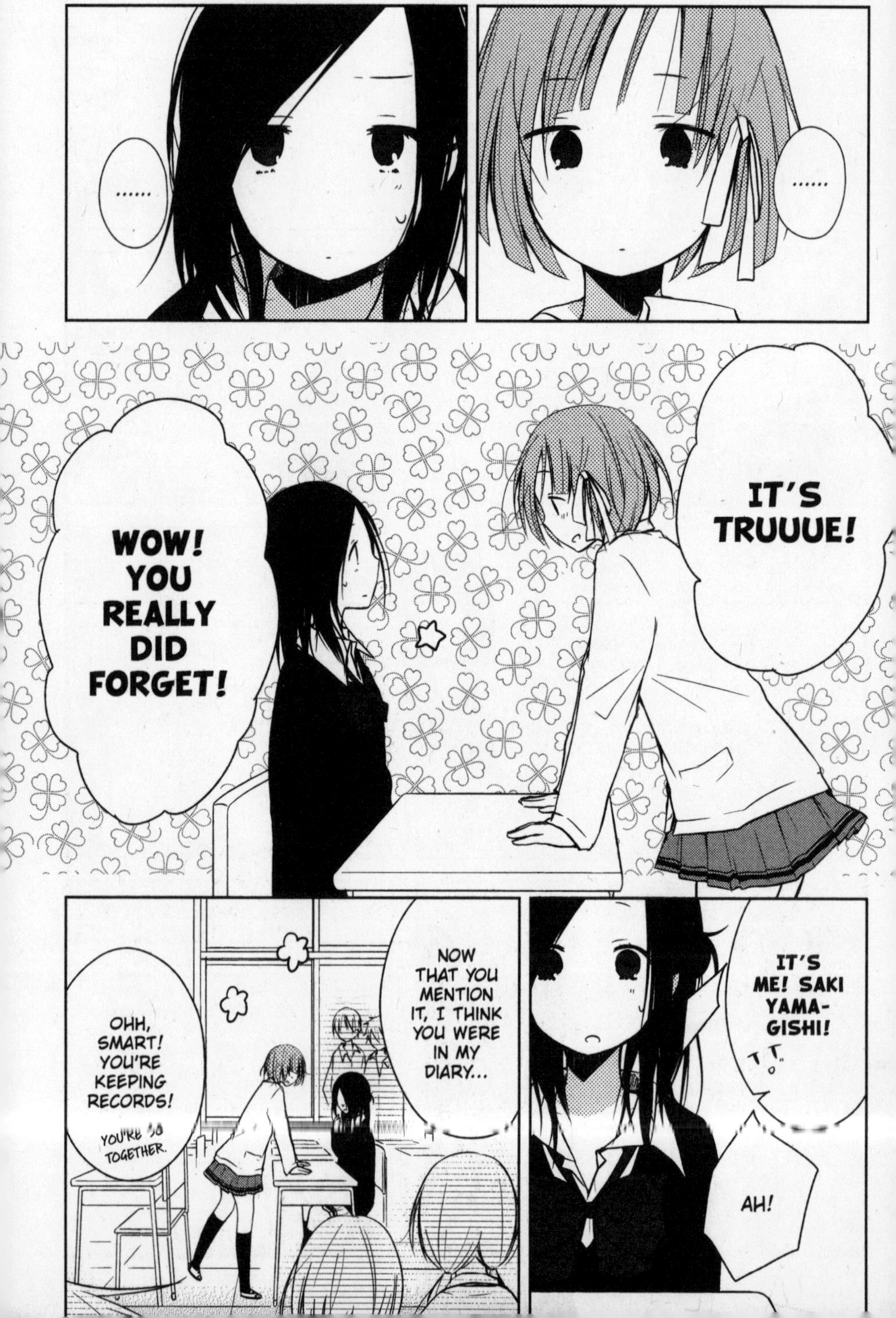
......
......
IT'S TRUUUE!
WOW! YOU REALLY DID FORGET!
IT'S ME! SAKI YAMA-GISHI!
AH!
NOW THAT YOU MENTION IT, I THINK YOU WERE IN MY DIARY...
OHH, SMART! YOU'RE KEEPING RECORDS!
YOU'RE SO TOGETHER.

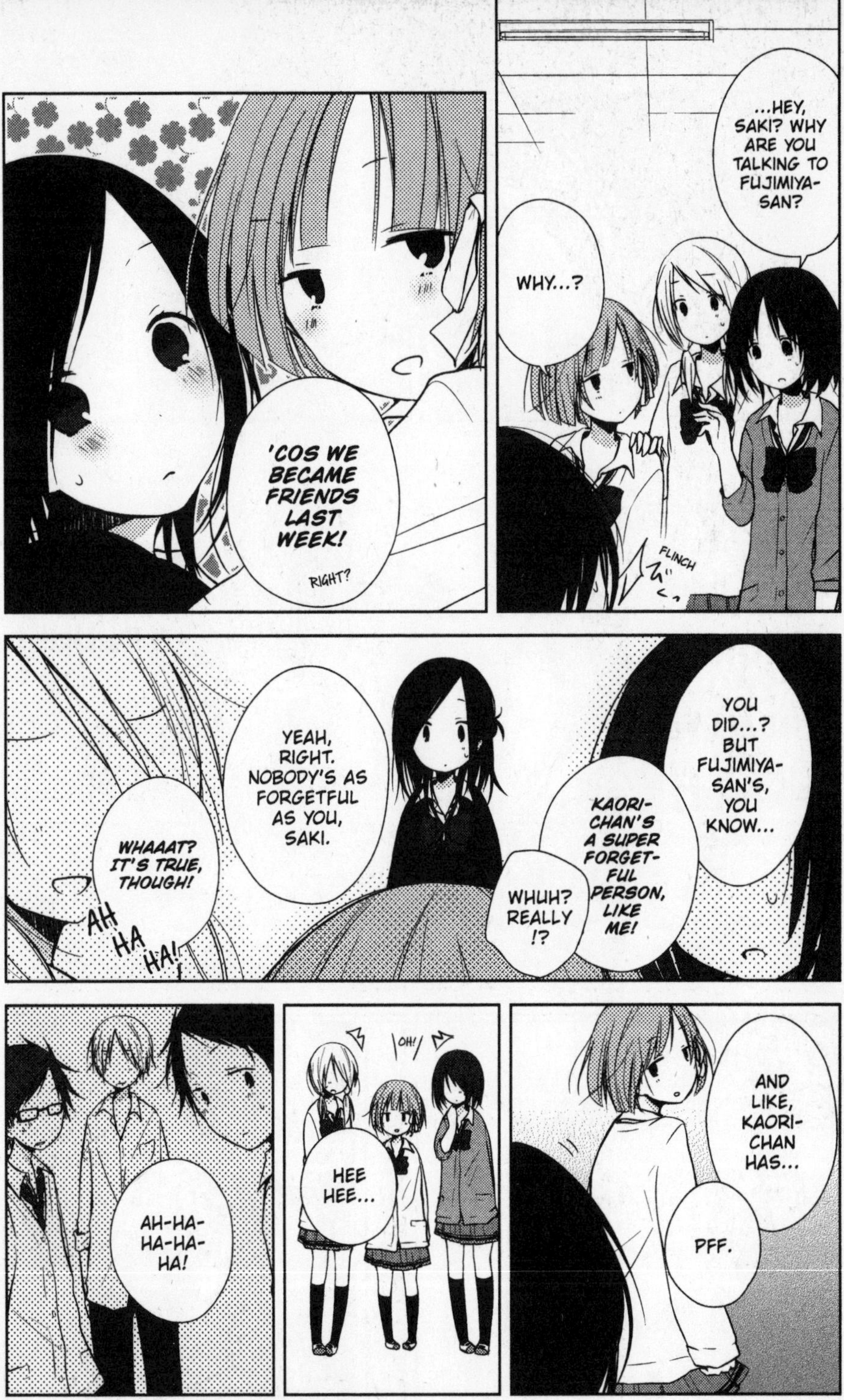
...HEY, SAKI? WHY ARE YOU TALKING TO FUJIMIYA-SAN?
WHY...?
FLINCH
'COS WE BECAME FRIENDS LAST WEEK!
RIGHT?
YOU DID...? BUT FUJIMIYA-SAN'S, YOU KNOW...
KAORI-CHAN'S A SUPER FORGETFUL PERSON, LIKE ME!
WHUH? REALLY!?
YEAH, RIGHT. NOBODY'S AS FORGETFUL AS YOU, SAKI.
WHAAAT? IT'S TRUE, THOUGH!
AH HA HA!
AND LIKE, KAORI-CHAN HAS...
PFF.
OH!
HEE HEE...
AH-HA-HA-HA-HA!

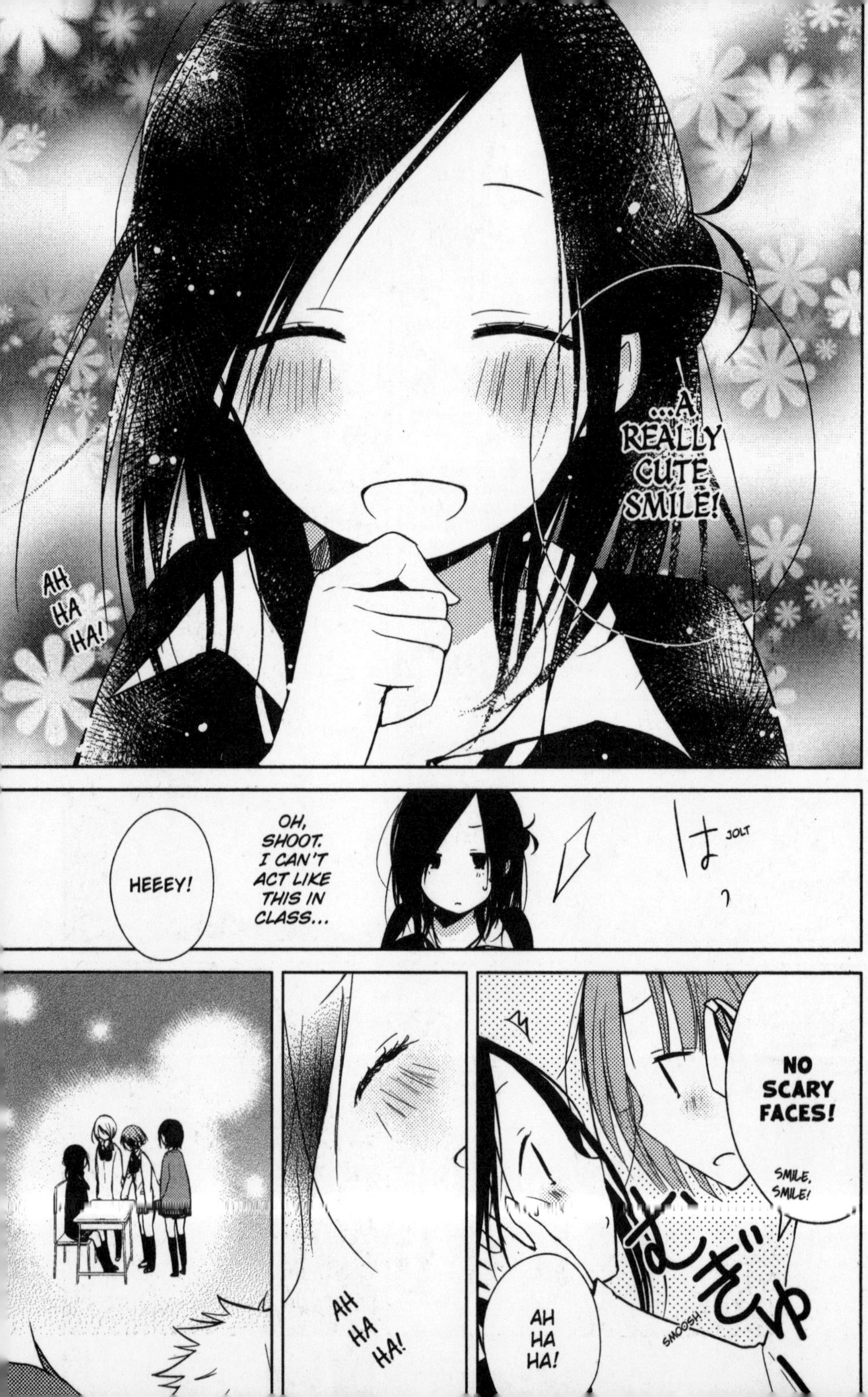
...A REALLY CUTE SMILE!
AH HA HA!
JOLT
OH, SHOOT. I CAN'T ACT LIKE THIS IN CLASS...
HEEEY!
NO SCARY FACES!
SMILE, SMILE!
SMOOSH
AH HA HA!
AH HA HA!

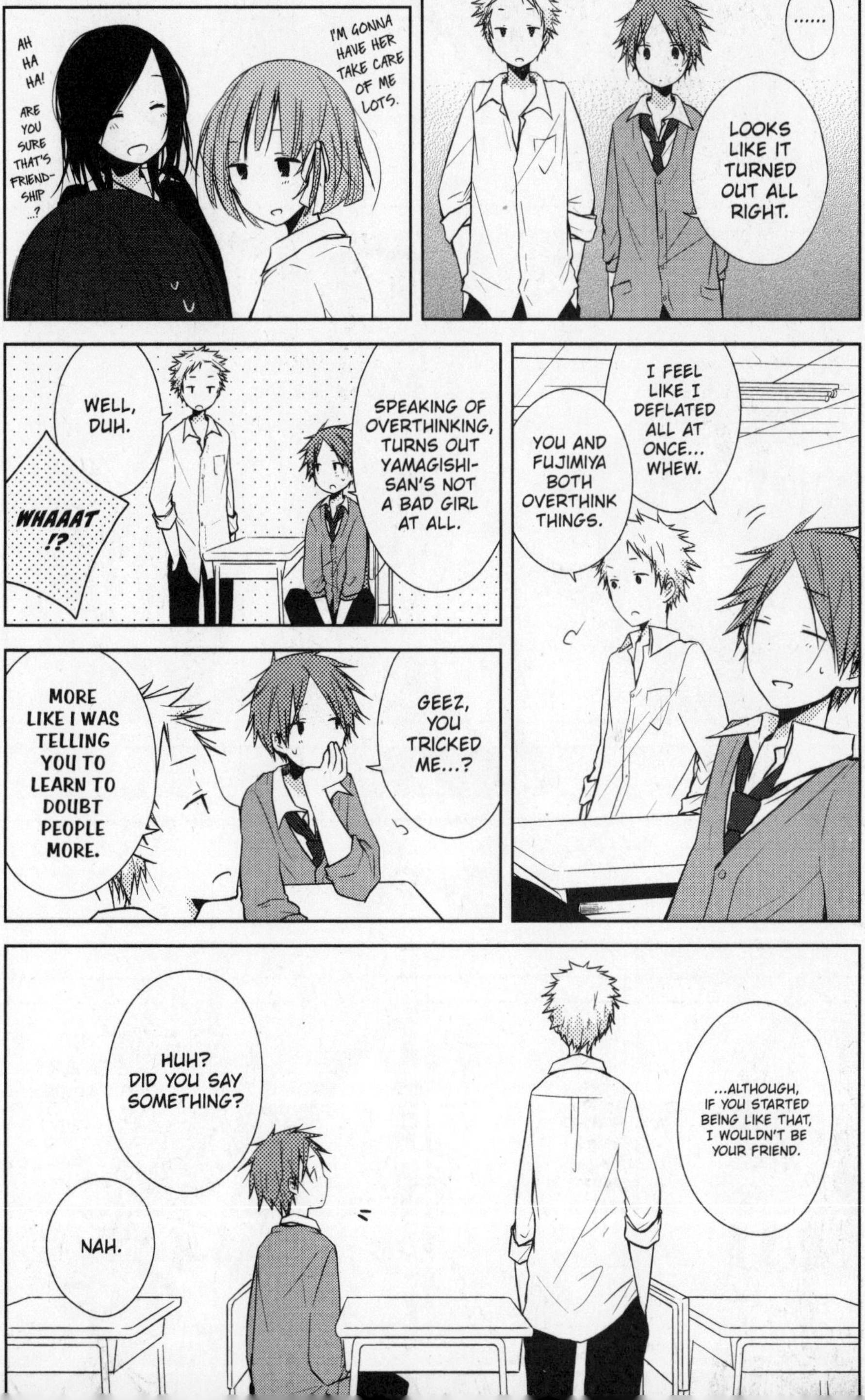
......
LOOKS LIKE IT TURNED OUT ALL RIGHT.
I'M GONNA HAVE HER TAKE CARE OF ME LOTS.
AH HA HA! ARE YOU SURE THAT'S FRIEND-SHIP ...?
I FEEL LIKE I DEFLATED ALL AT ONCE... WHEW.
YOU AND FUJIMIYA BOTH OVERTHINK THINGS.
SPEAKING OF OVERTHINKING, TURNS OUT YAMAGISHI-SAN'S NOT A BAD GIRL AT ALL.
WELL, DUH.
WHAAAT !?
GEEZ, YOU TRICKED ME...?
MORE LIKE I WAS TELLING YOU TO LEARN TO DOUBT PEOPLE MORE.
...ALTHOUGH, IF YOU STARTED BEING LIKE THAT, I WOULDN'T BE YOUR FRIEND.
HUH? DID YOU SAY SOMETHING?
NAH.

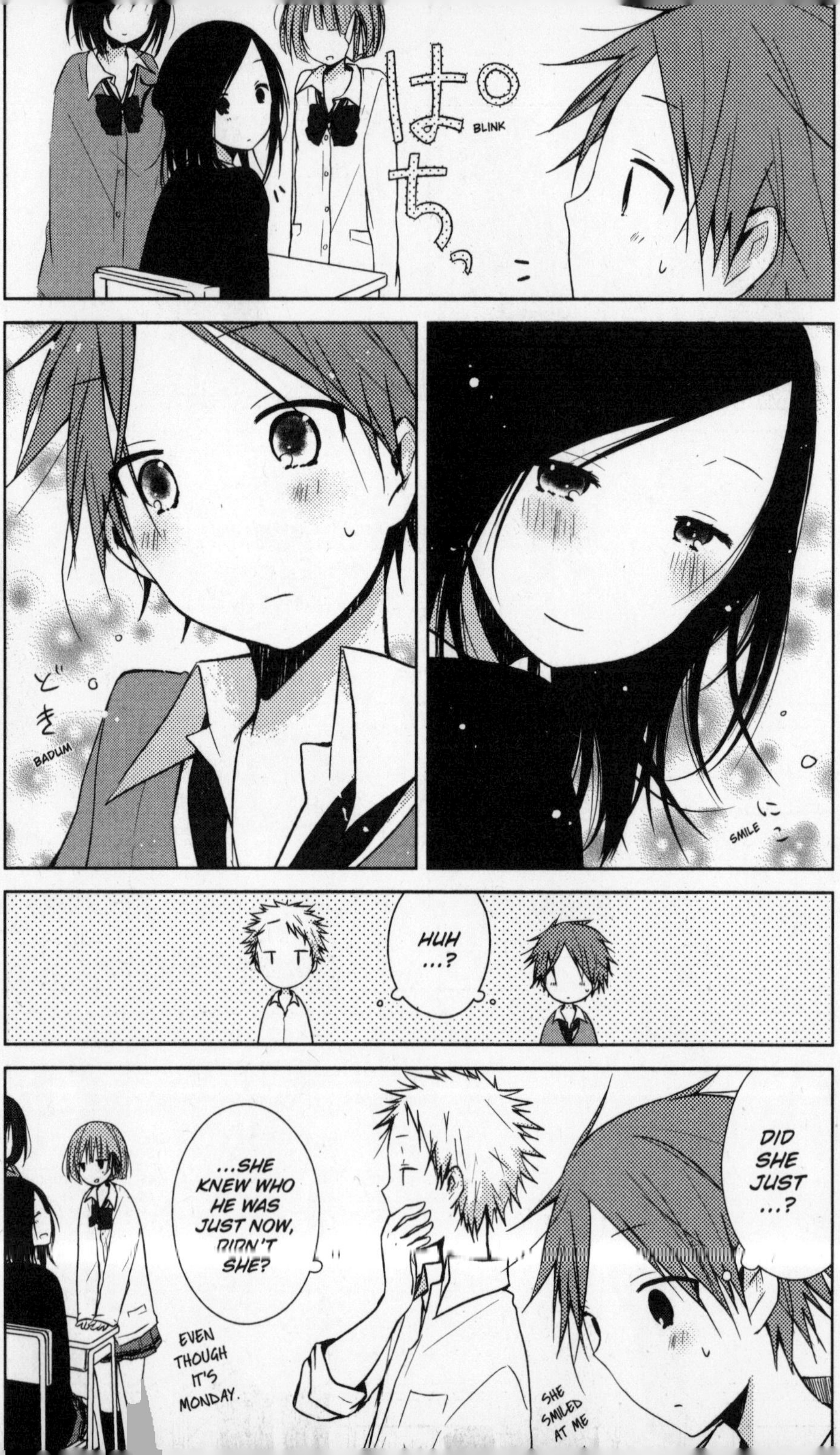
はちっ
BLINK
にっ
SMILE
どき
BADUM
HUH ...?
DID SHE JUST ...?
SHE SMILED AT ME
...SHE KNEW WHO HE WAS JUST NOW, DIDN'T SHE?
EVEN THOUGH IT'S MONDAY.

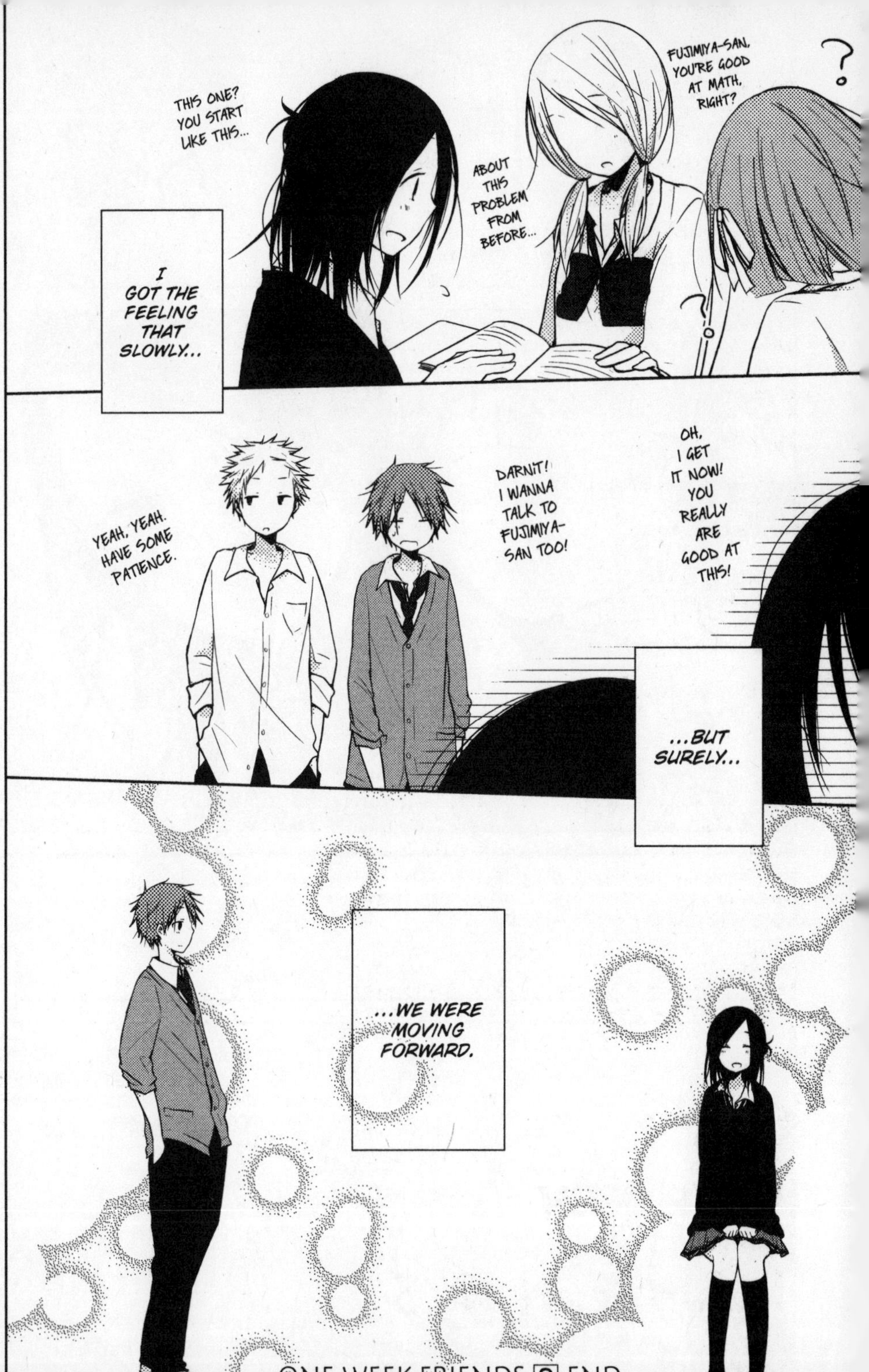
FUJIMIYA-SAN, YOU'RE GOOD AT MATH, RIGHT?
?
ABOUT THIS PROBLEM FROM BEFORE...
THIS ONE? YOU START LIKE THIS...
I GOT THE FEELING THAT SLOWLY...
OH, I GET IT NOW! YOU REALLY ARE GOOD AT THIS!
DARNIT! I WANNA TALK TO FUJIMIYA-SAN TOO!
YEAH, YEAH. HAVE SOME PATIENCE.
...BUT SURELY...
...WE WERE MOVING FORWARD.

ONE WEEK FRIENDS 2 END

TRANSLATION NOTES

COMMON HONORIFICS

no honorific: Indicates familiarity or closeness; if used without permission or reason, addressing someone in this manner would constitute an insult.

-san: The Japanese equivalent of Mr./Mrs./Miss. If a situation calls for politeness, this is the fail-safe honorific.

-kun: Used most often when referring to boys, this indicates affection or familiarity. Occasionally used by older men among their peers, but it may also be used by anyone referring to a person of lower standing.

-chan: An affectionate honorific indicating familiarity used mostly in reference to girls; also used in reference to cute persons or animals of either gender.

-sensei: A respectful term for teachers, artists, or high-level professionals.

nee: Japanese equivalent to "older sis."

nii: Japanese equivalent to "older bro."

PAGE 48
A **police box** (kouban) is a small neighborhood police station where you can ask after the lost and found, ask for directions, report crimes, get emergency services, etc.

PAGE 96
Yuuki calls Kaori "**Kaori-san**" instead of "Fujimiya-san" around her mother because her mother would be "Fujimiya-san" too.

PAGE 126
Being on a first-name basis: In Japanese, calling someone outside of family by their first name is sometimes considered a big step in the relationship. It's polite to check and make sure it's okay, as it can be off-putting if someone calls you by your first name when you aren't comfortable with it. In Kaori's case, if she's had no friends, a first-name-basis friendship would be even more special.

PAGE 131
Being on a first-name basis, part 2: For Yuuki, as a boy, being on a first-name basis with Kaori probably has some romantic connotations as well.

ONE WEEK FRIENDS

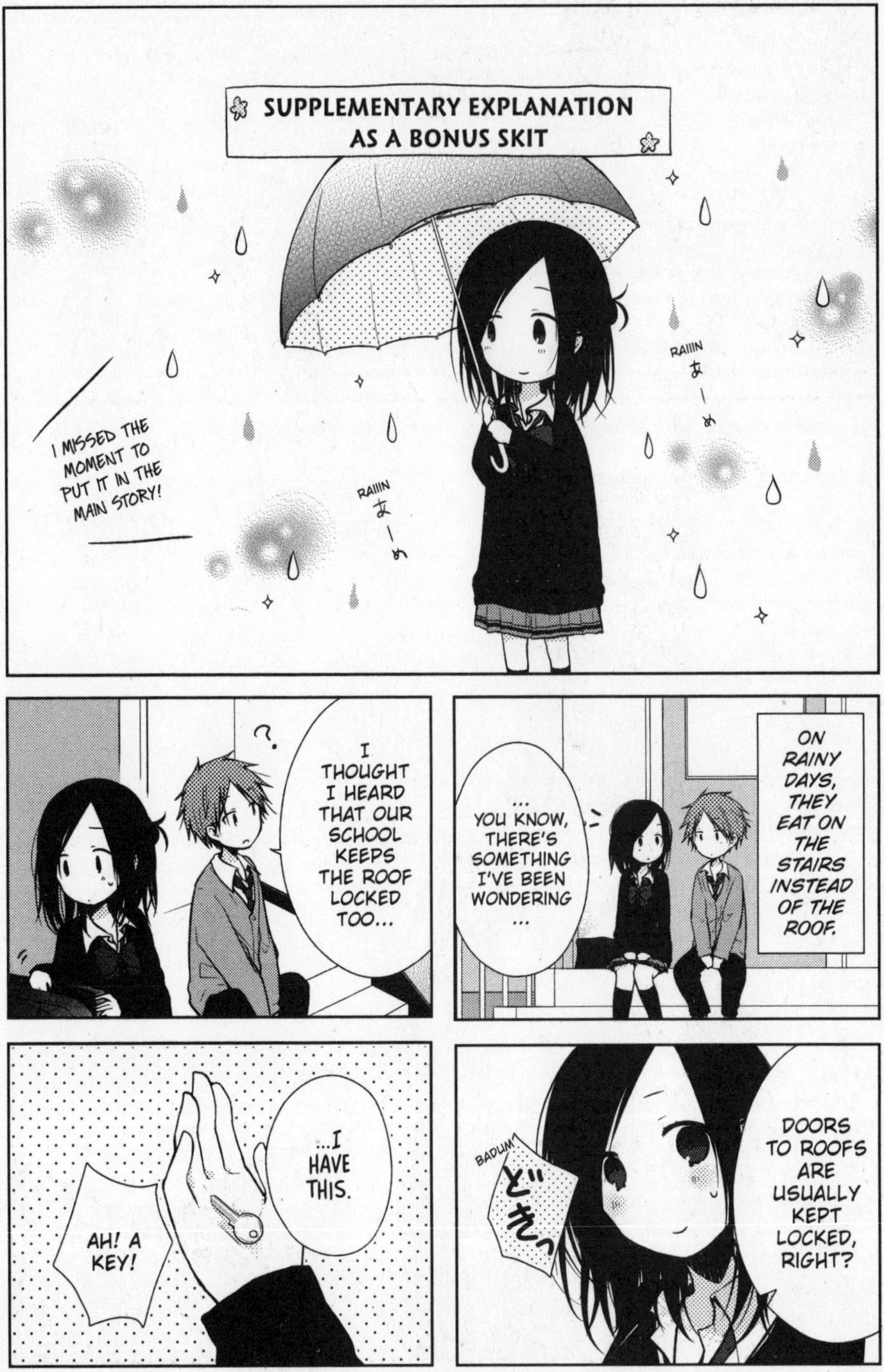
SUPPLEMENTARY EXPLANATION AS A BONUS SKIT
RAIIIN
あーめ
RAIIIN
あーめ
I MISSED THE MOMENT TO PUT IT IN THE MAIN STORY!
ON RAINY DAYS, THEY EAT ON THE STAIRS INSTEAD OF THE ROOF.
... YOU KNOW, THERE'S SOMETHING I'VE BEEN WONDERING ...
?
I THOUGHT I HEARD THAT OUR SCHOOL KEEPS THE ROOF LOCKED TOO...
DOORS TO ROOFS ARE USUALLY KEPT LOCKED, RIGHT?
BADUM
どきっ
...I HAVE THIS.
AH! A KEY!

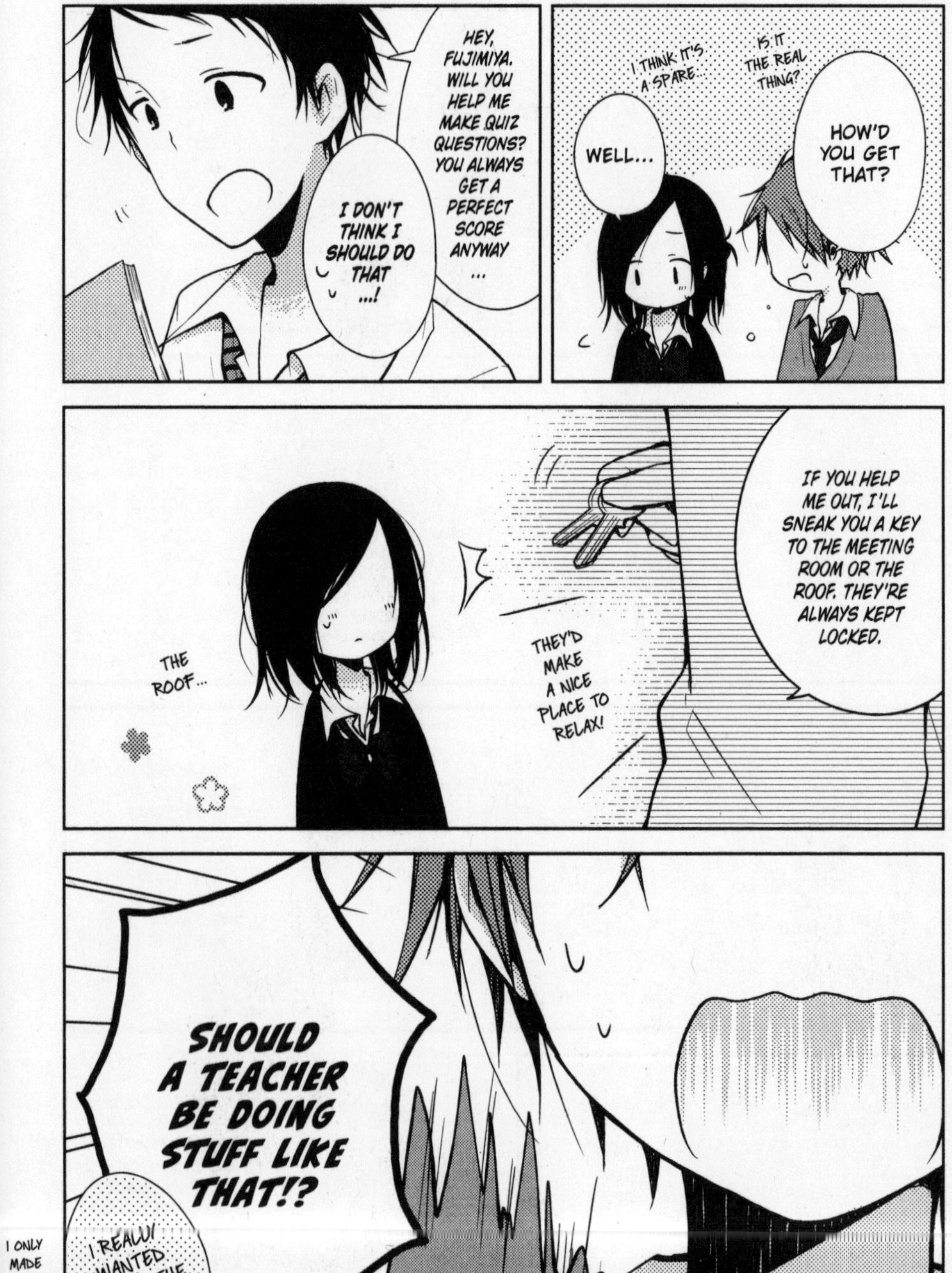
IS IT THE REAL THING?
HOW'D YOU GET THAT?
I THINK IT'S A SPARE...
WELL...
HEY, FUJIMIYA. WILL YOU HELP ME MAKE QUIZ QUESTIONS? YOU ALWAYS GET A PERFECT SCORE ANYWAY ...
I DON'T THINK I SHOULD DO THAT ...!
IF YOU HELP ME OUT, I'LL SNEAK YOU A KEY TO THE MEETING ROOM OR THE ROOF. THEY'RE ALWAYS KEPT LOCKED.
THEY'D MAKE A NICE PLACE TO RELAX!
THE ROOF...
SHOULD A TEACHER BE DOING STUFF LIKE THAT!?
I REALLY WANTED TO USE THE ROOF, SO...
I ONLY MADE UESTIONS THE ONE TIME!

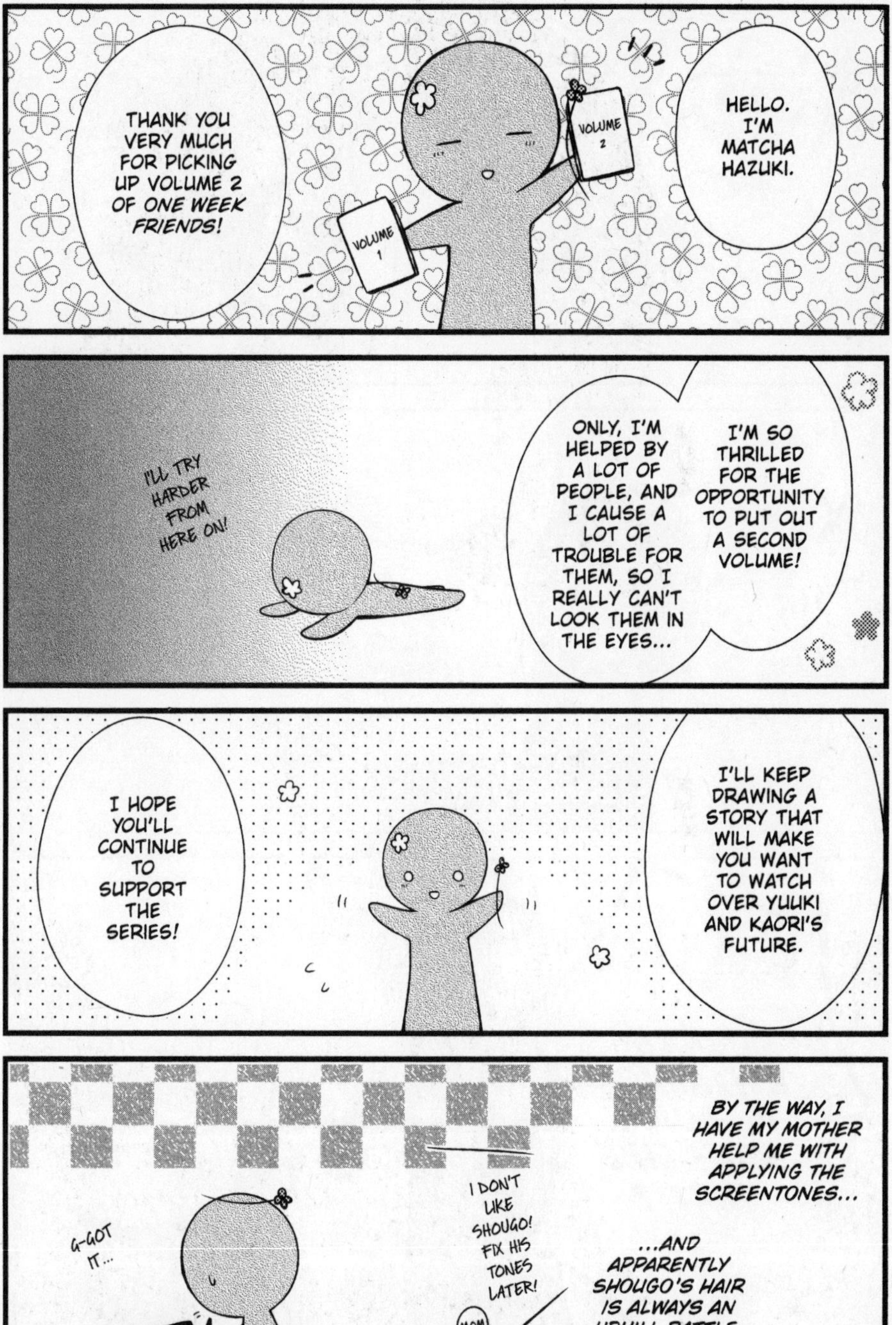
HELLO. I'M MATCHA HAZUKI.
VOLUME 2
VOLUME 1
THANK YOU VERY MUCH FOR PICKING UP VOLUME 2 OF ONE WEEK FRIENDS!
I'M SO THRILLED FOR THE OPPORTUNITY TO PUT OUT A SECOND VOLUME!
ONLY, I'M HELPED BY A LOT OF PEOPLE, AND I CAUSE A LOT OF TROUBLE FOR THEM, SO I REALLY CAN'T LOOK THEM IN THE EYES...
I'LL TRY HARDER FROM HERE ON!
I'LL KEEP DRAWING A STORY THAT WILL MAKE YOU WANT TO WATCH OVER YUUKI AND KAORI'S FUTURE.
I HOPE YOU'LL CONTINUE TO SUPPORT THE SERIES!
BY THE WAY, I HAVE MY MOTHER HELP ME WITH APPLYING THE SCREENTONES...
...AND APPARENTLY SHOUGO'S HAIR IS ALWAYS AN UPHILL BATTLE.
I DON'T LIKE SHOUGO! FIX HIS TONES LATER!
MOM
G-GOT IT...

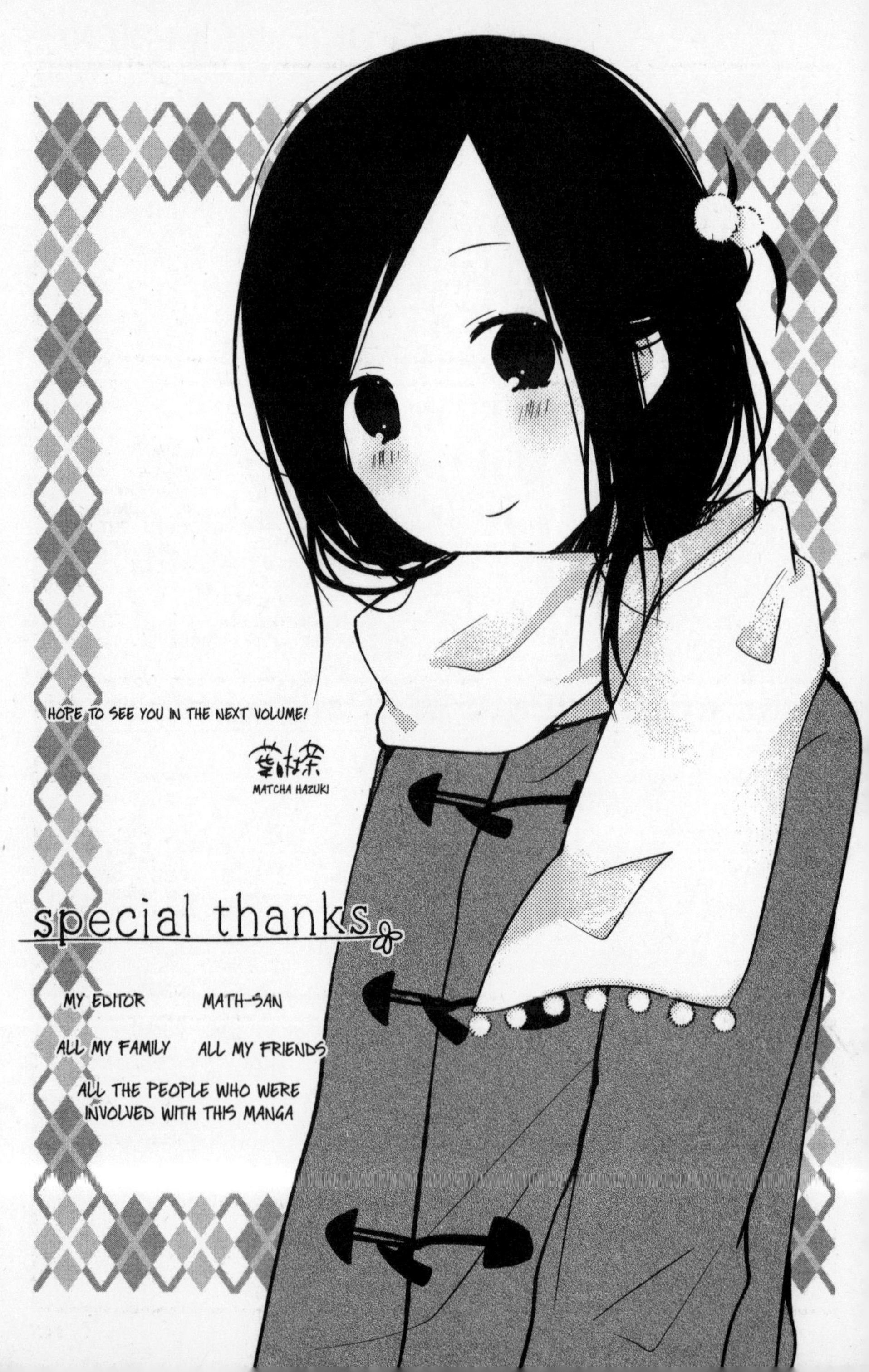
HOPE TO SEE YOU IN THE NEXT VOLUME!
葉月抹茶
MATCHA HAZUKI
special thanks
MY EDITOR
MATH-SAN
ALL MY FAMILY
ALL MY FRIENDS
ALL THE PEOPLE WHO WERE INVOLVED WITH THIS MANGA

NEXT ONE WEEK FRIENDS...

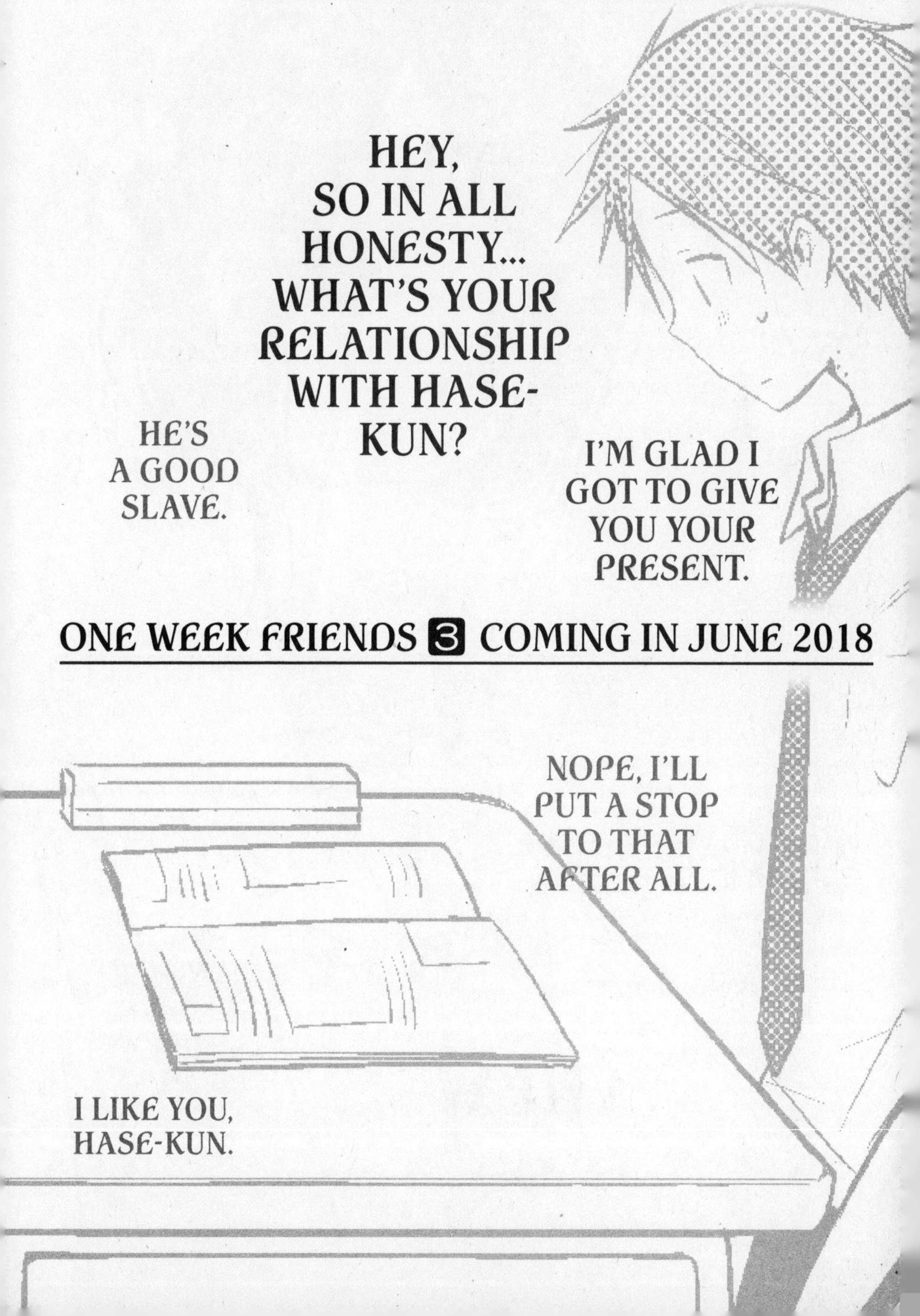
HEY, SO IN ALL HONESTY... WHAT'S YOUR RELATIONSHIP WITH HASE-KUN?
HE'S A GOOD SLAVE.
I'M GLAD I GOT TO GIVE YOU YOUR PRESENT.
NOPE, I'LL PUT A STOP TO THAT AFTER ALL.
I LIKE YOU, HASE-KUN.

ONE WEEK FRIENDS 3 COMING IN JUNE 2018

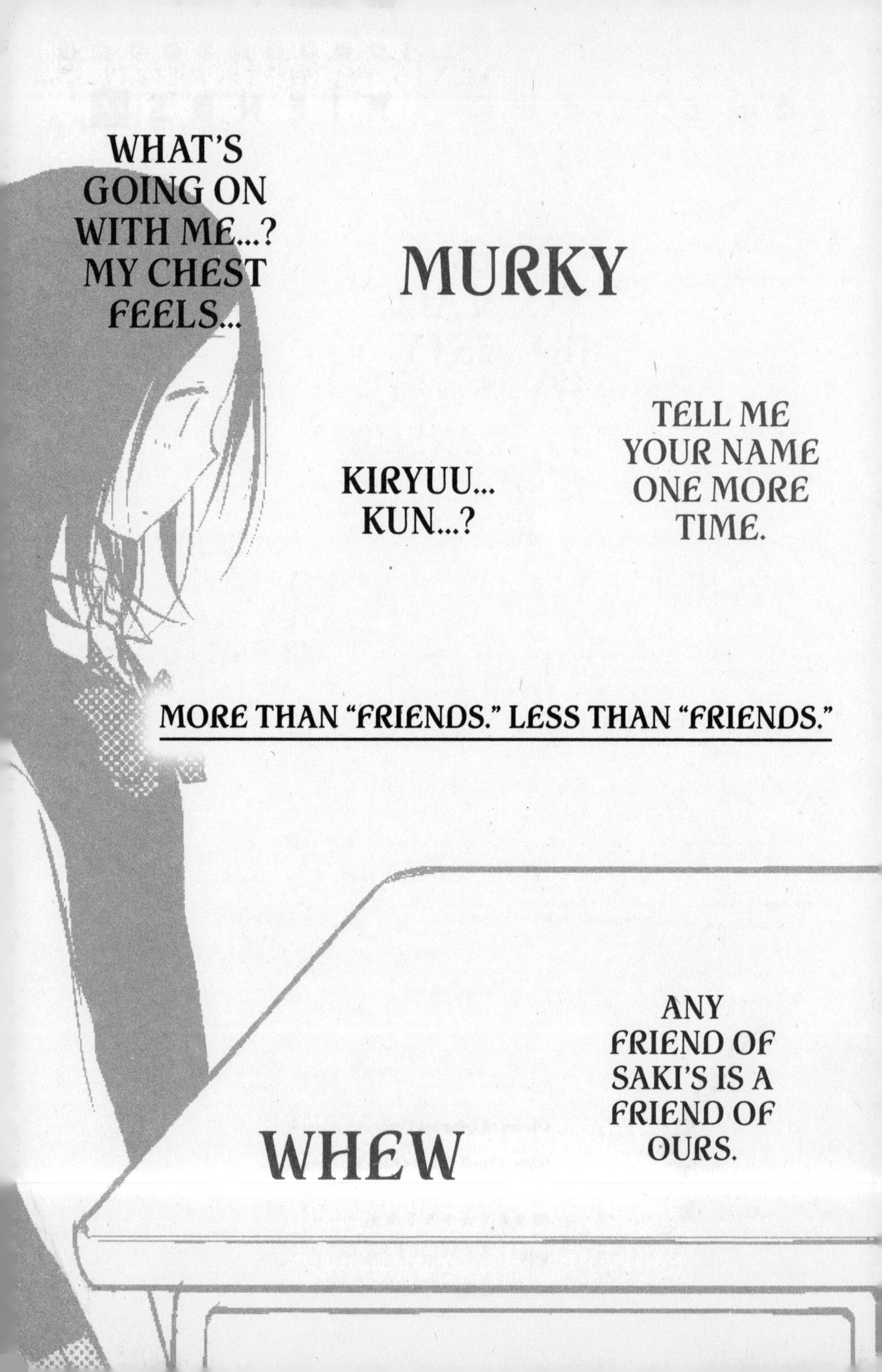
WHAT'S GOING ON WITH ME...? MY CHEST FEELS...
MURKY
TELL ME YOUR NAME ONE MORE TIME.
KIRYUU... KUN...?
MORE THAN "FRIENDS." LESS THAN "FRIENDS."
ANY FRIEND OF SAKI'S IS A FRIEND OF OURS.
WHEW

ONE WEEK F

MATCHA HAZUKI

Translation/Adaptation: Amanda Haley

Lettering: Bianca Pistillo

ONE WEEK FRIENDS Volume 2 ©2012 Matcha Hazuki/ SQUARE ENIX CO., LTD. First published in Japan in 2012 by SQUARE ENIX CO., LTD. English translation rights arranged with SQUARE ENIX CO., LTD. and Yen Press, LLC through Tuttle-Mori Agency, Inc.

English translation © 2018 by SQUARE ENIX CO., LTD.

Yen Press
1290 Avenue of the Americas
New York, NY 10104

Visit us at yenpress.com
facebook.com/yenpress
twitter.com/yenpress
yenpress.tumblr.com
instagram.com/yenpress

First Yen Press Edition: March 2018

Yen Press is an imprint of Yen Press, LLC. The Yen Press name and logo are trademarks of Yen Press, LLC.

The publisher is not responsible for websites (or their content) that are not owned by the publisher.

017954140

Printed in the United States of America